Book Two in the Legacy Series

Carlotta's Legacy

Betty Thomason Owens

Carlotta's Legacy

© 2016 Betty Thomason Owens

ISBN-13: 978-1-944120-02-3
ISBN-10: 1-944120-02-5
e-ISBN-13: 978-1-944120-03-0

Scriptures are taken from *The Holy Bible*, the Authorized (King James) Version.

This book is a work of fiction. Names, characters, places, and incidents are either products of the author's imagination or used fictitiously. Any similarity to actual people and/or events is purely coincidental.

Published by Write Integrity Press, 2631 Holly Springs Parkway, Box 35, Holly Springs, GA 30142

www.WriteIntegrity.com

Printed in the United States of America.

Dedication

For Isabele, Emily, Sophie, Teghan, and Lily Jane.

Acknowledgements

Pursuing a story can be fun, especially when the main character takes on a life of her own and takes you on the journey of a lifetime. My fellow critiquers followed along, picking at the story—asking the difficult questions—sending me deeper into the character, the beautiful setting, and the era. I'm so grateful for all of them and the many hours they logged working on this book. Thanks, Nike Chillemi, Patricia Reese Krugel, Marti Chabot, Tammy Doherty, and Celeste Charlene.

Thanks to my dear friend, Maureen Morales, for answering my questions regarding Catholic mannerisms and practices. Maureen is a high school friend whose sister Annette married my husband's brother, so in a roundabout way, we're family. Annette and Maureen are shining examples of the Catholic faith. Their obvious love for Jesus inspired me as I wrote this story.

The main setting for Carlotta's Legacy—the tiny village of Ginestra—is fictional, but the region of Umbria in the Province of Perugia, is not. Umbria is now on my bucket list. I discovered a wealth of information on YouTube in videos of nothing but scenery in Umbria (set to music, of course). I watched them over and over and wished I was the one behind the camera. These would be the scenes that greeted Rebecca every morning of her life in Italy. I'm grateful to these videographers and photographers for making so much material available.

Mere gratitude seems inadequate when addressing your favorite editor and publisher. If my pockets were overflowing, we'd all go to Italy for a month and do on-site research! Fay Lamb's expertise makes my writing so much better. Tracy Ruckman took a chance on me, for that I'm forever grateful.

Mom is my greatest fan, an avid reader, who passed down the "reading genes" to me. Love you, Mom! My husband Bob has supported my writing not just monetarily, but spiritually as well. Thanks for your presence in my life, your constant encouragement. I love you more every day.

Thank You, Heavenly Father, for Your love and forgiveness, and the opportunity to live for You and tell my stories.

Chapter One

4 November, 1929

Rebecca Lewis stared at the angry crowd gathered outside the bank where she'd worked as a secretary for only six weeks. It was Monday morning, almost one week after Black Tuesday.

What was she to do? Dare she cross the street, try to maneuver through that mob?

While she struggled to decide, her gaze fell on a familiar face behind the wheel of a brown Model A sedan—Robert Emerson, her best friend's husband. She waved to gain his attention then ran toward the car when he halted.

He opened the car door from the inside. "Jump in. I think we better hit the road."

She slid onto the seat next to him and closed the door as something hard hit the window.

Robert mashed the gas pedal and sped away.

Rebecca turned to gaze out the back window. "Thank you. I had no idea what to do."

He checked his mirrors then glanced at Rebecca. "I'm glad I happened along when I did. Apparently, someone recognized you as a bank employee."

With a quick look in his direction, she braced herself with a hand to the dash as he made a hard left.

"Sorry. Another crowd up ahead."

She laid a gloved hand at the base of her throat as her heart thumped. "Why are they doing this?"

"Panic. Everyone wants his money." His eyes met hers. "Where's your father?"

"He's in New York. Trying to recover something … or another."

"As is everyone—trying to recover something, I mean."

She watched his profile, the hard set of his jaw. The last few weeks had been especially hard on him and his family. "What about you? Woods-Sanderson?"

"We're all right, for now. Amelia was a smart lady. She diversified, invested worldwide."

"This is worldwide, isn't it?"

"Well, yes, but …" he pulled into his driveway. "I hope you don't mind if we cool our heels here. Nancy'll be worried. You know how she is about listening to the wireless."

Rebecca nodded. "I suppose I could use your telephone. Call my boss and let him know I tried to get there."

"Good idea. If you need backup, I'll be glad to put a word in."

She smiled at him as he exited the sedan and walked around the car. She knew to stay put. Ever the gentleman. Nancy was one lucky lady. Of course, she would call it blessed. Rebecca fiddled with the ring on her finger, hidden beneath her gloves. Had she made the right decision? Caught up in her thoughts, she jumped when Robert opened the door.

He grinned. "Sorry, did I startle you?"

She blew out a breath. "Yes, a little. I'm rather distracted."

"Nothing to worry about, you know. It'll all come to rights." He closed the door and offered his arm as they drew near the front steps.

Movement behind the stained glass of the front entrance brought her attention to Nancy, who stood in the foyer, peering through the window. She opened the door at their approach. "How bad is it? We've been listening to the reports."

Robert explained the situation as they walked through to the parlor. "Rebecca flagged me down out in front of Merchants Bank." He took Rebecca's coat and gloves and handed them off to Florence, Nancy's secretary. "Florence, please show Miss Rebecca to my office so she can use the telephone."

Rebecca followed behind Florence, even though she knew her way. She sat down at his desk and picked up the receiver. "Merchants Bank, please."

After her conversation had ended, she found Nancy alone in the parlor, pouring coffee. "Robert's upstairs visiting our sick little boy."

"Oh, no. What's the matter with Jack?" Rebecca sat across from her, crossed her legs, and arranged her skirt.

"Just a cold. It won't hold him down long." She handed her a cup.

Rebecca scanned the room as she sipped the hot coffee. They had made a few changes since she'd last visited. The soft blue color calmed, as did the presence of the pretty lady next to her. She examined her friend's face. The bruises were almost gone. Only someone who knew what she'd been through would notice.

Nancy sat back and gazed at Rebecca. "I see you looking at my face. Almost healed."

"I was thinking how wonderful you look."

"Liar." She smiled and sipped her coffee. "I'm a little worried about my leg. The doctor said it may never completely heal." She gave a soft sigh. "Something to remember him by."

"Oh, Nancy. I hope you aren't still thinking about him."

She stared into her cup. "I can't help it. Some days are just hard."

Rebecca couldn't help it either. She'd never forget the panic she'd felt when Robert called to tell her Nancy had been abducted by that hideous Nate. A man both she and Nancy had once considered a friend. What a fiend he'd turned out to be.

Robert's voice trailed in from the foyer. "I need to make a phone call. Then I'll join you ladies. Save me some coffee."

"Sorry, no can do," Nancy said, sending a mischievous grin toward Rebecca.

Rebecca returned her smile, still thinking about Nancy's ordeal. At least that part of their life lay behind them. He was dead and buried. Too bad he'd gotten himself killed in a car wreck. He should have suffered far more for what he'd done to her friend.

Rebecca turned her attention back to Nancy. What a dear. She had actually forgiven that scoundrel, and wouldn't let anyone else speak ill of him. Rebecca marveled at her resilience. Even now, in the midst of a major catastrophe, her eyes sparkled. She never missed the opportunity to assure Rebecca that her faith in God made all the difference.

"More coffee?" Nancy held up the pot.

"Just a little, if there's plenty."

"Oh, we can make more. Now tell me about this morning. What happened at the bank?"

Back in her tiny one-room flat, Rebecca pulled the curtains aside and peered out at the quiet streets, her skin prickling at the sight of armed police officers patrolling in pairs. Her decision to live downtown had seemed so perfect until this moment, in the aftermath of the rioting. Kip, the Emerson's chauffeur, had driven her home after dinner. They'd both been shocked speechless by the broken windows in the upscale north end of town. Even here, in the slightly less modish area, they'd had to swerve around battered and abandoned automobiles and folks cleaning up after the crowds had dissipated. And now the policemen. Rebecca couldn't say whether she felt safer or more troubled by their presence.

Behind her, the tea kettle whistled. She turned and lifted the pot from the stove then poured the steaming liquid into a prepared teapot. The light from a nearby lamp reflected in the facets of a half-karat solitaire diamond, catching her eye. She sank into a chair and gazed at the beautiful stone.

The ring had officially been back on her finger for only a

week after deliberating for months. It's not that she didn't have feelings for Riccardo. Lifting the framed photo from the table beside her chair, she gazed at the handsome young man in a dark suit and white hat smiling back at her. She closed her eyes as the memory of their last good-bye stole over her. She could almost feel the pressure of his arms around her. Wrenching her thoughts away from the scene, she laid the frame face down on the table.

Rebecca doubted her capacity for love at all. Was that fair to Riccardo? She reached for the teapot, poured the steaming liquid into her cup. Then she set the pot down again. Her upbringing hadn't exactly fostered affection—or trust. But the past was past. She must learn to look ahead and not back, as Nancy was so fond of saying.

Nancy had tried to reason with her, even tried to talk her out of marrying Riccardo. "You barely know him," she'd said.

"How can you really know someone until you've lived with them day in and day out?" Rebecca asked her. "You take a chance. You hope to make the right decision. Daddy says it's a crap shoot no matter how you go about it."

Nancy shook her head. "Oh, Rebecca, I only wish—"

Rebecca had interrupted her before she could start in again on another sermon. More than anything, Nancy wished for Rebecca to find the peace she had found. According to Nancy, you could only find it through religion. Rebecca had enough religion, and there'd be plenty more in Italy. She loved Nancy, and cherished her friendship, but when it encroached on her freedom of choice, she had to draw the line. She'd made her decision.

Besides, what other choice had she? Mother and Daddy had been thrilled by the possibility of an engagement to an Italian Conte, especially one so well off. At least, he'd been well off before the stock market came crashing down. How great a loss had he and his family suffered—if at all? Riccardo was a very stable individual. He was not the type to risk his family's future on fly-by-night schemes. Or borrow vast sums of money to invest.

An almost overwhelming sadness filled her as she remembered Daddy's failures. She knew better than to let her mind travel there. Her gaze drifted to the clock on the opposite wall. It was going to be a long night.

At half-past nine on Tuesday morning, Rebecca stood in the president's office at Merchants Bank as Mr. Audubon explained the situation. Though the temperature had dropped steadily in the last few days, beads of sweat popped out on his temples. As he spoke, he dabbed at the moisture with a folded handkerchief.

"And so, you see, Miss Lewis, we're forced to make cuts." He paused to dip his pen in a bottle of ink and signed something with his usual flourish.

She scanned the outer office through the window beside the door, noting the men working at their stations. Of course, none of them made eye contact with her. Even Carson, the head teller, manned the switchboard, instead of Mable Howard. Rebecca brought her gaze back to the president's rather florid face.

"The men have families to support," he said. No doubt, he'd noticed where her attention had been drawn. He cleared his throat. "Possibly, in a few weeks, we may be able to call you back." He handed her the signed slip of paper. "Hand this to Raymond. He'll pay you for your last day worked."

With a nod, she turned to go. There was nothing more to say.

On the street outside the bank, Rebecca glanced around then strolled toward home. What now? Two blocks down, on the other side of the street, a queue ended that wound all the way around the corner to the employment office. She kept her eyes averted as she passed. Would she end up in that line?

With that thought in mind, she turned and headed in the opposite direction, toward the Boston-Emerson Law Offices. Nancy called William Boston uncle, though he was not really related, simply an old family friend. He and Robert's father had served the Sanderson family as legal counsel for years. When Rebecca moved to the area following Nancy's accident, Mr. Boston recommended her to Mr. Audubon at the bank. He'd meant well. Perhaps she should have gone to work for Robert and Nancy instead.

Pushing those thoughts aside, she entered the plush offices of the law firm and smiled at the pleasant-faced receptionist, who was just ending a call.

The woman glanced up at Rebecca. "Good morning, Miss Lewis. Have you an appointment?"

Rebecca shook her head. "No, Miss Edison, I was just wondering if I could use the telephone. It's a local call."

"Why, of course you may. I hope everything's all right?"

Rebecca smiled into Miss Edison's sympathetic gaze. No doubt she'd overhear the phone call anyway. "I've been laid off, temporarily. I'm not sure what to do."

William Boston appeared in his doorway near the end of the hall. "Rebecca, is that you?"

Heat rose in her cheeks. She'd hoped to sneak in undetected. "Yes, Mr. Boston."

"Come in." He gestured to her.

She nodded to Miss Edison then walked down the hallway to his office.

"Have a seat and tell me what's happened." He sat and leaned back in his chair intertwining his fingers over his ample midsection.

Rebecca eased into the dark leather chair opposite Mr. Boston's desk, settled her purse on her lap, then folded her hands on top of it. "They had to let me go. Well, not just me, several of their employees have been laid off." Mostly the women. She held that part back.

He leaned forward, his hands gripping the edge of the desk. "Terrible run on the banks yesterday. Robert told me all about it this morning. I'm glad you weren't there."

She nodded. "So am I. But now what, Mr. Boston? With no job, I'll not be able to keep my apartment."

"Didn't I hear you'd decided to marry that Riccardo Alverá?"

A smile quirked her lips at the Americanized pronunciation of Riccardo's surname, with the accent on the second syllable, instead of the last. "It's Al-ver-AH. And yes, you heard right, but that was before the crash. Daddy lost everything. I don't know if Riccardo wants a penniless wife."

He crossed his arms over his chest. "Hmm. I'm not sure I think much of this man if he's only interested in your money."

"Is that not the way of things, sir?"

A deep furrow creased his forehead. "I don't think it is. If he truly loves you, he'll want you no matter what happens. If he doesn't, then he's not worth your time and sorrow, is he?"

"I suppose not."

"I know I'm meddling. That's just my way. How long 'til you'll have to move out of your apartment?"

"A couple of weeks."

"What about your parents?"

Rebecca resisted the urge to roll her eyes. Her parents had a bad habit of living in hotels. Now, no doubt, they were also looking for a place to lay their heads. "Not much to hope for there. Except possibly my grandmother's house in Westchester. Grandmother passed away last year, and I believe the house is still unoccupied."

"You could go there. And if all else fails, you have Nancy. She'll be happy to have you as a guest. But I predict you'll hear from that Count fellow soon. In the meantime, if I hear of anything, I'll let you know."

Rebecca pushed up from the leather chair and extended her hand. "Thank you, Mr. Boston. I appreciate your time."

He stood also and rounded the corner of the desk. "Can I have one of our couriers drop you somewhere?"

"No, thank you. It's not far."

After making that phone call, Rebecca strolled west along Main Street to the door of her apartment building, thankful she hadn't seen anyone familiar. She had no desire to talk. What a day this was turning out to be, and it wasn't even half over.

Her only hope now, she supposed, was to take Robert up on his previous offer, to work on a temporary basis at Woods-Sanderson. Something she'd never wanted to do, but she was officially desperate. So she'd made the phone call and left a message with his secretary.

Well, at least she'd have time to write that letter to Riccardo, break the news about their losses. If she mailed it tomorrow, how soon could she expect a response? Ugh. She hated waiting.

Minutes after she stepped inside her apartment, someone hammered on her door. Did they think she was deaf?

She opened the door to a man of about her height, but nearly thrice her width. The landlord.

He held out an envelope. "This telegram was delivered for you. The wife signed for it."

Rebecca's breath caught in her throat. Who could be sending a telegram? The landlord lingered. Did he expect a tip? She arched her brow at him. When he finally turned away, she closed the door and tore open the telegram then stared at the message.

COME TO NEW YORK AT ONCE.

Chapter Two

Heart racing, Rebecca paced back and forth, waiting for the train to be announced. On the ninth or tenth turn, she caught sight of Robert rushing toward her.

"Rebecca, thank goodness I caught you. Nancy would never forgive me if I let you get away without at least offering to accompany you."

Rebecca shook her head. "Absolutely not. You're not ready to be away from her. I'd never require that of you. Besides, I've made ocean voyages on my own."

He grinned. "I find that quite shocking, to say the least. But that's a subject for another time. I made calls, and I was unable to get any information at all. Are you quite certain the telegram was from your mother?"

"Yes. I know she sent it. It's probably her panicking over their latest losses." A whistle pierced the air as the train rumbled into the station.

Robert took her hand. "Well, you call us right away when you know what's going on, and let us know if you need anything. You can go to our offices in Brooklyn. Have them contact me, if you wish."

She nodded then stretched up to place a kiss on his cheek. "Thank you, Robert. Give Nancy my love."

"You bet, kid." He smiled, but his dark eyes didn't reflect pleasure. "Don't take any wooden nickels."

He was worried about her. Was this what it was like to have a brother—or family of any kind who actually cared what went on in your life?

She hurried onto the train and found an empty seat. After they were underway, she removed her gloves and folded them into her purse, making sure her ticket was easily accessed. Where was that pack of gum she'd purchased? In her coat pocket. She thrust her fingers in and met with paper. When she pulled it out, her lips parted. She sent a quick glance over her shoulder and back to the front then folded the fifty dollar bill and hid it away in her purse. Robert. She'd refused to allow him to pay for her train ticket, so he'd hidden money in her pocket. What would she do without those two? They'd been more family to her than her own flesh and blood.

Rebecca stared out the window at the countryside flying past. The colorful fall foliage was already giving way to the gray of winter. This had always been her favorite time of year, for the colors, the smells, and the promise of snow.

The conductor's voice rang out. She pulled the ticket from her purse and handed it to him as he drew near. After he punched it, she put it away again and noticed the telegram folded there. She'd read it at least a dozen times. What did she hope to find—something more than before? Why had Mother not given some hint? Had she been so broke she couldn't afford another word or two? Her mother could've called the Emersons, reversed the charges. She knew they'd get a message to Rebecca. Frustration rose in her breast and soured in her throat. What trouble had her mother gotten into this time?

Rebecca took a deep breath and exhaled. No sense in getting herself all worked up. She'd know soon enough. Settling back in the seat, she tried to relax and get some rest, but a fretful child behind her ended any hope of that.

Nancy would tell her to pray. "Turn your troubles over to the Lord," she'd say, patting Rebecca's hand. "Look at me— I'm a walking, talking miracle."

Rebecca knew that was true, but she doubted God cared about Rebecca Lewis. However, it was worth a try. She whispered a clumsy prayer. "Please help us, whatever Mother's gotten herself into this time, or help Daddy out of this hard place." She huffed out a sigh and shifted in her seat, glancing around as though others would know she was talking to God.

Someone gripped her shoulder. Rebecca turned to peer into a tear-stained child's face. A little boy, from the looks of it. His mother had nodded off, bless her heart. Rebecca smiled at the boy. He smiled back then withdrew as though shy.

His mother awoke with a start. "Oh, I'm so sorry. Is he bothering you? Trey, you turn around here and sit down."

Rebecca tried to reassure the woman but didn't want to encourage the child to repeat his attention to her. She knew from experience with Nancy's children, they could go on and on and on with whatever small obsession brought them a moment's pleasure.

After the longest four hours she'd ever endured, Rebecca disembarked at Grand Central Terminal, thankful for the money Robert had provided. She could take a taxi. Pressing through the crowd, she emerged in the station rotunda. Her eyes soon found the doors exiting to the street. She'd advanced only a few feet when her gaze lit on a placard with her name on it. How had Mother known which train she'd take? Perhaps Robert had managed to get in touch with her.

The uniformed chauffeur nodded when she introduced herself. "Yes, Miss. Mr. Emerson said I was to meet you here and take you wherever you need to go for as long as you're in the city."

Robert and Nancy. What would she do without those two? She smiled through her weariness. "And you are?"

"Burke, Miss." He tucked the placard under his arm and reached for her bag. She followed his trim figure through the doors to the street and finally to a black sedan. He opened her door and she settled inside while he stored the bag in the trunk. A few moments later, he addressed her from the driver's seat.

"Where to?"

His light, Irish brogue loosened a memory, lilting and familiar, a bit like her grandmother's. In demeanor, he reminded her of Uncle Gerry, who'd died of injuries suffered in the Great War.

"Sixtieth and Broadway."

Even at this late hour, a variety of traffic and noise populated the streets as Burke pulled to a stop in front of the building her parents called home these days. The Rand House. Genteel, but not grand or plush. Nothing like their former life. A doorman opened the door and stood aside for her.

Inside the faded lobby, she crossed to the desk and tapped the bell. After several minutes, a short, stout man approached the desk from the direction of the elevator. "May I help you?"

She gazed into his rheumy eyes, feeling none too confident of his ability to do so. "Mr. and Mrs. Lewis, please?"

He frowned as his gaze rolled over her. "Lewis? Hmm … are you a relative?"

She hesitated. Were those dollar signs in his eyes? "A … friend of the family."

He turned and stepped behind the counter then faced her again. "They've gone. Left here owing me nearly a month's rent."

She swallowed the panic rising in her throat. This was probably the reason for the telegram, but how was she expected to find them? She blew out a quick breath. "You have no idea where they've gone? It's imperative that I find them."

He drummed his fingers on the counter. "They owe you money, too? I heard they'd moved to an apartment in the West End, though how they managed that, I've no idea." He scrutinized her. "You sure you're not related?"

She lifted her chin and looked down her nose at him. "Are you sure they left no forwarding address?"

"Lady, they left owing back rent. Do you think they'd

leave a forwarding?" He dismissed her with a nod of his head. "Good luck finding them, Miss …?"

Heat warmed her cheeks as she turned her back on the man. She cast a glance over her shoulder as she passed through the open door. What a rude man. She had no intention of giving him information, though she couldn't blame him. Honestly. Would her parents never grow up?

Burke opened the door and as he did, he gestured toward the sky. "It's rather late, Miss. Might I suggest you allow me to deliver you to your hotel?"

Once settled, she waited until he sat in the driver's seat. "I'm afraid I have no hotel, Burke. I expected to stay with my parents. They have moved from their former residence, leaving no forwarding address. I only know they've possibly gone to an apartment on West End."

His patient gaze never faltered. "Mr. Emerson has given orders, Miss, for me to take you to the corporate suite at the Plaza."

She clutched her purse. Good gracious. The Plaza. She glanced down at her coat and travel-stained gloves. She wasn't dressed for such luxury. "I suppose we must then." Her voice came out in a whisper.

Burke glanced at her in the mirror. "He said you'd be worried about your appearance, Miss, but you mustn't. We know how to get around that."

As he maneuvered the vehicle through the streets, she wondered how the big hotels were faring in these difficult days. Were they suffering, too? How many patrons could afford their usual fees? In front of the familiar facade, she peered through the window as Burke spoke to a footman.

After retrieving her bag, he opened the door and stood aside for her to exit the vehicle. He lifted the bill of his cap. "Call the front desk in the morning, Miss, whenever you need me."

With a nod, the footman took the bag from Burke and led Rebecca to a side door. "This way, Miss."

The footman handed over her bag to a bellman with whispered instructions. Aiming a polite smile at her, the footman returned to his post. Under normal circumstances, she'd press a coin into his hand, but he seemed not to expect it, so she faced the bellman.

"This way," he said with a pleasant smile as he led her to the elevator. So far, they'd managed to circumvent the main lobby. "Sanderson Suite," he said to the elevator attendant.

The bellman refused her money, after showing her to the room. "Not necessary, Miss."

Rebecca strolled around the quiet suite of rooms, taking in the plush comfort. She'd been here before, in this very suite, with Nancy. They'd spent the night in New York after shopping all day, long ago, and far away. She'd taken the luxury for granted back then. Now her tiny flat could easily fit in the suite's bathroom.

She picked up the phone and gave the operator Nancy's number. When the phone rang back in, she picked it up and waited while the call connected. "Nancy?"

"Did you find your parents?" Nancy's voice calmed Rebecca.

Rebecca gave a short laugh. "No, they've moved."

"Moved? Without letting you know? Where are you, then?"

"I'm at the Plaza. Thank Robert for me. It's lovely."

"You're most welcome, Rebecca. Is there anything we can do to help you locate your parents?"

"No, I'll be all right. I just wish Mother had the foresight to send me a forwarding."

"It would've been more convenient, but things will work out in the morning. You'll see." After promising her continued thoughts and prayers, Nancy hung up.

Rebecca stowed her few things in the closet then drew a bath and sank into its sudsy warmth. Leaning back, she took in her surroundings. Funny how quickly one learns to appreciate nice things. The shiny, white bath trimmed in black and white tiles, gleamed. It was so easy to relax in such a pleasant place. Her heart pricked just a little as she remembered the telegram. What did it mean, and where would it take her tomorrow?

6 November, 1929, Ginestra, Umbria, Italy

His meeting ended, Riccardo Alverá shook hands with Mayor Modesti then turned toward the ancient mahogany door. He flinched at the sound of a woman's voice calling him— Francesca Boccali—the mayor's secretary. For a moment, Riccardo stood still, half tempted to pretend he hadn't heard.

"I know you heard me," she said.

He turned to find her nearly at his heels, drawing on her coat as she walked. He forced a smile and took hold of the door knob. *"Ciao, Signorina.* I was just on my way—"

She ran her hand beneath her shoulder-length, blond locks and allowed it to cascade over her collar. "I know. You are always on your way somewhere. Well, today, I am on my way along with you. At least be a gentleman and walk me to my car."

He opened the door and stood aside for her to pass through then followed with some reluctance. She had a degree of magnetic charm, and most men thought her attractive, but the signorina's personality grated on Riccardo.

"Will you stop and have a coffee with me?" she asked as they walked toward the narrow piazza. The bell in Santa Maria's ancient tower tolled, sending a flock of pigeons into the air.

He shook his head. "No. It is late. I am expected at home."

Nearly as tall as he, she smiled into his eyes. "Of course you are. Well, at least tell me you will be at the Festival of the

Olives on Saturday? I am riding in the parade, as usual, but—"

"You know I am going to be married?"

"What has that to do with me? Will she be here? Does she not allow you to attend festivals in her absence?" She took a step back and signaled her driver then removed a thin metal case from her purse and chose a cigarette. "Who is she, anyway? No one has ever seen her. We are beginning to doubt she exists at all." She narrowed her eyes. "Perhaps she is a figment of your imagination." She clicked open a golden lighter and lit her cigarette, releasing the smoke.

Her smug expression turned Riccardo's stomach, but he would not be baited into a quarrel with her. "Whatever you wish to believe, Signorina." He set his hat on his head and gave her a curt nod. "For now, I bid you good day." He dodged as her driver pulled the car along the curb. He'd never liked that guy. There was something about him. He was … oily.

Ignoring Riccardo, the man jumped out of the car and opened the door for Francesca.

Hands in his pockets, Riccardo turned and strode toward his car. By the time he arrived, he was whistling a merry tune. He was not about to let that woman ruin his day. He had better things … he paused as another thought speared his conscience. If he was going to publicize his engagement news, he should probably tell his mother.

He'd held off telling her, because he knew it would set her off. He could well imagine it.

"Who is this woman? Is she Italian? No? Is she at least a Catholic?" Then she would grab her rosary. "Oh, my heart, my heart!"

He chuckled in anticipation. He started his car's engine and drove through the narrow street.

Another reason he'd hesitated to tell Mamma—Rebecca's reluctance to set a date. Then she'd confided in him that she was not even wearing his ring. She felt guilty, because she was uncertain of her feelings for him.

A flock of goats impeded his passage over the bridge. He sat back and waited. He must get Rebecca here as soon as possible. The longer she stayed away, the less she trusted her own feelings.

The road clear, Riccardo took off again. He knew why she had trouble. She'd grown up a product of a distressed marriage. But Riccardo was determined to have her as his wife. He would not give up.

So, back to the issue at hand. Mamma. Humorous imaginings aside, the time had come to tell her.

Chapter Three

A fire alarm pierced Rebecca's pleasant dream, clanging, clanging. Where's the fire? She forced her eyes open. Not a fire alarm—the phone was ringing. She hadn't had a phone in so long she'd forgotten what one sounded like. Confused, she sat up as it rang again. She stumbled to the desk and picked up the receiver, glancing at the clock. Gracious, what time was it?

The operator asked her to hold for Mr. Emerson.

"Rebecca? Did I wake you?" Robert's perky morning voice.

"Er ... yes. What is it?"

"I'm sorry to call so early, but I have information. Have you a pen handy?"

She grabbed pen and paper. "Yes, go ahead."

He gave her the address for The Gardens West Apartments. "They're staying with friends, or in a friend's apartment. I'm not certain. Oh, and breakfast is on the way."

"I can see you smiling, Robert. You know how wonderful you are, don't you?"

She barely had time to freshen up when there came a knock at the door.

"Room service."

Her stomach reacted happily to the feast presented. Eggs Benedict and half a grapefruit topped with a maraschino cherry. Hot coffee and real cream. Yum. Once she'd eaten her fill and completed her toilette, she called the front desk and ordered the car.

In front of the full-length mirror, she smoothed the skirt of her gray wool suit. With the last-minute addition of the rosebud from her breakfast tray pinned onto her lapel, it appeared business-like and quite appropriate for whatever this day held.

Burke was chipper and energetic. He'd had his morning coffee, no doubt. He stowed her bag in the trunk and opened her door. "Where to, Miss?"

The Gardens West seemed a bit high-end to Rebecca. She leaned her head back to observe the five-story apartment building. How had her parents managed to secure such a place, when they owed back rent elsewhere?

Burke followed her inside, carrying her valise. He set it down near the desk and tipped his hat to her.

Swallowing the lump in her throat, she bid farewell to him for the time being. She'd no idea what lay ahead, nor how long 'til she'd see him again.

The building's stout doorman could have been a gatekeeper at an ancient castle. He was quite stern and looked as if he did not approve of her at all. He announced her to someone over a telephone then directed her to the elevator at the rear of the lobby.

She picked up her bag and followed his directions.

An attendant stood like a stone statue, barely acknowledging her presence. "Fourth floor, Miss. Turn right. You'll want number 403."

The door opened before she knocked, but Rebecca did not recognize the face of the woman who opened it. A housekeeper, perhaps?

After closing the door behind Rebecca, the woman led the way down a narrow hall to the first door on the right. "You may wait in here. I'll take your valise, if you wish." She avoided eye contact.

What was that about?

Rebecca found herself in a very comfortable parlor, well-furnished in bright florals and colorful stripes. An entire wall held large windows, one of which was open, allowing a slight breeze. Unfortunately, the view was of a brick wall with windows into a neighboring apartment building. One could almost reach over and borrow a cup of sugar.

Turning about, she was pleasantly surprised to find a fireplace with a beautifully carved screen. A large vase of white silk blossoms anchored the mantel. Whose home was this? Though tastefully decorated, it was certainly not her mother's style.

Quiet voices echoed outside the room. Rebecca's heart paused its beating when her mother appeared in the doorway. "Mother, what's happened?"

Mother's eyes and nose were swollen and red, her lips trembling. She twisted a handkerchief between her fingers. "Oh, I'm not sure …"

"Where's Daddy?"

Mother bit her lip as fresh tears flowed. "He's … he's gone."

Rebecca's breath caught in her throat. Had he finally left her mother as he'd threatened so many times? "Oh, Mother, I'm sorry."

Mother shook her head. "No, dear. You misunderstand me. He's dead. Daddy's dead."

The silence in the room thrummed in Rebecca's ears as she struggled to make sense of her mother's words. Daddy— dead? How could that be? But gazing into her mother's face, she knew it must be true.

Stifling hot, Rebecca removed her jacket, folded it, and laid it over the back of a chair. The rosebud had long since wilted, along with her hair and makeup. She dabbed at her eyes again.

"We couldn't find him," Mother said, her face to the window. The sound of her voice, as it bounced off the glass, made Rebecca think of early recordings, tinny and hollow. "He'd been gone for over twenty-four hours. I thought he may have gotten confused. We've lived here such a short time." She glanced over her shoulder at Rebecca. "He was drinking again. Distraught, you know. We lost it all. Everything. It was so final." She turned back to the window. "That's when I sent you that telegram. I was in a panic, and the police wouldn't do anything."

Rebecca stepped forward and laid her hand on her mother's shoulder.

Mother took a stuttering breath and huffed it out. "It was so hard, waiting. You know I'm no good at waiting."

"What happened?" Rebecca was no good at waiting either. She wanted to know the truth, no matter how hard it was to say.

"They came last night—the police. They'd found a body. Said it was him." She blew her nose. "I couldn't go. They wanted me to—" A sob wracked her body.

Rebecca bowed her head. While she'd been relaxing in luxury, her Mother had suffered alone. But wait, had no one gone to identify him? She looked at her mother. "So … we don't know for sure it's him?"

Mother nodded. "I asked Victor to go." She turned and stepped toward Rebecca. "You remember Victor—Daddy's partner?"

Rebecca swallowed the negative comment that settled in her mind. Partner in failure. Two addicts struggling to make something out of nothing. Risking everything they could pool together. The big take. A shiver ran up her spine. "Victor identified him?"

"Most definitely. Yes." Mother crossed to a table behind the sofa and picked up a small leather notebook.

Rebecca recognized it immediately. Daddy's. He never went anywhere without it.

Mother held it up. "Water soaked. He drowned."

Rebecca's hand flew to her mouth as a moan escaped. Pain gripped her, from the inside out, stealing her breath.

Finding the nearest chair, she sank into it. She was barely aware of her mother's voice asking for handkerchiefs.

The housekeeper, introduced to her earlier as Mrs. Hawkins, pressed one into Rebecca's hand then set a stack of fresh ones on a nearby table. "I'll bring tea," she said.

Mother sat across from Rebecca and waited until she calmed a bit. "Someone saw him jump," she whispered. "The police told me. The witness reported it, but they hadn't been able to find a body."

Rebecca's hands shook as she blew her nose. Mother sat in silence for some time, gazing out the window.

After Mrs. Hawkins brought the tea tray, Rebecca stared at the English Ironstone teapot and matching cups sitting primly on saucers. Odd, what thoughts come to mind at such a time as this. What had become of their possessions? Their china, their knickknacks, collected over the years, from all parts of the world. Mother said they'd lost everything. All of it, gone. And now Daddy, too.

With a shake of her head, she poured their tea and handed Mother a cup then lifted her own and inhaled its aroma. Mother started talking again, but Rebecca soon lost track of her conversation.

This never-ending day had progressed to nearly half-past-five. Impatient, Rebecca folded and refolded a handkerchief in her lap. She should be busy. There was much to do, but Mother insisted she stay in the parlor when their friends, Ann and Lars Nielsson, arrived.

They sat across from Rebecca on the sofa. Ann held Mother's hand and spoke softly, while Lars nodded and made notes on a slip of paper in his palm. "We'll take care of everything," he said. "You needn't worry."

Mother addressed Rebecca. "This is how he'd want it, don't you think, dear?"

Rebecca forced her gaze to meet her mother's. "Yes, Mother." Her gaze swung around the room, searching for a phone. She should call Robert. She excused herself. "I'll be right back."

She found Mrs. Hawkins, who led her to the study, a warm, dark room across from the parlor. Mrs. Hawkins turned on the lamp then left the room. Behind the desk, framed photographs bespoke happier times. Mother and Daddy on cruises, or in exotic locations. Mother and Daddy with friends, seated at tables, sharing drinks or dinner. She recognized Monte Carlo and Palm Springs. There was one picture of Rebecca, dressed in cap and gown, just after receiving her college diploma.

It was now so late she decided to call the Emerson home instead of the office. As soon as she heard Nancy's voice on the line, Rebecca struggled. *Suck it up, kid. You're a grownup. You can do this.* "Daddy's dead." She forced the words out.

"Oh! Oh, Rebecca, I'm so sorry. I knew I should have gone with you."

"I'm all right. I will be, anyway. We do recover, don't we?"

"Yes, we do." Nancy took a breath. "Tell me what happened."

"I can't. Not yet."

"Oh, dear—" Nancy's voice broke.

For a moment, Rebecca went silent, fighting for control.

"We're coming. When is the funeral?"

Rebecca gave a soft sigh. "Day after tomorrow."

"We'll be there. I'll have Robert call you."

Rebecca replaced the receiver and sat back in the big leather desk chair, letting her hands hang down on either side. Her eyelids drooped. She drifted off.

A strange noise woke her sometime later. It sounded almost like a clap. She found Mrs. Hawkins staring at her.

"I hate to wake you, Miss Lewis, but your mother needs you."

A bit shaky and not quite awake, Rebecca stood and followed the housekeeper to the parlor.

"Here she is." Mother held out her hand. "My dear, Victor has come, and this is his wife, Allouette."

Rebecca bit back a smile. Really? Allouette? Taking in the woman's face and figure, she had no doubt where Victor had met his third wife. Or was it the fourth? She pushed her hand forward to be squeezed in Victor's viselike grip. She winced. "Victor, how nice to see you again."

He muttered something about the tragedy binding them all together.

After his voice trailed off, Rebecca turned her attention to his wife. "Allouette, you said?"

The woman smiled. "Lou, for short. I feel like I know you already. Your mother's told me so much about you."

Rebecca glanced at Mother.

"Shall we sit?" Mother said, gesturing for Mrs. Hawkins to serve the coffee.

Trying to follow their disjointed conversation was comic relief for Rebecca. Victor and Lou often talked at the same time, over the top of each other's words. Mother seemed to deal with it well, choosing to answer whichever one finished first. Rebecca's head throbbed.

Within the hour, more friends arrived. How many did they have in New York right now? She'd hardly had time to process things.

How had Daddy drowned? Had he really committed suicide? She gave a shudder and glanced around the room, but no one was looking at her.

If only Nancy and Robert were here with her now.

Her gaze settled on an eight-by-twelve portrait of Daddy. It sat atop a baby grand piano in the corner of the parlor. He was wearing his favorite three-piece gray wool suit, a felt fedora in a lighter gray, clasped in his hands. He'd always removed his hat for a photograph. He was quite proud of his wavy, brown hair.

This was to be his memorial photo, she supposed. Mother told one of the newcomers there would be no viewing. The body had been in the water too long. How could she say something like that out loud?

After talking to Robert on the phone the next morning, Rebecca marked another item off her list. She'd managed to accomplish a good number of things already, since her mother was still abed. She glanced at the clock. Nearly noon. There were errands to run. Her mother had talked of shopping for new black dresses and hats. Wasteful, in Rebecca's opinion. But she hadn't a single black dress in her possession. She was not a fan of black. Her complexion was too pale to look well in it.

Her reflection in the mirror troubled her. If only she'd taken the time to get her hair done. It was far too long. She'd have to pin it back and hope a hat would hide the imperfections.

She was just wondering whether to go in and wake Mother, when someone knocked at the door. All morning, they'd received offerings of food from neighbors and friends. Mrs. Hawkins had quite a time finding space for everything. This time however, a delivery boy held a bouquet of white chrysanthemums. Rebecca set it on the piano near the photo. The card was from the Emerson family. She smiled.

The funeral director had told Mother they'd probably not receive many flowers. "Times are hard," he'd said, as if they didn't already know that.

When Mother finally put in an appearance, she was dressed and ready to go. They took a cab, though it was only a short distance, but Mother was in no mood for a walk.

If Rebecca had been allowed any say in the matter, she'd never have chosen the small shop Mother insisted upon. They seemed a bit snobbish for Rebecca's taste. She did manage to find a simple black dress that suited her.

Modeling it in front of the store's full length mirrors, she wondered if Mother planned to stiff the store's proprietors for these goods as she had done the hotel owner.

"Good thing I've some money put away," Mother whispered.

Rebecca breathed easier. She almost felt guilty for the thoughts she'd entertained. After changing back into her gray suit, Mother beckoned to her.

"Here, try this hat. It'll cover that mop of red hair. You really shouldn't let it grow so long. It doesn't suit you."

Suppressing a groan, Rebecca tried on the hat. She was satisfied, but Mother was not. The saleslady brought three more. One was quite nice, but it boasted a carmine ribbon.

"We can change that out," the lady told Mother. "Or better yet, cover it up with a wider black ribbon you can remove later."

"What a good idea," Mother said, peering at Rebecca's reflection in the mirror. "We'll take it."

While they waited to settle the bill, Mother pulled on her gloves. "I don't understand why we've heard nothing from your fiancé."

Rebecca looked at her. "I haven't told him."

"Why not? He's a right to know, don't you think?"

"I meant to write him."

Mother paid the clerk and collected her purse. "Write? A letter will take a month."

Outside, they hailed a cab. Once seated, Mother ordered the driver to take them to the nearest Western Union. "You'll send the man a telegram, Rebecca. Honestly. Sometimes I wonder about you."

Rebecca opened her mouth to object then remembered the fifty dollar bill in her purse. She'd been saving it for the train trip home. Surely she could spare a bit for a telegram. Mother was right. Riccardo should know.

Mother sat back with a huff. "I suppose we'll have to postpone again. Poor man. How long has he waited? Four years?"

Rebecca closed her eyes a moment before she opened them again to look at her mother. "I wanted to be sure."

"The man is patient."

The cab stopped in front of the telegraph office. Mother clutched Rebecca's forearm. "That's a good sign. Your father never would've waited that long." Her eyes brimmed with tears. She released Rebecca's arm to reach for a handkerchief.

Rebecca darted a look at her mother's face. "I'll be right back."

Chapter Four

Mourners huddled beneath umbrellas at the graveside, reminding Rebecca of a crop of black mushrooms. She nearly gagged when Allouette whispered in a not-so-quiet voice, "The sky is weeping for our sorrow."

Rebecca dare not meet Nancy's gaze. Odd that she'd even think of laughing. Did that make her a bad person? She focused on the shiny wooden box, her father's final place of rest, and sobered.

She'd only attended a couple of funerals, but Rebecca was fairly certain this one for her father was out of the ordinary. It had not been held in a church, but at the funeral parlor. No preacher spoke. Several of Alton David Lewis's closest friends shared anecdotes from his too-short life. One of his friends played the violin as the casket left the building. Mother's question, "This is how he'd want it, don't you think, dear," drifted into her mind more than once.

After the ordeal had ended at the cemetery, everyone withdrew to Gardens West, where she could spend time alone with her friends. They sat in the study, away from the noise of Mother reminiscing with Daddy's friends while someone played jazz tunes on the piano.

Nancy stirred cream into her coffee. "What will your mother do after this?"

Rebecca sighed. "She won't talk about anything. I've tried. She says it makes her head ache."

Robert patted her hand. "She will have to face it now. Whether she likes it or not."

Nancy glanced around the study. "This is quite comfortable. How did they come to live here? I thought you said they were struggling."

"It belongs to friends." Rebecca's gaze took in the room. "They're out of the country until spring. According to Mother, they like to have someone staying in. I'm not so sure Mrs. Hawkins agrees."

"Victor told me your father disappeared after he received a troubling letter," Robert said, his gaze intent on something outside the window.

"Robert," Nancy said, "a bit insensitive, isn't it?"

He focused on Rebecca, flashing his dazzling smile. "I'm sorry. It's the lawyer part of me raising its ugly head. I'm always trying to figure things out."

Rebecca set her cup down. "It's all right. I assumed the letter was from the bank. They'd just received a notice of foreclosure ... regarding the Newport properties. Could've been something to do with that. I believe he was trying to work out some sort of deal."

"Ah, I see." He leaned forward, elbows on his knees, fingers intertwined.

Rebecca watched his expression, the flexing of his jaw, the slight furrow above his brow. She'd no doubt he understood all too well. What must he think of her father? Oh well, she'd better toughen up. There'd be lots of judgment going on in the near future. She'd heard it already—only a coward would end his own life and leave his women to deal on their own. The worst part of it? She felt the same way, and that left her with a load of guilt. She'd loved Daddy, but she'd had little respect for him.

Was she strong enough to face the unknown future? She'd spent a lifetime, short as it was so far, trying to overcome the mess her parents had made of their lives.

Nancy curled her fingers around Robert's hand. "We'd better get started, don't you think, if we're going to catch the six o'clock train?"

Robert gave a slow nod and glanced at Rebecca. "I wish you were coming with us, Rebecca. I hate to leave you with … what comes after."

Rebecca stood. "So do I—wish I were going with you—but, this is where I need to be for now. Good thing I'm unemployed." She faked a smile.

Nancy rose and pulled Rebecca into an embrace. "Come back to us as soon as you can. You'll always be welcome."

Robert dropped a kiss on Rebecca's cheek. "Call if you need anything. And don't hesitate to call on Burke. He's at your disposal."

"Thank you." As they drew apart, she and Nancy locked eyes for a moment.

"I'll be praying for you every day," Nancy whispered, her voice thick with unshed tears.

Rebecca smiled, her own eyes damp. "I depend upon it."

After seeing them to the door, she tried to slink away to her room, but Mrs. Hawkins waited for her. "Your mother desires your presence in the parlor, Miss."

Rebecca closed her eyes briefly then offered the housekeeper a brilliant smile. "Thank you. I'll go at once."

"Go, Riccardo!" The children screamed, jumping up and down.

Riccardo gave the ball one final kick, sending it squarely into the goal. He raised his arms in the air. "Yes!" Too bad it wasn't a real goal on a real field. He shook hands with his cousin Paolo before picking up one of their game balls and jogging across the park to the terrace overlooking the lake. Every year, his mother's family gathered here to celebrate the olive harvest. This year, the clan's mood emulated the weather. There was a definite chill in the Umbrian air. In all of Italy, for that matter.

"Heads up," Paolo called as he kicked another soccer ball

in Riccardo's direction. Riccardo caught it with his toe, tossing it up into the air. He juggled both as he approached the family's villa, finally tossing one of them back to Paolo.

Paolo caught it midair then juggled it with his feet. "*Ciao*, cousin. See you next week at the tournament."

Riccardo still chuckled as he approached the table where his uncles continued a debate that had begun at breakfast.

"It will be over by year's end. You'll see." Uncle Vittorio pounded the table with his fist as he spoke, his balding pate reflecting afternoon sunlight. "The market will bounce back. Keep your eyes on the Americans. It's their game right now."

Uncle Berto caught Riccardo's eye. "What do you say, about it, Riccardo?" He ran his fingers through his full head of salt-and-pepper curls then pointed toward the sky. "I think we're in for a long, hard time of it. Do you disagree?"

Still holding the soccer ball, Riccardo crouched beside Uncle Vittorio's chair. "I hope you are right, Uncle V, but I don't know. Perhaps it will be somewhere in between the two."

"Ah, you are a politician, Riccardo," Uncle Berto said. "You know how to placate. Sit down, have a glass with us."

"No, *signori*, I must go. Mamma wants to be home before sunset. Another time, perhaps."

Uncle Berto snorted. "Your Mamma is training you up to be a good husband, is she not?" He and Uncle Vittorio laughed heartily.

Riccardo pretended to join in, but it rankled him. How was he to behave? Should he deny Mamma's few requests to make himself seem more the man? He thought not. Besides, he had a big hurdle coming up with the meeting he planned to have with his mother. How was she going to feel about Rebecca?

He planned to tell her on the road home from the lake. She'd be angry, especially when she found out he'd put off telling her for several weeks. But with Mamma, you needed to choose your timing carefully. As he slid into his seat and closed the door, he opened his mouth, Rebecca's name on the tip of his tongue.

"My sisters are idiots!" she announced.

Riccardo turned to look at her. "Mamma, what are you talking about?"

She launched into a long monologue about how one of his aunts had sold a priceless antique vase that had once belonged to their great-grandmother. Apparently both of his aunts had decided it was the right thing to do. They had not sought Mamma's opinion—no mystery to Riccardo—they knew what she would say. At first, he tried to calm her but soon lost interest. She finally stopped talking and fell asleep.

As soon as they pulled up in front of the house, before their driver could get out of the car, Claudio, who usually cared for the horses, ran out to meet them. *"Buonasera, Signore*, you have a telegram from New York."

It had to be Rebecca. Had she changed her mind again? *"Grazie*, Claudio." He suppressed a grin. No doubt, Claudio had been at the house visiting his new wife, Eva, who was training in the kitchen.

After he'd seen to Mamma's comfort, Riccardo strode to the table in the foyer and picked up the envelope, ripped it open, and read the short message.

DADDY PASSED AWAY. WILL WRITE WITH DETAILS—RL

With some reluctance, Rebecca donned the black dress again. She and Mother were due at the attorney's office this morning to settle her father's estate. Rebecca dreaded the meeting since they'd now know exactly how far in debt he'd left them.

The doorbell rang as she made her final preparations. When she walked into the foyer to set down her purse, she found a gorgeous fall bouquet of white chrysanthemums and dark red roses, interspersed with baby's breath and maidenhair fern. A card lay on the table, addressed to her.

Our deepest condolences, Riccardo

"Breathtaking," Mother said, as she entered. "Who sent them?"

Rebecca held up the card. "Riccardo. And his mother, apparently."

"Red roses." She reached up to touch Rebecca's cheek. "He loves you."

Did he really, or was it obligation because she was his fiancée? Rebecca set the card on the table and reached for her purse. When had she become so cynical? Life as a bitter old maid loomed before her. A wrinkled one. She massaged the tight spot between her brows then faced Mother. "Burke's downstairs."

Mother stopped in front of a mirror beside the door to make a few last minute adjustments to her hair. Perky gray curls formed a border beneath the brim of her cloche hat. A black lace scarf draped her neck. "Well, let's go. We don't want to be late."

"I'd prefer not to go at all." In the elevator, she leaned close to Rebecca and whispered, "Why should we be concerned with what Daddy owed? We can't possibly pay it all back."

Rebecca took a deep breath to steady her nerves and stay her tongue. There were so many things she wanted to say right now, but it was not the place or the time. The elevator attendant, the same statue she'd met upon her arrival here, announced the first floor lobby. They disembarked and headed to the front door.

"Good day, ladies," the doorman said, as he opened the door for them.

Rebecca faced him with a smile. "Good afternoon, Stoddard."

A spark lit his eye as he acknowledged her greeting by

touching the bill of his cap. Perhaps he wasn't such a drudge after all. Knowing her parents, they'd never noticed him, much less bothered to learn his name.

Burke waited beside the sedan, his usual pleasant expression in place. Mother ignored him, but Rebecca thanked him as she settled on the cushioned back seat. "You know the address?"

"Yes, Miss Lewis. Traffic's a bit thick, but we should be there in plenty of time."

"Irish," Mother whispered.

Rebecca glowered at Mother, but she had already turned away, staring out the window. No use reminding her of their own lineage.

As the meeting progressed, Rebecca's stomach twisted into knots. A recent loan document held Mother's signature. With accumulated interest, sale of the Newport property would not be enough to cover the balance due. Rebecca watched Mother's face for a sign of life. Did she understand at all?

As he gathered the papers into a neat stack, Mr. Stuart looked pointedly at Rebecca. "Your mother will receive a summons once the sale of the property is final. Your father's other creditors will no doubt add their amounts due to this list." He folded his hands on the tabletop. "There are things you can do, Miss Lewis. If you have a private attorney, you may want to speak to him."

A summons. Other creditors. A bit numb, Rebecca nodded and rose from her chair. "Thank you, sir."

Mother refused to discuss it with Rebecca. All the way home, she talked of her plans for Rebecca's upcoming nuptials. "We need to get right to work. You know how long these things take. We've a trousseau to purchase, and … we'll need to secure passage. When shall we go? April's a wonderful time, but it's a bit chilly for a voyage. How about May? That will give us plenty of time to make our plans. What do you think?"

Rebecca closed her eyes, wishing she could also close her ears. Had the woman not understood a word Daddy's solicitor had said? They were over their heads in debt. How could she think of a wedding? She swiped at a tear with her gloved finger. All her dreams had just been tossed out the window like dirty dishwater. She opened her eyes.

Mother sat in silence, gazing at her. "I don't think you've heard a word I've said, Rebecca. We really do need to talk about this. It's your future. It's … our best way out of this mess. We can go to Italy." She smiled and reached to take Rebecca's hand. "You love Italy."

Rebecca's gaze drifted to the rearview mirror. Burke's attention was on the traffic, but she knew he'd heard everything. She hated when her mother aired their laundry in front of … anyone. Would Burke mention their conversation to his employer? Because Rebecca knew his employer. Robert would ask Burke point blank.

"I need time, Mother. Surely you can understand that. We're still in mourning."

Mother squeezed her hand. "That's just it, dear. We don't have time."

As Burke maneuvered their vehicle through the lunch crowd, Rebecca stared at the faces of those passing by. Could she do this? Could she leave her country behind forever, to live among people she didn't really know? Yes, she loved Italy. She had always loved it. But it had been fun—a holiday: skiing in the Italian Alps, where she'd first met Riccardo, sunbathing on Mediterranean beaches, and trekking through Tuscany. She'd spent a brilliant week in Sperlonga, studying the caves and the Roman ruins. Visited Riccardo's beautiful seaside villa. Warmth crept into her heart at the memory of him. Could she give herself to this man, forever? Love him as he deserved to be loved? Her mouth went dry. She wasn't sure she could really love anyone. Besides, she needed to tell him their situation. She had still to write the letter.

He may not want her anymore.

Chapter Five

1 December, 1929, Umbria, Italia

"*Americana*!" Mamma wailed, gesturing wildly. "And not even of the Catholic faith. How can you bring such a one as this into our household? All the generations who have ever lived in this house will spin in their graves because of you."

Riccardo almost laughed out loud. Mamma was so dramatic at times. But he didn't. He sat in silence as she railed against Rebecca, a woman she barely knew. At some point, she'd take a breath and notice he hadn't spoken. That's when he'd hit her with round two, Rebecca's mother.

"You could have your pick from so many nice, Italian girls. Just the other day, that Francesca woman from the mayor's office told me how well she thinks of you."

Riccardo rolled his eyes. "Mamma. I am not interested in any of these women. I already know who I want as my wife."

When she started in again, he held up his hand, in much the same way as his father had always done. "I am not finished speaking, Mamma. You know I love you. But I love Rebecca, too. And I believe she is the one God has chosen for me."

Mamma's face turned the color of a good marinara sauce. She patted her breast. "My heart! Oh, you have broken my heart, using the Lord's name in vain. Surely He would never choose such a one for you, someone who is not of your faith."

Riccardo kept his voice firm. "She will be, Mamma. You will see. She'll come to church with us. She only needs direction in her life."

He did not doubt this.

His mother rose from her chair and stomped out of the room.

Riccardo leaned forward, elbows on his knees. Could he do this? One man, on his own, with two strong-willed women living under this roof, and another only a short distance away? Was he crazy even to consider it?

He got up and crossed to the window, gazing out at the distant mountain peaks, now covered in their winter blanket of snow. He pushed his hands into his pockets. Would Rebecca adapt her life to theirs? Already, she was withholding information from him. He'd received her very proper letter, telling of her father's death, and he'd thought little of it. Then, a few days later, he'd received a letter of several pages, from Mrs. Lewis. Her story had differed somewhat. Perhaps Rebecca was embarrassed about their situation, and the way her father had died. This was what he'd told himself. Why else would she not tell him the truth? If she truly loved him, wouldn't she confide in him?

He rubbed his chin, already rough with new growth, though he'd shaved in the early morning. The sound of his mother's voice drifted in from the back of the house. She was in the kitchen, helping with the evening meal. He was glad. Work—this was how she dealt with her troubles. He turned and strode from the room. Perhaps he should do the same.

New York City

A chill wind buffeted Rebecca as she stepped outside. She tightened her coat's belt and tied a wool scarf over her shoulders. A black wool cloche kept her ears warm. She glanced both ways then turned toward Broadway, with no particular destination in mind. Soon, the cold air and exercise helped to clear her sluggish mind. She could concentrate on the problems at hand. The morning's mail had included a letter informing them the Newport property and all of their household belongings would be sold at auction on January 24, barring inclement weather. She supposed by then, Mother would have emptied her secret coffers, so there'd be no other income to declare. Legally, she should be safe.

Mother hoped to depart New York no later than mid-May. Rebecca fumbled with her ring, twisting it round and round. She'd mailed Riccardo's letter the day after the meeting with the lawyer. To speed things up a bit, she'd paid extra for air mail, once the letter reached England via Cunard Line. If she could just manage to hold off making any important decisions until after she had a return letter from him—but Mother wouldn't leave her alone. She wanted an answer right away. What difference did it make if they weren't to leave until May? They'd still have to find temporary lodgings.

She hadn't told Mother yet, but she planned to spend Christmas with the Emersons at Perry's Landing, owned by Robert's grandmother. Rebecca had never been to Perry's Landing, but she'd heard so much about it and really wanted to go. Perhaps they'd invite her to stay with them until she left? But no, she couldn't do that. She couldn't leave Mother on her own, though there was probably no reason to worry. The woman was like a cat; she always landed on her feet.

Pausing to wait for a stop light, Rebecca took in her surroundings. It wouldn't do to wander off and get lost. Once she was confident of her route and the traffic had cleared, she set off again.

A scene played in her mind, of Riccardo as he read her letter. How would he react? She tried to imagine his expression, but all that came to her was the look in his eyes as he'd confessed his love and longing for her. Had it really only been a year since they'd all spent Christmas together in Upstate New York? Mother and Daddy, pretending to be the happy couple, hosting a large gathering at a friend's lake house. Rebecca was quite sure Riccardo hadn't been fooled by their ruse. But he hadn't let on.

After walking for nearly three blocks, she stepped into a

small coffee shop. Finding an unoccupied table by the window, she ordered a cup of coffee. The aromatic brew warmed her as she gazed out at the street and ruminated. She didn't mind being alone. In fact, she rather enjoyed it. It was nice to complete a thought without interruption.

The low hum of conversations comforted her, until she overheard her father's name. Trying not to call attention to herself, she glanced around the small room, her ears tuned to the sound of the woman's voice she'd heard.

"… so sad, and now his widow is leeching off the Fergusons. I heard she doesn't even pay rent."

"Shocking," the other woman said.

Rebecca heard no more of the conversation. She left payment and a tip on the table beside her empty cup and crept out, hoping no one recognized her. What had she done to deserve this? Must she go through her entire life in humiliation?

Perhaps she was just as bad, looking for sanctuary with a man she barely knew. She hadn't exactly been honest with him. Her letter had barely skimmed the surface, but she couldn't seem to pen the words. She'd told him Daddy had drowned, not bothering to mention he'd taken his own life. And she hadn't mentioned the sorry state of their finances only that they were in "rather reduced circumstances."

Breathless from walking so fast, she stood at a corner, waiting to cross. Since there was no traffic light on this street, a policeman directed traffic. After what seemed an eternity, he waved in her direction.

If only Riccardo were here now. He would hold her in his arms and comfort her. But he wasn't here, and she could not let herself depend on someone else for her comfort. She'd always been on her own. What if this was her lot in life? Perhaps she didn't deserve anyone. Guilt pricked her, completing its usual task.

When the light turned, she crossed the street. Music reached her ears—a familiar song—something she'd heard as a child attending church with her nanny. She sought the source of the music—a beautiful old church with its doors standing open. Why would they have the doors wide open on such a cold day? She crept nearer, listening as someone played the song on a pipe organ. Curious, she wandered to the front of the brightly-lit sanctuary, and genuflected then sat down in the pew. She wasn't sure why she'd knelt. She wasn't Catholic, but her nanny had been, and Rebecca had always mimicked the woman's behavior in church. It had seemed right and proper at the time. She glanced around, taking in her surroundings.

The large stained glass window in the rear of the sanctuary depicted the scene when the dove landed on the savior's head. Rebecca admired its beauty and craftsmanship. As the song continued, something stirred in her breast. A feeling … or perhaps a longing … or was it only her imagination? She closed her eyes and prayed. The music quieted, leaving peace in its wake. Feeling somewhat better, she stood and walked out of the church.

Within sight of the Gardens West, she noticed a car parked out front. An odd premonition set her heart racing.

Stoddard opened the door. "You'll be glad of the warmth now, won't you, Miss? Your cheeks are rosy with the cold."

Rebecca smiled as she unwound her scarf. "It was rather nippier than I'd expected." She glanced over her shoulder, to the curb where the car was parked. "Do you know whose vehicle that is, Stoddard?"

He gave her a quick nod. "Ah, yes. It's a Mr. Lansdowne. I believe he's an attorney, here to see your mother. He's just this minute gone up."

Alarm bells ringing in her breast, Rebecca hurried to the elevator, but had to wait for it to descend. Why was an attorney visiting Mother, and why had Rebecca heard nothing about it?

Mrs. Hawkins opened the door. Rebecca dashed through, already removing her coat and scarf.

Taking her coat, Hawkins whispered, "He came unannounced, Miss. Your mother wasn't expecting him."

Rebecca followed the sound of the voices and found them in the formal parlor. A tall man of apparent middle age, quite well-dressed, stood as she entered.

Her mother introduced them. "This is my daughter, Rebecca." Facing Rebecca, she said, "Mr. Lansdowne was just about to tell me why he has come."

Rebecca sat beside her mother on the sofa, facing Mr. Lansdowne. His expression was impossible to read. He must be a very good lawyer.

He drew a letter from his lapel pocket and slowly unfolded it as he spoke. "As I told your mother, Miss Lewis, I represent the Fergusons, owners of this apartment. I have here, a letter from Blanche Ferguson. She has asked me to inform you, they are returning to town earlier than planned and will need the full use of their home. You are requested to vacate the premises by December 15."

Rebecca stared at the man's face, wondering what thoughts were coursing through his mind at this moment.

"Oh, dear," Mother said, patting Rebecca's hand. "Well, I suppose we must. Before Christmas?"

Rebecca lifted her chin. "That's no problem, sir. But tell me, why did Mrs. Ferguson not write to us directly, instead of going through her attorney?"

Mr. Lansdowne cleared his throat and looked into her eyes. "She asked that I make the call myself. Since you are amenable to the request, perhaps we can proceed without further delay. You see, she has also required an ..." he broke off to glance around the room, then brought his gaze back to Rebecca's. "An inventory of the contents of the apartment."

"An inventory?" Rebecca hoped she had misheard. But no. Judging by the discomfort depicted in the man's eyes, she had heard correctly. She darted a glance at her mother, who had gone rather pale.

Rebecca bit back the retort sitting on the tip of her tongue, instead giving a calm answer in an even tone of voice. "Of course. I quite understand, Mr. Lansdowne. You will wish to do this before we leave, I expect?"

He set the folded letter on the table then drew a clipboard from a valise at his feet. "Right now, if it's not inconvenient."

Rebecca stood.

Mother followed. "Please, feel free to do whatever needs to be done. We'll try to stay out of your way." Her voice trembled with each word.

He left the room, clipboard in hand.

Rebecca closed her eyes and drew in a deep breath, letting it out slowly. There were at least fifty things she'd like to say to her mother right now, but she held her tongue. Mother's pained expression stopped her. The woman was already suffering. "Why don't you sit down? I'll make us some tea."

Mother pulled out her handkerchief and held it over her mouth with trembling fingers.

Mrs. Hawkins appeared at the door, her eyes on Rebecca. "May I see you in the kitchen, Miss?"

Rebecca patted her mother's hand then followed the housekeeper. In the kitchen, with the door closed, Rebecca filled the tea kettle and set it on the burner to heat. Then she turned to Mrs. Hawkins.

"I'm afraid this is my fault," she told Rebecca. She laid her palm on her breast as she drew in a shaky breath. "It was before you came. I was rather alarmed by … some of the goings-on. There were all sorts coming in here, visiting with your father—God rest his soul." She turned away to reach for the tea.

Rebecca watched as the woman spooned tea leaves into the pot. When Mrs. Hawkins faced her again, Rebecca touched her arm. "I'm sure I would've done the same. You were only looking out for your employer's interests."

Mrs. Hawkins nodded. "I wrote Mrs. Ferguson a letter and told her some of what was happening. But when you came, you were so kind and levelheaded. I knew everything would come out all right. I sent a quick note to my employer, but by then, I suppose it was too late." She poured the boiling water into the teapot and set the kettle back on the stove. "I'm really sorry, Miss. I hope you can forgive me."

Rebecca gazed into the woman's eyes and smiled. "There's really nothing to forgive. You were doing your job. I understand that. But if you need forgiveness, you have it. I hope Mrs. Ferguson appreciates you."

Mrs. Hawkins turned away, but not before Rebecca had seen the flush rising in her cheeks. Most likely, the Fergusons cared little for what happened to their help.

Rebecca and her mother waited in the parlor for nearly an hour as the attorney moved around the apartment. She wondered why he was doing this, instead of calling on a subordinate. Mother must have been thinking the same thing.

"Why would a prominent attorney take inventory of someone's household goods?" She sipped her tea for a moment then giggled.

Rebecca sent her a frown.

Mother set her cup down. "Perhaps he's been demoted to a lesser position since the crash. Or maybe he's casing the joint. He means to—"

"Mother!"

Mother's brow furrowed. "Well, one has to make the best of every situation, don't you think? If I'm not finding something to laugh at, I'm crying, and I'd really rather not, if you don't mind."

Such was Mother's way of coping with difficulties. Rebecca stood and paced to the window. She looked out at the day, now shadowed by gray clouds. Weariness washed over her. Instead of finding ways to entertain herself, Mother should be thinking about what they were to do now. More likely, she expected her daughter to do that. Rebecca turned just as the parlor door opened, and Mr. Lansdowne stepped inside.

"I have only this room left to inspect. Then I'll be on my way." Mother started to get up, but he asked her to keep her seat. "Please don't trouble yourself. I'll only be a moment. Then I'll need to have you sign some papers."

Rebecca's heart sped up. Why would they need to sign something? She moved slowly toward the sofa and sat down. Was he going to send them a bill? Well, let him do it. They could add it to all the others, queuing up in Daddy's estate.

The minutes ticked away until he sat down and shuffled through the list clipped to the board. Then he pulled a folder from his valise, removed a sheet of paper, and glanced over it before handing it to Rebecca.

It was a simple acknowledgment of the "perfunctory inventory performed at the request of the owners of said property." It required Mother's signature, and Rebecca signed as witness.

"Now," Mr. Lansdowne said, as he returned the papers to his valise, "you will be required to reimburse any items taken from the pantry during your stay. Mrs. Hawkins has kept a very accurate list. Other than that, everything seems in good order." He latched his valise and held it on his lap. "I thought perhaps Blanche had overreacted. That's why I came myself. I'm her brother as well as her lawyer. I hope I haven't made you ladies too uncomfortable."

Mother cackled. "Oh dear! Poor Blanche."

Rebecca smiled at Mr. Lansdowne. "Thank you for letting us know. And we were due to leave soon, anyway." She glanced at her mother. It wasn't really a lie.

"Yes, of course we were," Mother said.

Mr. Lansdowne rose to go.

Rebecca stood also. "I hope you have a very nice holiday, Mr. Lansdowne."

He smiled and nodded. "You do the same, Miss Lewis."

"What of your apartment in Springfield?" Mother asked Rebecca at dinner. "Can we go there?"

Rebecca shook her head. "I had to let it go, Mother. I lost my job. I couldn't pay for it." Besides, it was only one room. They'd kill each other within a week. No need to mention that.

Mother frowned as she pushed peas around on her plate. "Well, there's Victor and Lou. They did say if I needed anything … and they sent an invitation to Christmas dinner." She perked up a little. "They'll have a fancy dinner. Wouldn't that be just the thing to lift our spirits?"

Rebecca set her fork down and gazed at her mother. "You should accept their invitation."

"Only me? But what will you do?"

"I'll go to Springfield. I can stay a few days with Nancy. That will give me time to come up with some kind of plan. Perhaps by then, I'll have a letter from Riccardo."

Rebecca called Nancy after dinner. She didn't tell her what had happened. One never knew who might be listening on a party line. "I'm coming to Springfield day after tomorrow."

"Wonderful," Nancy said. "You'll stay with us, of course. Then we'll all go together to Perry's Landing for the holidays. I'm so glad. I can't wait to see you."

Rebecca released a sigh as she cradled the handset. At least Nancy still loved her. She could always stay in Springfield and find another job. Mother would be disappointed, of course. She had her heart set on going to Italy, getting away from all the gossip and difficulties. But would it be any better there? Italy was also suffering from this depression. And they had always been a poor country.

Mrs. Hawkins made their last few days easier, pressing and packing their clothes and keeping hot coffee brewed.

Rebecca ran errands and interference, as Mother made impossible demands on the overworked housekeeper. "Mother, she doesn't work for you, remember? She has to make sure everything is ready for her employers."

"Oh, pshaw," Mother said. "She's used to it. You're much too friendly with the help. They'll take advantage of you in a second. Steal you blind. You'll see when you have your own household to run."

Rebecca turned away before she did something really disrespectful, like an eye roll or an outright belly laugh. Who had run the household those last several years? Naive little Rebecca, that's who. What would have happened, had she not stepped in? And no one had stolen anything or taken advantage of anyone.

She didn't respond to Mother, just plastered on a smile and continued her work.

On their final day at Gardens West, a telegram arrived from Riccardo. Rebecca drew a deep breath before opening it with trembling fingers.

> I LOOK FORWARD TO YOUR ARRIVAL IN THE
> SPRING. LETTER TO FOLLOW.
> ALL MY LOVE, RICCARDO

He still wanted her.

Betty Thomason Owens

Chapter Six

15 May, 1930

Rebecca stood at the railing of the *RMS Olympic* as New York Harbor faded into the distance. "I shall never see you again," she whispered, grateful for the wind that snatched her words and dried her eyes. "Of that I am quite certain." With one gloved hand, she gripped the cold metal railing and with the other hand, she stuffed a folded envelope into her coat pocket.

Slowly, the number of passengers at the rail thinned until only a couple of cigar-smoking men stood with their backs to the wind. Rebecca tucked a strand of hair behind an ear and released her hold on the rail. Her steps faltered only once as the steamer's engines settled.

A trill of feminine laughter echoed from some nearby doorway, dislodging a memory of another long-ago voyage. A much happier time, when money flowed like water from an artesian well. Before the crisis. Before life happened. She swiped at another tear and gave herself a mental shake. Why was she so maudlin? Daddy would call her schmaltzy and box her ears. She faced a door that led to an interior corridor.

A young man in an unfamiliar uniform opened it then stood aside allowing her to pass. "Ma'am."

Yes, things had changed. Besides the fact she was old enough to be called "ma'am," the words, "C Deck" on the overhead sign assaulted her vision. Her stomach took a nose dive. She'd never even visited the lower levels in the past. Pausing again at her cabin door, she hunched her shoulders to loosen the tension and drew a long, slow breath of air, decidedly stale, with a hint of mold. What was the hurry? In fact, if she could think of any errands that needed attending—

The door swung open.

Too late.

Rebecca forced a smile. "Hello, Mother."

Mother had already removed her hat and slipped out of her coat. "There you are. I was a moment away from sending for you. Come inside. It's really quite comfortable."

Rebecca followed her into the room, scanning its interior as they progressed. It seemed almost Lilliputian. Two berths on the right side wall, one upper, one lower, a narrow sofa on the other, and a dressing table in between. No facilities. Not even running water. She bit down on her lower lip and focused on the one point of grace—a porthole. At least they'd be able to see daylight.

With a quick nod, she advanced toward the table, removing her hatpins then the hat. "It's … satisfactory. After all, it's only for a few days." Eight or so very long days stuck in a sardine can with her mother. The one person who held the power to twist Rebecca's nerves in a knot.

"Well, it's not first class, of course," Mother said, gazing at her image in the dingy mirror. "But it's the best we can do right now. And no one need know about it. We'll keep to ourselves." She picked at her graying hair, pulling it back into shape after being smashed beneath a cloche hat. "I'm told the double berths are left over from the war when the ship was used to transport soldiers. The addition of a sofa provided for a third man to sleep here."

Tucking the hatpins into her burgundy cloche, Rebecca set it on the dressing table giving herself a moment to gather her thoughts. After a quick breath, she pasted on a smile and turned to face her mother. "That's comforting, in a way. If our soldiers could endure it, surely we can also. Who is there to question it anyway?"

Perhaps it would've been easier had Rebecca not spent the

last few days with the Emersons at their country house. Though Nancy said they had cut back and were living frugally, the place still dripped of luxury. Not that Rebecca blamed them. If you can afford it, why not enjoy it?

Mother touched Rebecca's arm. "May I assume you heard what I said, or shall I repeat myself again?"

Rebecca pushed her thoughts aside and concentrated. "I believe you were asking about dinner?" This was as good a guess as any, since food was a subject high on her mother's list of interests these days.

Mother gave her an indulgent smile as she reached up to tuck a stray curl behind Rebecca's ear. "My darling, you really must learn to pay attention. What will Riccardo think of your lapses?" A slight furrow creased her brow. "Especially in view of recent events."

Rebecca sat down on the edge of the sofa and removed her shoes then stretched her aching feet and wiggled her toes, hoping to bring them back to life.

"If he'd been made aware of all our circumstances, which he has not, he would understand my distraction." She licked her lips and glanced around, hoping for a drink of water. A pitcher and two glasses sat on the dresser.

Mother fiddled with the hem of her jacket, her eyes averted. "Actually, he does know."

Rebecca's hand trembled as she poured water into her glass, splashing droplets on the paneled wall. She set the pitcher down. "What?"

"He deserves to know," Mother huffed out. He's your fiancé." She pulled a washcloth from their supply and mopped up the mess then draped the damp cloth over the side of the cabinet. "I wrote to him."

Rebecca's imagination kicked into high gear. She'd seen enough of her mother's letters to be really afraid of what she'd written to Riccardo. "What? When?" Riccardo hadn't said anything about it. Perhaps it was recent?

"Quite some time ago."

Rebecca sighed. "I believe that's my decision to make."

"You don't think he needs to know ahead of time, so he can make the necessary preparations? After all, we can no longer pay for the wedding, and that poor man's waited long enough. Longer than he should have, if you ask me."

But no one's asking you. Rebecca had to bite her tongue to keep from lashing out at the woman. Slow and steady, she drained her glass and set it down when she really wanted to scrub her fingers through her hair and scream at the top of her lungs.

Mother was bored without Daddy. She was constantly sticking her nose in Rebecca's business. Ironic, really. As a child, Rebecca had longed for her parents' attention. Parents who cared when she fell and scraped a knee or brought home a blue ribbon from the spring meet. She'd envied her classmates when their mommies showed up with cookies or cake on their birthdays. And now ...

After a long, slow breath, she faced her mother. "Riccardo and I agreed on a simple wedding. There's really nothing to afford, other than food for the reception, and we can find ways to save on that."

As she struggled with the latch of her suitcase, Mother darted the occasional glance at Rebecca. "Even that will be difficult, dear."

Rebecca's breath escaped with a "whoosh," leaving her empty. A physical blow to her abdomen must feel quite similar. "You spent *all* the money?"

Mother gave a slow nod, hazel eyes brimming, lower lip quivering. "It's not like I threw it away, dear. I put off telling you until we were underway, because I knew you'd be upset." She pressed her hands together as if to pray. "I didn't want you to cancel everything."

After a moment, Rebecca slid close to rub her mother's arm. "It's just too much to bear."

"Your Conte was very sympathetic. Said he'd take care of everything."

Rebecca pressed well-manicured fingertips beneath her chin to keep it from crashing to the floor. "Oh, Mother, you didn't. I hope he hasn't paid for this … this voyage … and—"

"Oh, no. He did offer, but I told him we were well able to make the trip on our own. I'm just thankful I had the foresight to sell your grandmother's house and set the money aside before the bank devoured everything. How embarrassing would it have been for you to arrive with no trousseau?"

Set the money aside. Mother had kept that money hidden in one of Daddy's old cigar boxes and stashed it in her suitcase. Good thing, too. They hadn't been allowed to reenter the Newport house once the bank foreclosed on it.

A soft knock sounded at the door. Mother stepped forward. "That'll be our tea." She opened the door and stepped aside as a young woman in a trim black dress and crisp white apron delivered a tray laden with breads, cakes, and a tea service.

"Will that be all, ladies?"

At Rebecca's nod, the woman quietly left the room.

Rebecca turned her gaze on Mother. "How did you manage to have tea delivered in third class?"

Mother hummed a little tune as she poured the tea and handed a cup to Rebecca. "I slipped the woman a little something to bring it to us, just this once. I don't know about you, but I've no wish to venture forth this evening."

They sat side-by-side on the sofa and stared at the wall as they sipped tea and nibbled the snacks.

Rebecca had a very good idea why her mother preferred not to go out. Tired as she was, the humiliation of sitting down to eat in the third class restaurant would no doubt be her undoing.

Rebecca tried not to think about the letter her mother had written to Riccardo. She had planned that conversation with him so well, rehearsed it a hundred times in her mind, each time, wondering how he would receive it.

She fingered the letter in her pocket. Now she would never know. She hadn't been allowed the opportunity to watch his face as he received the bad tidings. News that should have come from her lips. She'd never know how he really felt about it. Because he would never tell her.

Riccardo ran a comb through his hair, sculpting it with the heel of his left hand. He set the comb on his dresser, smoothed his carefully trimmed mustache, and straightened his tie. One very good looking man stared back at him from the mirror. On the way out the door, he picked up his new brown fedora. Outside his room he halted, checked his wrist, then returned to pick up his watch. It wouldn't do to go off without the wristwatch Rebecca had given him their last Christmas together. After fastening the band, he lifted a framed portrait from his bureau. A few more hours and he'd be gazing into those amazing blue eyes.

He replaced the picture and strode toward the hallway where Mamma's voice echoed, giving last minute orders to her kitchen staff. How would she handle herself in the coming days? She'd made her opinion quite well known to him on several occasions—she was none too keen on his choice of a bride.

He descended the stairs and crossed the tiled entryway to peer out the open front door to the drive. Tito had already pulled the car around and was busy dusting the shiny black Rolls Royce with a chamois.

A soft sound brought Riccardo's attention back to the foyer where a small black-haired boy peeked at him from the entrance to the servants' hall. "Chico, tell Nonna to send *la signora* to the car."

Chico's gapped-toothed smile flashed white against his sun-browned face as he skittered away without a word.

Still, a quarter of an hour passed before his mother joined him in the drive. No apology, of course. Carlotta Teresa Dominici Alverá never apologized for tardiness. A small smile quirked his lips at her approach.

"Buongiorno, Mamma." Resting his fingers on her shoulders, he dropped a kiss on each cheek and smiled into her scowl. "Are you ready?"

He caught the momentary flicker of a smile before she turned toward the car where Tito stood with the door open. That she could never resist his smile was a well-known fact. Riccardo assisted her then followed Tito to the opposite side.

Dust swirled in their wake as Tito followed the long, sloping drive to the road. Riccardo ran his fingertips along the sharp crease of his trouser leg. He'd dressed carefully, choosing a milk chocolate brown suit, ivory white shirt, and dark brown silk tie shot through with red and gold threads in a herringbone pattern. Gold cufflinks glinted at his wrists, reminding him of *Papá*, who had given them to Riccardo upon graduation from university.

His gaze came to rest on Mamma's profile, certain she would speak her mind one more time. She wouldn't look at him until she was ready. He glanced at his watch. The drive to the train station in Foligno required over an hour. He preferred she not wait until the last few minutes of the drive.

"Ti amo, Mamma," he whispered then watched as her head turned slowly toward him.

"You say this, but then you go against my wishes for you." A deep furrow creased her brow. "To marry outside the Church." She pressed her fist against her breast and exhaled. "It crushes my heart. I cannot breathe."

He reached for her clenched fist and massaged her fingers until she relaxed. "Mamma. You speak as though Rebecca is a heathen. She is not. She has a warm and open heart. You will see. If you invite her, I am quite certain she will accompany you to services."

"Americana," Mamma whispered, withdrawing her hand.

He gave a low chuckle.

After a moment's silence, Mamma turned her face to the glass again. "I suppose I will have to speak English all the time."

"No, Mamma. This too, we have discussed. Rebecca speaks fluent Italian." He glanced at his watch as they passed a sign indicating ten kilometers to Foligno. "We're making good time, Tito, grazie."

Tito touched his cap. *"Prego,* Signore."

Mamma released a pent-up breath. "What of the mamma? Does she also speak the language?"

Riccardo shook his head. "I am uncertain of her abilities. But you must not worry." He shrugged. "Mrs. Lewis is able to make her own way, wherever she goes."

"Lewis. What kind of name is this? English? I do not trust the English." She pulled a white cotton handkerchief from her purse and dabbed her nose.

"I rather think the original family was Welsh."

Her eyes widened, causing her narrow brow to all but disappear beneath the brim of her hat. "Scottish—even worse. Ruffians. How will I bear it? What are you doing to us? Mingling our good Italian bloodline with—" She covered her face with her hanky.

"Mamma. You are scaring Tito. He will think these ladies are villains before they even arrive."

Tito grinned into the rearview mirror.

"Besides, I think you are forgetting. Papá was a Spaniard."

Mamma sucked in a quick breath. "Half—only half—and

that was Castilian." She tucked her hanky into her sleeve then folded her hands in her lap. "For your sake, *mio figlio,* I hope you are right about this girl. I will do my Christian duty. I will be a good hostess. As long as you know my objections."

"Oh, I know your objections, Mamma."

At last, Tito pulled into an empty spot outside the train depot at Foligno. He jumped out to assist the signora.

The noise and activity announced the approach of the afternoon train. After the preliminary blasts of the horn, Riccardo held out his arm for Mamma. They made their way to the platform. The steam evaporated almost as soon as it was emitted, leaving heat waves in its stead. Beads of sweat broke out on Riccardo's brow. Was it from the temperature or the excitement he could barely contain?

Seventeen months had passed since Rebecca bid him farewell at the train station in Upstate New York, near the small town where they'd spent Christmas. Both her parents had been with them. Even then, distress dug a deep furrow in her father's brow. Riccardo had attributed the man's bloodshot eyes to alcohol, but now he wondered. An odd feeling squeezed at his heart. Was he making a mistake?

Rebecca stepped from the train to the platform, pausing briefly before reaching back to help her mother. As soon as Mother stood beside her, Rebecca scanned the crowd. Where was Riccardo? The place filled quickly with disembarking passengers. "I don't see them yet. Must be running late."

"We are a tad early, according to the orderly," Mother called, dabbing at her neck with a limp hanky. "Goodness, it's hot. I do wish you'd chosen to meet at the coast. It's so much cooler there."

Rebecca's attention wandered as she continued to scan the thinning crowd. A couple of blasts announced the train's imminent departure. In that moment, she caught sight of a dapper young gentleman in a brown suit, a well-dressed woman at his side. The woman's face was hidden behind a black lace shawl draped over a black hat, typical of an Italian widow. Riccardo's countenance lit as his gaze found Rebecca's. She made sure her own expression matched his.

She touched her mother's arm. "There. I see them."

"About time," Mother said, a little too loudly. "I feel as though I'm melting."

Riccardo relinquished the woman's arm, removed his hat, and gave Rebecca and her mother a polite bow. "Welcome to Umbria, Signora and Signorina Lewis. May I introduce my mother—Signora Dominici Alverá. Mamma, this is Signora Lewis, and of course you know Signorina Lewis."

His mother gave a stiff nod and offered the barest of smiles.

Rebecca drew in a breath and released it slowly. *And so it begins.* Riccardo, in his polite way, had tried to prepare her for a possible cool reception from his mother.

Before Rebecca could react, he took her fingers in his and raised them to his lips. With a healthy dose of the usual mischief dancing in his dark brown eyes, he whispered, "Cara, what is my life without you?"

A flash of gold at his wrist caught her eye. He wore the watch she'd given him for Christmas. Warmth spread through her, loosening the cords of her heart. "Hello, Riccardo." She smiled into his eyes and forced herself to breathe normally. She would not give in to silly nerves.

An attendant approached with their luggage. Riccardo gestured toward a man standing nearby. "Tito, come." They began their descent from the platform while Tito, a short but thickset man in black livery, transported their belongings to the car. After packing the luggage in the boot, he stepped to the passenger-side door and waited.

"Shall we go?" Riccardo waved toward the car with an

open palm. He shepherded the ladies to the automobile then assisted Rebecca and her mother as Tito helped Signora Alverá.

There were more carriages than automobiles parked near the depot. There was even a donkey cart, hauling luggage to a nearby *pensione*.

"Welcome to Italy," Riccardo said, a smile firmly in place.

Had he been watching her? From her seat beside her mother, and directly across from her soon-to-be husband, she observed him. He held his hat on his lap and seemed completely at ease. When his gaze found hers, she turned away. Their long journey had left her weary and unprepared for close contact with anyone, especially Riccardo. The only possible problem would be keeping her mother from talking too much.

He came to her rescue by acting the part of the tour guide with an ongoing narrative of their surroundings.

She kept her eyes on the changing scenery. Rows of dark cypress trees opened to wide fields of yellow, white, and purple wildflowers.

"Too early for poppies," Riccardo said, as though reading Rebecca's thoughts. He pointed out a road that led to Assisi. "One day I will take you. There is the Basilica of San Francesco d'Assisi, the monastery, and several beautiful cathedrals."

La Signora sniffed as if she doubted their interest in the faithful sites. What had given her such a low opinion of them? Did she know how Daddy died? How he'd wasted his fortune and left his family destitute? Was this the reason for the woman's contempt?

When their vehicle lumbered over a rough patch of road, Rebecca grabbed at the door.

Riccardo reached out to steady her, his gaze meeting hers. "We are nearly there, cara. If you will look ahead, you will see it around the next bend."

Under scrutiny from both sets of Italian eyes, Rebecca faced the window, waiting for that first glimpse.

Finally, the car slowed. Tito turned into the drive, and passed beneath a wooden sign. *"Tres Viti Verdi,"* she read aloud. She turned questioning eyes on Riccardo. "Three green vines?"

He smiled and cleared his throat. "My great-great grandfather traveled throughout France, Spain, and Italy, searching for the perfect vines. He arrived here with the best from the three countries and planted them there." He pointed to an arbor on the hillside. "From the three vines, he developed all those you see."

"Oh my," Mother said. "What an interesting man he must have been."

"He was a wonderful *Italiano, mio bisnonno*," Signora Alverá said, her voice so quiet, Rebecca barely heard. It was the first thing the woman had uttered since their initial introduction.

Chapter Seven

After a quick tour of the Alverá's nineteenth century country villa, Rebecca and her mother followed Riccardo to a shaded portico off the dining room. A round table held fresh bread, cheeses, and a variety of brined olives, along with a bottle of wine, and a small bowl of fresh-cut roses. No servant attended them as they dined. Rebecca was struck by the simplicity of the table and their surrounds. Certainly the family could afford the best of everything, but they were not extravagant.

Riccardo watched her, a small smile quirking his lips.

She tilted her head to peer at him. "What?"

"I can't believe you are really here."

Mother cleared her throat. "I'm sorry to interrupt, but now that we are here, may we know your plans, Conte?"

Riccardo darted a look toward the house then graced Mother with a dazzling smile. "I was getting to that. I thought perhaps Mamma would like to be here when we discuss it." He paused to glance at the door again. "Evidently, she is delayed."

"We can wait," Rebecca told him as she spread mascarpone cheese on her bread.

He set down his glass. "No, no, it is all right. Today, you will rest. Once we have finished our luncheon, I will see you to the cottage." Turning his attention to her mother, he continued. "After the wedding, you may stay in the cottage, Signora. It is your home for as long as you need it."

Mother dabbed at her eyes with her handkerchief. "Thank you, Riccardo. That means so much."

With some difficulty, Rebecca managed to swallow the bite she'd been chewing. Mother was certainly turning on the charm.

He offered them more wine. When they both refused it, he set the bottle aside and relaxed in his chair.

"Tomorrow evening, we have planned a dinner. An introduction, if you will, among our family and friends. This is the only thing for you to do tomorrow, so you may rest as long as you like. The following day, we will go into town. While I take care of business, you may do a little sightseeing, a little shopping, perhaps? Then on Saturday, as we have discussed in our correspondence, Signora Lewis, we will have a private ceremony in the garden, where our illustrious Mayor will officiate."

He lifted Rebecca's fingers and brushed them with a kiss. "You will also meet him tomorrow night. We must be very grateful to him. He has secured a special license for us."

Her heart stilled. She peered into his eyes. "Was there a problem?"

"Not really, though I did wonder if I would have to meet you in Southampton to be married by the ship's captain."

She opened her eyes wide.

He chuckled. "No, no—I am teasing, cara. There was a slight snag regarding the annulment. This is all. Your papers were in good order. Mayor Modesti took care of everything."

She swallowed hard. Good thing she hadn't followed Daddy's advice to keep her former marriage a secret, though it had only lasted three days. Daddy was unfamiliar with the Roman Catholic faith—Riccardo's religious background—now to be hers, also. They would not look kindly on such deception. After a calming breath, she spoke in what she hoped was a calm voice. "So it's common knowledge. I mean, does everyone know—about the annulment?"

He shook his head. "Strictly on the Q.T. Only the mayor and I know." Still holding Rebecca's fingers, he dismissed the subject with a wave of his free hand then glanced from her face to Mother's and back again. "Have you any more questions? Have I done well?"

With a grateful nod, Mother reached across the table to pat his hand. "You have." She drew in a breath, releasing it with a sigh. "Now, if you don't mind, I am beyond tired. Where is this cottage?"

A lavender-scented breeze wafted through the open window, tickling Rebecca's nose. She sneezed and opened her eyes. After a moment, memory returned. They were in the cottage near the main house at Tres Viti Verdi, Riccardo's home, surrounded by his vineyards and olive groves. As another puff of air billowed the silk and lace curtains, she rose and crossed the room.

Lavender bloomed below the window and all around the base of the house, providing a clean, fresh scent, and repelling bugs and scorpions, according to Eva, the servant assigned to them. Beyond the lavender beds, chickens clucked contentedly as they scratched in the dirt.

When the bedroom door opened, Rebecca turned to see Eva standing on the threshold, bearing a tray of food.

"Buongiorno, signorina," she said, setting the tray on the side table. "I hope you slept well?"

Was it still morning? Rebecca padded across the room to sit in a sage damask chair next to the table. The tray held a typical Italian breakfast on plain, white china. A couple of slices of fragrant bread, a small bowl of strawberry preserves, and a steaming cup of strong coffee. A red rosebud in a crystal vase completed the tray's perfection. She lifted the cup to her lips and tasted it. Delicious.

Eva made the bed while Rebecca ate. The slender maid's wavy dark blond hair was cut in a short style. Her hazel eyes purveyed good humor and intelligence. She moved with grace and confidence to accomplish her duties.

After spreading preserves on a slice of bread, Rebecca glanced up at her and asked, "Is my mother awake?"

"Signora Lewis is awake and says to tell you she is reading a book in the arbor." Eva fluffed the pillows and smoothed the bedspread. "She said you wear the green dress today, signorina. I have ironed it for you."

As the maid spoke, Rebecca sank her teeth into the heavenly-scented bread. She closed her eyes in bliss, savoring the taste. "Thank you, Eva." She didn't even bother to object to her mother's choice of clothing for the day.

Eva hesitated. "Is there anything else I may get for you? Would you like me to fix your hair?"

Rebecca shook her head. "No, thank you, perhaps later, before dinner." The maid gave a quick nod then left the room, silent as a cat. Rebecca heaved a sigh. How long had it been since anyone had waited on her so proficiently? They'd let most of their servants go nearly five years before. Then after the crash ... and after Daddy ... Rebecca laid the bread down. She still had difficulty believing he was gone. After spending most of December and early January with the Emersons, she and her mother had managed to live frugally in a small flat in Springfield. Rebecca had taken a temporary position as a corresponding secretary at Woods-Sanderson & Associates. Of course, Robert had most likely created the position, but for once, she hadn't cared. She'd made enough money to support them until time to leave.

Coffee cup in hand, she stood, and strolled back to the window. She would not have blamed Riccardo if he had wanted to break their long-standing engagement. How many times had she put him off, hoping things would improve? And then the crash came. Instead of getting better, the bottom fell out. And Daddy jumped off the Brooklyn Bridge.

She squeezed her eyes shut. The bright sunshine filtered through her closed lids, turning them deep red. She was reminded of something Nancy had said in her letter. Rebecca turned back, set the cup on the tray, and crossed to the dresser. She'd hidden the letter in the bottom of her jewelry box. Now she pulled it out again. Her fingers trembled as she drew the folded paper from the envelope.

My dearest, dearest friend,

My heart is heavy for you. I hope you know you will always have a home here with us, if ever you need it. Please, please, please! Consider what you are doing. Don't feel compelled to marry out of necessity. Not for yourself, not for your mother. You have friends who love you and are pledged to help you.

Marry for love, dear friend.

My prayers continue for you as you make this decision. Remember all we've talked about. As the sun steals through the smallest cracks and penetrates the darkest regions, so the Son will always find you. No matter where you go, or how far away you find yourself, He will be with you. This is my prayer for you. Never forget.

Rebecca ran her fingertip over Nancy's beautiful script. Then she refolded and slipped it back into its envelope and hid the envelope in the jewelry box. Rebecca and Nancy had been fast friends since that long-ago day on board the *Queen Mary*. Nancy had since found her knight in shining armor. Though they'd suffered through some troubles, their marriage had become stronger. Rebecca had secretly hoped to find someone just like Robert Emerson. Someone who would love her regardless of her past, and disregard her willful nature, of course.

She jumped at a soft knock on the door.

"Rebecca, are you awake?"

Mother. "Just a minute, I'm getting dressed." She closed
the jewelry box lid then donned the green dress, slipped on a
pair of sandals, and ran a comb through her hair. Her mother
would probably not approve of her appearance. One last glance
in the mirror convinced her of that, but she didn't care. She
strode to the door and opened it to find her mother thumbing
through a paperback novel.

Mother gave her a thorough scan. "You look as tired as I
feel. I'm glad they haven't any plans for us until evening." She
headed for the front door, still talking. "Do you know they bake
their own bread here? The smell woke me up at the crack of
dawn. Wonderful, heavenly smell."

"Are we going somewhere?"

Mother glanced over her shoulder. "I thought we might
take a stroll. Have a look around."

Stepping outside the cottage door, Rebecca was
immediately struck by two things. The heat of the day, though
it was still morning, and the vastness of the property
surrounding them. Nerves tap danced in her midsection. After
Saturday, this would be her home. Forever. She swallowed a
lump in her throat, sucked in a deep breath of country air, and
set off behind her mother.

A dark-haired lad raked the gravel path that led from the
house to the garden. He stopped and removed his cap at their
approach. With a dip of his head, he greeted them.
"Buongiorno, Signora, Signorina."

"Buongiorno," Rebecca said. Everyone seemed so friendly
here. She wondered if they were curious about her and Mother.
What did they really think of Riccardo's decision to marry an
American?

She followed Mother along the path to the kitchen garden
where herbs and flowers bloomed side-by-side among bean and
squash vines. Honeybees and bright yellow butterflies flitted

from bloom to bloom. Next, they strode down a well-worn trail to a low stone wall where a couple of cows and some sheep wandered. Rebecca leaned against the wall and gazed back toward the house.

Tres Viti Verdi's two-story main house was built in the traditional style with curved arches and pale yellow stucco walls. Grayish brown stonework adorned the arches. Red clay tiles lined the roof. Wisteria vines draped the rear portico of the main house as well as that of the cottage.

Riccardo's quick tour last night revealed several recent renovations, including two spanking new bathrooms. These, he had done for her. He'd confessed as much in one of his latest letters. Rebecca suspected his mamma did not approve the changes. The woman's lips had pressed into a flat line as Rebecca admired the newfangled hardware and colorful tile work.

Did she really prefer hauling in water to fill a copper tub in a drafty upstairs closet? This is what they'd been used to. Though Riccardo never complained, he had hinted at how outmoded the structure was and how he had always planned to modernize the facilities. The timing made it seem as if Rebecca had required it, which she had not. But she was nonetheless grateful.

"It's so peaceful here." Mother's words came out as a sigh. "Too bad it's so hot." She left Rebecca at the wall and headed back to the cottage. "I'm bound for the shade and a tall glass of icy something, I hope." She paused, glancing over her shoulder. "Will you join me?"

Rebecca pushed away from the wall and sidled after her. She tried to picture this as her life. Mother living close by, probably interfering in every possible way. Would the two mothers get along? Or would they simply tolerate one another? By the time she arrived in an arbor that shaded the back of their cottage, Eva was just leaving.

"I've ordered lemonade, I think," Mother spoke into the novel she had already begun to read. "My Italian's a bit rusty."

"You could've waited for me."

"Oh no, I need the practice, I suppose, if I'm to have a prolonged visit."

A prolonged visit. Her words set Rebecca's teeth on edge. How long until she became bored? What then? She had no money, no prospects. She'd lived the high life, traveled the globe, and partied with the world famous. Now she planned to retire in a country villa? Rebecca couldn't imagine it. But she held her tongue.

She sat in the nearest chair and ran her fingers over its smooth, dark wood. The table and four chairs were fashioned from grapevines, stripped of their bark and tightly woven into sturdy furnishings. The chairs included thick canvas-covered cushions and were ample enough in width to be truly comfortable. She sat back and stretched her legs out in front of her.

A moment later, she heard the unmistakable tinkle of ice on glass as Eva approached, bearing a tray.

Mother accepted a glass and held it against her temple.

Rebecca smiled into Eva's eyes. "Grazie, Eva. When should we prepare for dinner?"

"I can tell you that," Riccardo said.

Rebecca turned at the sound of his voice. "You're very sneaky. I didn't hear your approach."

He leaned forward to drop a kiss on her upturned lips. "One of my many talents, cara."

Her lips still tingling from his touch, Rebecca fiddled with the fabric of her skirt. He had an undeniable magnetism. Did he affect everyone this way, or just her? She wondered how many heads he'd turned. Had he entertained others in her absence? She'd never expected him to wait only for her. According to Daddy, no man could do that, nor would they want to.

Eva left to get another glass for Riccardo.

He laid his hat on the table then pulled out a chair and sat beside Rebecca. "I hope you ladies slept well?"

Mother set her glass down and propped her elbow on the arm of her chair. "I slept like a baby until visions of freshly baked bread filled my brain. What a wonderful aroma."

Riccardo's infectious laughter echoed in the yard. Rebecca had always admired his exuberance. Her gaze traveled over his trim, but muscular frame. He was jauntily clad in tan jodhpurs, dark brown riding boots, and a white cotton shirt, open at the collar. His jet black hair lay in neat waves, held in place with a modicum of pomade.

"Have you been riding?" she asked.

Eva returned with a glass, which she filled from the pitcher she'd left on the tray. After handing the glass to Riccardo, she returned to the main house.

Riccardo took a long draw from the ice cold lemonade. "I have. I stopped by this morning, to see if you would like to accompany me, but Eva said you were still sleeping. I did not wish to wake you."

"I'm so glad you didn't. I slept wonderfully well for the first time in … a long time."

Riccardo locked his gaze on hers, revealing more emotion than she cared to think about at the moment. She concentrated on her glass, sipping slowly, savoring the taste.

Mother slapped her book closed and set her glass on the tray. "I think I'd like a nap. Well, dear Conte, when do we need to arrive for dinner?"

"Dinner is at eight o'clock, Signora, but I hope you will arrive at seven and join us for antipasto as our other guests make their entrance." He rose and offered his hand.

She laid her hand in his and stood. "I shall see you at seven, then."

After Mother had gone, and Riccardo returned to his chair

beside Rebecca, neither of them spoke for several minutes. A hen cackled in the distance, announcing the birth of an egg. Such a homey sound, Rebecca almost believed she was back in the U.S.

Sensing Riccardo's gaze on her, she lifted her eyes to his and smiled. "Dare I ask what you're thinking?"

He grinned. "I could sit here all day, *mi amor*, watching you." He reached for her hand and held it to his lips.

Why could she not thrill at his touch? Shouldn't she? Any normal woman would swoon at his looks alone, much less those beautiful brown eyes. And the sensuous lips pressed against her palm, gave her little more than a tingle. She leaned forward, intent on rising. "But you won't, because you are a very busy man."

He rose and drew her into an embrace, all in one smooth move. "I won't, because you are too tempting, mia cara." He released her and leaned to pick up his hat. "And because *pennichella* approaches," he finished with a dazzling smile. "*Italianos* must have their nap."

Chapter Eight

Strains of a vaguely familiar concerto filled the air as Rebecca followed a flagstone path to the main house. Near the side entrance, Riccardo jogged out to meet her. "I was just coming to escort you, cara."

His gaze flowed over her like warm honey sending her stomach into a little flip-flop. Maybe all she needed was time with him. His obvious affection for her would surely melt the coldest regions of her aching heart. If only she could trust him.

When he offered, she settled her hand in the crook of his arm. Together, they walked the short distance to the door. It was nice to be on the arm of such a handsome man. She'd almost forgotten the sensation.

At the steps, he paused and pressed his lips to her ear. His mustache tickled her earlobe. "You look amazing tonight. I think I must protect you. Someone may try to steal you away from me."

Always the tease. She let her gaze roam over his physique. His tuxedo fit to perfection. "You don't look so bad yourself." But of course he already knew that. She could tell by the look in his eyes, but she couldn't help the smile or the warmth that crept up her neck and into her cheeks.

He led her through the door, where Mother's tinkling laughter greeted her.

"Your mother has already found friends, I see." Riccardo arched his brows and tipped his head toward Mother, who had cornered a smartly-dressed older couple near the front window.

Rebecca giggled. "The Baldassarris. We met them in Venice several years ago, I think. I didn't realize you knew them."

"They are cousins of my father's. Also they have a small interest in the vineyards." He introduced her to one of his Dominici cousins from Todi and several of the Alverás of Collazzone. She met a banker and his wife, evidently old friends of Riccardo, and two elderly ladies who lived nearby, the Baronessa Serafini, a widow, and her sister, Violetta Rossi.

After she had greeted the Baldassarris and endured her mother's effusive praise, Riccardo turned toward the entranceway and lifted his chin to peer over her head. "Ah, there is the mayor. Come, I will introduce you to him." As they walked, Riccardo whispered in her ear, "You must not laugh at him, cara. He is very short, and everyone knows it, but you mustn't let on."

He was so silly at times. But he made her laugh, and she needed to. She suspected he knew that and set out on purpose to keep her heart light. Or was it just his elation? His happiness overflowed. Was he so pleased and anxious to make her his wife? She jerked to attention as they drew up in front of the illustrious mayor.

They waited while Mayor Modesti ended his conversation with another guest. Rebecca allowed her gaze to sweep over him, taking in the diminutive public figure. She did her best to keep her impressions of him under strict control.

Mayor Modesti wore thick-soled shoes to add an inch to his height, bringing him to nearly four-foot-ten, still well below Rebecca's five-foot-six in two-inch heels. At Riccardo's introduction, she offered her hand. The mayor gave a curt bow, brushed her fingertips with his mustachioed lips then turned his full attention on Riccardo. Rebecca took a backward step in order to watch the mayor in action. He reminded her of a Chihuahua.

"Not to distract from your pleasant evening," he told Riccardo with a cursory glance at Rebecca. "But I was wondering if you have heard the grumblings. I know you read the papers."

Riccardo responded by placing his hand on the mayor's shoulder. "No, no, you are right. It would distract from our pleasantries. I see Mamma coming to announce the dinner." He grinned at Rebecca over the mayor's expertly coiffed head. "And you know my lovely intended, she speaks fluent Italian. I would not wish to bore her so early in the evening."

The mayor nodded and gave another quick bow. "Apologies, Signorina."

Rebecca moved into the crook of Riccardo's arm as he led her to the dining room where she was seated next to him with the mayor on her right. Mother sat across from her and Riccardo's mother sat at the opposite end of the table.

After a blessing from the eldest of the Alverá clan, a white-haired man seated to the right of Signora Alverá, a very noisy meal followed. They were an exuberant lot, at least. Rebecca enjoyed the banter since it freed her to observe them.

Her gaze wandered the room, admiring the Signora's tasteful decor. Simple, yet elegant. Candles glowed, crystal and silver sparkled. Lovely white roses cascaded from a broad silver vase.

With the exception of the mayor seated next to her, who discussed the rise of socialism with his other neighbor, the conversation never touched on any serious subject. Rebecca had Riccardo to thank for it. A truly gracious host, everyone adored him. Several of the women, two of them married, had eyes only for him. Should she be jealous? She glanced in his direction and found him watching her, his dark eyes aglow. Had he guessed her thoughts?

She fingered the edge of her linen napkin. When had she become so diffident? The old Rebecca exuded confidence wherever she went, her self-worth never in question. In her youth, she had never expected a young man's full attention, nor had she cared. But age brought anxiety, spurred on by a very large dose of truth as she witnessed constant turmoil in her parents' marriage. Now she understood much of that. The demise of their well-feathered nest had caused friction and conflict that couldn't be easily ignored. They'd both sought solace in the approval of others. And left Rebecca to deal with the consequences and the ever-decreasing funds.

Her mother's loud peal of laughter roused Rebecca from her inner musings. Mother was in her element. Other than the plain black sheath dress she wore, one would never guess she was in mourning. A few chairs away, Riccardo's mother carried on a quiet conversation with one of her elderly cousins, Signora Dominici. What must they think of her mother's behavior?

After dinner, most of the party moved out onto the large terrace to enjoy their after dinner drinks and sweets. A few of the couples danced to music provided by a trio of instrumentalists. Through the open windows, Rebecca noticed the mayor still seated at the table in heated conversation with one of the men.

When Riccardo claimed her for a waltz, she asked him about it. "He seems such a serious man."

"Too serious. He fears his own shadow." He nuzzled her cheek.

She drew back to look at him. "I admired the way you steered the conversation away from difficult subjects at dinner. Was there a rule—no politics, no religion?"

"Only one rule, given to each of them as they entered my home this evening." His gaze pierced hers. "Let us speak only of love tonight."

Warmth flooded Rebecca's body as he spun her around on the terrace. What would her life be like married to this man? At times, he was a quiet stream, its surface smooth as glass. But she had seen the ripple effect, usually displayed as mischief. She had seen him angry, really angry only once. It helped to know his temper had a low flash rate.

She glanced at the faces around them. Though younger than most of them, clearly he had earned their respect. No doubt, he would need their acceptance in the days going forward. Even she could sense the unrest among the Italians. How different would it be for her, as an American, to answer to a dictator like Mussolini, rather than a president, in a society where expressing your dissension could earn you jail time? Or worse.

Perugia, Umbria, Italia

Like many other Italian cities, Perugia crowned a hilltop. As Tito navigated the main roads, Rebecca took in the gorgeous views of blue mountains in the distance while Mother kept up a constant rattle of words on Riccardo's other side. Rebecca had decided the man was a saint.

After taking care of the necessary paperwork to finalize their marriage license, Rebecca, her mother, and Riccardo walked across a wide piazza.

"I have business to attend," Riccardo told them. "No need for you to follow me about. I thought you might like to visit the market, and then we can meet later for lunch."

Rebecca and Mother wandered among the booths of the marketplace. The bustling market brought the locals in to buy and trade their goods, mostly produce, but also handcrafted items. Not quite Bloomingdale's or Macy & Company, but Rebecca deemed it a pleasant diversion.

Before he left, Riccardo offered them spending money. Her mother was inclined to receive it, but Rebecca refused outright. "No, thank you. We don't need it." She hoped the forced smile she offered would reassure him she really didn't need the money. The arch of his brow and slight quirk of his lips told her he wasn't fooled. He was well acquainted with her stubborn pride.

As soon as he was out of sight, Mother gripped Rebecca's elbow and gave her arm a shake. "Why did you do that? You know we haven't any money to speak of. Honestly, Rebecca."

"I'm not married to him yet."

"You have just secured your marriage license, isn't that enough? Your pride won't even buy you one of those lovely pastries over there. What a waste."

Rebecca smiled and pulled Mother away from the food. "That's a good thing, Mother. If you keep eating everything in sight, you'll need a new wardrobe. And who will pay for that?" She knew the answer to that question. Mother would have no trouble asking for money from either Riccardo or Rebecca.

Mother huffed but strode alongside her to the far end of the bazaar where they found some lovely scarves and handmade jewelry. "Should we buy something for the Signora? After all, she has given up her future home to me."

Rebecca stopped and looked at her. "What are you talking about?"

"Eva—did you know she speaks English? She said this is why the Conte assigned her to the cottage. Anyway, she told me the Signora would normally move into the cottage when her son married. His wife would become the Contessa and the 'Signora della Casa,' the mother-in-law, would give place to her. But since I will be living there, she has no place to go. I got the feeling Eva does not approve of me." She leveled her gaze at Rebecca. "I hope you will not be uncomfortable sharing your home, your domicile with your husband's mother still there. She's a strong willed woman. Will she be able to give up control to you?"

Rebecca nibbled her lower lip while fingering the beautiful silk scarves. "I've no desire to displace Signora Alverá. She's welcome to continue as usual."

Mother clasped a bracelet on her wrist and held it up to admire. "This one is lovely. See how the lavender stones catch the light." She got the vendor's attention. *"Quanto costa?"*

After haggling back and forth, Mother settled on what she thought was a good price. She counted out the coins then turned back to Rebecca, her face alight with triumph. "Good thing I had a little money squirreled away."

But she had not forgotten their former topic. She gave her head a shake. "No, my dear. You mustn't make the mistake of giving in to your mother-in-law for the sake of peace in the household. She may take it as laziness on your part, or ignorance. It would only reinforce her opinion of 'Americanas.'"

Her mother was right. "I'll talk it over with Riccardo then. He'll know what's best."

The bells in a nearby church tower tolled the noon hour as Riccardo strolled across the square. He waved to them and gestured to a small cafe where he laid claim to a table beneath an olive tree. Bright red and purple petunias spilled over the wall at the base of the tree.

Riccardo threw up his hands at their approach. "Where are all your purchases? I felt sure you'd be burdened with shopping bags by now." A wry smile on his face, he held a chair for Mother then seated Rebecca. He called to a waiter and ordered espresso and a light lunch before pulling another chair from a neighboring table for himself.

Mother showed off her bracelet. "I found something that will match the dress I'm wearing for the wedding tomorrow."

"Bello." His gaze found Rebecca's. "And what of you, mia cara? Did you find nothing?"

The waiter returned with steaming cups of espresso. Rebecca stirred cream into hers. She had no intention of revealing her thinning financial status. "I'm a thoughtful shopper. I like to look around and see what's available then decide if I want any of it."

Riccardo glanced at her over the rim of his cup. "I can see

that. You are practical, I think."

"She's careful," Mother said, breaking off a generous portion of bread. "Almost too careful. You'll have to help her out of that." She stabbed at Rebecca with a blood red nail. "Now may be a good time to ask those questions."

Riccardo's brow arched raising his hairline in an almost comical fashion. "You have questions, cara? About the wedding, perhaps?"

Rebecca shook her head. "I am concerned your mother may feel uncomfortable with her situation once we are married. I understand it is the usual custom that the mother moves into the cottage."

He settled back in his chair, propping his right ankle on his left knee. "Yes, it is the usual practice among the aristocracy. And she would have done it." He glanced at Mother then back at Rebecca. "But there is no rush, I think." He waved his hand in the air. "We will be away for a couple of weeks. Then, after we return, if she is uncomfortable with the … er … situation, she can always go to the coast for a bit. But to be honest, I do not see her unhappy once we are all settled in. She will have more time to spend in her garden, which she loves. This, I see as a good thing."

Rebecca nodded, her gaze following the path of a flock of pigeons in the distance, soaring above the rooftops only to settle once again on the cobblestones of the piazza. She was not truly convinced that the Signora would be content to share her home.

Riccardo lifted her chin with his fingertips and gazed into her eyes. "*Mia carissima,* do not let it trouble you. Mamma knows what is expected of her. This is the way of life." He signaled to the waiter and settled their bill. "Now, let us go and see what interests you among the vendors before they pack up for the day."

Chapter Nine

Riccardo led the horses around to the front of the cottage and waited for Rebecca. After their morning of shopping in the village, he thought she might enjoy a ride around the property. He smiled at the memory of her childlike expression when he'd bought the beautiful lace shawl. Was this really the same Rebecca he had known for several years? The fiery, confident woman he'd proposed to?

No. She had changed. Either her father's death had affected her or possibly the loss of their fortune. He slapped the loose end of the reins against his knee. Perhaps a combination of the two events in her life. Devastating events were life-changing. The Lewises, along with many others of the new rich Americans, had had a very public humiliation. Riccardo was familiar with their history and knew exactly how they'd come into such a vast fortune. A fortune Rebecca's father had frittered away. What kind of man wastes his family's future?

A passage from Rebecca's letter after her father's death still haunted him. *In view of the circumstances, you're under no obligation to continue our engagement.* He'd been reminded of a contractual agreement. Either she had lost interest in him, or she was in deep emotional pain. After several days of prayer and deliberation, he'd decided it was the latter. She was hurting, and he wished only to comfort her.

The door of the cottage opened, and Rebecca strolled out wearing the riding outfit he'd bought her. His eyes roamed over her form. As she approached, he nodded his approval. It fit her like a glove. She tugged at the brim of her hat, probably trying to hide the blush, but too late, he'd already seen it. He chuckled as he gave her a leg up into the saddle. "You look lovely."

She gazed down at him from her perch. "If I gain even an ounce of weight on our honeymoon, I won't be able to wear this anymore."

He laughed as he mounted his horse. "Then you must be very careful, cara. Because I hope to see you in it. Often." He slapped the reins and urged his horse forward. She brought her horse alongside his. They rode in comfortable silence for several minutes. He watched her out of the corner of his eye. She would be a good companion.

They rode through the vineyards where he introduced her to Benito Campi, the head laborer at Tres Viti. "Everyone calls him Poppi. He is the grandfather of the vines." He grinned as Poppi gave her a polite bow. "He is also the grandfather of most of the children you see on Tres Viti. If you have not already guessed, cara, most of our servants are of one family."

Her eyes on Poppi, Rebecca smiled and dipped her head. "You are very blessed to have such a wonderful family, Poppi. How convenient that you may all live and work together."

Poppi chuckled and touched his brow. "Be careful with this one, Ricci. She has intelligence."

Her gentle laughter echoed in the vineyard. The sparkle in her eyes provided him a glimpse of the old Rebecca. She leaned toward him. "Good advice … Ricci."

"All right, so now you know my nickname. To Poppi, I will always be a boy of ten." He tipped his hat to the man. They turned their horses back onto a path that led through the olive groves. He gave her a sideways glance. "At least it's better than Connie."

She chuckled. "Yes, perhaps it is. I hadn't thought to call you that. Not in your mother's hearing, anyway. I seem to recall, you didn't think she'd appreciate it."

He reached for her hand and brought it to his lips. "She would be puzzled by it. This is all. Her English is perfunctory, at best."

"I can understand that. She does live in Italy, and I believe you told me she rarely travels."

He glanced at her. "She does not like to travel."

"I imagine she would consider my desecration of your title disrespectful."

"Hmm. She might. She would most definitely require an explanation." He rested his hand on his thigh, keeping her fingers captive. She didn't seem to mind.

Her chin jutted forward. "It was an honest mistake."

He tugged her hand, drawing her toward him. "I know it was. Tannenbaum's accent is atrocious. Conte—Connie—they sound so similar." With a low chuckle, he released her then urged his horse forward. How he loved to tease her. They continued at a canter until they reached the crest of a hill. Here, near the edge of an olive grove, he halted the horses again. The view that lay before them was of verdant fields sloping down to the river. "Here are the wheat fields."

After several moments with only the twittering of birds and the sough of the wind through the wheat, she spoke. "Have you always grown wheat? I don't remember your mentioning it."

"Once, these fields were grassy meadows for the cattle and other livestock. We mowed it into hay in the fall. But our illustrious leader requires all of us to grow the wheat. He doesn't want to lean so heavily on imported grain. He believes we must learn to feed ourselves."

An almost imperceptible shadow crossed her face—a veiled look in her eye that vanished in an instant. He would have missed it had he not been watching her so closely. "Do you harbor reservations about your new country, cara? I wouldn't blame you, if you did."

She raised her eyes to his. "Should I?"

He removed his hat allowing the breeze to cool his scalp. Already, the heat was rising. They should turn back. He blew out a breath and met her gaze. "We can only hope and trust in God, Who is Supreme Ruler."

Her gaze held his for several seconds. What thoughts passed through her mind? Ah, well, in the next few days, he'd have more time alone with her. He set his hat on his head, gathered the reins, and turned his horse toward home. "We should get out of the heat. *Andiamo*—let's go."

On the return journey, he showed her where the old winery had stood. "It burned fifteen years ago."

She glanced around. "Where is the new one?"

He shook his head. "We never replaced it. Now we sell most of our grapes. We specialize in fruit for the eating and for making the fresh juice. Tres Viti grapes are well known for their sweetness. Before the crash, we got a good amount of money for them." He shrugged. "Now, not so much."

She smiled into his eyes. "It'll bounce back."

"I hope so. I'm not so certain as you."

She averted her eyes and urged her horse forward. If he mentioned money or the future, she would often turn away or change the subject. He rubbed his chin with the back of his hand. He must try to reassure her, build up her confidence. But how, when his own suffered in this deflated economy?

7 June, 1930
Dearest Nancy,

Today, I will marry Riccardo.

I have done as you asked. I have prayed and listened for God's answer. I believe this is the right thing for me to do. Riccardo is a good man, and he loves me. I have no doubt I will come to fully love him in due time. This may seem barbaric to you, since you were fortunate enough to marry for love. Remember how you balked at your Grandmother's plans for you? Turns out, she knew more than you thought.

You know my heart, dear friend. I am and always have been pragmatic about life. Everything will fall into place. I will always remember your offer of hospitality. If things go terribly wrong, perhaps I shall need it someday. For now, let me return the offer to you. When you come to Italy, you will have a home here. I am smiling, because I know you will come. Tres Viti is lovely. I imagine us walking through its vineyards, talking and laughing at our memories. Perhaps you will visit us at the villa in Sperlonga. You would love that, too.

As for leaving my home country, you know I have always loved Italy. I know I can be happy here. The politics of this place make me a bit uneasy, but Riccardo assures me the situation is in God's hands. We may certainly trust in that.

It is funny, don't you think, though we are the best of friends, neither attended the other's wedding. I hope you will wish me well. I am thinking of you and wishing you the very best. I hope to see you again before we are old and white-headed.

All my love, Rebecca

She folded the letter and sealed it in an envelope. After writing the address on the front, she laid it on the desk for Eva to post. Outside, birds twittered as the sun's first rays broke over the distant mountains. Crickets still crooned outside her window. She stood and crossed the room. She'd slept little, but she was not worried about it. Today, she was a bride.

She fingered the silk chiffon of her wedding dress. The sales clerk had called the color, "a whisper of peach." The dress was belted at the waist and fitted to below the hips where it flared into a graceful scarf hem below the knees. Rebecca loved the lace insert at the bodice and elbow-length flared sleeves.

It was just the thing for an afternoon wedding the clerk

had said. "In the bright Italian sunlight, it will appear ivory. Is it not perfect?"

This was the first clue her mother had informed the clerk of Rebecca's former marriage. Mother disagreed with Rebecca's insistence that she couldn't wear white.

No regret or dismay troubled Rebecca's heart. She'd made a stupid mistake when she'd run off with Georgio. But she'd long ago forgiven herself. Oh, what a lark they'd had. Her lips curled in the smile that always came with his memory. Yes, he'd married her for her money, but she'd cared not a whit. Young and dumb, she'd given no thought to the future. She had lived in the moment. She hugged herself, drew in a deep breath, and exhaled. Georgio had been a passionate man.

To this day, she didn't know the exact amount of money Daddy paid him to go away. Funny how she hadn't cried when he left. All she'd really cared about was that Daddy had come to her. Yes, he was angry, but his presence spoke volumes. He'd gotten the "foolish marriage" annulled as quickly as it had happened. And they'd promptly forgotten it.

Until Riccardo proposed.

She told him because it was the right thing to do. She could never pretend to be a blushing bride, all dressed in white; it wasn't her way. She'd owned up to it, no matter what Daddy—or Mother—said. Daddy tried to convince her to lie. "Don't be daft, darling. Wear the white dress. Why should you have to punish yourself for a silly mistake everyone's already forgotten?"

Everyone, except Rebecca.

Voices echoed in the courtyard. She crossed to the window. It was barely light, yet the servants were already preparing for the wedding, setting up tables and chairs. Though the ceremony would be private, with only a few witnesses, the reception would include family and all of the servants. This informal gathering was exactly what Rebecca would have wished. No big, fancy event for her.

A soft knock on the door and Eva entered, bearing a tray. "Buongiorno, signorina! You are already up. I will draw your bath while you have your coffee."

With Eva and Mother's help, Rebecca was ready at quarter past noon. As they prepared to go to the garden, the door opened and Signora Alverá entered. In place of her usual black or dark brown, she wore gray, with a black lace shawl draped over her shoulders. She held a beautiful bouquet of cream-colored roses with sprigs of lavender throughout, and bright green grape leaves twisted around the stems.

She reached for Rebecca's hand. "Today, you are my daughter." She gave the flowers to Rebecca then kissed her cheek. "May the Lord bless you and make you prosperous in His ways." After settling the shawl over her hair and face, she turned to Mother. "They are waiting for us in the garden, Signora Lewis."

Rebecca watched as the two women walked out of the house. Eyebrows arched, she gazed at Eva. "What just happened?"

Eva laughed as she made a last minute adjustment to Rebecca's veil. "She really is a wonderful woman, signorina. She will love you. You will see."

Rebecca pursed her lips. She sincerely hoped so.

Eva left her at the edge of the garden. Rebecca drew in a long, slow breath as she scanned the cobbled path that led to the arbor where everyone waited for her. She released the breath and stepped forward. If only Daddy was here to support her. He'd make jokes to lighten her mood as he walked her up the path toward her destiny.

Her heart skipped as she caught sight of Riccardo. "Well, at least one of us is wearing white," she whispered. His linen suit complemented his warm, brown complexion. As she drew near, his gaze slid over her. That confident smile of his brought on a severe case of nerves. Her footsteps faltered. Nancy should have been here to stand beside her, lending her strength. Nancy had such a deep well of strength. Rebecca swallowed the lump in her throat and ordered her feet to move forward. As if sensing her fear, Riccardo met her halfway, his hand outstretched. She bit down on her lower lip to stop its trembling and laid her hand in his open palm. He drew her fingers into the crook of his arm and led her into the shade of the arbor.

For Rebecca, the next few minutes took place in a dream. At times, she was underwater, hearing words spoken from the surface. She forced herself to concentrate and make the right responses. Throughout the entire experience, Riccardo never released her hand. His gaze held hers, drawing her back to the real world. When Mayor Modesti pronounced them man and wife, Riccardo lifted her veil. She heard her Mother's soft intake of breath as Riccardo's lips caressed Rebecca's for a precious moment in time.

Chapter Ten

Riccardo laughed as the guests raised their voices in the traditional Italian toast.

"*Per cent'anni!*"

He leaned close to Rebecca. "How about it, cara? Can we make it that long?"

She gave him a coy smile. "Perhaps, if you are a very good boy."

"Oh well, if that's all it takes, there would be so many centenarians around, the world would be full of them." He gave her hand a squeeze. "I do want to grow old with you. Perhaps not that old."

A shadow crossed her face, not quite a frown, but almost. He brushed her cheek with his knuckles. What was she thinking? He wanted to kiss her but drew back. Plenty of time for that later. Now, he must please his guests.

After a meal of many courses including antipasti, soups and salads, pasta, roasted chickens, and a huge array of breads and cheeses, Riccardo led his bride in the traditional bridal dance. The dancing continued as servants cleared the tables and brought out the desserts and the traditional sugar-coated almonds.

Then it was time for the after dinner drinks and the final round of toasts to the bride and groom. It was all great fun, but he wasn't sad to see it end. He had waited too long for this woman.

Mayor Modesti was the first to leave. "I am so sorry I cannot stay to see you off." He bowed over Rebecca's hand. "You have all my best wishes, Contessa."

Riccardo signaled to Tito, who gave him a nod then left

the garden to bring the car around. Riccardo loved to drive his bright red Alfa-Romeo, especially along the coastal highway. He hoped Rebecca wouldn't mind having the top down.

He smiled into her questioning eyes. "Tito will bring the car now, but we mustn't be in a hurry. You have one or two things still to endure. By the way, you must remain seated, my love." He rose from his place and stood behind Rebecca, his hands on the back of her chair.

Moments later, four young men surrounded her, two Dominici cousins, and two field hands who took hold of the legs of her chair and lifted her into the air. Her hands flew to her mouth, her eyes wide.

Riccardo touched her arm. "You may want to hold on."

The other guests jumped to their feet and began to clap and cheer. Rebecca grabbed hold of the seat of her chair as the men hoisted her upward three times. Then her mother handed her the bouquet of roses.

"Toss the bouquet, cara," Riccardo called, clapping his hands in the air.

Still aloft, she tossed the bouquet then grabbed hold of the chair's seat again. Riccardo laughed to see her white knuckles, but her face reflected an almost childlike joy. Loud cheers and laughter drew his attention to one of Poppi's granddaughters, who had caught the bouquet. He congratulated the girl with a kiss to each cheek before following the young men who carried Rebecca to the car.

Beside the Alfa-Romeo, the men lowered the chair so she could climb in. Riccardo helped her settle in to the seat. Amid the loud well-wishes of the entire wedding party, he jogged around to the driver's side, jumped in, started the engine, and began the slow descent toward the road.

"You are a very good sport, my love." He turned to find her eyes filled with merriment. He'd half expected narrowed slits and arched brows, a sure sign of her displeasure. On purpose, he hadn't warned her about his family's traditional "wedding march." Thank goodness he was taking her away for their honeymoon, or they would have to endure an evening of pranks from the young men.

She tied a white silk scarf around her hair and settled back. "I quite enjoyed it."

"I suppose I should have warned you."

She shook her head. "No. The surprise made it more fun." She drew out a mirror and repaired her lipstick. "Will we make it to Sperlonga tonight?"

"With no delays, we can be there by nightfall. This is my plan. But there may be goats or sheep in the road. An overturned lorry or a landslide. Here in Italy, you never know. We will see." He mashed the accelerator as the road straightened.

June, 1930
Villa Carlotta, Sperlonga, Latina, Italia

Rebecca sat on the ancient stone wall of the terrace, gazing into the distance as the sun rose over the Tyrrhenian Sea. She loved this section of the Mediterranean. A soft morning breeze swept a curl into her face and tickled her nose. She tucked the curl behind her ear and relaxed against the balustrade to watch as below her, seabirds floated on the air currents, seeking sustenance.

It was going to be another beautiful day. If only they could stay here forever, never returning to the work and drudgery of the farm. Oh, what a fairytale that would be.

A shaft of yellow sunlight illuminated the multi-level white terrace, trimmed in magenta bougainvillea and bright red geraniums. A hummingbird hawk moth flitted from blossom to blossom. Rebecca had once heard they were a good omen. She stretched her arms above her head and gazed at the sky.

"Please let it be true," she whispered. Add on Nancy's

prayers and maybe ... just maybe ... she had a chance at a decent life.

Ricci's voice drifted from the open windows, singing in his bath. She giggled at the ridiculous Italian ditty. Sometimes he reminded her so much of a little boy then he would suddenly change back into a grownup. She hugged herself at the memories of their first night together as man and wife.

She'd assured Nancy she could come to love him. She'd hoped, even dreamed, the words would come true. Now she knew it was possible. But would their passion cool and leave emptiness, or adoration in its wake? She hoped the latter. She blew out a frustrated breath. Would she ever be free of these doubts?

What did she know about love? Real love. Given her parents' examples was she capable of loving someone? The concept of forever love seemed unattainable. Just when it came within her grasp, it skittered away like a frightened bird.

Ricci stepped onto the terrace, towel-drying his hair. "Boungiorno, *mia sposa*, love of my life. How are you this fine morning?"

She rose at his approach. "Wishing our time here did not have to end."

He laughed as he caught her in his arms. "Let us not think of the end, my love. Let us savor every moment, make it last. How about breakfast at our favorite cafe, eh?"

Half an hour later, they descended the steps to the village and traversed the cobbled streets to the quaint corner cafe called Latte Dolce. They sat outside and enjoyed a lingering breakfast while planning their day.

Along with the delicious espresso, Rebecca drank in the sights and sounds, the history of the place. One could almost sense the past, with its legions of Roman soldiers. The Romans had given the place its name, from *spelunca*, meaning caves. When she had first come here as part of a students' tour to study the grotto and its history, she'd been caught up in the Homeric tale of Odysseus. What a romantic she'd been.

"Would you wish to visit the grotto again?" Ricci asked, touching her arm, snatching her out of her fanciful tour of the past.

Rebecca turned her hand to fit inside his. "I have no desire to go back there. Let's enjoy the sea while we can. The weather is so fine."

There were no servants at the seaside villa, so Ricci had made arrangements with one of the area restaurants to deliver their meals. Today, lunch was provided in a basket to be enjoyed on the beach.

The shoreline was filled with people, luxuriating in the sun. Their colorful umbrellas looked like giant beach balls scattered about the sand. Rebecca glanced around. "How is it they have so much free time? When do they work?"

Ricci laughed at her questions. "You are not in America, cara, where it is work, always work." Carrying the basket, he led her to the dock where he rented a skiff. "Too many on the beach today," he said as he helped her into the boat.

As soon as she settled in, he set off. She grabbed hold of the sides as he swung the boat around. "I thought you liked crowds."

The muscles in his arms bulged as he worked the oars, propelling them forward. "Not today."

She watched his face as he scanned the shoreline. Finally, he seemed to find just the right spot. He put in at a stone jetty. Above them, the walls of the city rose against the bright blue sky. Sperlonga had a shape similar to a turtle. She smiled at the idea of a giant sea turtle suddenly awakening and crashing into the sea, sending a great wall of water to cleanse the bed where he'd lain for centuries. In the end, only the beach remained. She closed her eyes and gave her head a quick shake.

She was becoming Nancy. What a goof Nancy had been in

school, the little dreamer. But Rebecca had loved her so. Nancy was such an innocent back then.

Ricci found a flat rock where there was plenty of room to spread a tablecloth and lay out the meats and cheeses. Fresh-baked bread and strong tea completed the meal.

Once they'd finished eating, she repacked the basket then lay on her back beside Ricci on the smooth, warm surface of the rock.

"Tell me about your childhood, Becca."

She thought he was sleeping until he spoke.

She loved the way he said her name. It was sweetly familiar, almost like a caress. "I've talked about my life before."

He turned his head to look at her. "Not really. You gave me the condensed version. I want to know you, Becca. Who you really are." His voice sounded husky, as though he'd been asleep.

She sniffed. "You might not like that person."

He reached his hand toward her, touched her cheek, and smoothed her hair away from her eyes. "No. I love you. Nothing you tell me will change that."

She closed her eyes. "Some would say I had an idyllic childhood. I was an only child. We had plenty of money." She paused to draw a breath. "But I was raised by a nanny. A beloved nanny, but she was not my parents. They were always running off together to some exotic place. I craved their attention."

"You didn't feel loved."

She nodded then pushed up onto her elbow, so she could see his face. "I adored them when I was little, though they continuously pushed me away."

"What about later, when you grew older?"

She glanced up as a flock of white pelicans flew over, headed out to sea. "When I was ten, they said I was too old for a nanny. They sent me to a boarding school. I learned there were benefits to having absentee parents. I wanted for nothing. Whatever I asked for, they sent me. I suppose it was guilt on their part. I didn't care." She turned over on her stomach. "I told myself I didn't care. But I did, really."

He pulled her to him, traced the line of her jaw with his finger. "You still care, I think."

"I wish things could be different. I loved … Daddy." Her voice broke. She lay her head on Ricci's chest. "He seemed proud of me. Of the way I turned out. He wanted me to be happy. He told me so, shortly before—"

Ricci held her as she cried silently. She sat up, ran her fingers through her hair, and swiped at her eyes. "I'm sorry. I thought I'd cried all my tears."

He sat up next to her. "I still cry a little when I think of Papá. It's been seven years." He pushed up from the rock and grabbed the basket then held out his hand for her. "Come. Let's go back."

She climbed into the boat. "What should I call your mother?"

"I think you should ask her, cara."

She shook her head then cut him a sideways glance. "She doesn't like me—and don't say she wouldn't like anyone who married her precious little boy."

He grinned as he used an oar to push away from the jetty. "I wasn't going to say that. I was only going to say she will learn to love you."

"Right. But she would not have to learn to love me if I was Italian, a good Catholic, and titled, with land and money."

A frown creased his brow before a slow grin eased it away again. "Oh no, she would settle for Italian and Catholic."

Their last Saturday in Sperlonga, Ricci took Rebecca to Maria Assunta, an ancient, but beautiful church along the main road. The moment she stepped into the interior, her face changed. She genuflected before entering the pew. Though the service was conducted in Latin, she made all the right moves. Was he missing something here?

He forced his attention to remain on the Padre, but as soon as Mass ended, he faced her. "You are very familiar with our traditions."

"My nanny was Catholic. She took me to Mass every week. Religious holidays, too."

Outside the church, he took her hands in his. "You are full of surprises, mia sposa."

She laughed as she fell into step beside him. "Nanny would be proud. She'd say she prepared me for my marriage to you. But I often thought her taking me to the Catholic Church was one reason she was dismissed."

"Your parents were not religious?" They continued to wend their way through the narrow streets flanked by ancient buildings. Their footsteps echoed on the cobblestones.

She shook her head. "Mother was raised in a very strict Baptist church. Daddy ... I don't think his family attended any religious services." Her gaze drifted to a faraway place.

"And you evidently know your Latin."

She paused to look at the display in a shop window. "One of my favorite subjects in school. I was involved in a Latin Society—a club. It was fun."

"Fun? Latin?"

This brought a giggle as she turned to gaze into his eyes. "The sponsor was quite handsome. Only a few years older than his students. So, yes, fun."

He joined in her laughter. This was his Rebecca, teasing, laughing, eyes sparkling, with a spring in her step. He was falling in love with her all over again.

By the time they'd returned to the villa, the day was half spent. Dinner was warming on the stove, a simple Italian beef stew and crusty, warm bread. Afterward, they walked on the beach and planned the last few days of their stay in Sperlonga.

"On the drive home, I thought we could take a different route. It is longer, but if we leave early, we will have plenty of time."

"Unless there are goats or sheep or overturned lorries …"

She was mocking him, but it was nice to know she remembered what he'd said on their wedding day. "You are learning, signora."

"I'm a quick study. Why are we taking a different route?"

"I want to show you one of my favorite places—Bracciano."

"That's a lake, isn't it?"

"It's a lovely place. They have a very good restaurant where we can have our dinner."

She made no reply, but dug her toe into the sand then gazed at the horizon.

"Is something bothering you?"

She leaned against his side.

He draped his arm over her shoulders.

"I'm a little concerned about Mother," she confessed. "Is she driving your mamma crazy in our absence? She can be … overbearing at times."

He arched his brows at her, faking surprise. "Really? I had not noticed. But you needn't worry, cara. Mamma is up to the challenge. She can give back." They had arrived at the base of the many steps that led to the villa. He allowed her to go in front of him. "But I think you may be right. Perhaps I should make a phone call to see how it is going."

She slowed then turned to gaze down at him. "Maybe you shouldn't. What if … things aren't going well?"

He stepped closer to her, until he was on a level with her. "*I parenti su' comu e denti, sempri mordono.*" He grinned then planted a kiss on her lips. "Relatives are like teeth—they always bite."

Chapter Eleven

Carlotta Alverá sat on the edge of the sofa fingering her rosary, anxiety churning in her breast. She lifted her chin and brought her gaze back to Eva's. "You are certain?"

Eva sat across from Carlotta, her back straight, hands folded in her lap. "Who else? Only Signora Lewis has been in there. Detta and I moved all of the signorina's ... I mean the young signora's things into the main house, as you ordered."

Carlotta's fingers paused. She dropped the rosary into her pocket. "All right then. I thank you for telling me this. I must now decide what to do about it." She gazed into Eva's hazel eyes, more green than brown today. Leaning forward, Carlotta laid her hand on Eva's. "Do not worry about it, my dear. This is not your fault."

Eva bit her lower lip and nodded. "Grazie, Signora. I am so worried. I was thinking maybe I had miscounted. And then we found those bottles." She shook her head.

Carlotta pushed up from the sofa. "What have you done with them? The bottles, I mean."

"They are in a box beneath the kitchen sink for now." She covered her mouth with trembling fingers then drew in a breath and released it. "What shall I do with them?"

"I would like to see them. Bring them to the ... er ... to the potting shed. I'll meet you there in a bit."

After Eva stepped quietly through the door on her way to the cottage, Carlotta went to her desk and drew out paper and a pencil. She kept a very accurate inventory of their wine. She must check the bottles to make sure they were from Alverá stock. She could then go and subtract those from her inventory. Once everything was documented, she would need to decide what to do about it. Should she tell Riccardo? Or should she first confront Signora Lewis?

She huffed out a breath. To please Riccardo, she had tried hard, very hard, to be friends with that woman. Signora Lewis kept to herself for several days after the wedding. Then she'd visited Carlotta early one morning to ask permission to invite friends to her cottage. When she told Carlotta their names, well, of course it was all right. A Duca was always welcome, even if he was French. And his friends, the Marchese and Marchesa of Adelfia—how could she turn them away? In fact, she had made them a dinner and welcomed them with open arms. The duca was charming, a widower who spoke only a little Italian.

How the Signora Lewis had flirted with him. Had the woman no shame? She had only been widowed what? Seven months or so. Shocking! Carlotta peeked out the window toward the cottage. Probably too early for the woman to be awake.

A moment later, Eva walked across the yard, carrying a wooden box. Carlotta turned away from the window. She must put on her gardening shoes and take her gloves so no one would question her trip to the potting shed. Not that it mattered, since Signora Lewis slept late most days. She paused at the outer door to whisper a prayer. "Santa Maria, Madre di Dio, help me in my weakness. I don't know what to do."

She found Eva in the potting shed, removing the bottles from the orange crate. She glanced up as Carlotta entered. "Ten bottles, Signora."

Carlotta sighed. "Oh, dear. Well, let us see if they are all ours." One at a time, she examined the bottles. Though Tres Viti no longer had an official winery, Poppi still produced a few bottles for their personal use. The rest they bartered for with the neighboring vineyards.

With each bottle she examined, Carlotta's heart grew

heavier. These were all from her wine closet. Which meant Signora Lewis, or someone, had gone into the main house to access the wine cellar. When had anyone done that? She laid her palm against her forehead. "Well, none are from our older collections. That is one thing for which to be thankful."

Eva placed the last bottle in the box. "What shall I do with these?"

Carlotta blew out an exasperated breath. "Send them to Poppi. Say nothing of where they are from. I will deal with this."

After Eva's departure, Carlotta wandered through her kitchen garden then down the path toward the rose garden. She must clear her mind.

Was her new daughter-in-law aware of her mother's indulgences? She sat on a stone bench in the midst and drew in a deep, rose-scented draught of air. Her regal Golden Lady was in bloom. She fingered the silky petals and bent to inhale its perfume. The scent was delicious, like spiced apples. A light breeze cooled Carlotta's brow and in that moment, her mind cleared. She knew what she must do.

The main house at Tres Viti was awash with light as Riccardo pulled the car into the lane. "I believe we are expected." He smiled into Rebecca's eyes.

"What are you smiling at?" Rebecca demanded. "Are you so happy to be back? Perhaps you were tired of so much time alone with me."

He searched her face then relaxed as he killed the engine. She was only kidding. "I think you know how I feel about that, cara." He flashed his most provocative smile. She let her head fall back and laughed out loud. It was good to hear her laugh with such abandon.

Tito approached to open Rebecca's door. "*Buono sera, Signora.*"

Riccardo ran around the car to assist her.

She glanced around him to address Tito. "Buono sera, Tito. How is the family?"

"Very well, Signora. Grazie."

Riccardo gave orders to Tito and Alfredo, the other young man who accompanied him. "After you bring in the luggage, put the car in the garage. Tomorrow, you will have time to clean it up, no?"

"Si," Tito answered then the two men went to work unloading the Alfa-Romeo.

Mamma stood in the doorway, a crocheted shawl draped over her shoulders. "I am so glad you are all right. When you are so late, I worry."

Riccardo released Rebecca's arm to drop a kiss on his mother's cheeks. "Now, Mamma, I am sure you have prayed to St. Christopher. Why then must you worry?" He held out his hand to Rebecca and caught her gaze. "Come in, my darling." His glance interrupted an odd expression in her eyes, so fleeting, he thought he may have imagined it. Was she nervous? He gave Mamma a long look, hoping she'd pick up on his meaning. *Have mercy on her.*

With an almost shy smile, Rebecca faced his mother. "Buona sera, Signora."

He watched the two women for a moment then followed Tito up the stairs, calling to Rebecca over his shoulder, "I'll make sure our things are stowed away properly."

On the landing, he heard his mother say, "You needn't be so formal, Rebecca. We are family, now."

He smiled and shook his head. This was going to be interesting.

Rebecca didn't know what she had expected, when Signora Alverá objected to being addressed as "signora." Mamma, perhaps? But no, she wanted Rebecca to call her by her given name.

"You have a mother," she'd said. "I don't want to cause problems. So you may call me Carlotta."

Rebecca forced a smile. "Thank you, Carlotta. That's very thoughtful. Where is my mother, by the way?"

Carlotta glanced at the stairs where Ricci had gone then, rearranging her shawl, moved away from the door. "She was tired. She said to tell you she'd see you in the morning."

Typical Mother. An uneasy feeling wound its way into Rebecca's heart. Carlotta was hiding something. She had already noticed a certain set of the woman's mouth when she was holding something back. Just like her son, she was not good at duplicity.

"Cara," Ricci called from the top of the stairs. "You must come up and see that we have all your things."

"Please excuse me, Carlotta."

With a barely discernible nod, Carlotta left the room.

Rebecca ascended the stairs to a place she had never been—Ricci's room. Or suite of rooms, as it turned out. The expansive master bedroom flanked by three large windows, included a sofa, two chairs, and a small dining table near the windows. A four-posted bed stood in the back corner. A rather large crucifix hung on the wall above the bed. Rebecca turned around to gaze toward the front. The morning views out those windows must be wonderful.

Ricci took her hand and led her to an adjoining room, another newly renovated and very large bathroom. On the same wall as the bathroom door, another door led to a dressing room with a walk-in closet.

"You like it?" Ricci asked, watching her.

"It'll do." Though she tried, she couldn't hold back the smile. Of course she liked the room. "It's marvelous. Very traditional."

Tito and the footman, whose name eluded Rebecca,

reentered carrying the last of the items from the boot of the car. How had Ricci managed to fit so many things in there?

He grinned at her apparent distress. "We don't have to put everything away tonight. Eva can help you tomorrow."

Rebecca took a moment to thank Tito. "Grazie, Tito, and I'm sorry, I've forgotten his name." She nodded to the footman.

Tito bowed. "*Di niente,* Signora. And his name is Alfredo."

Rebecca nodded to Alfredo and the two men left the room. With a silent vow to remember Alfredo's name, she turned back to Ricci. "Will Eva have time? I thought she would continue at the cottage."

He wrapped his arm around her waist and pulled her to him. "No. Eva is for you. We have others to tend to the cottage."

"Tell me about them—the Campi family—I know I'll never get all the names straight, but at least I will have a vague idea."

Ricci sank into one of the large chairs and pulled her onto his lap.

She settled against him, prepared for another long narrative. He loved to tell the history of this place.

"When Poppi was a boy of about twelve, his parents both died in a cholera epidemic. My grandfather took him in and taught him everything he needed to know about the vines. When he was old enough, my grandfather found him a wife from a neighboring family. This is how Nonna came to be with us."

Rebecca drew back to look at Ricci's face. "It was an arranged marriage?"

He nodded. "They soon fell in love. They had seven children, six still living. The eldest is Alberto, the footman you just met. He also oversees the care of the horses, among other things. Sometimes, you will hear him called 'Berto.' He is married to Isabella, and they have five children. The oldest, Sandro, also helps with the horses. You will not usually see Isabella, she stays home with the younger children.

"And then there is Claudio, who is in the army. Eva is married to Claudio. They have no children, though he has one by a former marriage. You have already seen Chico, the little snoop who hides beneath the tables and peeks around the corners."

Rebecca chuckled. "I had no idea Eva was married. Of course, I never asked."

"Maria is the third child. She is married to Tito. They have three children. The eldest is Corrina who works in the kitchen. Maria's sister Giada is next. She is called Gigi, and she has a bambina, several months old. Gigi's husband is also in the army. But I think he will be home soon. Lorenzo works in the fields with his father, and Lucia, the youngest of the girls, works in the kitchen."

Rebecca repeated their names, hoping to commit them to memory. "And there was another—you said they had seven children?"

"Their youngest child, Stefano. He died after falling off a wagon during grape harvest. He was only eight."

She drew a quick breath. How awful to lose a child in such a way. She almost wished she hadn't asked about him.

Ricci caressed her cheek. "Now, my love, it has been a long day, and we are both very tired." He kissed her then helped her stand so he could rise. "I hope you will sleep well this first night in your new home."

She glanced around the lovely room. "I think I shall."

A breeze billowed the curtains in the darkened bedroom. Beside Rebecca, Ricci slept, his breathing deep and even. If only she could go to sleep so easily. She turned onto her back and stared at the blackness outside. There was a chill in the air as the wind whistled around the eaves.

She climbed out of bed, donned her robe, then stood at the window. She could smell the moisture in the air. Well, Ricci had mentioned they needed rain. She drew a chair to the window and sat, hoping to grow drowsy enough to return to bed. She exhaled and let her shoulders droop. A sudden spate of raindrops hit the window and splashed on her face. She jumped up to lower the sash but not before she'd breathed in a delicious draught of rain scented air. So refreshing and now she was more awake than ever.

After stepping into her slippers, she crept from the room and down the stairs. She was just wondering if she could find her way to the kitchen when a light flashed on at the end of the hallway. She waited, listening. Perhaps someone else couldn't sleep. She crept forward, not wanting to startle whoever it was.

Carlotta looked up as Rebecca entered the kitchen. She was pouring milk into a pan. "Would you like some?"

Rebecca nodded. "Please." If only she could read the woman's expression and know whether she was welcome. One thing she had already learned, Carlotta was a lady and given to hospitality. More than likely, Rebecca would never know how the woman really felt.

Carlotta poured in more milk then set the pan on a burner and lit the gas. After returning the pitcher to the refrigerator, she motioned to a shelf where the dishes sat in neat stacks. "Hand me another cup." She watched as Rebecca chose one and handed it to her. She placed it on the counter. "I hope I didn't wake you."

Rebecca shook her head. "No. I couldn't go to sleep. Too wound up, I suppose."

Carlotta concentrated on stirring the milk. "I would think, after such a long day, you would be very tired."

"I dozed a lot … in the car."

Carlotta raised her eyes to Rebecca's. "I do that, too. But with my Ricci driving, I'm surprised you could sleep."

Had the woman just made a joke? Rebecca chuckled. "I was very tired after we left the lake."

"What did you think of Bracciano?"

"It's beautiful. I wished for more time to explore it further."

"In the fall, the Dominicis gather at the lake." She turned off the gas and poured the steaming milk into the cups then set the pan back on the stove and poured water into it from a kettle. She handed a cup to Rebecca then gestured toward the table in the center of the room.

The long wooden table was flanked by two benches. Rebecca slid onto one and Carlotta sat across from her.

After blowing on her milk, Rebecca took a sip. "So do you spend the day at the lake and return home?"

Carlotta shook her head. "No, no. We rent a villa, and we all stay together. We stay for …" she gave a shrug. "Three days or so. We take time to celebrate our families."

Rebecca gazed into the steaming milk. How different from her own upbringing where family was something one avoided.

Their conversation stilled as thunder rolled and rumbled. Carlotta shook her head. "Holy Father, protect the grapes." She made eye contact with Rebecca. "We need the rain, but the storms I don't like. And times are so bad. We don't need more bad news."

"The grapes are your biggest crop?"

Carlotta lifted her cup. "The grapes, they are everything. We have a few olives. We are starting to grow the wheat, but it doesn't like the field, I think." She sighed and finished her milk. "I grow the gardens, and we have meat and eggs and milk." She gestured toward the cabinets and a door Rebecca supposed must be the pantry. "We have all we need for now. Thank the Lord. Sometimes I forget."

After they'd finished their milk, Carlotta washed the pan and the cups, an act that spoke volumes about the woman's character. Rebecca dried the dishes and put them away. In the morning, the kitchen would be bustling with servants. Someone could easily clean up two cups, a couple of spoons, and a pan.

Together, they climbed the stairs. At the door to her room, Carlotta paused. "You rest in the morning. You don't need to begin your duties so soon. We will talk tomorrow. *Bene la notte*, Rebecca."

Rebecca stood for a moment, watching until Carlotta entered her room and closed the door. Then she crept inside the room she shared with Ricci. His mother's simple kindness had touched Rebecca deeply. As she lay down and waited for sleep, she rehashed the past hour spent with her mother-in-law. Perhaps she had accepted the inevitable. Strange to think this feisty little woman may be easier to live with than her own mother.

Chapter Twelve

Riccardo smoothed his hair back and replaced his hat. He stood on the crest of the hill overlooking the river, but his thoughts were far away. Four years away, when he had first met Nelda Lewis, Rebecca's mother. He only spoke to her for a matter of minutes, but in that short time, he had formed an opinion, not only of her, but of the Lewis family. So he was not shocked by his mother's revelation.

Mamma crossed herself three times during her conversation with him this morning. He chuckled at the memory of her discomfort. "You know I don't like to speak ill of others. Especially family. But I have prayed, and I spoke with Father Antony. He said I should tell you the truth then let you make the decision." She made the sign of the cross and glanced up to heaven. "Father, forgive me if I speak out of turn."

Only a few days before, she'd been more than happy to share her preconceived opinion of the "Americanas." Now she was afraid of speaking out of turn? What had happened?

"I love you, Mamma." He'd planted a kiss on her forehead and held her in his arms. Sometimes he had to remind himself to do that. She was a widow, and there was no one but him to hold her when she needed comfort. He leaned his cheek against the top of her head. "You aren't speaking out of turn. Father Antony is right. As head of our household, this is something I need to know. I will speak with Signora Lewis today."

Mamma took a backward step but kept her hand on his arm. "You think you should talk to Rebecca first?"

"No, Mamma. I think she knows."

Long after Mamma returned to the house, Riccardo

considered his options. Had he made a mistake in inviting Signora Lewis to live at Tres Viti? At the time, it had seemed the most logical solution. Rebecca would not have to worry about her mother. But had he strung a millstone about their necks?

His hands clasped behind his back, he strode down the hill toward the cottage. He'd left word with Detta, Eva's replacement, he would return in an hour's time to speak with Signora Lewis. When he arrived, his mother-in-law was sitting outside on the terrace in the shelter of the arbor, a book in one hand, a folding fan in the other.

He pulled out a chair and sat. "Buongiorno, Signora."

She gave a curt nod and closed her book.

Did she suspect what he'd come to talk about?

"Why don't you call me Nelda?" She flipped open the fan and waved it back and forth to stir the air.

He couldn't help noticing the dark circles beneath her eyes. And she'd been less diligent with her hair. He cleared his throat. "Are you unhappy here, Nelda?"

The fan stilled. Her gaze drifted to the distant fields. "Why would you ask that?"

"So many bottles of wine, Signora."

Her mouth opened, but she didn't speak. Instead, she pressed her lips together. Tears brimmed her eyes. "Does Rebecca know?"

He paused then shook his head. "No. I saw no need to involve her. This conversation is between us."

She nodded as a smile twisted her lips. "Between us and whoever informed you about the wine bottles. I can guess who that was."

Riccardo sat forward, elbows on his knees, fingers intertwined. "Just be thankful that 'whoever' is a person of discretion." He let that sink in before continuing. "I return to my former question, Nelda. Are you unhappy here?"

The movement of her fan quickened as she considered his question. A breeze rustled the leaves of the grapevines overhead. Doves cooed in their cote, and hens cackled. Sounds Riccardo rarely heeded, but he heard them now. They spoke of peace, tranquility, home. He could see they made no such impression on Nelda Lewis.

She raised her eyes to his. "I have never been content to stay in one place overlong, Riccardo. I suppose it is a shortcoming on my part." She laid her fan on the table and sat forward. "I've had an offer, actually, and I think I shall accept it."

Riccardo rested his chin in his hand and waited for her to continue.

"My friend, Eugene Lambert, has offered me the use of his flat in Nice. He has no need of it right now."

"Lambert, the Duc of Archambault?"

She nodded. "You know him?"

"I've heard of him. He visited in our absence, I believe."

"Yes, along with the Marchese and Marchesa of Adelfia. Your mother prepared a very nice dinner for all of them. As he was leaving, he made the offer. He called again yesterday and made sure I knew he was serious."

Riccardo sat back in his chair. "When would you leave?"

"He departs from Rome tomorrow afternoon. I could accompany him." She fingered the fan. "I will need a ride to the train."

"So soon? Are you quite certain?" What would Rebecca think of this?

Nelda glanced over her shoulder toward the cottage door. "I have already asked that new girl to begin packing my things."

"Then I will make the necessary arrangements." He rose to go.

She grabbed his hand. "Thank you, Riccardo ... for

everything."

"You will speak to Rebecca?" At the alarm in her eyes, he clarified the question. "To tell her you are leaving?"

Her eyelids fluttered then stilled at half-mast. She dropped his hand and rose from her chair. "Of course."

Riccardo walked away from Nelda, his head spinning. The woman had no morals. She didn't even try to make excuses or to stir his sympathy. He'd been prepared to accept an apology, at the very least. And what about her daughter, did she even care what Rebecca may feel?

His heart ached for Rebecca. No wonder she doubted herself after a lifetime of continuous disappointment.

Riccardo was well acquainted with the Duc's reputation as a womanizer. But the man had a fortune and several lucrative properties. Nelda could live quite well if that was truly her plan. He just hoped she wouldn't end up back here at some future date. He rubbed the back of his neck, thoughtful. He was tempted to tell Rebecca, but it was her mother's place to do so.

He caught sight of the women setting up the dinner tables in the orchard. Already, it was time for the men to come in from the fields. Mamma made her way across the lawn, carrying a large bowl. She never missed helping with the noon meal. It was her favorite part of the day when everyone gathered together like one big, happy family.

How would his Rebecca fit into this scene? He strode toward the house to see if she wanted to join them. He found her in their room, going through some of her belongings. "I thought you might like to join us outside for the noon meal, cara."

She glanced at him and smiled. He loved the way her eyes twinkled when she looked at him, as though she was truly happy. He wanted to sweep her up in his arms and kiss her until her toes curled. Perhaps they could skip dinner and …

"Wonderful, I'm starving." She crossed to the mirror and checked her appearance. "Am I presentable?"

He swept her into his arms and kissed her. Then he pulled back to gaze into her eyes.

She leaned against him. "I'll take that as a yes."

Hand in hand, they crossed the lawn to the table. "Traditionally, the women servants wait on the men first, then feed the children and themselves," Riccardo told her. "After dinner, the men take a nap before returning to their labor. The women never stop until their work is done." As they approached the table, the men stood until Rebecca sat, then returned to their places. Everyone waited quietly as Riccardo bowed his head and blessed the food.

After dinner, Rebecca returned to the house to finish putting things away. She wanted to get this done so she could fully concentrate on what she needed to learn from Carlotta. She intended to fit quickly into her new position as *la signora della casa.*

The bedroom complete, she moved downstairs to the room that would be her study. Here, she would keep up with the household receipts and correspondence. This was a lovely room—*her* study, with *her* beautiful cherry desk, *her* lovely blue velvet settee. Furnished by Riccardo, of course. Wonderful, thoughtful man.

Setting down the box she carried, Rebecca stepped to the bank of windows lining one wall, allowing a view of Carlotta's rose garden. The sweet scents of lavender and roses drifted in on the afternoon breeze.

The back wall held family photographs. Wonderful, lively photos depicting people who actually cared for one another. Ricci had proposed taking them down, but Rebecca wanted them. She slid her fingers over a beautifully carved frame. They gave her a sense of belonging. She wanted to know these people, memorize their faces, hear their stories.

A murmur of voices came to her as the women worked in the kitchen. A peaceful, pleasant sound. Yes, she was going to love this place.

The day passed quickly. She settled the last crystal figurine in her curio cabinet. She and Ricci had added several new pieces to the family's collection while on their honeymoon. After closing the glass door, she stepped back to approve the arrangement.

She glanced over her shoulder when she heard a soft knock at the door. Her mother stood on the threshold, looking tired and a bit peevish.

Rebecca turned to face her. "Hello, Mother."

Mother stepped through the door and closed it behind her. "I need to speak with you."

Stifling an impatient sigh, Rebecca gestured toward the settee. "Of course." A heavy smell of peppermint drifted past Rebecca's nose as her mother sat. Had she started drinking again?

Mother waited until Rebecca was settled. "It won't take long. I know you're busy."

"I have time for you."

Mother arched her brows as though she didn't believe it. She drew a breath and released it through smiling lips. Her green eyes pierced Rebecca's. "I'm going to Nice. Eugene has invited me to stay in his flat on the Riviera. You remember his flat. We stayed there in '24."

Relief ran like cool water through Rebecca's veins—followed closely by the usual heavy dose of guilt. She fiddled with the locket at her throat, a long-ago gift from Daddy. "But Mother, how will you live?"

Mother's lips tightened into a straight line. Her eyes glazed over, as they often did when she was about to tell a lie. "Eugene is happy for me to stay in the flat. He doesn't like for it to be unoccupied. I won't need anything. Not really."

Rebecca resisted the temptation to pledge her help. She had no right to do so without consulting Ricci. She licked her lips and smoothed her skirt, finding it difficult to sit still. "When do you leave?"

"In the morning, I'll take the early train to Rome. Tito will drive me. There's no need for you to go."

Rebecca opened her mouth to object, but Mother held up her hand.

"I'd prefer if you didn't go. We can say our good-byes here."

Mother had never cared for drama. Rebecca fingered the deep tufts in the blue velvet of the settee. "When will you return?"

"This is a permanent move." She glanced out the window then brought her gaze back to Rebecca. "You belong here. I am stifled. There's absolutely nothing to do. No society to speak of. I wonder if you will be able to bear it."

"I think I shall. I'm quite happy at the prospect of country life." The admission shocked Rebecca a little, but it was true. At least it sounded true. For the first time in a very long time, she was happy.

"How charming for you." Mother pushed away from the settee. "I hope you will never have cause for unhappiness, my dear."

Rebecca followed her to the door then paused. "Oh, wait, I—we bought you something—in Sperlonga." She crossed to her desk and picked up a book. Somehow, it didn't seem like enough. Not now. She held it out to Mother.

"*Years of Grace*. I've heard of it." Mother turned it over in her hands and looked at the back cover. "It's just out, isn't it?"

"I believe so."

A smile lit Mother's face. "Well, I shall have something to read on the train. Thank you, dear. And thank Riccardo for me."

"But surely you'll dine with us tonight?"

Mother shook her head. "I think not. I've a lot to do, and I mean to turn in early. I hope everyone will understand."

"Of course. Well, I'll see you in the morning, then."

With a nod of her head, Mother turned to go. Rebecca stood in the doorway, watching her and feeling rather numb.

After they watched Tito drive away bearing Mother and all her worldly belongings, Rebecca accepted a good-bye kiss from Ricci, on his way to the vineyard. "*Ciao, bella.* I will see you at dinner."

Carlotta looked at Rebecca. "I don't think you had time for your morning coffee."

Rebecca pressed her lips into a smile. "If that's an invitation, I accept." She followed Carlotta into the house.

A few minutes later, Carlotta hummed as she poured coffee into two cups. "I hope you are not too sad that your mother is gone."

"No," Rebecca said as she sank into the chair opposite Carlotta. She added cream to her coffee and stirred it slowly. At her mother-in-law's bidding, she helped herself to fresh bread and cheese from a tray in the middle of the table. "In a way, it's an answer to prayer."

Carlotta's fingers paused as she added sugar to her coffee. Her brow creased in a frown. "Why do you say answer to prayer?"

Rebecca shot a glance at Carlotta. What must she think of a daughter making such a statement regarding her mother? "I'm sorry. I didn't mean to sound disrespectful of my mother. But she can be ... difficult."

"You will miss her now, I think."

Carlotta's words sounded more like a question than a statement. Rebecca shrugged. "I'm used to being away from my mother."

"I see. You maybe don't know her so well." She lifted an embroidery hoop from the work basket at her feet and tugged at the needle.

Hmmm—had Carlotta become acquainted with Mother while Rebecca and Ricci had been away? Perhaps they'd become friends. Rebecca frowned into her coffee. Surely not. She watched her mother-in-law who now concentrated on a difficult stitch in her work, one brow arched above the other. Did Rebecca really want to know what the woman thought of Nelda Lewis? Probably not. She brushed crumbs from her fingers and dabbed at her lips with a linen napkin.

Quiet as a mouse, one of the servants removed the used dishes and refilled their coffee cups. Gigi—or Lucia? She tried to remember what Ricci had said about them. Surely, in time, she would remember their names.

Carlotta cleared her throat. "The staff will give the cottage a good cleaning today. And tomorrow or the next day, I will move in my things."

Rebecca's eyes flitted to Carlotta's face. Was that a hint of sadness in her voice? She sought to reassure her. "There's no hurry. Unless you are eager to go."

Carlotta peered at her for several seconds then dropped her gaze. "I think I am in the way here." She swiped at an invisible tear. "It is tradition, no?"

Aha. Just as she'd suspected. Carlotta didn't really want to leave her home, even though the cottage sat less than half a city block away. Before she shed any more fake tears, Rebecca sought to reassure her. "Well, yes, I have heard that. But there really is no need for you to move, unless you wish to do so."

"It is you who may wish me gone before many days pass."

Rebecca met Carlotta's shining gaze. That was a distinct possibility. But for now, perhaps the best thing to do was to give her time. More than anything, she wanted them to be friends. Was it possible? She offered her a smile. "If that day comes, I promise you'll be the first to know."

Carlotta set the embroidery hoop on the table and rested her hands on top of it. "Well then, perhaps we should discuss the running of the household."

For a few moments, they sat in silence as Carlotta worked and Rebecca waited. The servant woman returned to freshen their coffee, her eyes flitting back and forth between Carlotta and Rebecca. What did the servants know about their new contessa? If this house was like most others, there was plenty of gossip. She brought her gaze back to Carlotta's peaceful countenance. Why the sudden change in her? Had Riccardo spoken to his mother and asked her to be civil?

Rebecca opened her mouth to speak, then closed it again.

Her mother-in-law settled her stitchery on her lap and raised her eyes to Rebecca's face. "Yes? What is it you wish to say?"

"I know you didn't like me at first—that much was obvious. But when we returned from our honeymoon, you were nice to me. What changed your opinion?" She heard a feminine gasp from the area of the kitchen. Were they eavesdropping now? Probably.

Carlotta straightened her spine, never dropping her eyes from Rebecca's and spoke in slow, but perfect English, as though she wished to be fully understood. "Because you are my son's wife, and he obviously adores you, I have made an effort to be nice to you. To defer to you as Contessa, because it is right. It was my upbringing, to give respect. I promised Riccardo I would be hospitable to you … and to your mother … as our guests. But now, you are la Signora della Casa."

Rebecca suppressed a smile. "But you are *la padrona*." This time, she was certain she heard titters from the kitchen.

Carlotta raised her chin. "I see you know a bit about respect. So I apologize for what I have said about you." She turned her head toward the kitchen door and cast her words in that direction. "In the kitchen."

There was no holding back the smile this time. Rebecca shook her head. "Then we are at peace?"

"We were never at war. It is just that I refuse to kitty-cat around. I must say what I think."

Rebecca eyed Carlotta, "Kitty-cat?"

Carlotta's brow wrinkled and her lips pursed. "Walk soft?"

"You mean pussyfoot around? I don't want you to do that. I prefer that you speak your mind. If you don't like something I'm doing, say so, and say it in Italian." She switched to the specified language. "I understand you quite well."

Carlotta pushed her palm against her forehead and smoothed her hair back then responded in Italian. "I am glad of that, because speaking so much in a foreign language has given me a headache." Then she smiled. A real smile that made it all the way to her eyes.

Chapter Thirteen

Mid-July, 1930

Rebecca pinched herself several times in an effort to stay awake at her mother-in-law's missionary society meeting. She'd already stifled four yawns and counted to a hundred in Latin, backward and forward. Honestly, how many times did they need to explain how to piece together crocheted granny squares?

Ten long minutes later, the chairwoman wrapped things up, asking everyone else to leave except for those who still had questions. Thank goodness, Carlotta headed toward the door, not the dais where several clueless women congregated. Rebecca trotted after her mother-in-law.

Her eyes on Carlotta's receding backside, Rebecca nearly rammed Father Antony. She drew back, her hand to her throat. "Please excuse me. I didn't see you."

He smiled and nodded. "I can see that. But I am glad we have very nearly run into each other. I have wanted to speak with you."

Uh oh, was she in trouble? She ran a swift memory check. No, she couldn't remember doing anything that might be against church law. But she wasn't really all that familiar with their rules. She brought her attention back to the priest.

He gestured toward the outer door. She set off in that direction and he fell into step beside her. "Signora Alverá ... er ... your mother-in-law, tells me you are interested in Catechism classes." His arched brows seemed to question, though his statement had not.

Rebecca cleared her throat. "Why ... yes ... I did ask her about it."

He halted his steps, his brows meeting in a solid line over his nose. "You are interested in converting to our Roman Catholic beliefs?"

She paused, too, her gaze darting ahead to Carlotta, who stood in conversation with two of her friends just beyond the outer arch. Well, this was as good a time as any. She smiled and nodded. "Yes, Padre, I am interested."

He clasped his hands at his waist and beamed at her, revealing several overlapping teeth. "Ah, good. We have classes beginning in the fall. I apologize for the fact that ... well, we have not so many new converts in our small town, you see. So you will have to attend classes with the children." He covered his mouth with a fist and cleared his throat. "We will send you a letter with everything you need to know."

Her smile ebbed away. She plastered it back on. Classes with children. She sensed humiliation in her future. Gazing at Carlotta again, she blew out a sigh. Humility was a good thing, right? "Thank you, Padre."

After he left, she hurried to catch up with Carlotta. Within hearing distance of the ladies, she overheard one of them talking about an Americana. Why did they always make it sound like a curse word? Rebecca slowed her steps and backed up to the wall. Eavesdropping was wrong, but her curiosity was piqued.

The older woman's raspy voice echoed in the passageway. "I don't know how you have endured this. What will happen when they have children? Have you thought about that?"

Another voice chimed in. "And she was napping during the meeting."

Rebecca's breath caught in her throat as she waited for Carlotta's response. Only a few weeks had passed, but she hoped her mother-in-law's opinion of her had changed. She'd worked so hard, attended every Mass, delivered bread to the poor.

Carlotta kept her voice low, but Rebecca heard every word. "I will thank you not to speak ill of my daughter. You do not know her. But if you will open your hearts, you will get to know her. And then you will love her, I think."

My daughter—did she know Rebecca stood near enough to overhear—or was she speaking from her heart? This was Carlotta. She could say all she wanted against someone in her family. But no one else was allowed to do so. She became a lioness, defending her cubs.

After a couple of calming breaths, Rebecca moved away from the wall and rushed outside, as if she had come a long distance. "There you are. I hope I haven't kept you waiting too long. I was delayed by Father Antony." She made eye contact with each of the two ladies and graced them with a smile a politician would envy. She wanted to burst out laughing at the looks on their faces but managed to control herself. What a day she was having.

"What a day." Riccardo said as he leaned against an ox-drawn hay cart. The lone ox munched contentedly on the sun-dried hay at its feet. "I don't know what to do, Poppi."

Along with a good-sized crew of servants and neighbors, Poppi forked dried hay into mounds.

Riccardo removed his hat and smoothed his hair back. "Vittorio wants me to run for chair, but with all this talk, I don't know." Riccardo had agreed to fill his father's old position on the local association of landowners, usually referred to as the committee. The committee met weekly with the mayor to discuss the many new rules and regulations passed down from the present regime. In the days of the monarchy, when Papá had attended, they mostly sat around, smoked, and talked. It was a pleasant pastime. These days, it could become heated, especially when someone brought up one of the many new taxes.

Poppi stopped long enough to mop his brow with a damp kerchief. "I think you have no choice, Ricci. As long as you are a part of the committee, perhaps you can help make changes."

Riccardo drew in a deep breath and exhaled with a loud sigh. "I'm just complaining. You know me."

Poppi grinned as he stuffed the red kerchief in the pocket of his overalls. "Better than anyone. You will moan and groan." He forked up a load of hay and hefted it on the pile. "And then you will do what is right."

The hay cart creaked as Riccardo pushed away from it. He slapped his hat against his thigh, and set it on his head. "My past is catching up with me. That's all. Like a runaway train."

"Il mio amico," Poppi said, gripping Riccardo's arm. He looked him square in the eyes. "This, too, will pass."

Riccardo gazed into the distance, nodding in agreement. "I know you are right."

"I usually am." Poppi followed this admission with a chuckle. He let go of Riccardo's arm and returned to work.

Riccardo lifted his hat to acknowledge the nearby workers before turning to stride down the path toward the road where he'd left his car.

His mind wandered as he drove into town. The landscape of the countryside surrounding Tres Viti hadn't changed much over the years, but Riccardo had. After his father's passing, he'd had to grow up and take responsibility for the property and his mother's welfare.

But his past had dogged him. He'd never done anything really bad. He'd never partied excessively or gambled. But the women, they would not leave him alone. At first, it had been fun. Like many an Italian lad, he'd played the Casanova. Until he met a certain redhead. She'd ruined it for him. He tried, but he couldn't forget her. So he'd pursued and won her.

By the time he reached the outskirts of town, thoughts of Rebecca had lifted his spirits. Funny how that always happened.

"Something smells wonderful," Rebecca said as she wove through the kitchen to check on the meal.

Ricci had called before leaving town to warn them he was on the way, and he had invited several people to join them for supper. Apparently, this was something he'd often done. Carlotta barely blinked an eye. The women in the kitchen chopped more vegetables and tossed them into the pots.

Rebecca helped Gigi set the table then ran upstairs to change before their guests arrived. She assumed he'd invited the usual suspects. He had several friends on Mayor Modesti's committee with him, and lately, they'd had a lot to discuss, so it made sense to adjourn to someone's home.

After changing into her favorite dinner dress, navy blue with cap sleeves, Rebecca sat for Eva to do her hair. The heat and humidity made it nearly unmanageable. Eva swept it up and back, pinning it into a French twist.

"It looks lovely, Eva. Grazie." As Rebecca touched up her lipstick, she heard the sound of multiple automobiles in the drive. "Sounds like our guests have arrived." She stood and smoothed her skirt before rushing to the stairs.

She had hoped to greet them at the door, but Ricci had already ushered them in. Oh well, she could make a grand entry. All eyes turned to her as she descended the stairs. Ricci's inner circle of friends, along with their wives. She released a breath. His closest friends had come to accept her. Well, almost. They no longer treated her like a visitor from another planet.

Ricci stepped forward and offered his hand. "You look enchanting, Signora Alverá." His eyes sparkled as he smiled into hers. "Thank you for doing this on such short notice."

Rebecca greeted the friends by couple, Paolo and Anna Angelucci, Giuseppe and Ambra Carbone, Tomas and Moro

Giontelli.

"Signori y Signoras," Carlotta called from the dining room. "The food is ready. Please pass through."

"First, one feasts with their eyes," Ambra said, as she took the chair held for her by Giuseppe. "What a beautiful table, Carlotta."

Carlotta beamed from her place near the head of the table. "You can look at it all you want, but I hope you will eat it, as well."

"Oh, she will eat," Giuseppe answered kissing his fingertips in the classic Italian gesture. "My wife loves to eat." For this, he received a playful slap from Ambra.

After Ricci spoke a blessing over the meal, they passed the colorful vegetable dishes.

Rebecca's mouth watered at the platter of bright green basil nestled among thick slices of tomatoes with globs of bright, white goat cheese and brined olives. She could eat from this platter and be fully satisfied. As long as she had bread.

Her eyes wandered to the warm focaccia now being passed. She'd enjoyed watching the women make the focaccia—smoothing out the dough—punching it with their fingertips, then slathering it all with olive oil and herbs. Oh, the smell as it baked. Manna from heaven.

She glanced around the table, watching everyone eat with enthusiasm, dipping the bread in bowls of olive oil. How these folks remained so small puzzled her.

A cool breeze off the mountains wafted through the dining room as the meal progressed. Rebecca's attention was drawn to the tall, ruggedly handsome Paolo. He was a passionate man, concerned that so many of his workers were talking of immigrating to the United States.

"All this talk of freedom and becoming rich in America. I don't believe it. Are they not also experiencing this depression?" He smoothed his neatly trimmed mustache and licked his lips.

"Their difficulties are multiplied," Tomas agreed with a
nod of his head. "I was reading about the great drought in the
Midwest. Their crops are threatened." He lifted his hand in the
air. "How will they recover if they can't grow their own food?"

Anna turned to Rebecca. "Have you seen evidence of
great wealth available to the immigrants of your nation?"

Memories of the deplorable conditions of the slums of
New York and Boston crowded into Rebecca's mind as she
considered Anna's question. These were places Rebecca had
only seen from inside a cab. The Irish ghettos were the worst,
but the Italians had it little better.

She gazed into Anna's imploring eyes. "There are many
who are starving, and there isn't enough work for those who
are already there. But America is known for its resiliency. I've
no doubt it will bounce back in time. If one has the energy and
the resources to survive these tough economic circumstances,
then I suppose it is possible."

Ricci clapped his hands. "Bravo! My wife, the politician."

To his left, Giuseppe raised his glass. "Salute."

Paolo scowled into his glass as he swirled the liquid. "It is
too serious for me to laugh. We must find a way through this."

Ricci's expression sobered. "You are right, Paolo. We
must if we are to survive. But, once again, we are being asked
to take up arms. Our strong, young men are being sent into
battle, and for what?"

Carlotta pushed away from the table, her eyes on Rebecca.
"I believe this is our cue to withdraw, my dear."

The men rose as their wives followed Carlotta to the
parlor.

Rebecca looked with longing at the stairs as she passed. If
only she could disappear into her room. She prayed the men
would not tarry long over their after-dinner drinks and
conversation. She was expected to join the women, of course,

but she preferred to hear the men's discussion. She had little in common with these women. Two of them were already mothers. She sat on the overstuffed sofa next to Ambra.

Carlotta strained tea into cups then passed the cups to each of their guests. Rebecca had learned early on that this was a ritual her mother-in-law preferred to do herself.

Gigi set a tray of sweets on the table.

Rebecca selected a thin slice of lemon pound cake, her favorite.

The women talked over the drone of the men's voices. Rebecca tried to give them her full attention. She was at ease only with Ambra, who also had no children.

She studied Ambra as the young woman spoke in an aloof manner, no doubt picked up among her society friends. Rebecca was well acquainted with women of that caste. Goodness, she'd been one for a number of years. Ambra wore her dark hair in an up-sweep. Her delicate, well-manicured hands had probably never done a day's work. Her husband was a Duca, which made no difference during this crisis. It only seemed to grease the slide into genteel poverty. Because they'd lived such an extravagant lifestyle, they were now bleeding money. What's more, everyone knew it. Rebecca sipped the tea as her gaze slid to her mother-in-law's hands gripping a pink china cup. Her nails were neat and well-tended, but her hands were work-worn, tanned by the sun.

"You must give him goat's milk," Carlotta said in reply to Moro, who'd made a remark about her baby's colic.

"I refuse to keep a goat," Ambra said. "Ever since one ate my husband's favorite shirt right off the line."

Carlotta laughed out loud, a sound so rare, Rebecca nearly dropped her teacup.

Ambra chuckled then dabbed at the corners of her eyes. "I would have served that nanny goat up for dinner if my cook hadn't intervened. So now, it is banished to the cottage of one of our laborers, far away from the main house. The creature never knew what hit her."

Rebecca smiled though she didn't know why it was so funny. The sound of chairs scraping against tile announced that the men were finishing up. A moment later, Ricci's frame filled the doorway. His relaxed smile warmed her heart. He was pleased with whatever he and his friends had discussed. As the other men entered the room, Rebecca set her cup down and brushed imaginary crumbs from her skirt.

Within moments, the lot of them had dispersed amid calls of "Ciao" and many cheek-kisses. Rebecca smiled and waved then turned to make her way up the stairs. Carlotta had already withdrawn, probably to the kitchen.

"Where are you going?" Ricci called after Rebecca.

She turned to gaze at him. "My pillow is calling my name."

He laughed but waved her back. "Come take a walk with me. Your pillow will wait for you."

"A walk? But it's dark out."

He gestured again. "Come, come. The moon is full. The night is lovely."

He was right. The temperature was perfect, the humidity low. A large summer moon hung in the sky, illuminating the gravel drive and surrounding countryside. Ricci took her hand as they strolled down the lane so recently traversed by their friends' automobiles. She could still smell the dust and oil as she walked, wondering why he had drawn her away.

"I have been asked to take over as chair of the committee," he told her in a quiet voice as though he wished to keep it a secret from the creatures of the night.

She glanced up at his face. "What does that mean?"

"It is a position of honor, mainly. I would report directly to Mayor Modesti. A sort of spokesperson—a liaison— between the mayor and the community."

"I see. Sounds as though it would suit you."

"You think so?" He caught both her hands and intertwined his fingers with hers.

She looked into his eyes. He was very handsome in the moonlight. "Of course, you're a natural leader."

He was quiet for a moment, their gazes still intertwined. "So ... you think I should accept?"

It was obvious he had already made up his mind. He wanted the position, the honor, the approval. She leaned against him and smiled into his sparkling eyes. "You want to do it, so yes, I think you should."

He lifted her chin and kissed her then pulled her into his arms. She leaned against him, drawing strength from him. When had he become so much a part of her? It had happened so gradually, she hadn't realized it. She breathed in his scent, listened to the beat of his heart, and understood for the first time, the meaning of two becoming one.

Chapter Fourteen

17 September, 1930
Dearest Nancy,

    I am devastated.

    I hoped to have wonderful news to share with you, but late last evening, that hope ended. The doctor has just left. He advised several days of bed rest. Riccardo and Carlotta are enforcing his orders. Only hours into it, and I am desperately bored.

    Please tell me you can come next spring or summer. I long to see you. My ears ache to hear authentic American English, especially the cultured Yankee variety.

    Oh, my dear, I love it here more than I ever thought I would. But this last ordeal has broken my heart. Carlotta has taken it in stride. I am quite certain she will go to Mass in the morning and pray for me. Though she will never say so, I think she truly believes my misfortunes stem from my bloodline. I was not born Roman Catholic. Though I've gone with her to Mass. I've prayed the prayers. I've pledged my undying obedience. I even plan to take the classes. But still she says, "One cannot change one's colors." I'm not certain what that means. Perhaps you can enlighten me?

    Tomorrow, Nonna, the "grandmother" (Poppi's wife) will try to teach me how to knit. It is good to have something to do. This is what Carlotta says. Pray for me, dear Nancy. And if you have any mercy at all, you will write me one of your long letters.

Yours always,

"R"

After the ink dried, Rebecca folded the letter, but hadn't the strength to tuck it into the envelope. She laid it aside and leaned back on her pillow. Was her weariness due to the miscarriage or her state of mind? She'd never felt so discouraged.

For a few golden weeks, she'd rejoiced in her impending motherhood. Odd, for one who'd never really desired a child. When faced with an actual pregnancy … joy had filled her soul. But as usual, life turned around and spit in her face.

Riccardo stayed by her side throughout the ordeal, holding her hand, speaking words of comfort. But he hadn't suffered as she had. How could he? The child had not been a part of him. Rebecca understood that, but still she'd expected more from him. She'd finally trusted herself with him, as she had with no other. Together, they had produced life.

She laid her hand on her abdomen, now empty of its precious burden. Would she ever bear another?

The doctor had seemed uncertain. He wouldn't make promises. Time will tell. God's will be done. He'd said all the usual things. Not much comfort there.

Riccardo pledged his everlasting love, whether God blessed their union with children or not. Tears rolled down her cheeks at the memory of his words. What would his love for her cost him?

A soft knock on the door was followed by Eva's inquiry, "Signora?"

Rebecca swiped at her damp cheeks. "Come in, Eva."

Eva entered, closed the door, then took a step forward. "Oh, you are crying." She moved swiftly to get a clean handkerchief from the drawer then returned to the bed.

Rebecca dried her eyes and blew her nose. "I'm sorry. I'm a mess."

Eva sat in the chair beside the bed. "No, no—you mustn't apologize."

"I'm not the type to wallow in my sorrow. If only I could be up and busy. I know I'd soon feel better."

"You must rest, my friend. It won't be long, just a few more days. Now, what may I bring you? Books? Tea? A leg of lamb?"

Rebecca tried to hold back the laughter, but it proved impossible. Though it hurt, she laughed out loud. Eva had such a gift and had come to mean so much to Rebecca.

Eva picked up the folded letter and stuffed it in the envelope. "I will have someone post this for you." She stood and crossed to the door. "Then I will bring you tea and something to read."

After she left, Rebecca lay very still, wondering at the goodness of these people. They had taken her in—a total stranger—and treated her as family. Loved her, as one of their own. All her life, she'd longed for this kind of love. She drew in a deep, ragged breath and sighed.

When Eva returned with tea and several books from the study shelves, Rebecca smiled at her.

Eva set the tray on the table then straightened the bed and adjusted the pillows. "Ah, good, you are feeling much better. As we made the tea, Nonna prayed. She also sent your favorite raisin cakes to tempt you. And tomorrow, she will teach you to do the knitting." When she had the tray in place, she stood aside. "You will recover, Signora. I know this because I have been through it also."

Rebecca searched Eva's face. She was always so upbeat. No one would guess she'd suffered at all. "I'm sorry, Eva. I didn't know."

"It is all right. I didn't tell you so you would feel sorry for me. It is so you will know it gets better. I am content for now, and I pray that one day, I will have another chance. I pray this for both of us. And we can light a candle for one another."

Rebecca relaxed against the pillows and smiled at Eva. "Thank you for telling me. It does help. And tell Nonna I look forward to her lessons."

Riccardo left the committee meeting as soon as it had ended. He didn't stick around for small talk. He had not the heart for it today. Before leaving town, he stopped in at the church and lit a candle. His heart ached for Rebecca. After two weeks, she still seemed so depressed. Sure, he'd wanted the baby as much as she, but it hadn't been real for him. She'd known the child. Felt its presence.

He was about to get into the car when he heard Francesca Boccali calling his name. He ignored her frantic waving. "I will not be delayed by her again," he said under his breath as he jumped in and sped away.

He had a lot to think about on the way home and meant to spend the entire time meditating the news he'd heard this morning. The prolonged meeting had been a total bore for Riccardo. Did they not understand he was a working man? He had many things to oversee at home if he was to make a success of Tres Viti. And Il Duce was making it more and more difficult to turn a profit. Now he wanted even more land producing wheat.

What of the cattle, the horses? What were they to eat? There was far too little hay and pastureland already.

Leaving town in the dust, he did not even look back. He must figure a way to get through the next few years, with all the demands on his time. There was even a rumor the officers would be called up again, to train raw recruits. This, he could not fathom. How could any of them possibly make a living if they were constantly called away for this and that? Of course, most of the old order nobility had servants to do all the work. He laughed out loud at the thought. With mounting expenses,

Riccardo had to limit his work staff, and he was not the only one. Many of his friends confessed the same needs.

Il Duce's answer was to have more children. Tax breaks for everyone who produces at least five offspring. Riccardo banged his palm on the steering wheel then shook his head. Was this to offset the dwindling citizenship? Did he not see what was happening? How many Italians left the country daily because they'd lost everything in the stock market crash? And because they had no desire to serve a dictator.

What would the man require of them next? Would he take their land? Would he turn their children into chattel? Their fears were fast becoming reality. Already, the schools were changing, training young minds to accept everything that issued out of Il Duce's mouth.

He blew out a sigh. At least the man had enough sense to honor the Church and set Rome apart. If he'd not done that— Riccardo shook his head—he didn't like to think about what would have been.

Mamma would say, "Riccardo, you are not speaking in faith." And she was right. He must turn his fears and anxieties into prayers for his country, his people, his home. As he turned onto the lane that led from the main road to Tres Viti, he prayed the prayers he'd been taught all his life. And then he prayed from his heart. He spoke to God in a way he'd never done before. It was as if he spoke directly to Him, and God listened and heard.

Finally allowed to leave her bed, Rebecca hummed as she donned the clothes Eva laid out for her. She intended to have a normal day. Well, as normal as it could be at this late hour.

She buttoned the pale blue shirtwaist dress and smoothed the skirt over her too-flat tummy. Would she ever swell with child? She glanced at the crucifix adorning the wall above their bed. Peace flooded her body as faith rose like the tide within her.

"Whatever you require of me," she whispered, "I will do."

As she slipped on her shoes, she heard the sound of a car's engine in the drive. Was Ricci just now returning from town? She stopped to glance in the mirror then crossed to the window. No, that was not his vehicle. The car's rear passenger door opened, and a blonde woman got out. Dressed in a dark red suit and shiny black heels, she smoothed the long hair that fell in waves across her shoulders.

A moment later, the woman sent her right hand aloft in a greeting.

Rebecca stepped to the side of the open window to enhance her view. Ricci approached. She heard his voice but could not make out his words. A smile wreathed his face.

The woman relaxed against the side of the car. Ricci stood in front of her, his arms crossed over his chest. He seemed intent on whatever the woman was saying.

He reached up and pushed at the brim of his hat then shook his head slowly. Rebecca sank back behind the curtains when he sent a glance toward the house. Who was this woman? Should Rebecca go out there or at least go to the front door?

Before she could decide what to do, the woman pushed away from the side of the car. Rebecca heard a definite "Ciao." Then the woman took a forward step and planted a kiss on Ricci's lips. Not the traditional cheek smack, first one side then the other, but a full-on mouth-to-mouth.

Rebecca's own lips parted as she sucked in air. She reeled away from the window, grabbing at the bedpost to steady herself. What had just happened? Was Ricci having an affair with this woman? Right in front of their home? Where servants could see? Where Rebecca could see?

The car's engine roared and the tires crunched on gravel in a slow retreat. The front door opened and Ricci greeted someone. Then his footsteps sounded on the stairs.

Rebecca collapsed in the chair, but nerves wouldn't let her stay. She stood up again, trembling and struggling for breath.

He gave a soft knock on the door then opened it. "You're up. Wonderful. Do you feel like joining me for—" His gaze took in her expression. "What is it? Are you ill?" He rushed to her side.

Before he could touch her, she sidestepped him. "No." She shook her head. "I'm not ill." She forced her gaze to his face. "Who was that woman?"

He blanched. "You saw that?"

Her breath came in short bursts. The vision of an angry bull played across her mind. "Yes, I saw that. What were you thinking?"

He straightened his shoulders, his lips parted. "Wh … what was I thinking? You think *I* did that?" He gestured toward the window. "She kissed me! Did you not see me step away from her?"

No, Rebecca had not seen that if, indeed, he had stepped away. Reason cautioned her to calm down, but she wasn't listening to reason right now. Her blood boiled. "Why would she do that, if you had not led her to believe she could?"

Ricci stepped forward, his eyes flaming, his voice low. "I did nothing to encourage her. In fact, I did everything I could to discourage her."

Rebecca convulsed at the anger in his voice. It was too much. Too soon after her loss. She couldn't deal with the emotion.

He tried to comfort her, tried to hold her in his arms, but her nostrils filled with a strange perfume.

She jerked away from him. "Don't. Not with her scent on you. I can't stand it." She turned her back on him and rushed into the bathroom, closing the door. She leaned against the sink, her head in her hands. Her heart thumped against her breast. How could she deal with this on top of everything else?

Her head ached, she ached all over. She peered into the mirror. Shocking. She looked like a ghost. Her pupils were dilated, making her eyes appear black and scary. She hardly recognized herself.

Could she blame Ricci if he welcomed the attentions of another woman? He certainly had plenty of opportunity. Most days, he left before daylight. After breakfast, he spent his mornings in the fields. Except for the days he was required to attend those meetings. And who knows what went on there?

He was a handsome man with a ready smile. Women loved him. They always had.

She jumped when he rapped on the door.

"Rebecca, this is ridiculous. Come out so we can talk." After a moment, when she didn't answer, he said, "How can you think I would do such a thing?"

He huffed out a breath, his footsteps receded, and the door opened and closed.

She sank onto the edge of the tub and wept.

Chapter Fifteen

Riccardo stopped outside the door to the bedroom, chest heaving, hands trembling with emotion. He had not come so close to losing his temper in a long, long time. He closed his eyes and collapsed against the wall, his gut roiling. Was he angrier at Francesca for what she had done or at Rebecca for believing he would ever betray her? Releasing a sigh, he threaded his fingers through his hair then pushed away from the cool plaster of the upstairs hallway and descended the stairs. He needed fresh air.

Thankful no one was about, he grabbed his hat from the hook beside the door and headed to the stables.

Lancelot snorted a greeting as Riccardo approached. He smoothed the horse's muzzle then reached for a bridle on a nearby hook.

Sandro, one of Poppi's grandsons, jogged up. "You want me to saddle him, Signore?"

Riccardo cast a forced smile over his shoulder as he slipped the bridle over Lancelot's ears. "I can do it, Sandro." The boy's crestfallen expression bade him to reconsider. "Well, all right. You do it, please."

Beaming, Sandro lifted the saddle off its perch while Riccardo led Lancelot out of his stall. As the boy worked, Riccardo wandered to the front of the barn. Two brown and yellow cats stretched out in the sun. He knelt beside them and scratched their ears. Doves cooed in the eaves above his head as a small dust devil spun a wild dance on the path in front of him. The heartache deep in his chest threatened to steal his breath away. He closed his eyes and bowed his head.

When the *clip-clop* of hooves sounded on the cobbled

stones of the entranceway, Riccardo stood. Sandro handed over the reins.

After checking the straps and cinches, Riccardo reached out to ruffle the boy's hair but decided against it. He gripped his shoulder instead. "You've done a fine job, Sandro."

"Grazie, Signore. I'll be here when you return."

After mounting his horse, Riccardo gave the boy a thumbs-up. He followed the line of cypress trees down the slope to a dry creek bed, crossed over to the other side, and onto a narrow lane that cut through the pasture. On even ground, he urged Lancelot into a run. His hat blew off, but he didn't care to stop. He'd pick it up on the way home.

By the time Rebecca made her way down the stairs, the house was quiet. At this hour of the day, most everyone was resting. She crossed the tile floor and stepped outside where she stood for a moment to get her bearings. A walk was just the thing to clear her head and calm her nerves. A fresh breeze stirred the leaves of the fruit-laden olive trees as she strolled along the gravel path.

Though she tried not to think of it, the morning's quarrel with Ricci kept bouncing around in her mind. The two of them were quite a pair. Her temper flared easily, and Ricci's, though slower, could be volcanic in strength. Like a dam bursting. An old memory surfaced of him blowing up at a handsome young naval officer who'd repeatedly flirted with her. She'd been flattered by the man's attention at first but then irritated when he continued to pester her. After a battle of words failed, Riccardo had decked the slightly looped officer with one punch.

Rebecca grasped an olive branch and held tightly to it as her heart spasmed. Oh, Ricci. His words outside the bathroom door echoed in her mind, "How can you think I would do such a thing?"

Years of experience, maybe? Never being able to trust her parents—knowing both of them had been unfaithful to each other?

Ricci had never let her down. He'd always kept his word. An honorable man. One she could trust.

Until the blonde woman kissed him. Right there in front of his house. Out in the open for everyone to see. Everyone. A niggling doubt weaseled its way into her mind. She squeezed the olive branch so tightly, its bark cut into her skin. She released it and moved forward out of the olive grove to the edge of the pasture. Was it possible the woman had done it on purpose?

Who was this woman, anyway? Rebecca's thoughts traveled back to the dinner party, the second night after her arrival in Umbria. Several women in attendance seemed to flaunt their friendship with Ricci, as though they had something to prove. She had noticed but paid little mind, because at the time, he'd had eyes only for her.

Had the blonde woman been among them?

Rebecca stood gazing at the field of dry grass undulating in the breeze. A dark object caught her eye. As she drew nearer, she could see it was a hat. She picked it up. Ricci had a hat just like this. She strode up the dusty lane, searching the fields for any sign of him. As she topped a rise, she saw his horse, grazing in the tall grass. But Ricci was nowhere to be seen. She fingered the hat, her heart beating faster. He could be hurt. He could've fallen from his horse. She called to him. "Ricci!"

Her feet moved faster. She sped down the hill, calling his name, "Ricci! Ricci, where are you?"

Lancelot raised his head to watch her with deep brown, soulful eyes. He tossed his head and snorted, but there was no other sound. She stepped through the tall grass, her eyes on the horse and stumbled on something large. Losing her balance, she tumbled forward. Hands caught her. Strong arms supported her.

"Whoa!" She fell into Ricci's arms. Her breath caught in her throat. "I was afraid … something had happened to you."

His face was only inches away from hers, brows arched in surprise.

She shook her head. "Why are you lying on the ground?"

He steadied her with his hands until she was sitting then pushed himself into a similar position. "Thinking." He nodded toward the hat. "I see you found my hat."

She nodded and placed it on his head, slightly askew. She giggled but saw no answering glint in his eyes. He must still be angry with her. She dropped her gaze. "I'm sorry, Ricci. So, so sorry."

"I'm sorry, too," he whispered.

Her eyes snapped to his. "Why are you sorry? You said it was her, not you."

His shoulders drooped. She heard him draw in a breath, and her heart nearly stopped. Had she been wrong? Was he going to confess an indiscretion?

"That we fought. That you have so much trouble trusting me. For whatever has caused this, I am deeply sorry."

His hat still sat crookedly on his head, looking slightly ridiculous. She fought the urge to giggle again. When she gazed into his brimming, bloodshot eyes, her heart melted. She rose to her knees and faced him, touched his cheek, felt the wetness of his tears. "Oh, Ricci, I do love you so."

Leaning forward, she touched her lips to his. At once, his arms encircled her as he returned her kiss with a passion that roared over and through her, like a wave of the ocean.

Time slowed, as overhead, clouds scudded by. Rebecca lay with her head propped on Ricci's arm, watching the display. Somewhere near at hand, a thrush sang. Lancelot munched on dry grass. Ricci snored softly. Rebecca smiled and heaved a sigh. Could life get any better?

She sat up as Ricci stirred and stretched.

His voice husky from sleep, he said, "We'd better get back before they send out a search party." He pushed up from the ground, brushing at the clinging grass. She handed him his hat then grasped his hand. He pulled her to her feet and into his arms. "Ti amo, mia sposa."

"Likewise," she whispered, melting into his embrace.

They strolled up the winding lane, Ricci leading Lancelot. She glanced up at him. "Who was that woman?"

He grimaced. "Do we have to talk about it?" His shoulders slumped and the corners of his mouth took a downward turn. "She is no one to me. But I can understand your interest in her." He blew out a breath. "She is Francesca Boccali, secretary to Mayor Modesti. She is also secretary of our land use committee meetings." He halted his forward motion and turned to face Rebecca. His eyes bored into hers. "She wants me. But she cannot have me. Because my heart belongs to someone else."

Rebecca lifted her chin, her gaze challenging his. She was taking a chance—a big one—but she had to know. "Has she ever had you?"

His gaze never faltered. "No. Never. Not in that way."

She closed her eyes and breathed deeply. "Not in *that* way. No doubt you have flirted with her."

He tilted his head to the side and glanced away. "Not seriously. She is not my type." He slid his arm about her waist and pulled her forward. "Come on. Let's get back. I am very hungry." Their bodies bumped together as they walked along, side-by-side.

Rebecca continued on to the house after Ricci left her to take Lancelot to the barn. Still, her mind would not let go of what had happened. Why would this … this Francesca woman do something like that? And why would she choose to do it in front of the house where she knew they could possibly be seen? Did she believe she could win Ricci away from Rebecca?

She gnawed her lower lip as she slipped up the stairs to freshen up before dinner. Upon entering her dressing room, she found Eva there, putting away clean laundry. Rebecca turned aside and sifted through her dresses, looking for something to wear. Behind her, Eva laughed out loud.

Rebecca drew back and glanced over her shoulder. "What is so funny?

Eva covered her mouth and giggled again. She gripped Rebecca's shoulders and moved her in front of the mirror where she could see dry grass and straw sticking out of her hair.

"Hah!" Rebecca drew in a quick breath. "Oh my goodness." Her eyes met Eva's as they both dissolved into loud, giggling laughter.

Riccardo opened the door to their bedroom, puzzled by the feminine laughter he heard coming from Rebecca's dressing room. He rapped on the door. "Are you all right in there?"

The door opened and a smiling Eva exited, barely suppressing another giggle behind the palm of her hand. "Buona sera, Signore."

He watched her go then peeked around the door to find Rebecca, seated at the dressing table, applying powder to her nose. "Dare I ask what was so funny?"

Rebecca glanced at him from the mirror then pointed to a small pile of dry grass on the tray beside her brush and comb. "Eva found this in my hair."

Ricci chuckled. "I suppose I had better check mine also."

She rose from her chair. "Here, let me."

He turned and bent his knees so she could see.

She picked a few pieces out. "Not bad. You better hurry, though. Eva said dinner is ready."

They were only slightly late. After huffing out a couple of impatient sighs and complaining that the roast would be tough from overcooking, Mamma bowed her head, Riccardo's cue to bless the food.

"Bless us, oh Lord, and these thy gifts, which we are about to receive from thy bounty through Christ our Lord. Amen." The words were rote, repeated at every meal, but tonight, Riccardo felt their meaning most keenly. He made eye contact with Rebecca. Her face reflected joy, contentment. They had come much too close to losing something precious. Even more precious to him than the child she'd carried for so short a time.

He gritted his teeth at the memory of Francesca's actions. He must ensure nothing like that ever happened again.

"Riccardo?" Mamma said. "Will you carve the roast? I'm starving from the long wait."

He shook off the reverie and sliced the meat as Mamma rambled on about the Festival of the Olives.

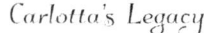

Chapter Sixteen

The clerk at the dry goods store in Foligno peered at Rebecca over round, wire rimmed glasses. "I don't know if you are permitted to buy on the Alverá family account."

Rebecca fought the urge to roll her eyes. Not again. She was certain this was the same clerk with whom she'd dealt before. Why was he questioning her? She drew in a breath and exhaled. "I am Signora Alverá, wife of Riccardo Alverá. I've been here the first of every month for the last several months."

He continued to stare at her as if he couldn't interpret her accurate Italian. "I am sorry, Signora, but please, I must be very careful of our accounts."

Rebecca shifted her purse from one arm to the other. She was so tempted to turn and walk from the store, but she'd spent nearly an hour ticking off all the listed items. She was beginning to understand why Carlotta had given her this task. "Must I bring a letter of introduction every time I shop here?"

He tilted his head to the side as if thinking it over.

The click of heels on the tile floor behind her, alerted her of another's presence, but she dared not take her eyes off her purchases. She wouldn't put it past the clerk to begin returning them to the shelves. A feminine voice rang out in the lilting accent of the locals.

"Luigi, give the Contessa what she asks. We have not all day."

Rebecca pivoted, just enough to see a young woman, her blond hair pulled back and tied with a stylish red bow. Scarlet lips quirked out a curt smile, never warming her cool blue-green eyes. Something about her seemed so familiar. Rebecca faced the clerk again as he began to ring up the purchases.

Still, he watched her, like a cat preparing to pounce. Once he'd managed to load all the goods in boxes, he presented her with a ticket to sign. After examining the signature for a full minute, he waved to a boy near the back of the store. "Peppe will help you to your car."

Rebecca retrieved her basket and turned with care, not wanting to stumble over the woman standing directly behind her. "Mi scuse, per favore."

The woman stepped aside then forward, never looking at Rebecca nor acknowledging her apology.

As she stepped out of the shadows at the front of the shop into the late morning sunlight, Rebecca couldn't shake the feeling she'd seen that woman somewhere before.

Tito helped Peppe situate the boxes in the boot. Rebecca gave the boy a nod of thanks as he returned to the shop.

When Tito stepped around to open her door he stopped, his eyes focused over her shoulder.

Had his complexion blanched, or was it a trick of the sun? Rebecca turned to look as the blonde stepped out of the shop.

Her cool gaze swept over Rebecca, triggering a chill that danced up her spine. Then the woman gave a slight nod and moved away, her spiked heels clicking on the cobbled pavement.

Rebecca faced Tito. "Who is that woman?"

He reached down to open the door. "She is secretary to Mayor Modesti, Signora." He kept his face averted as he stepped aside for her to enter the car.

So that was Francesca Boccelli. Or was it Boccali? Rebecca huffed out a sigh. Why did she have so much trouble with these names?

The drive back to Tres Viti gave Rebecca plenty of time to think. She couldn't help wondering why Francesca was so cold and unfriendly. Rebecca had never done anything to the woman. Except to marry Ricci, of course. Deep down, she knew this was probably the root of the issue. The woman was a poor loser.

Rebecca understood Francesca's attraction to Ricci. He was not only handsome, but also good natured and intelligent. He had charisma, and if she was inclined to climb the political ladder, no doubt she would set her sights on a man like him. But she should have the grace to back off since he was already taken.

Only a few months had passed since their marriage. Perhaps the woman needed more time to heal. She'd made her feelings known and had been rejected. How long before she moved on?

Rebecca had to admit, the woman was attractive, though somewhat overbearing and … sour-faced. Surely, there would be another one to catch her fancy. Someone more important than a mere conte, somone who owned even more land and money than the Alverá family.

A sugar daddy. That's what Francesca needed. Rebecca bit back a smile.

When Tito halted near a narrow stone bridge, Rebecca glanced out to see two young shepherds herding sheep across the road. She took in her surroundings. The ancient bridge probably dated back to Roman times. It spanned a tributary of the Tiber River. Gently rolling pastureland lined its banks. Her gaze followed the path of the gravel road they traveled as it wound up the hill on the other side of the river. Beyond that, she knew the road held many twists and turns before it flattened out again and intersected with the lane leading home.

She was just beginning to wish she'd brought a book along when, a dog chased the last fluffy sheep across the road, and Tito started the engine. Before very long, Tres Viti's entrance appeared. Tito made the turn.

As the car rolled down the lane leading to the main house,

the various laborers halted work to greet her with a nod or a wave. Rebecca returned each one, feeling a little like royalty. But she knew her place well in this tiny kingdom. She was definitely not the queen of this hive. Not yet, anyway.

Dappled sunlight danced amid the branches of the olive trees as Carlotta spread a cloth over one of the outdoor tables. During olive harvest, everyone pitched in to help. They had to move quickly to remove the olives and get them to the mill. Olives for the oil must not heat up.

Riccardo's rich baritone rang out as he led the pickers in a rousing chorus. Carlotta's gaze settled on Rebecca who was clad in her everyday dress and sweater. Rebecca crossed the yard carrying a cloth-covered tray, set it on one of the tables then called out to Maria, a smile lighting her eyes.

Carlotta tried not to worry, but sometimes she couldn't help herself. Though the doctor had given Rebecca a good outlook, she still had no news to share. And she wasn't hiding a condition, poor thing. She was no bigger around than a fence post. Carlotta had come to love Rebecca, truly she had, but had Riccardo brought a curse on himself by marrying her?

She gazed into the bright afternoon sunlight as she helped Gigi smooth a cloth over another table. As she reached for a stack of plates, a breeze brought a chill from the mountains, but the sun warmed the south-facing hillside. She loved eating outdoors on such a day.

More women walked down from the kitchen, bearing platters, bowls, and pitchers. The time had nearly arrived.

Stepping to her place at the table, she sat in the chair and waited for the others to assemble.

Carlotta's heart throbbed painfully. But why? She fingered the rosary in her coat pocket and mouthed a prayer. Scanning the faces around the tables, she prayed for each one. She loved them all. Her gaze settled on Riccardo's handsome face, wreathed in smiles. Especially that one, so like his father. When her neighbor passed a platter of herb-roasted chicken, Carlotta helped herself to some and passed it on.

When all the dishes had been around, Riccardo raised his teacup. "To Mamma!"

"La Signora!" The others exclaimed, raising cups all around the table.

Carlotta forced her lips into a smile and lifted her cup also. In her mind, the day sparkled and shimmered. It was as though time had slowed. But wings of panic beat in her breast so hard, she struggled to draw a breath. Heat bore down upon her, as if the sun had drawn nearer the earth, touching her face with its white-hot breath.

She set her cup on the table with trembling fingers and gazed at Riccardo. He smiled back at her as he bit into a chicken leg. The noise at the table escalated. They were a lively bunch, happy to be taking a break from their work. Carlotta relaxed against the chair back and forced herself to breathe deeply. When she lifted her gaze again, she found Rebecca's eyes upon her. The girl rose from her chair and stepped to the thermos jugs where she dampened a dishtowel in the cool water. Unnoticed by anyone else, she approached Carlotta and laid the cool cloth on the back of her neck.

"You are overheated from so much work," she whispered in Carlotta's ear, "Or perhaps you are dehydrated. Would you prefer water to drink?"

Carlotta clutched Rebecca's hand and forced a smile. "I am better now. The cool towel helps."

Rebecca returned to her seat and resumed conversation with her neighbors. Carlotta sipped the tea, thankful for her daughter-in-law's discretion.

"Mamma, you've barely touched your food. Are you all right?"

Carlotta looked to her left, straight into Riccardo's face.

She hadn't noticed his approach. "I'm fine. Just not so hungry."

He crouched beside her chair. "Why don't you go back to the house and rest? We have plenty of help here. Do you need me to walk you there?"

"No, no. I am fine, really. I will finish my drink and have a bit of this bread." She really was better. She could feel the strength returning to her limbs.

Riccardo stood, his hand on her shoulder. "You have only to ask, Mamma."

She patted his hand. "I know. I will rest this afternoon."

The men lay on the ground beneath the trees and napped while the women cleaned up after the meal.

One of the older children seated the little ones in a circle beneath a live oak tree and read them a story.

Carlotta stopped to tousle Chico's dark hair, sending a smile to the others as they listened. Chico was a darling child, though a bit precocious. He tended to get away with most anything he wished to do. He was Claudio's son by a first marriage. His mother had been killed in a car accident when Chico was only seven months old, so the child had been raised by Poppi and Nonna. And, of course, all the aunts and uncles and cousins had a hand in his upbringing. No one spoke of his dead mother. She had run around on Claudio while he was soldiering in the army.

Claudio had met Eva when he'd returned home on leave. Carlotta paused in her work. Eva had married Claudio, only a few months before Riccardo's and Rebecca's marriage. Poppi and Nonna had hoped the union would keep their eldest son closer to home. But he was a soldier at heart, and he could not be still. Now he was being sent farther afield, into the north of Africa. Eva had taken the train to Bari to spend a few days with him before his departure. It would be hot in Bari, but they had the ocean breezes. Carlotta longed for one of those right now.

She lifted her hands and pushed her straying hair away

from her face. Even now, beads of sweat stood on her brow. Using the corner of her apron, she dabbed it away then brushed her skirt before starting toward the house.

Rebecca joined her, offering her arm. "Let me walk you."

Carlotta sent her a thankful glance. "I really am much better now. Thank you."

Refusing to be put off so easily, Rebecca linked her arm in Carlotta's. She had never seen a sign of weakness in the woman. Something was definitely wrong. Could she persuade her to see the doctor? Knowing Carlotta, probably not.

After reaching the house, she helped her mother-in-law out of her coat. Carlotta settled into her favorite chair near the fireplace. It seemed odd to Rebecca that the woman had been overheated when the outdoor temperature could not have risen above the mid-fifties. There was a definite chill in the air, and Ricci had said it was good they were getting the olives harvested a few days early, ahead of the rain.

Rebecca stirred the fire then stepped away to remove her coat. As she hung it on the peg beside the door, a sudden dizzy spell threatened her balance. She leaned against the wall for a moment until it passed. She'd been plagued by dizziness since her miscarriage. The doctor said she needed to build up her blood. He prescribed plenty of bone soup. Nonna had been most happy to comply. As the spell lightened, Rebecca glanced over her shoulder at Carlotta. Her eyes closed, she seemed to have drifted off. Rebecca lifted a knitted afghan from the sofa and draped it over her mother-in-law. It wouldn't do for her to catch a chill.

Rebecca joined the ruckus in the kitchen, helping the women clear up the mess from the meal. She loved having work to do, keeping her hands busy, but most of all, she enjoyed the camaraderie with the women.

"You will like the festival, Signora," Nonna said, as she

scrubbed the wooden table. "The men dress in traditional costumes and follow the wagons as the band plays."

Rebecca smiled at the thought of Ricci marching in a parade. "And what of the women? Do they also dress up?"

Nonna giggled. "Only the young women, Signora." She reached out to pull her youngest daughter, Lucia, into a tight hug. "Like this one. Young, and still unattached."

Lucia's cheeks flushed.

Rebecca smiled at the shy girl, only slightly taller than her mother. She was a beauty and would no doubt attract a suitor soon enough.

The kitchen spotless, the women took a break before beginning supper preparations. Rebecca checked on Carlotta, who was still resting, then ascended the stairs to her room. From the window, she could see the men working in the olive trees. She should go and see if there was something she could do to help, but weariness drew her to the bed.

How wonderful the bed felt, soft and warm. She yawned and kicked off her shoes then snuggled into the pillows. Just a short nap. That's all she wanted, a few minutes of rest.

Ricci woke her, sometime later. He was already cleaned up and dressed for dinner.

She smiled into his eyes. Then as she came truly awake, exclaimed, "Oh dear, I've overslept. Your mother will be fretting about overcooked food."

"Perhaps, but I would not worry too much, my beautiful wife. After all, is it not you who is La Signora?"

Chapter Seventeen

Rebecca held on tight as the wagon bumped over the dirt lane leading to the olive mill.

"It is tradition," Carlotta had told her. "We ride to the mills and watch our olives being pressed."

Carlotta couldn't go. She didn't feel up to it. So Rebecca sat on the wagon beside Ricci, holding on for dear life. And what an adventure her life had become.

Ricci smiled into her eyes. "We are almost there, Becca. It is not unlike the hayrides in your country, no?"

Rebecca frowned as she sorted through the negatives in his sentence, spoken in English. He liked to stay in practice. "Yes, it is a little like a hayride, except we have horses, not oxen—in my experience, anyway."

"We are rustic here in the foothills," he said with a chuckle. "But life is good, no? It is about to get better. There is nothing so fine on earth as the taste of freshly pressed olive oil." He kissed his fingertips and grinned down at her.

"Mmm …" She could only imagine. The natives used olive oil like butter. They put it on everything. It was also used as a preservative. Two smells would always remind Rebecca of Italy. Olive oil and garlic. Oh, and lavender, of course. How could she forget that?

"Once upon a time," Ricci said, "most villas had their own olive presses. Rugged stones, turned by oxen or perhaps a donkey. But now, we come here." He guided the oxen in behind the wagon driven by Poppi and drew to a halt. Then he jumped down and reached for Rebecca. She laughed to see the sparkle in his eyes when he held her a bit longer than necessary. He grabbed her hand and led her out of the way as

Tres Viti's team descended on the wagons and unloaded the olive-filled burlap bags.

"It is essential to get them to the mill quickly, so they don't heat up," he told her again.

"What happens if you're delayed getting your crop milled?"

"They ferment," Ricci told her. "You don't want that. Spoils the flavor."

Rebecca watched as the huge stone wheels turned. The bright green color of the oil surprised her. Ricci handed her a slice of fragrant, still-warm bread to dip in the fresh oil. She closed her eyes and savored the taste. It was alive with flavor.

The harvest had been a good one, the atmosphere around the mill as festive as a party. Neighbors called greetings to one another and shouted invitations. "Come home with us!"

His face alight with good humor, Ricci returned the greetings but also made apologies. "Not tonight, my friends, but we will see you at Spello." He turned back to Rebecca. "Spello is the best of the festivals. We will go on Saturday if Mamma is well enough. Her cousins live nearby, and they will be expecting us." He slid his arm about her waist. "Come. I see Tito has arrived. I thought perhaps you'd enjoy riding home in the automobile."

She raised his hand to her lips and kissed it then held it to her cheek. "You are so thoughtful, my husband."

He kept his eyes on his feet as they crossed the cobbled path. "I have a surprise for you as well. I hope you will like it."

She watched him as they made their way to the car. Had he remembered her birthday? He was very good at keeping secrets, so she didn't prod or try to guess. But she was curious. She'd long ago dropped the habit of reminding people of her birthday. She'd suffered too many disappointments. Occasionally, Daddy had surprised her by remembering. Of course, Nancy always did, even when she was thousands of miles away. Rebecca had tucked Nancy's latest card in her drawer. Was it unfair of her to expect Riccardo to know it was her birthday without being reminded? Possibly.

She greeted Tito and slid into her seat, gazing around the interior of the auto. Hmm … nothing in there. Once they were underway, she looked at Riccardo. "What is this surprise?"

He chuckled. "I love telling you ahead of time just to make you squirm."

She scoffed and batted his arm. "You're such a brute."

"Oh, this I know very well. But you will not think so when you see what is the surprise."

She pressed her lips together and tucked her full skirt beneath her legs. It was chilly in the car.

Riccardo pulled her to him and encircled her with his arms. "Is this better?"

She snuggled against him, inhaling his scent—sweat, garlic, and the fresh, minty smell of olive leaves. Turning her head, she gazed out at the snow covered peaks in the distance. The beauty of their surroundings always took her breath away. Would she ever tire of it?

This region was called the "green heart" of Italy, because of the live oaks that never lost their leaves. And there was still so much to see. Busyness with the harvest and Ricci's new post as committee leader, had prevented travel.

So she'd begun a list, which included castles and lakes, Assisi and Spoleto and Ponte delle Torre—The Towers Bridge, all within close proximity to Tres Viti. Perhaps they could spend their winter and early spring sightseeing.

Slowly, the car ascended the drive and pulled to a halt in front of the house where a garland of some sort hung between the portals on either side of the door. Rebecca glanced at Ricci's face. Was this part of the surprise?

He got out and came around to her side, opened the door, and offered his hand. Still watching his expression, she stood.

Perhaps they hung a garland for olive harvest? After all, it was quite a celebration.

Inside, her senses were jolted by the wonderful aromas from the kitchen. Did she smell cake? Her stomach responded with a low rumble. Ricci helped her out of her coat and hung it beside the door. "Let's go up and change for dinner."

Hmm ... it was early yet, barely noon. They usually sat down to a large meal at one o'clock. He definitely had something planned. She'd play along. In their room, he headed for the bathroom, closing the door behind him. She gazed around, wondering what to do next.

Eva knocked then entered. "I have your blue dress ready. Is that all right with you?"

Rebecca narrowed her eyes at Eva. Did she know the secret? "The blue one is fine. Thank you."

Eva stepped to the dressing room and switched on the light. "How did you like the mill? Did you taste the fresh oil?"

Rebecca entered the dressing room, unbuttoning her dress. "I found it interesting. The oil is so much greener than I expected."

"It is a lovely color, no?"

Small talk. Rebecca couldn't abide it when she was preoccupied. She slipped into the dress then sat at her dressing table. Eva ran a comb through Rebecca's hair and anchored the sides with ivory combs. "Will there be anything else?"

"No. You may go."

Eva paused a moment, an odd flicker in her eyes. She picked up the discarded day dress and hung it over her arm before turning away.

Rebecca applied a light coat of lipstick then blotted her lips on a tissue. Perhaps she'd been too curt with Eva. She hurried to the dressing room door. "Eva?"

Across the room, the maid halted, her hand on the doorknob. "Si, Signora?"

"I'm sorry. I'm distracted." She glanced at the bathroom door, now standing open. Ricci must have gone down ahead of her. Turning back to Eva, she smiled. "Ricci told me he had a surprise for me and wouldn't say what it was. So, of course, that's all I can think of."

Eva shrugged. "I understand, Signora. There is no need for you to apologize to me." She managed a small smile before leaving Rebecca alone.

Rebecca sighed. Eva hadn't been quite herself since she'd returned from Bari. Was it normal and natural for her to suffer melancholy this long? Several weeks had passed since she'd returned. Surely, by now, she would be over the separation anxiety. But what did Rebecca know about it? Since her marriage, she had never spent a night alone. How awful it must be for Eva.

Ricci waited for Rebecca at the bottom of the staircase, his face a handsome blank. Though she tried, Rebecca couldn't read his expression. What did the dear man have for her? Still, he said nothing, just took her arm and led her to the kitchen where she was met by Nonna. Carlotta, whose face was also a blank, stood directly behind the cook.

Nonna stepped forward, holding an apron in her hands. "Signora Rebecca, here is your apron."

Rebecca raised her brows and glanced at Ricci. He grinned but said nothing.

Nonna tied the apron around Rebecca's waist. "In *Italia*, the one with the birthday provides the food for the guests." She stepped aside, sweeping her hand toward the kitchen where her family stood waiting.

Rebecca blinked. This was not good. Did they know she couldn't cook? Finally someone remembers her birthday, and … oh, boy. Perhaps she could assemble antipasti? Would they settle for sliced bread and olive oil?

Nonna burst out laughing then everyone joined in.

Rebecca drew in a deep breath and quietly released it as first one, then another, of the kitchen servants produced steaming platters and heaping bowls of food.

"Maybe next year, eh?" Ricci said, offering his elbow to Rebecca.

"Wait," Nonna called, reaching to untie the apron. Holding onto Rebecca's hands, she stretched to kiss Rebecca's cheeks. "Best wishes to you, Signora."

Rebecca's heart warmed as everyone took their turn with kisses and the traditional *"auguri!"*—best wishes!

"Admit it," Ricci said. "We had you fooled."

She smiled into his eyes. "You did. I was very afraid, and you should be, too. My cooking is to be feared."

He laughed out loud.

Carlotta drew alongside and led the way to the table. "Today, the staff will join us for your celebration."

After a wonderful meal sprinkled liberally with merriment and laughter, Lucia and Gigi left. They returned a short time later, carrying a tiered birthday cake between them.

"I knew I smelled cake," Rebecca said.

Nonna folded her hands together. "Gigi is learning the art of cake decorating from the baker at Faldi. She is doing well, do you not think?"

Rebecca nodded. "It's almost too lovely to cut."

"But we will," Ricci said. "And then, cara, you will open your present."

"There's more? I thought this meal was my surprise."

Carlotta shook her head. "Oh, no. We have for you the perfect gift."

It was a large gift, with an odd shape. Rebecca admired the artful job of wrapping, but her curiosity propelled her to destroy it quickly. She removed the ribbon and tore away the paper to reveal a beautifully tooled, fine leather saddle. She sucked in a breath and gazed at Ricci, who stood watching her. "You remembered."

He nodded as she ripped the rest of the paper away. "Oh, Ricci. It's amazing."

"I knew you would like it. I told Mamma it was to replace something very special you had lost. You must share with her the story."

Rebecca ran her fingers over the smooth mahogany-colored surface and blinked away tears. She cast a quick glance around the room, to include all those present. "I was given a saddle very much like this the year I turned twelve. I had a favorite horse—a beautiful red filly. Her mane was almost the same color as my hair."

"What was her name?" Carlotta asked.

Rebecca paused and swallowed the lump that rose in her throat. "Ursula. I haven't thought about her in a very long time. I rode her as often as I could whenever I was home from boarding school."

Carlotta interrupted. "But what of the saddle? Who bought that for you?"

"My grandfather. He also gave me Ursula. She was a thoroughbred but wasn't fast enough for the races, so he brought her to me, along with the saddle he'd had made for me by an artisan of his acquaintance." She gripped the cantle and smiled. "It was a Western saddle, rather than an English dressage saddle. Granddad said it was safer. He was of the mind that women should still use a sidesaddle. But, since times were changing, he wanted to give his granddaughter the best available." She looked up at her audience and realized they were still watching.

With a soft laugh she hoped would lighten the mood, she planned her next words carefully. Her stomach still twisted in knots at the memory of coming home after Granddad's death, to find Ursula had been sold, along with her beautiful saddle.

Her step-grandmother, angry that all her husband's money had been left to his no-good son, moved quickly to liquidate everything within reach. Granddad had never transferred Ursula's ownership. On paper, she belonged to him.

Rebecca sucked in a ragged breath and released it. "She was sold with my grandfather's personal belongings after his death. I never saw her again."

Carlotta rubbed Rebecca's shoulder. "Oh my dear, such a loss for a child to bear. Not only the death of a beloved grandfather but also an adored pet. But now, you mustn't frown anymore. Alberto will take your saddle to the stables, and you and your husband can go riding, watch the sunset, no?"

Though the day had been a long one and she was tired, Rebecca smiled into Ricci's warm brown eyes as he reached for her hand. "Why don't you go up and change, my lovely wife. We will do as Mamma says."

Rebecca's eyes flitted to her mother-in-law's. Of course, we will do as Mamma says.

A strange sensation washed over Rebecca as she climbed the stairs to their room. What did it matter? Why not make the woman happy? One more glance over her shoulder revealed the truth to Rebecca. Carlotta was unwell. She was definitely "off the beam," as Daddy used to say. Rebecca's heart constricted as she pushed her steps forward into the dressing room and changed into her riding outfit. Tres Viti without Carlotta—it was inevitable some day of course—but Rebecca hoped it was a distant someday, for Ricci's sake ... and for hers.

Riccardo had one more surprise for his wife's birthday—one his mother had provided. He marveled at the wisdom and grace of God as he prepared for their ride. When Rebecca descended the stairs dressed in her riding clothes, he admired her with a low whistle then chuckled at her response. She'd lost weight after the miscarriage, so the outfit wasn't as snug as it had been.

They donned jackets, scarves, hats, and gloves then proceeded to the stables where Alberto and his eldest son, Sandro, had the horses ready.

Riccardo turned to observe his wife's face when she saw her saddle on the horse Mamma had secured.

Her eyes lit as her lips parted. "I have never seen this horse. Has she been here all along?"

"She was delivered while we attended to the olives, my love. Mamma's gift to you."

"Oh—oh Ricci!" She moved forward, covering her mouth with gloved fingers, her eyes questioning. "For me?"

He nodded. "You remember her cousins, the Dominicis—they raise fine horses."

"She's ... beautiful. Perfect." Her gaze locked onto Riccardo's. "Is she really mine?" At his affirmative nod, she glanced back toward the house. "I must thank her."

"We can ride by her window on the way. She will be expecting you."

Rebecca circled the beautiful chestnut mare, stopping to stroke the animal's thick winter coat. Her mane was a mass of expertly rendered braids. "She's prepped for show, isn't she? What's her name?"

"Stella Rossa."

"Red Star," she whispered. "An appropriate name." The horse nuzzled her new mistress, touching Rebecca's arm with a velvety nose. Rebecca giggled and spoke quietly to her before turning to Riccardo. "Shall we go?"

Riccardo moved to help her into the saddle. Once Rebecca was in place, he stepped around to Lancelot and mounted. "How is the saddle?"

"Wonderful. I think it's even better than the one I lost."

Sitting tall in his saddle, he turned Lancelot toward the house. They rode along the lane, stopping below the parlor window where Mamma stood. Rebecca kissed her fingertips to Mamma then cupped her hands together, thanking her.

As they rode along the lane, Riccardo watched Rebecca's face. The sun, low on the horizon, set her skin alight with a coral glow. Her hair curled beneath her hat, nearly matched the coat of the horse she rode. His heart swelled with love for her. He had loved Rebecca since the day they'd met, but that seemed like a child's crush compared to what he felt now.

It was quiet on the hillside as they rode, except for the soft clopping of the horses' hooves and the squeak of Rebecca's new leather saddle.

She turned her gaze on Riccardo. "You are quiet."

"I am enjoying the view, cara."

Her eyes lit with humor, but she didn't respond. Instead, she touched Stella's mane, lifting one braid to examine it. "I have never been so happy, Ricci. No one has ever done such wonderful things for me. You don't know—" her voice broke, she looked away.

Riccardo reached over and clasped her hand. "My beautiful wife, I have told you how much I love you."

"Sometimes I feel so unworthy of your love."

He tightened his hold on her fingers. "Why is that? Don't you know I adore you?"

She brought her eyes back to his face. "You shouldn't. Not adore, Ricci. Be in love with me, but don't put me on a pedestal, please. I can't—I will let you down—I know I will."

He let his head fall back as a chuckle rumbled in his chest. "Cara, you give me so much pleasure. I do not adore you as a deity, if that is what you fear. I know you are not perfect, and I don't expect it of you. I only meant to express my great love." He drew up his horse, and she stopped beside him. He wanted to be certain she understood his intentions. "You have nothing to prove or maintain. Only be yourself and I will love you." He leaned toward her and she met him halfway. Their lips touched, but only momentarily. Stella spooked at the sound of a car's engine revving. The animal took two small jumps forward before Rebecca brought her under control.

Riccardo gazed toward the end of the lane where a dark sedan pulled away from the edge of the road then disappeared around a curve. A chill wind buffeted his cheekbones. Who would be parking there at this time of day? It was too dark for him to make out the license plate or any markings on the car. He faced Rebecca. "Time to return, I think. The sun is going down." He turned his horse and waited until she came alongside.

"Do you know who that was?"

He cast her a reassuring smile. "Probably someone lost their way and had to stop and consult a map." At least he hoped that was the case. Why would anyone be watching Tres Viti?

Chapter Eighteen

Music, uniquely Italian, echoed off the centuries-old walls of the village of Spello. Built in medieval times, the fortified city teemed with life for this festival of olives. Rebecca stood beside Carlotta watching the ox and donkey-drawn carts in the procession. Men, dressed in traditional bright flannel shirts with kerchiefs about their necks, drove the carts, or marched beside and behind. Some played instruments, strumming guitars and mandolins. Others played small accordions, ocarinas, and reed-pipes. Women in brightly colored peasant costumes danced around them.

Carlotta soon grew tired. Rebecca found her a seat on a bench then stood directly behind her, watching the revelers. When would Ricci return? He'd looked so handsome dressed in a red plaid shirt, with a black kerchief knotted at his neck and a black beret set at a jaunty angle on his head. She'd giggled as he gave her an exaggerated wink from his position in the parade. But after he marched past, she lost sight of him.

As she searched for him, she noticed a vendor who sold colorful cups of espresso. She bent and spoke into Carlotta's ear, "I'll be right back."

Perhaps this would revive her mother-in-law. They'd spent a day and a night with Carlotta's family who lived nearby. Rebecca had found the guest bed somewhat lumpy. What little sleep she achieved was restless. Now she was stiff, sore, and just plain sleepy.

Cups in hand, she made her way through the lively crowd. As she approached the bench where her mother-in-law waited, a movement near a green door caught her attention. With a flash of red plaid, Ricci appeared. Rebecca stood still, watching him.

Ricci settled his beret on his head and glanced around. Just as his eyes met Rebecca's, the green door opened again and a woman stepped out. A blonde woman. Rebecca froze in place. What was *she* doing here? And why were they in that place together?

Then two other men stepped through the green door. Mayor Modesti and a man Rebecca didn't recognize. She nearly lost her grip on the espresso. Thank goodness Ricci had not been in there alone. No matter what he'd said, she did not trust Francesca.

A moment later, Ricci stood beside her. "Here, let me take one of those. Where is Mamma?"

Now Rebecca felt the need of a place to sit down. Her knees had turned to jelly. She forced herself to concentrate on Ricci's face. "Seated near the fountain. She is very tired. I thought the coffee may revive her."

"Good idea." He took one of the cups then offered his elbow.

Rebecca linked her arm in his as the crowd pressed in. They found Carlotta looking a bit forlorn, but she brightened at their approach. Ricci squatted in front of her and offered the coffee.

"Oh, how wonderful. I was just thinking how much I could use a cup."

Ricci patted her free hand as she sipped the espresso. "It was Rebecca. I am only the deliveryman."

Carlotta laughed. "And a very handsome one you are." She moved her gaze to Rebecca. "Thank you, my dear. But you look weary, too. Perhaps there is room on this bench for one more."

Ricci stood and drew Rebecca close. "I will go and find Tito. Then we can leave. We'll have lunch along the river."

As Rebecca observed his high-spirited interaction with

others along the way, she became more curious than ever about what had gone on in that meeting.

"Did you get a souvenir?" Carlotta asked, bringing Rebecca's attention back to her. "You must get something to take home. Something to remember your first festival of the olives."

Rebecca had intended the colorful espresso cup as a souvenir, but perhaps it was a bit too common. With a smile of thanks to Carlotta, she pushed through the crowd toward the vendors. Some of the best olive oils were available for sale, but she had no need of them since Tres Viti had an excellent product of their own. She found hand-carved wooden toys and had almost decided on a beautifully crafted miniature mandolin when the sparkle of glass caught her eye. She could add to their growing collection.

Approaching the vendor, she bent to look at the beautiful array of glass figurines. From behind Rebecca, a familiar voice spoke. She turned to find Francesca so close, their noses almost touched. Rebecca drew back. "Did you say something to me, Signorina?"

Francesca's lips quirked around the cigarette in her mouth. She withdrew the nasty thing and blew out a cloud of smoke. "You know I did. I said good day to you, *Contessa*."

A slight chill touched the back of Rebecca's neck. She didn't like the way the woman stressed "Contessa" as though she considered her unworthy of the title, but she refused to be baited. She offered a polite smile. "And good day to you also, Signorina. I hope you are enjoying the festival."

"Very much. It is a lovely day." She took another long draw on her cigarette and this time, turned her head aside before exhaling the smoke.

Her cold, blue gaze sent shivers through Rebecca. "Well, I … I must be on my way. My husband will be looking for me."

Francesca's arm darted forward. Her fingers closed over

Rebecca's wrist. "Have you ever considered what you are doing, Signora—to your husband?"

Too shocked to withdraw her hand, Rebecca could only stare at the woman.

Francesca dropped her cigarette and tamped it out with the toe of a black patent-leather shoe. "You are like poison to him. You will cost him everything, Signora. You and your Americana ways."

"I beg your pardon?"

"You know what I am speaking of. You cannot even give him an heir. But it is not just that. In the coming days, you will see. Because of you, he stands to lose everything that is important to him. Why don't you do him a favor—sail back home to your America—before you bring ruin upon the heads of the entire Alverá family?" She dropped Rebecca's wrist. "*Buono sera, Contessa.*" Turning away, she was soon swallowed up by the crowd.

For a moment, Rebecca's feet refused to move. Staring at the partially mashed cigarette on the pavement near her shoe, she could still make out Francesca's dark red lipstick on the butt, as a tiny plume of smoke curled up from the ashes.

Riccardo searched the crowd for a glimpse of Rebecca's red hat. He'd insisted she wear it today so he could easily find her. He caught sight of it bobbing slowly along, as she walked toward the place where Mamma waited. He strode as quickly as possible through the press, reaching the bench at the same time as Rebecca. Her eyes met his. What was that look? Why was she so pale? He reached for her.

"You are tired, my love. Here. Let me take your package. What have you bought? A souvenir of your first festival?"

She gave him a tremulous smile but made no reply. He turned his attention away and reached his hand toward his mother. "Come, Mamma. Tito waits for us."

He led the two women to the car. When he had them safely inside the automobile, perhaps then he could find out the reason for Rebecca's strangeness.

Within minutes after leaving, Mamma had dozed off. Riccardo turned to his wife seated next to him. He touched her cheek. "I'm sorry I was unable to be with you. I hope you enjoyed the festival."

The smile on her face didn't match the flint in her eyes. "I did miss you very much. I saw you coming out of that green door with the others. Was there a meeting?"

"Not a formal one. Modesti wanted me to meet Antonio Guerra, the new adjutant. This is all. He was in Spello for the festival, a guest of the Modesti family. I invited him to Tres Viti on Thursday evening. Then you can meet him also."

"What does an adjutant do?"

Rebecca's voice sounded distant, as though she feigned an interest. He tucked his forefinger beneath her chin and tilted her face to his. "Cara, what is troubling you? Are you angry with me?" He felt the sideways movement as she slowly shook her head.

"No, Ricci. Not angry. Just … disappointed, I guess. I had hoped to spend more time with you today. Lately, you're always so busy." She sent him a wisp of a smile as she fingered the flannel of his shirt. "You are so handsome in your red shirt and black bandanna."

He grinned. "Ah, I see the problem now." Mamma snored softly, so he leaned forward to kiss Rebecca's lips. Then she snuggled into his side and laid her head on his shoulder. He wrapped his arm around her as contentment filled his breast. The day this woman walked into his life had been his most blessed day. With a low chuckle, he remembered she had actually skied into his life.

She lifted her eyes to his. "What are you laughing at?"

"A wonderful memory." He shifted in the seat. "I was

thinking perhaps we should go to the mountains after Christmas. We can go skiing, if you like." A momentary something flashed in her eyes. What was that? "Becca?"

"That sounds wonderful, Ricci, really."

She was hiding something. But what? He would have pressed her further, but Tito turned off the road onto the path that led to the river where bright sunlight glinted off blue water. If it was not too windy, Riccardo planned for them to have their lunch outside.

Tito pulled the car onto the grass and braked to a halt. He got out and opened the door. "Wait here," Riccardo said to Rebecca. "I will see if it is warm enough for us to have a picnic. We may have to eat in the car."

After opening the boot, Tito addressed Riccardo. "I parked to block the wind, Signore. I think we will be sheltered if we set up our chairs beside the automobile."

Riccardo helped with the preparations then woke Mamma.

As Rebecca passed the cups of steaming coffee poured by Tito, she took in the scenery. It was a fine day, though chilly. Sun warmed the metal of the black automobile, making their picnic comfortable. Seated in their folding chairs, she and Carlotta snuggled beneath a warm wool blanket. They enjoyed a meal of meat, cheese, and bread dipped in olive oil while watching the shimmer of sunlight on the water.

"Did I see you talking with Francesca Boccali in the marketplace, Rebecca?"

Carlotta's question came so out of the blue, Rebecca nearly choked on a bite of cheese. She took a quick sip of coffee to wash it down. All eyes turned to her—even Tito's. She cleared her throat, wondering how to answer. Just then, an eagle dove into the water, emerging with a large fish in its mouth. Hoping for a reprieve, Rebecca pointed. "Did you see that?"

Ricci's keen gaze swept over her. "What is this about the Signorina Boccali?" His eyes narrowed. "Did she speak to you?"

Without thinking, Rebecca heaved a sigh. She hadn't meant to show distress. Ricci was sure to pick up on that. She must act quickly. "She asked if I was enjoying my first festival. Afterward, she bid me good day." She blinked her eyes. It wasn't really a lie.

The seconds ticked away, seeming more like long minutes to Rebecca, before Ricci turned his attention back to the water. Was he fooled? She drained her cup and set it aside. Probably not, but at least he would not press her further. What did he care, anyway? Was he afraid Francesca would tell Rebecca something? Perhaps the impromptu meeting behind the green door was more than just an introduction to an adjutant, whatever that was. Why would they have to meet in private, anyway, unless they were hiding something?

Riccardo watched Rebecca for a moment before turning back to the view before him. Sometimes he wished it was possible to read minds. However, he suspected there was a very good reason why God had left that out of the human psyche. He sat forward, looking at Tito. "I suppose we had better get started."

It took only a few minutes to pack their things. Soon, they were back on the road again. He waited until Mamma had dozed off then took Rebecca's hand and spoke to her in English. "There are several things we need to discuss, my love."

An odd light sparked in her eyes. Perhaps he had confused her or maybe said the wrong thing?

She waited a moment before speaking. "Why are you talking to me in English?"

He gave her his most charming smile. "Because I prefer to

speak privately."

She nodded her understanding, but still, she watched him. Like a hawk.

He patted her hand. "You asked about the adjutant's duties earlier. It seemed as though you were only being polite, so I didn't answer. But the adjutant is a military position. Our small town has come under scrutiny. Therefore, we merit an adjutant."

"Under scrutiny? What does that mean?"

"There has been some dissension within the committee. Someone of the old order—the aristocracy. Most, like me, try to blend in, but some can't seem to do so."

"I see." Her gaze faltered then fell to her lap.

He was being insensitive. He had worried her, though not intentionally. "We mustn't worry, my love. We must—"

She joined in with, "We must have faith. I know."

"And on a more cheerful note, I have it on good authority, Signorina Boccali has requested an official leave of absence."

The dark clouds lifted from Rebecca's expression. "A leave of absence?"

He nodded. "A family emergency of some sort. She doesn't know exactly how long she will be away."

"Away? As in out of town?"

"Yes. More than this, I don't know. I wonder though, if the timing is significant. The adjutant comes; the secretary goes away." He shrugged.

When she leaned into his side, he lifted his arm so she could snuggle closer. It was wonderful to see her smile again.

Chapter Nineteen

5 December, 1930, Tres Viti Verdi

Riccardo's Uncle Vittorio arrived with his family to spend the holidays. Rebecca took an immediate liking to this gruff old Italiano. He seemed pleased with her also. In an odd way, he reminded her of Nancy's grandmother, Amelia. Perhaps it was his frankness.

"You are a new convert, I hear," he said only a few minutes after making her acquaintance.

"I am." She watched his face for the usual judgmental stare. Instead, he gripped her arm and nodded. "Welcome to the family, Rebecca—may I call you Rebecca?"

She smiled into his dark eyes. "Of course. May I call you Uncle Vittorio?"

He guffawed then pulled her into a one-armed embrace. He looked past her to Ricci. "Riccardo, you have a winner here. I think you'd better keep her."

Ricci was swinging one of his young cousins in the air. He set the little boy down and cast an appreciative smile toward Rebecca. "Oh, I plan to, Uncle V."

Because this was her first Christmas in Umbria, Uncle Vittorio insisted Ricci take her to Assisi on the seventh of December for the celebration.

"There is nothing like it anywhere. You must experience it," Uncle Vittorio said to Rebecca.

"You can see the light of the bonfire from here, Uncle V," Ricci said.

Uncle Vittorio smoothed his palm over the bald spot on his head. He grinned at Ricci. "I know that. Have I reached this old age and not learned that? But you should take her. This way, she will never forget. The girl must see the faithful things, and she will remember."

On the way to Assisi, Ricci told her about the ritual. "They build an amazing big fire. You can see its glow all around."

"What's the purpose of it?"

"It simulates the star that once guided the three kings to the manger."

Rebecca kept her eyes on Ricci's face as he spoke. Most of his attention was on the road. Since they had many guests at home, Tito had stayed behind to help.

The eerie sound of bagpipes greeted Rebecca and Ricci as they found a place to stand and watch the festivities. The glow from the immense fire lit the walls of the old fortress. Rebecca was reminded of a scripture she'd heard recently about a city on a hill. "Ye are the light of the world. A city set on a hill cannot be hid." Of course, many Italian cities sat on hills. On this particular night, Assisi sent a bright light into the darkness.

Afterward, Ricci led her back to the car. Was it silly that she kept scanning the area, even in the deep shadows, looking for Francesca? Though everyone told Rebecca the woman had left the country on an extended leave, she still had trouble believing it.

Farther away from the fire, the night air held a deep chill. Her teeth chattered. Ricci seemed unaffected. He continued to talk as they strolled along a narrow street. "When the weather warms a bit, we'll come back and spend a few days here. There is so much to see. I know you will love it."

She could see the car by the time he noticed she was shivering.

"I'm so sorry. I didn't realize you were chilled." He swept her into his arms and hugged her tightly, warming her.

His kiss on her lips sparked another kind of warmth. She giggled.

He pulled back to look at her. "Is this funny? Are you laughing at my kisses now?" His eyes sparkled in the soft glow of a street lamp.

She relaxed against him. "It wasn't a ha-ha-funny laugh, Ricci. It was a feel-good giggle."

He chuckled as he kissed her forehead. "I see. I'm glad I can still make you feel good, cara." He released her but kept her fingers in his grip as he led her the final few feet to their car. Before leaving, he tucked a wool blanket over her legs. "It is a bit chilly on this hill." He dashed around the car and got in. Soon, they were tooling down the road toward home.

Rebecca turned to watch the glow of the fire against the indigo sky. She still heard the bagpipes and the chanting of the brothers, reverberating in her mind. Uncle Vittorio was right. She would remember this night always.

The Christmas celebration began in earnest on the eighth of December. Everywhere she went, Rebecca heard the greeting, *Buon Natale!* The familiar smell of roasting chestnuts filled the air in the marketplace. One thing she missed—there were no decorations—not even at the villa. She secretly longed for the colored lights and bright red ribbons of home.

As Rebecca absorbed the rituals and took part in the prayer services and numerous small celebrations, she wondered. Perhaps the Italians had it right. For them, the season was sacred rather than materialistic. As a child, when she had attended the midnight mass with her nanny, she'd wondered at the beauty and deep respect the parishioners held for this holiday. In Italy, life revolved around the central theme of faith. At least, among the faithful, and the believers were certainly in the majority here.

On the seventeenth of December, they celebrated the first *Novena,* a special prayer service held every day for nine days. The family filled two pews.

"I will pray for you a special blessing," Uncle Vittorio whispered to Ricci and Rebecca. His brow arched into what was once his hairline. "One day your children will fill these two pews." His belly shook with silent laughter.

Behind them, several of the Dominici cousins giggled but were immediately silenced by their mammas. Warmth flooded Rebecca's cheeks as Ricci squeezed her fingers. Still, she loved this gruff old uncle. He held nothing back. You always knew where you stood with Uncle Vittorio.

The next few days passed as quickly as a puff of wind for Rebecca. Several of the cousins would leave after Christmas Day to spend Epiphany at home with their children. This was when Italian children received small gifts from La Befana. In Italy, it was more important than Christmas Eve.

After a bustling day spent entertaining Ricci's family, Rebecca tried to hide her disappointment as she eyed the Christmas Eve table. How different it seemed. No brown sugar encrusted ham with pineapple rings and cherries. No beautifully decorated Christmas cookies and cakes. Just a huge tureen of fish soup with a side of crunchy bread. No meat. And of course, a panettone, an Italian version of fruit cake. The soup was hearty and tasty, but her appetite longed for the rich Christmas goodies of home. Perhaps next year, she could introduce Christmas cookies. Why not? She knew the children would love them. Nancy would be happy to send her some recipes.

Ricci seemed to sense her mood. He smiled at her across the table and sent a look that warmed her heart, but only for a moment. Guilt crept in unannounced. She was behaving as a child. How could she be unhappy surrounded by family and friends? God had blessed her in unexpected ways. She allowed her gaze to drift around the table as she committed these moments to memory. How many Christmases had she spent alone or in the company of those who cared little for her? She had been given an incredible gift.

The celebratory meal ended, exhaustion set in. Her feet were like lead as she ascended the stairs to their room. So much stimulation left her weary, but in a good way. The pungent odor of pine greeted her as she pushed the bedroom door open. A fire burned on the grate, and candles glowed around the room. The table held a large bowl of freshly-cut boughs complete with pine cones. Now she knew the reason for the look in Ricci's eyes at the dinner table. He had done this. What a wonderful man she'd married.

Ricci turned the invitation over in his hands. Perhaps this was just the thing to lift Rebecca's spirit. She'd made a valiant effort, but he knew she struggled with homesickness during the holidays. His feeble attempts at decoration were like weak patches on an old tire. She'd been grateful, but it had fallen short.

He strode into the house and straight to her study where she was certain to be at this time of the morning. She looked up as he entered. Her blue gaze held expectancy. He rounded the desk and rested the heel of one hand on its edge as he leaned down to plant a kiss on her brow. "Buongiorno, my lovely wife."

She didn't voice the question in her eyes. "Buongiorno. You're back early."

He crouched beside her and held out the embossed envelope. "I have something for you."

She searched his face as though she didn't trust him. "What is it?"

"Why don't you open it and find out?"

Rebecca accepted the envelope and slid the blade of a letter opener beneath the flap. Her brow furrowed as she removed the flat card and held it up so she could read it. A hint of a smile quirked the corners of her lips. She raised her eyes to his face. "A New Year's Gala?"

He nodded. "In Foligno. I thought you might like it. Several of our friends are also going. We can travel together. It will be fun."

"Fun." She whispered the word as though trying it out. "I suppose it's fancy dress?"

He smiled. "Oh yes, formal." Was this the reason for her hesitancy? Did she worry about her wardrobe? He touched her cheek. "You can go shopping … get whatever you need."

She licked her lips. "It's kind of short notice."

He shook his head. "No, no. You can go with me in the morning. I have business in Perugia. Bring Eva with you. She can help you find something."

Her eyes twinkled as her lips relaxed in a smile. "How long will we be away for the gala, overnight?"

He nodded. "Yes, it will end late, so we'll stay overnight at a pensione. We'll be home in plenty of time to prepare for Epiphany." He rose and held out his hand. "Come. You can go and ask Eva if she is free to go with us tomorrow."

Rebecca smiled into Ricci's eyes as excitement danced up her spine. A New Year's Eve gala. She couldn't be more surprised by his offer. And she could go shopping. She'd just completed December's accounts, so she knew money was a bit tight, but there was enough for a little splurge. She could surely find what she needed in Perugia.

She found Eva in the kitchen, where the women were singing hymns as they worked.

Several voices sounded in chorus at her entry. "Buongiorno, Signora!"

Rebecca smiled and greeted them. Crossing to Eva, she asked, "Would you be able to go with me tomorrow, to Perugia?"

Eva stepped back, her eyes wide. "Perugia? Of course, if

you need me to go."

"I need to find a dress for a formal New Year's dance. My husband suggested you may be able to help me."

"Oh, yes. I do know of a couple of shops," she replied, dipping her hands in a pan of warm water then drying them.

"You should fix her hair up nice so she'll know how it will look." Carlotta called from her seat at the table, where she helped Lucia fold napkins. "You know, when she tries on the dress, she'll see it as it will be."

Eva nodded.

Rebecca sent a smile around the room, knowing their conversation had grabbed everyone's attention. "Good idea. Perhaps you'd like to accompany us?"

Carlotta gave her head a quick shake. "No. I am too old for shopping. You will have a good time, the two of you."

"Be sure to stop at Sianara's for lunch, Eva." Nonna said. "You remember those cannolis?" She kissed her fingertips as several of the others sent up a chorus of "mmm's."

Rebecca made a mental note to bring back cannolis for the kitchen staff, though in her opinion, Nonna's were the finest around.

Early the following morning, Rebecca sat while Eva did her hair then donned the suit she planned to wear for shopping. When Ricci came down for breakfast, Rebecca joined him.

He gaped at her. "Well, this is a pleasant surprise. I'm not used to seeing you at such an early hour."

"I didn't want to delay your leaving," she said then blew on her coffee to cool it.

"Ah, yes. It's the shopping that has you up so early. Perhaps we should go more often."

Beautiful winter vistas greeted them at every turn. Even though clouds hung low, hiding the peaks of the mountains, the evergreen Umbrian countryside delighted Rebecca. And Eva entertained her with stories of a childhood spent in the outskirts of Perugia.

"I have family there still," she told Rebecca. "And one of the shops I'll take you to is run by my aunt. I'm certain she'll have something of interest to you. And my cousin sells fine shoes. Perhaps we'll have time to visit there also."

"I don't really need new shoes," Rebecca said, just above a whisper.

"Oh, you must have new shoes to go with your dress," Ricci said, his eyes doing their mischief dance.

She cast him a warning look.

He responded with a low chuckle.

Eva's aunt was obviously very capable and used to working with the elite. She had a good inventory of ready-made dresses and suits, hats, and the latest in women's undergarments. She was especially keen to sell "the young contessa" on the latter. Perhaps she was unimpressed with the quality of Rebecca's underwear. Not an encouraging thought.

Eva helped keep the older woman focused on the task at hand, and they soon found a suitable gown. The deep burgundy color suited Rebecca's complexion and the crepe de chine fabric would be comfortable for dancing. A snug fit, it could be taken out when Rebecca regained her lost weight, which she was certain she would do at some point. Her mink stole would look well with it, also. While trying on the dress, she decided she'd need shoes after all.

Ricci met them just after noon at Sianara's, a lovely little cafe, where they ordered the cannolis to go then enjoyed a meal of river trout and roasted vegetables. The Alverás held to the meatless regime until after Epiphany.

"You will love la signora's dress," Eva told Ricci.

Ricci smiled at Rebecca. "I have no doubt of that. How was your aunt?"

Eva exchanged a glance with Rebecca. "She is very well,

and I think she was quite impressed with the new contessa."

Ricci smiled around a large bite of vegetables.

"She wasn't so impressed with my undergarments." Rebecca kept her voice low enough to only be heard by her table mates.

Eva snickered into her napkin.

Ricci laughed out loud. "I hope she sold you on the latest Italian under fashions. I've heard she has a penchant for such things."

Chapter Twenty

December 31, 1930

Well, it wasn't Guy Lombardo, and this wasn't the Ritz, but the orchestra at the New Year's Eve bash in Foligno wasn't half bad. Rebecca scanned the crowd of dancers, looking for familiar faces.

Sometimes she missed her friends back in the States. It hadn't seemed to matter where she went, she always knew someone. She had lived in Italy for nearly a year, and her sphere of influence was … well … underwhelming.

"You are very serious," Ricci said. "Are you not enjoying the party?"

"Oh, yes," she whispered in his ear. "I was just thinking how quickly the time has passed. In a few minutes, it'll be 1931."

He leaned his head against hers as they turned in time to the music. "And in only a few months, we will celebrate the beginning of our second year of marriage. This is what I am thinking of."

She smiled, though he couldn't see her. They hadn't even been married a year, yet so much had happened. Her life was so changed. A year of living in one of the most beautiful places in the world with a wonderful man who loved her. She should be ecstatic. And she would be, if only. But she shut those regrets out and hummed *Dream a Little Dream* as the orchestra finished up before their break. How nice that they played so many American hits. But it was not really surprising. The United States influenced the world in so many ways.

Ricci's circle of friends joined them at the table. Rebecca still thought of them as Ricci's friends. She'd never felt completely accepted by them. Perhaps they didn't know what to make of her. Either that or she kept a distance between them. A wall.

She watched them as they laughed and joked together. Was it odd she felt more at home with the servants? Not really, when she thought about it. She'd been raised by servants, after all. In her parents' absence, she'd taken her meals with them, celebrated holidays with them.

An outbreak of laughter captured her attention. She'd pulled another Nancy, letting her mind wander, and now she had no idea what was so funny. But she joined in their laughter anyway. If she remembered, she'd ask Ricci about it later.

Before the band returned, the ladies got up as one to go and powder their noses. Ambra stopped next to Rebecca's chair. "Come on, Contessa. I believe your nose is shiny, too."

Rebecca giggled as she retrieved her pocketbook. Ambra had always been an ally. They walked arm-in-arm to the ladies room, but before they went inside, Ambra paused.

"I was hoping for a moment in private with you." Her eyes shone with emotion.

Rebecca couldn't imagine what must be on her mind. "What's going on?"

Ambra took a deep breath and suddenly Rebecca knew. It was the small hand gesture. Ambra's fingers rested for just a moment—below her belt—on the slight bulge of her tummy. Rebecca forced her eyes to meet Ambra's. "You're going to have a child."

Ambra's warm smile, the glowing eyes, these were all sure signs of impending motherhood.

She giggled and squeezed Rebecca's fingers. "I knew you would guess. A little hint is all you needed." Then she sobered. "I feel almost as though I should apologize."

Rebecca leaned forward to kiss Ambra's cheek. "Oh, no—don't you dare. I'm so excited and happy for you. That's the most wonderful news." She swallowed the golf ball sized lump in her throat and repented for the thoughts she was thinking. "Ten Hail Marys before bed, I promise," she whispered as they entered the ladies' room.

Ambra turned to look at her. "What did you say?"

With a nervous giggle, Rebecca waved her hand. "I was making a mental note to pray for you later."

"Oh, thank you. That's so wonderful."

Rebecca grimaced as she headed for an empty stall. Tack on ten more Hail Marys.

Riccardo stood, along with the other guys at the table, as their wives filtered in from the powder room. The orchestra had also returned. They were getting ready for the final hour of 1931. Rebecca slid into her seat, an undefinable look on her face. After lowering into his chair, he leaned forward to whisper in her ear. "What's up?"

She sent him a radiant smile that didn't quite make it to her eyes. "Girl stuff. We can catch up later."

He nodded, more curious than ever. He knew her well. She did not indulge in girl stuff. Something was definitely up. The music started. *Dulce y Amable.* Sweet and Lovely. Perfect. He stood and held out his hand for Rebecca. "Dance with me?"

It seemed the night could not be better. His lovely wife in his arms, her nearness reminding him a dozen times why he'd fallen for her, beautiful music, good friends. Then his gaze fell on the face of Francesca Boccali, across the dance floor, in the arms of a tall, slender someone. Darkly handsome. Familiar. Riccardo swallowed.

After the song ended, he headed back to the table, hoping Rebecca wouldn't see them. This could be disastrous.

As he suspected, Francesca had seen Riccardo and was headed their way. Could he get Rebecca out in time? He placed his palm at the middle of her back, trying to steer her toward the door.

She glanced over her shoulder then halted. "Giorgio?"

Too late. Riccardo looked at Rebecca, who was staring at the man headed directly for them.

Giorgio De Campo stopped in front of them, his eyes on Rebecca. He bowed. "Ciao ... Rebecca." He rose to his full height, slightly above Riccardo's and made eye contact with him. "Conte. It is good to see you again."

Feeling Rebecca's stare, Riccardo acknowledged Giorgio's greeting.

Beside Giorgio, Francesca flipped open a cigarette case and removed one then offered one to Giorgio. He also took one and held it between his first two fingers. Her lighter flared. Francesca held it for Giorgio to light his then she lit hers and clicked it shut.

Riccardo wanted to move away from their nasty cloud of smoke, but he wasn't going anywhere without his wife.

Giorgio grinned at Rebecca. "Am I too late finding you?"

Rebecca made no comment. Riccardo wished he could see her face. She took a backward step, bumping against Riccardo. Instead of moving away, she leaned against him, just barely, but enough that he knew she wanted him to stay. He laid a hand on her shoulder, applied gentle pressure to reassure her.

The music had started up again. Giorgio gave a curt laugh. "For a dance, Contessa."

Riccardo felt her head moving in a negative gesture. "You are right, Signore, it is too late." She reached for Riccardo's hand. "It is the last dance, which belongs only to my husband."

Riccardo drew in a deep breath, not caring that the air was tainted with cigarette smoke. He placed his other hand at Rebecca's waist. "Shall we go, cara?"

He lifted his chin toward Signorina Boccali and Giorgio. "If you will excuse us." They moved to the dance floor. He wished someone could have taken a picture of Signorina

Boccali and Giorgio De Campo in that moment and preserved their expressions. Giorgio's confusion and Francesca's fury. Had they really expected Rebecca to accept his presumptive invitation?

Rebecca leaned against him as they maneuvered through the steps of the dance, her eyes probing the depths of his.

He bent his head to drop a kiss on her brow. "You are amazing, my love."

She gave a little laugh and snuggled against him.

The music ended. The bells tolled the midnight hour. He bent to kiss her.

She wound her arms around his neck and whispered, "I love you, Riccardo Alverá."

Rebecca had about a hundred questions to ask Ricci as soon as they were alone. No doubt, he had a few for her, too. He sent inquisitive looks her way from time to time, but she determined to make him wait. She did not wish to discuss this in front of his friends.

They walked in silence as all of them returned to the pensione. Overhead, millions of brilliant stars twinkled against the dark sky. Quiet voices echoed in the narrow streets as others made their way home from the party.

Ricci held her hand.

They walked easily together, but her mind was a cluttered mess. She tried to organize her thoughts as they drew near the place they were staying. Ricci knew Giorgio. How had that come about? And how had Francesca come to be with him? This could not be a coincidence.

Inside their room, he turned to her. "I suppose you are wondering how I came to be acquainted with your former husband?"

She plopped down on the edge of the bed, kicked off her heels, then stretched her toes. "I'm wondering several things right now."

He sat in the chair opposite her and slipped his shoes off. "I met him several years ago."

"Can you narrow that down a little more? Exactly when did you meet him?"

His brow furrowed as if he tried to understand what she was asking. "I believe it was '28, or perhaps early '29. We met on the slopes."

Around the time she'd first told him about Giorgio. She tapped her fingertip on the bedside table. "I see. Was it a chance meeting?"

He arched his brows. "A chance of what?"

After an eye roll, she began removing pins from her hair. "Did you meet him by chance, or were you looking for him?"

He relaxed in the chair but kept his eyes on hers. "I admit, I watched for him whenever I went to the mountains, my love. I was curious. This is all. When I heard someone call out the name, I was compelled to introduce myself."

It sounded innocent enough. She would probably do the same, given the opportunity. *If* Ricci had an ex-wife. She'd been blessed with an especially active curiosity, which she'd mostly outgrown. "What about Francesca? How did she know about him?"

Ricci sat forward, propped his elbows on his knees, and cupped his hands together. "One can only think she may have read the letter Modesti had her type when we applied for a marriage license. She is his secretary, after all." He covered a yawn.

Ah, Modesti's letter. Rebecca gazed at Ricci through lowered lids. He was getting tired. She should let him off the hook. For tonight anyway. She laid her hairpins on the table. "Perhaps we can discuss this in the morning after you've rested."

He stood, drew her up and into his arms. "I like that idea.

I'm too tired even to think."

She leaned against him for a moment then pushed away. "On the other hand, I could keep pestering you for answers. Sleepiness works on you like a truth serum."

He was already removing his clothes and within seconds, had climbed into bed. "Does it? Well, have fun sweetheart. Be gentle with me." He chuckled softly as he drifted off.

Rebecca stood beside the bed shaking her head. It was so unfair that he could go to sleep in an instant. She'd probably lie awake half the night, thinking about what had happened. After hanging up her dress, she slipped into her nightgown, and curled up beside him.

The first thought to pop in to Rebecca's mind when she awoke—she'd forgotten to say twenty Hail Marys. She turned over onto her back, gazed at the yellowed plaster ceiling and began to recite the prayers. She must have been really tired to have fallen asleep so quickly when there was so much to think about. For good measure, she threw in a short prayer for Ambra.

Jealousy churned in her breast at the memory of Ambra's excitement. Just a few weeks ago, Eva had confessed that she was in the family way. Though Rebecca was thrilled for them both, she couldn't help the almost overwhelming sadness.

She looked at Ricci, sleeping peacefully beside her. She wanted to whack him with her pillow.

After a warm bath, she brushed her hair and got dressed. All the while, her mind whirled with questions. Why had Francesca done this? There was no way it was coincidence. No way.

She stepped to the window and gazed out, massaging her temples. What was the woman's objective? What could she possibly hope to gain? She glanced at Ricci again. He was a worthy prize.

Was she only trying to humiliate Rebecca? Or had she something more sinister in mind? Rebecca shook that one off.

Ricci stretched and opened his eyes. "Ah, good morning, my beautiful wife."

She arched her brow at him. He'd better not make any advances. She was in no mood.

Tossing aside the covers, he got up and stumbled into the bathroom. She spent the time packing their bag so they could leave as soon as possible. She'd had enough of this place.

Ricci stepped out, wrapped in a towel. "Did you sleep well?"

"Yes, actually. I didn't expect to." She pointed to his clothes. "I laid out your things."

"I see." He didn't move, just stood there, gazing at her. "I'm confused about something."

She pushed aside a wayward curl. "What?"

"Last night … you said you loved me. You were very—" He swayed as if he was dancing. "Warm. Inviting. This morning, I think you are mad at me."

She blew out a breath. "I'm not mad at you. I'm frustrated."

"I know the feeling."

Rebecca knew better than to look, but she couldn't help herself. The cute little puppy dog eyes got her every time. She giggled. That was it. She had no self-control where this man was concerned.

Chapter Twenty-One

Riccardo whistled as he carried their suitcase downstairs. Most of his friends had already left, but Ambra waited in the sitting room.

She greeted Riccardo with a smile. "My husband is doing what you're doing. Playing the footman."

Giuseppe crossed the threshold as Riccardo approached the door.

"Buongiorno, amico mio. Have you had breakfast yet?" He followed Riccardo out and to the car.

Riccardo hefted the suitcase into the boot and closed it. "No, we haven't."

"Join us, then. We were just going."

Riccardo looked up as Rebecca and Ambra strolled outside, dressed in their warm winter coats. The four of them crossed the street and entered a small, aromatic cafe.

Riccardo held out a chair for Rebecca. Her smile sent his heart racing. He signaled a waiter then sat down.

The waiter rushed over and filled their cups then took their orders.

His eyes on Riccardo, Giuseppe lifted his coffee cup. "Did Rebecca share with you our good news?"

Riccardo glanced at Rebecca then back at Giuseppe. "No, are you to be congratulated?"

"Yes. I must say, I'm surprised your wife didn't tell you." He raised Ambra's hand to his lips and kissed it. "But I suppose she had other things on her mind."

"Darling, please," Ambra whispered.

Riccardo watched the two, wondering whether to laugh at them or be worried.

"We met your former mister last night, Contessa," Giuseppe said, his eyes now on Rebecca.

Ambra sucked in a quick breath.

Rebecca's gaze found Riccardo's briefly as she dabbed her lips with a napkin. "Did you? How diverting. Yes, now you know my deepest, darkest secret."

"Oh, I hope not," Giuseppe said. He tore off a bite of bread and devoured it. "I will warn you, though. Francesca made the rounds this morning."

Ambra gripped Rebecca's hand. "I'm so sorry, dear. I asked him not to say anything."

Riccardo leaned forward, his attention on Giuseppe. "What exactly did Signorina Boccali say?"

"Just that she was so sorry to have made our Contessa uncomfortable last night. She had no idea we would be at the party." He grinned at Riccardo and winked at Rebecca. "She was lying, of course. We all knew it. But it would have been better if we had heard this from our old friend, Conte."

Riccardo hoped the matter would be dropped quickly, but since Giuseppe chose to pursue it to the end, he set down his cup and gathered his thoughts. "I wished to shield my wife from gossip. I suppose that is too much to ask in a small town."

Giuseppe chuckled. "When one is in the public eye, there is no such thing as privacy, Conte. You know that."

Rebecca examined her coffee cup, running her fingertip over the raised floral design around the base. She lifted her eyes to Ambra's and began in a quiet voice, "I was nineteen years old, still in school. I met Giorgio on Christmas holiday in the Alps. He was obviously after my money. We eloped. The marriage lasted a full three days. Daddy swept in and paid Giorgio to go away. The marriage was annulled. I never saw him again. Until last night."

Riccardo watched her face, admiring her control. What a doll she was. The kind of woman a man dreams of, but never thinks to find.

Ambra whispered something to Rebecca that sounded like another apology.

"Three days," Giuseppe said. "And it never goes away. Be warned, my lovely friend. There are some who will judge you harshly for such reckless behavior."

Riccardo pushed his chair back. "We need to be on our way. It's been a pleasure, as always."

"You're such a bad liar, dear Conte," Ambra said. "I am so sorry for any discomfort, but my husband is right about one thing. There will be talk. There will be judging. But we are armed with the truth at least." She looked at Rebecca. "I thank you for your honesty—one thing I've come to appreciate about you."

Riccardo helped Rebecca into her coat. Both couples left the small cafe.

Giuseppe and Ambra said their good-byes amid kisses and best wishes for the New Year.

Riccardo blew a relieved breath as they walked away. He took Rebecca's hand and led her to the car. "I hope the heat is working this time. But if it is not, I have a blanket behind your seat."

"Why thank you kindly, sir," Rebecca said, as she slipped into the seat.

He closed her door and ran around the car, wondering what was going on in that pretty head. He was fairly certain she'd have a barrage of questions for him. Questions she'd been thinking about since last night.

Rebecca waited until after Ricci maneuvered a hairpin curve on the drive home. The way he drove, the last thing she wanted to do was distract him. "I know I've asked you this before, but are you quite certain you never did anything to encourage that woman?"

He sent her a toothy grin. "Not intentionally, but you know what a handsome man I am." With a wave of his hand, he gestured toward himself. "I cannot turn this off."

She snickered. "Darling, be serious. Perhaps there was a time when you'd had too much to drink?"

"I love when you call me darling." He smiled at her then gave his full attention to the road as they entered another series of curves. "What you asked—that has never happened—I never drink too much. You know that."

"I know that is true now but when you were younger perhaps? A crazy youth?" She'd known plenty of those.

"I didn't know her then. But really, it only happened once. I vowed never to let it happen again. The drinking, I mean."

"Uh-huh. So you had no wild and crazy days?" She made an effort to keep her voice light. "No trail of broken hearts?"

"I would not say that." His brow furrowed. "Why are you asking?"

"I'm trying to reason it all out. Why is she doing this? Why doesn't she just let it go?"

He took a deep breath and exhaled. "I've thought about this a great deal. I think perhaps she is bent on revenge. I rejected her. This is something she is not used to, I think."

Rebecca toyed with a curl peeking out from beneath her hat. "How long ago was that when you rejected her?"

"Since she began working for the mayor. Every time I saw her." He pierced Rebecca with a sidelong glance. "Every single time. The last time—well, you know about that one. I assumed it would stop when I married you. It did not."

She didn't know he'd been subjected to that woman's forwardness for so long. Seldom did one hear of a woman making such advances. It was usually the other way around. She tugged at her skirt. Noticing a clump of dirt on her shoe, she bent to flick it away. "How do we react to this revelation of my past? You know she'll tell everyone."

"She doesn't have to tell everyone. She already revealed it to the right people. It will get around. Most likely, it already has. I think you handled it very well, cara. Calm and cool. You make me love you more with each passing day."

Eyes damp, she faced him. "You always try to divert me with compliments. But I can't help thinking I've brought disgrace on you and your family."

He took her hand in his and gave it a firm squeeze. "You think we are all so perfect? You have not gazed into our past, have you? We are all forgiven, cara. If you have confessed your sins, they are forgiven. You mustn't let this continue to plague you. We will get through it."

Easier said than done. Yes, she had made a confession and had been forgiven. But her sins still haunted her. Could it be her past indiscretions were the reason for her inability to bear a child? That was ridiculous. They'd only been married a few months.

She was weary of it all—this load of guilt—it wouldn't leave. Would she never be free?

They'd made a quick trip. Rebecca was happy to see the outline of the villa at Tres Viti. Home. The door opened wide as they pulled up in front of the house. Tito was the first to appear, then Eva and Chico. Where was Carlotta? She always put in an appearance.

"Buonasera, Signora," Tito said as he opened her door. He stood aside as Rebecca uncurled from the seat. The Alfa-Romeo was built for speed, not comfort.

Eva drew near, holding out her hands. "Come inside out of the cold. The wind brings a chill today."

Chico ran to the back of the car, watching as Tito removed the luggage.

Following Eva inside, Rebecca was barely aware of Tito and Ricci behind her. She looked around the room, taking in all the familiar sights. The warm fire burning, the polished wood floors, the arched doorways. Carlotta's empty chair. "Where is Carlotta?"

Eva glanced at Ricci. "She is unwell. She says to give her regards to you both and perhaps she may see you at dinner."

Rebecca looked at Ricci, waiting for his response.

He shrugged out of his coat and handed it to Eva. "I'll go up and see her."

"Give her my love," Rebecca said as she followed Eva to the kitchen. Most of the women were preparing the meal. Only Lucia was missing.

Nonna wiped her fingers on her apron and stepped to the stove. "Tea or coffee, Signora? You must be chilled from your journey."

"Buonasera, Nonna. What has happened?"

Nonna patted Rebecca's arm, which was the first clue that whatever had occurred, it was serious. "The doctor was here. He said she's had a light stroke."

Rebecca's breath caught in her throat. "A stroke?"

"A light one. Not much trouble. Only the bad headache and for a short time—last night—her speech was not so good."

Eva took Rebecca's hand. "Come, sit down. How about a cup of tea?" After guiding Rebecca to a chair, she spooned tea leaves into a pot.

As she poured hot water over the tea leaves, Nonna explained what had happened. "It was last night. She wouldn't let us call you. Only the doctor and you know I had to threaten her to get that far."

Ricci entered the kitchen in time to hear most of what Nonna said. "She is sleeping now. Tito said it was not serious, but it could happen again?"

Nonna nodded. "Yes, this is what the doctor says. But he doesn't know everything." She crossed the floor to his side. "We will take excellent care of her, and she will recover."

Eva placed a cup of tea in front of Rebecca. "The doctor did say she has a good chance at a full recovery. But she must rest for a few days. Would you also like a cup of tea, Signore?"

Ricci shook his head. "Grazie but no. I am going out to the stables."

Rebecca watched him go. Most likely, he wished to be alone.

"He feels guilty for not being here," Nonna whispered. "She knew he would." She sat across from Rebecca. "How was the party? Did you dance the night away?"

Rebecca smiled. Nonna had such a way of setting one at ease. "We certainly did. The orchestra was very nice."

Eva dried a plate and put it away. "Was your dress all right? Tell us about the fashions."

"So many beautiful dresses, you would never know there was a depression. And the shoes—"

Nonna covered her mouth with her hands. Nonna loved pretty shoes.

Rebecca described everything in great detail, knowing they would be enthralled. "My dress was perfect. We needn't have worried over choosing the right shade. I saw every color of the rainbow. Even a yellow one."

"Really?" Nonna slapped the table. "In the winter?"

Lucia stepped through the door. "She is awake and asking for you, Nonna."

Nonna got up right away, removed her apron, and hung it on a peg.

Rebecca stood also. "May I come with you?"

"Of course you may."

It wasn't difficult to keep up with the little woman as she bustled through the hall and up the back staircase.

Carlotta's face seemed pale against her pillow, but her eyes lit when Rebecca stepped through the door. "You're home." She turned to Nonna. "I was only going to ask if they had arrived. But since you are here, did the doctor tell you what I can have? I would give most anything for chicken soup."

"We have it prepared, Signora. I will send up a bowl of it." Nonna brushed a strand of hair away from Carlotta's eyes. "You are talking much better now."

"The words got mixed up for a while," Carlotta said to Rebecca. "It was the strangest thing. And my head was hurting so bad I needed to lie down. I never dreamed it was my heart."

Nonna patted her hand. "It wasn't your heart, dear one. It was the blood pressure, remember? The doctor said it is too high and you maybe had a clot."

Carlotta frowned at Rebecca as though she had difficulty understanding, or possibly remembering.

"I'll go get your dinner ready," Nonna said.

After she had gone, Rebecca sat in the chair beside the bed. "I'm so sorry we weren't here with you."

She spoke slowly, weighing her words carefully. "I was afraid at first. Nonna stayed with me. And you know the others are always close by. I asked them not to call Riccardo. I knew he would hurry home. I wanted so much for you to enjoy your evening together."

"You are very good to us."

"You did enjoy the party?"

"Oh yes. It was wonderful." No need to tell her about Francesca. That would add to her worries.

Heavy footsteps on the stairs told her Ricci was on his way. She bent to kiss Carlotta. "I'll leave you two alone."

Carlotta held on to her hand until Ricci walked through the door. "I dreamed of a child. I held him in my arms. I was so happy." Her eyes filled and overflowed.

Rebecca brushed away her tears, but she had no words. She met Ricci's gaze and read the sadness there. As soon as Carlotta let go of her hand, she left the room. She wanted to escape before she was completely overcome by emotion.

In her room, she dropped to her knees beside the bed and cried.

As the emotion subsided, she peered up at the crucifix and crossed herself. "Please don't think I'm ungrateful. You have given me more than I ever dreamed possible. But this is why, more than anything—" she stopped to mop her eyes and blow her nose. "More than anything, I want to give them a child. Please. Not for myself but for my loved ones." She rested her head on the bed and took a deep breath then pushed up from the floor and stepped into the bathroom to repair the damage before going down to dinner.

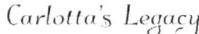

Chapter Twenty-Two

5 January, 1931, Tres Viti Verdi

"La Befana, La Befana," the children cried, dancing and pointing at the sky.

Rebecca laughed at their joyous faces and typical Italian drawl. "La Be-fah-nah!"

"La Befana, she is coming!" Chico sang out.

Rebecca squinted at the sky where he pointed. It looked a bit like a stork or some other large bird, but she wasn't going to spoil the fun. In the States, an old crone flying on a broom was something entirely different. Though the old Italian tale of La Befana was an odd one, she thoroughly enjoyed shopping for small gifts to leave on their pillows. Gifts the children believed were left for them by La Befana. In great expectation, they'd leave messages and small treats, instead of the cookies and milk American children left for Santa.

Later, sitting by the fire, Chico and the other youngsters listened wide-eyed as Rebecca told them about Santa Claus, also known as St. Nicholas. She decided not to tell them what large presents she'd received as a child. She didn't want to foster covetousness or envy in their young minds.

"But Signora, do you not celebrate the holy birth?"

Rebecca's heart ached a little, as she gazed into the large brown eyes of one of the youngest Campi girls. What would they think of her if they knew how she'd been raised? Mother and Daddy had done their best to keep the Christ child out of their holiday celebrations. This too, she would not share with these precious little ones. "Most Americans are Christians, and they do celebrate the Natale, as you do."

"Come now, children," Nonna called to them. "Time for

you to go home to your beds so La Befana will not pass over you. If she sees you are not sleeping, she will not leave your surprise."

Amid squeals and laughter, the children hurried from the room. Chico paused for a moment in front of Rebecca. "Thank you for the story, Signora."

Rebecca touched his chin. "You are welcome, Chico. Sleep well."

"You are very good with them," Carlotta whispered.

Rebecca had forgotten she was in the room. An inexplicable feeling, almost a desire, flitted through Rebecca's mind to draw close to Carlotta and lean her head on the older woman's knees. Was it the holiday season that brought on such melancholy? Or was it Carlotta's own need drawing Rebecca? Instead of giving in to the desire, Rebecca sent her a smile. "They make it easy."

Carlotta stirred then sat forward in her chair. "Your Christmases were like the ones of which you spoke? The Santa visited you?"

Rebecca gave a little chuckle. "Yes, as a child, I believed in Santa Claus. My parents and grandparents encouraged it. I didn't want to tell those children, but I received a great many gifts. Sometimes large gifts. I expected them and would've been angry if I had not received them." She grinned. "I was a very spoiled child."

Carlotta tilted her head and gazed at Rebecca. "I can imagine that very well. But you have grown into a fine young woman, Rebecca. You mustn't be sorry for what you have experienced. You are still growing into the woman God has in mind. Always remember that." She slid to the edge of her chair and struggled to rise. Rebecca rushed to help her, but Carlotta brushed her attempts aside. "No, no. I am all right. I am thinking to make some warm milk and get ready for bed."

The side entrance opened with a sudden rush of cold air.

Ricci stepped through and closed the door. "It is a fine cold night, ladies." He slipped out of his coat and hung it beside the door then removed his hat.

As he drew near, Carlotta patted his arm. "Are you the Santa Claus?"

He grinned and kissed her cheek. "Tonight, I am many things, Mamma." He did a little pirouette. "I am La Befana." He bent to peer into Rebecca's eyes. "I am Santa Claus."

Carlotta cackled as she shuffled toward the kitchen. "Let us hope you are also Riccardo."

Quiet weeks followed the holidays. Crisp, cold mornings kept the women inside, close to their fires. Rebecca caught up on all her correspondence. Tres Viti's files were in order, the logbooks neatly copied.

Ricci returned to his routine, mornings in town, afternoons spent working with Poppi. For Rebecca, reality set in. This was her life, for as long as they both should live. How did she feel about that? After downing the last remnants of her morning coffee, she stood and walked to the window. Carlotta's beautiful garden lay dormant. In the distance, a heavy mist crowned the blue-green hills. Spring was only weeks away. By then, perhaps she'd have good news for Ricci and the rest of the family. Her hands on her abdomen, she closed her eyes and allowed herself to dream as she wondered what it would be like to have a child of her own.

This pregnancy had advanced farther than before. She almost dared to hope. What a luxury it was to have hope. Each Mass she attended, she sent up earnest prayers, almost begging God to allow her to carry this one to term. Her arms ached to hold an infant. She imagined the praises of her family. Finally. She'd be worthy of their love.

"Signora."

Rebecca drew her hands away from her midsection and

spun on her heel to face Maria. "Yes?"

"Scusi, Signora, but you have a visitor." Maria stood aside and waited.

Rebecca hadn't heard a vehicle or anyone knocking. She followed Maria to the front parlor where a cheery fire burned and Ambra Carbone sat on the sofa.

Rebecca smiled as she crossed the room. "Ambra, what a wonderful surprise."

Ambra stood and they greeted one another in classic Italian style, with a kiss to each cheek.

Rebecca turned her smile on Maria, who waited at the door. "Please bring refreshments." After Maria brisked away, Rebecca gestured to the sofa. "Please, sit. I apologize—I didn't hear you drive up."

Ambra's eyes crinkled with her smile. "That's because I didn't drive up." Her smile widened into a grin. "Giuseppe is in the vineyard with your Ricci. I walked up to the house. I hope you don't mind."

"Not at all. You have only interrupted my boredom. I am so pleased you've come."

Maria reentered with a laden tray.

Rebecca inhaled the aroma of fresh coffee. Thank goodness her nausea had subsided. She could enjoy the tasty treats set before her.

"So, what have you been up to?" Ambra asked, before filling her mouth with a coconut macaroon.

For a moment, Rebecca was tempted to confess her condition. She opened her mouth to speak the words but couldn't do it. It was too soon, the news too private. Her eyes drifted to Ambra's swollen belly. If something happened … she couldn't bear the humiliation again. "Just catching up on paperwork. A real yawner. What about you?"

Ambra sipped her coffee and gazed into the fire as if she carefully weighed her response. "We have just returned from

Rome."

"Really? Pleasure or business?"

Ambra brushed at crumbs on her skirt. "Family. We spent two weeks with Giuseppe's family. And I must say, it has opened my eyes. I am quite alarmed."

Rebecca set her cup down and faced her friend. "Why? What has happened?"

"Giuseppe has several younger siblings who are in the school system, and even though they attend parish schools, they are being taught to honor the government above all."

A chill danced up Rebecca's spine. She leaned forward to refill their coffee cups. "I thought this was only happening in the public schools. How is this possible?"

Ambra drew a breath and released it, her eyes on Rebecca's face. "The boys call each other 'legionaries,' and tout the leadership of the Blackshirts." She frowned into her cup. "We have been somewhat protected here in our small community, but I see it advancing. In Rome, you know, the Blackshirts enforce Mussolini's statutes. My mother-in-law told me about a man who was made to drink an entire bottle of castor oil then they forced a live toad down his throat." She shuddered. After another pause to sip her coffee, she continued. "This, because he dared speak out against the government."

Rebecca had heard some of this before. There had also been public floggings and threats on family. Scare tactics condoned by the government. It wasn't current news, but they had never been closely affected by it as Ambra had been. What did the future hold for them as citizens? She dabbed at her lips with a linen napkin as another thought struck her. Into what kind of world were they bringing a child? She took Ambra's hand. "I'm so sorry. This must have been difficult for you, especially now."

Ambra turned her hand to grasp hold of Rebecca's fingers. "It was. And *Il Duce* wants us to bring more and more children into the world, so he can build Italy into a great world power. I tell you, it is most disturbing. Here in our small community, it is easy to ignore. We go about our lives as if tomorrow will be the same as yesterday, while all around us, the world is falling apart." A tear left a damp trail on her cheek. She reached to swipe it away then cast an apologetic glance at Rebecca. "I'm sorry to be in such a mood."

Rebecca smiled as she released Ambra's fingers. "You're not bothering me. This is something that troubles you deeply. It's best to talk about it, if you can."

"The worst part is knowing that, if this man stays in power—as he certainly means to do—our entire life is changed. Our world is not the same as the one our ancestors planned so carefully. They raised us with faith and hope … and love, expecting good things to come. Is this even possible anymore?"

Rebecca rested her hand on Ambra's shoulder. "Of course it is. If you have a strong enough faith, you can endure even this." She glanced toward the door. Should she send for Carlotta? Her mother-in-law would be better at this than she. Rebecca felt so green, so new to the faithful things. She hadn't even been confirmed. How could she encourage another who had grown up in the faith?

She swallowed and forced a smile. "We are taught that man can't steal our faith. It is a gift from God and what He gives, no one can take away. They can take our physical lives away—but not our faith—our belief in Jesus Christ. You have to put your trust in the things that matter."

Ambra closed her eyes and drew in a long, deep breath. As she exhaled, her body seemed to release tension. She relaxed against the sofa's back. Slowly, her gaze returned to Rebecca. A smile transformed her expression. "Out of the mouth of babes. I should be teaching you this instead of you reminding me."

Rebecca returned her smile. "Would you like more coffee?"

Ambra gave a quick shake of her head. "No, but would you walk with me back to the vineyards?"

"Of course. Let me get our coats." She stood and crossed to the wall hooks near the door.

Ambra rose also and followed her. "Perhaps on the way, we can visit this beautiful horse I've heard so much about?"

Rebecca assisted Ambra into her wool jacket then reached for her own coat. "Of course, if you're up to it. I'm sure Stella Rosa would welcome visitors today."

Riccardo saw them first. He glanced up as two women wound their way through the olive grove, their figures barely visible among the silvery green leaves of the trees. As they drew nearer, he recognized Rebecca with Ambra. He hoped their approach would silence Giuseppe's whining. The man could wilt ears of corn with his complaining.

"'Seppe, my friend, your better half is on her way."

Giuseppe paused in his conversation with Poppi to glance at Riccardo, who gestured toward the olive trees. "Yes, I suppose it is time for us to go."

Riccardo forced a smile as he made the expected offer. "Please stay and enjoy a meal with us."

Giuseppe waved his hand in the air. "Grazie, but no. We've been away too long already. I only wanted to stop in and make you aware of this situation." He stepped near and rested a broad hand on Riccardo's shoulder. "We must be on our guard, my friend."

Riccardo nodded. "Yes, you are right. We live in dangerous times. But please, do not alarm my lovely wife." He sincerely hoped the Blackshirts wouldn't bother with their small town. Why would they? What did Ginestra have to offer anyone?

"She may scurry back to her home in America. Perhaps you should think of this also."

"No, my friend." Riccardo offered him a crooked grin and a quick shrug. "I cannot leave my family. My home."

Giuseppe nodded his understanding. "I know you are right, but—" He had no time to finish whatever it was he meant to say since the ladies had arrived. He stepped forward. "Buongiorno, Contessa. I hope you are well this fine, cold day."

Rebecca smiled, her glance flitting from one man's face to another. "Yes, thank you. I am very well. And yourself?"

After the usual formalities, Giuseppe and Ambra moved toward their car. Riccardo took Rebecca's hand and led her behind them. They stood side-by-side as their friends got in their vehicle and pulled away.

Riccardo turned to gaze at Rebecca. How beautiful she looked, her cheeks rosy from the cold. "How was your visit?"

"We had a good conversation. How about yours?"

He gave her a wry smile as he lifted her fingers to his lips. "Not as entertaining as this moment, my love. It was the usual Giuseppe."

Rebecca smiled and leaned against him.

He loved how she did that, as if she needed physical contact with him. He draped his arm around her shoulders. "Well, cara, we should get back to the house. Mamma will have our dinner waiting."

Rebecca watched the distant road as the Carbone's vehicle inched along, leaving a cloud of dust in its wake. "Have you seen any more strange vehicles parked along our road front, Ricci?"

His eyes snapped to hers. The same idea had entered his mind, but he had quelled it. "No, not lately."

"Is Francesca back at work now?"

Why was she asking these questions? "What is in that

beautiful mind of yours, my love?" When she didn't answer, he touched her chin with his fingertips, tilted her face toward his. "No, she is still on leave. Why do you ask?"

She gave a slight shake of her head and turned to begin the walk back to the house. "Just a thought. I wondered if there was a connection, that's all. Silly of me, I suppose."

He followed, matching her stride. "You think she stalks us?" Hoping to put her at ease, he grinned as though he teased her. But the same thought had crossed his mind more than once. "Why would she do that?"

"Why, indeed? That is the question, is it not?" She smiled into his eyes.

He cared little about Francesca, other than the fact she'd been away, which afforded him a bit of relief at committee meetings. He needn't avoid her barbs and stares. He could come and go without the worry that she'd follow him. As he and Rebecca started up the path that wound through the olive trees, Riccardo circled her waist with his arm and pulled her to him. "I don't believe we have even hugged today, my love." After a moment, he pulled back so he could see her face. "All this talk of intrigue. I hope you are not fearful. You know you are safe with me, do you not?"

She leaned against him, lifting her eyes to his. "I feel very safe at this moment."

He would have kissed her had he not seen Poppi's approach.

"Are you still newly wedded?" Poppi called as he moved past them. "If you are late for dinner, you'll think you are still a young boy when those women at the house are done with you."

Riccardo laughed. "Poppi is right. We'd better hurry. I've no wish for a tongue lashing today."

Chapter Twenty-Three

Spring, 1931

The breeze that ruffled Riccardo's hair held a hint of spring. Heavy-hearted, his gaze swept the mountains, still wearing their snow caps. He scanned the horizon to a distant river valley, settling on a wisp of smoke from a lonely dwelling. As a boy, he had tried to pinpoint the residence, even made up stories about its inhabitants. That was a long time ago.

The bray of a donkey pierced the air, followed by an echo through the vale.

Riccardo crouched to wrap his fingers around a shock of dry grass. It pulled easily from the damp loam. They'd had a good amount of rain this winter. The clump of grass forgotten, he stood, replaced his hat, and strolled down the slope toward the vineyards. With each forward step, his mind moved away from the weather and the condition of the fields.

What was happening? His future had once looked so bright—a beautiful wife, a respected position in the community—God's blessings seemed boundless. He hadn't worried too much about the drought, politics, or the world situation. Given time, a year or two, those things could change. But something was amiss. Something closer at hand. Mayor Modesti had been distracted at this week's meeting. This was so unlike him.

Riccardo paused to gaze at his feet, though his mind was elsewhere. His thoughts had returned to the conference room and the faces of the men at the table as Mayor Modesti stumbled through the latest proposal on land use. Yes, something was wrong, but Riccardo had no idea what it was. He'd tried to get a moment alone with the man, but Modesti had brushed him off.

Poppi whistled a jaunty tune in the vineyards below the place where Riccardo stood. Hands in his pockets, Riccardo set off again. His steps were slow and deliberate, almost like a child's. One who had done something worthy of punishment and now must face his Papá.

Had he done wrong? Near the crest of the hill, he crouched for a moment, elbows on his thighs, hands dangling between his knees. "Father, if I have done wrong, I pray you will show me, that I might make it right. I know I'm not perfect—far from it—but I've tried hard to do what's right. Now Mamma is ill, though she tries to hide it, and Rebecca—" His voice cracked, as anxiety broke like waves over his soul.

His Rebecca, the love of his life, had lost another baby. In true Rebecca fashion, she'd taken it hard at first then released it and bounced right back. Or so it seemed. But had she really? And now that Eva could no longer hide her condition, how would Rebecca survive it?

She'd cried herself to sleep again last night. She didn't know he'd heard. Riccardo drew a deep breath and released it. How could he convince her, she was not responsible for this loss? He didn't despise her. If anything, he loved her more deeply. He wanted a child—of course, he did. But more than that, he wanted Rebecca healthy and free of guilt. His heart ached for her. Cut to the quick.

He finished his prayer with the sign of the cross then rose and took a deep breath. No use wallowing in his misery. Tomorrow would be better. One foot in front of the other, moving forward.

The trail through trampled grass brought him closer to the path that led from the vineyards to the stables. He caught sight of Rebecca, her head covered by a bright silk scarf, knotted beneath her chin. A puff of wind troubled the fabric of her dark blue skirt, flattening it against her legs. Arms crossed over her chest, she looked like a waif, pale and thin. His heart stilled as he watched her.

With quick strides, he rushed to meet her. If only he could find a way to relieve her suffering. He held out his arms and she ran into them.

Weary, Rebecca leaned into Ricci's warm embrace. Like a morning mist in the noonday sun, all the words she'd planned evaporated. None of it held any importance. She inhaled, breathing in Ricci's scent—of loam and olive branches, soap and spicy aftershave—then released the breath with a sigh. What if Francesca had been right? What if Rebecca was the ruin of Tres Viti and the Alverá family?

She had never told Ricci what that woman had said to her in the market at Spello. It seemed like a lifetime ago. He'd had so many things on his mind these past few months. Political upheaval, their financial situation, Carlotta's health. Then more recently, Rebecca's loss of another baby.

Somewhere in the distance, an eagle's cry pierced the air. Rebecca opened her eyes and lifted her face to Ricci's. He covered her lips with his own. For a moment, they blended into one creature, one heart. No matter what Francesca or anyone else said, though Rebecca's presence brought destruction and loss, they were part of each other. As he would be so quick to tell her, they would face it together.

"Cara," he whispered, releasing her for a moment to gently frame her face with his palms. "You know I love you more than life itself. I would give my life rather than see you suffer so much pain." He dropped his hands and took a backward step. "I think Dr. Manfredi is right. I think you need time to recover. Perhaps we should go to Sperlonga for a few days."

She shook her head. "No, Ricci. Not yet. Let's keep that for later, as we planned, for our anniversary. Right now,

Mamma is not well, and Eva is …" she drew in a breath and exhaled. "I want to be here for Eva."

He reached for her hand and pulled her alongside as he started toward the house. "I'm not happy with you, you know."

She met his gaze. "What? Why?"

"You didn't tell me. You kept this one secret for so long, Becca. Why?"

Tears brimmed her eyes again. She swiped at them with her fingertips. She had managed to carry this one nearly four months. She'd begun to hope, feel excitement, and make plans. "I didn't want to get your hopes up, only to have you disappointed."

He stopped to tuck a strand of her hair beneath her scarf. "Don't do that again. We must share our disappointments, our heartbreaks. This is our strength—how we survive—you cannot bear it on your own. It will destroy you." He set off again, drawing her hand into the crook of his arm. "About our holiday in Sperlonga, perhaps you are right. We will go in June. We will take Mamma with us. She loves the sea. And …" he halted for a moment, his steady gaze on her.

In the sun's light, she found flecks of green in the depths of his eyes, along with an ample sprinkling of mischief. What was he thinking?

His lips quirked into a sideways smile. "She loves nothing better than a house filled with guests."

Oh no, surely he wasn't planning to invite his friends. "What guests? Who else will be there?"

A chuckle rumbled in his chest.

"Ricci? You said no secrets, remember?"

"Er … only for the painful things. This is not one of those."

She was not about to let him off the hook. She arched a brow and pierced him with a look meant to dislodge whatever secret he harbored.

He leaned his head back and laughed out loud. "All right. I'll tell you. Your friends, the Emersons, will be here to help us celebrate."

Her breath caught in her throat. Rebecca stood still as his words sunk in. The Emersons. Nancy. Robert. "Really? They're coming here?"

He nodded. "Yes, my lovely wife. They are coming. Since the first of the year, we have planned it. We were keeping it for a secret. But you insisted—"

She wrapped her arms around his neck and pressed against him. "You are a wonderful man, Ricci." Then planted a quick kiss on his lips before she turned and started down the path on her own. "Are you coming? I have many plans to make."

Rebecca marked another day off her calendar, resisting the temptation to count the remaining days until the seventh of June. "Deep breath," she whispered.

Sliding the calendar aside, she looked at the tray on the corner of her desk. Carlotta was doing her best to fatten up Rebecca. Freshly baked bruschetta spread with mascarpone cheese and sprinkled with chopped olives and chewy bits of prosciutto. She reached for the white porcelain cup and sipped the strong, hot coffee, thick with cream.

Her appetite had improved in the last couple of weeks. She was gaining strength daily, spending time outdoors in the spring sunshine, working in the garden, and riding with Ricci. She even accompanied the women to the river to help with the laundry. Amazing to think they still washed clothes in the same way as their ancestors. They insisted it was easier.

"The clothes are so much cleaner," Lucia told Rebecca. "And the time together with my sisters … it is a gift."

Rebecca loved the camaraderie among the Campi family so much more than she enjoyed the society of the women at Santa Maria's. She no longer wondered why Carlotta spent her days working in their midst. It was the love and their strong faith that drew Rebecca. They prayed over everything and spoke to God, to Mary, and to Jesus, in the same way they spoke to an esteemed friend or family member. Though she had now been confirmed into the Roman Catholic faith, Rebecca had never gained the depth of grace she'd witnessed here among the servant women. She wondered if she ever would. It seemed an unreachable goal, but she had made a promise, and she meant to keep it. If God ever blessed her with children, they would be raised in the Catholic faith.

She had just finished the second slice of bruschetta when hurried footsteps sounded in the hall, followed by a knock at her door.

She wiped her fingers on a napkin. "Come in."

"Signora Rebecca," Lucia said before the door had fully opened. "It is time. Eva is calling for you."

Rebecca stood quickly. Eva was having her baby. She wanted Rebecca with her. Rebecca had agreed to Eva's request several weeks ago, when it was in the future—but in the present—her courage fled.

"Signora, come, please." Lucia beckoned to her.

"Okay." Rebecca grabbed her sweater and pushed herself forward, willing her feet to follow Lucia. "Has the midwife been called?"

Lucia glanced over her shoulder. "Already, she is with Eva. She waited to call you. Now it is soon. We must hurry. She wishes for you to be with her."

To occupy her mind, Rebecca donned her sweater while they walked. Not that she needed it. The weather was quite warm. Her fingers shook so badly, she could barely manage the buttons. Close behind Lucia, she hurried down the path to the lovely brown cottage Eva shared with Nonna and Poppi.

Lucia opened the door and rushed inside. Rebecca had expected noise, but it was quiet in the cottage, except for the muted voices of the women. Shouldn't there be screaming? She'd always heard there was screaming. When Lucia pushed open the bedroom door, Rebecca's eyes were drawn immediately to Eva's face, damp and slightly florid, but she seemed at ease. Had she already given birth?

Eva reached for Rebecca. "Come, dear friend—" She grimaced then groaned.

Lucia led Rebecca forward to a chair beside Eva's pillow. Eva squeezed Rebecca's hand so tightly Rebecca gasped. The pain of squished fingers must be nothing compared to what Eva endured. Rebecca suppressed a shudder and forced deep breaths, willing herself to relax. She allowed her gaze to scan the room, pausing to smile at each of the eager faces. Nonna, Gigi, Maria—even Isabella, Alberto's wife. Lucia, the only unmarried daughter, stayed outside with the children. A sweet smell drifted through the room, a relaxing scent of lavender and roses … and something spicy … sandalwood?

The midwife's quiet voice directed Eva. "Push. But not too hard. Now breathe. Relax. You are doing very well." This was the same woman who had visited Rebecca when her last baby miscarried.

Twice, Eva tried to talk to Rebecca. Both times, she was interrupted by pains. She didn't cry out, but her faced drained of color and her eyes glazed over.

It was not as bad as Rebecca had feared. No screams. Surely, Eva must not be hurting too badly. But in the final moments, as the baby was born, Eva let out a wail that brought tears to Rebecca's eyes. The room spun and her stomach threatened to give up its contents. Until she heard the baby's cry. Eva laughed out loud and gripped Rebecca's hand even harder.

"It's a boy!" Nonna said, clapping her hands. "Another handsome boy, just like his Papá."

Maria opened the door just enough to give Lucia the news

so she and the children could run tell the men. The midwife bundled the baby in a soft blanket and brought him to Eva.

Rebecca's eyes brimmed again at Eva's expression as she beheld her son for the first time. But that was as far as it went. Rebecca would not allow herself to think of what she had lost. Someday, God willing, she would experience this, too.

"Rebecca," Eva whispered. "Would you like to hold him?"

When Rebecca held the tiny boy, tenderness filled her heart. A love sparked within her breast. She was loathe to give him up. She lost track of time, sitting and watching, feeling, and trying not to feel. Nonna took him away to be bathed and coddled. His name was Alessio, and Rebecca was in love with him.

Chapter Twenty-Four

June, 1931

Only the greatest restraint kept Rebecca from bouncing up and down like a six-year-old as the Emerson's car ascended the drive. Since he had business in Rome, Robert hired a car and driver for their visit. Flanked by Ricci and Carlotta, Rebecca waited beneath the portico as the chauffeur guided his vehicle to the front of the house. Tito and Alberto ran forward to assist with the luggage, while many of the other members of the household staff stood in a line outside the door.

Rebecca could stand it no longer. She rushed forward, throwing herself into Nancy's embrace. Tears rolled down her cheeks, but she didn't care. To her, it seemed that years had passed since last they met, instead of only one. It had been a strange, wonderful, eventful year for Rebecca.

After introducing her friends to Carlotta and Riccardo, she led them inside. "I'm sure you'll want to freshen up. Then we can meet back down here and have lunch on the terrace." She showed them to the guest room then returned downstairs to help with the final preparations. They would have a simple, traditional meal in the shade of the ancient grapevine.

Ricci strode out, stopping to kiss her cheek. Rebecca smiled a greeting. "After we eat, perhaps you'd like to show Robert around the property."

"Are you trying to be rid of us?"

She lifted her gaze to his. "You catch on quick. If he's not too tired, he may like to go for a ride. He loves horses."

"Ah, a fellow equestrian. Well then, I will certainly make the offer. And then you will have plenty of time to visit with your friend." His eyes flashed with mischief. "What will you find to talk about?"

Rebecca grinned as Carlotta approached, carrying a platter of sliced vegetables. She set it down then rearranged some of the flatware. "I hope your friends like our way of cooking, Rebecca."

As if on cue, Nancy stepped outside, followed closely by Robert.

"We're not finicky, Signora," Robert said.

Rebecca stifled a grin as she watched her mother-in-law's expression. *"Pignolo*, Carlotta—they are easy to please."

Carlotta's smile seemed genuine.

Rebecca breathed out a sigh. She so wanted Carlotta to accept her friends, even though they were Protestant Americans.

"Something smells delicious," Nancy said, eying the plate of marinated vegetables. "Your home is lovely, and I love dining al fresco."

Ricci stepped forward and pulled out a chair for Carlotta. "Mamma, come and sit, so the others may be seated."

After they'd filled their plates, Ricci addressed Robert. "If you are not too tired from your journey, we can go riding this afternoon."

Robert nodded. "I like the sound of that. I could use some exercise."

"We have plenty of that here," Ricci said. "You are welcome to take your fill."

The meal ended, the men sidled off, deep in conversation about the current price of grapes.

Carlotta excused herself, and Rebecca suggested a walk. It was quite hot in the sun, so she led Nancy along a path through the trees to the rose garden.

"The roses smell so sweet," Nancy said, bending near one of Carlotta's prize-winning vines. She beamed at Rebecca. "It's wonderful to see you settled in such a beautiful place. Dare I say happy?"

Rebecca hooked her arm through Nancy's as they walked. "I'm happier than I ever expected to be. Happier than I deserve."

"Oh, I don't know about that. I think everyone deserves happiness."

Rebecca eyed her friend. "You would."

Nancy giggled then sobered as she studied Rebecca's face. "You've fallen in love with him, haven't you?"

Pursing her lips, Rebecca nodded. "He's the kindest man I know."

Nancy paused, a twinkle in her eye. "Really? May I assume you're no longer carrying a torch for Robert?"

Rebecca laughed out loud. "I think I'm finally over him, yes. He's all yours."

"Good to know."

At a stone bench, they sat to take in the view. Rebecca pointed out the olive groves and farther afield, the vineyards. "Did you ever think I'd be a farmer's wife?"

Nancy's eyes widened. "Not in a million years. But you're not really, are you? Or is it true what's being said about Italian aristocracy?"

Rebecca drew in a deep breath. "I'm afraid so. Many have already left the country rather than change their ways. If their loyalties lie with the former king, they can be deported to Africa. They lose everything, anyway."

Nancy shook her head. "So tragic. What about Riccardo?" She gestured toward the villa. "It would be such a shame to lose this place."

"So far, we've been safe. He's trying to fit in, but I don't know how long he'll be able to keep that up."

Nancy's gaze held hers. "You worry for him, I'm sure."

"It's kind of a pattern for me, apparently." She picked a sprig of lavender blossom and rolled it between her fingers, releasing the minty fragrance.

"You do at least have experiences you can fall back on," Nancy said. She pushed a few stray hairs from in front of her eyes as she spoke. "You've learned how to economize. That's a good thing."

"That's something I never expected to have to do. But I have no regrets."

Nancy slipped her arm around Rebecca's waist. "We're quite a pair, aren't we?"

Half an hour later, they walked back to the house. Rebecca showed Nancy into the servants' parlor where they found Alessio in his cradle. Rebecca pulled aside the baby's blanket for Nancy, revealing the infant's slumbering face.

Nancy leaned forward to look at him. "What a handsome boy. And look at all that hair." She gazed into Rebecca's eyes. "He must be such a comfort to you."

Rebecca nodded, fingering the baby's soft curls. "I knew you'd understand." She sighed as she replaced the soft blanket. "Eva's been a wonderful friend. And now she shares this joy with me."

Nancy touched her hand. "I pray for you every day."

"I know you do. I'm so happy you're here. Ricci and I have made so many plans you may need to go home to rest."

Riccardo dismounted and held on to Stella's halter as Robert stepped down. When they stood side-by-side, he swept his hand forward. "This is the valley I told you about." He gestured due east. "That stream empties into the Tiber. It provides much water in all but the driest of seasons."

"You've got a beautiful place here." Robert pivoted to make eye contact. "Pardon me if this is prying into your private business, but are you going to be able to hold onto it?" He cleared his throat. "I am a lawyer, you know, as well as a businessman. I can be nosy. Just ask my wife."

Riccardo met Robert's gaze. "You are welcome to ask whatever questions you wish. The truth is … I am in danger of losing all of it, my friend. In this country—at this time—you do what you are told. Dissension can get you very quickly punished. If I speak out or even show my true feelings in this case, most likely, I will be sent to Africa, without a return ticket."

"Surely … in a hole-in-the-wall place like Ginestra, you could go unnoticed? Keep your head down, get through unscathed?"

Riccardo paused then kicked at the dirt with the toe of his boot. He brought his gaze back to Robert's. "I'm uncertain what you mean by 'hole-in-the-wall.' If you mean insignificant, there is no such place in Italy. Not when Il Duce is seeking to tax our every breath."

Robert was silent for several moments then crossed his arms over his chest. "Then you are in a pickle, my friend. Let me think about it, see if I can come up with something of use to you." He smiled into Riccardo's eyes. "That's what I do. I solve problems. It's an inherited trait."

A tiny flame of hope flickered in Riccardo's heart. Could something be done? He tugged at the brim of his hat then rubbed his palms on his thighs. "You will keep it quiet, though? Do not speak of it, even here."

Robert's jaw clenched as he worked his mouth. Riccardo watched the man's eyes as he scanned the valley below them.

Robert straightened his back, dropped his arms to his sides, and faced Riccardo again. "I understand completely. You have my word."

They shook hands then remounted and rode across the ridge and down the path to the vineyards. As they rode, Riccardo's mind processed Robert's suggestions. What if it was possible to secure the land, so that Riccardo wouldn't go down in history as the Alverá heir who lost Tres Viti? Of course, it wouldn't be his fault—not really.

They drew up again, just below the stables, as Robert admired the stand of wheat, still green, undulating in the afternoon breezes. "This is the mandatory grain field? The one you told me about?"

Riccardo removed his hat and ran his fingers through his hair, allowing his scalp to cool. "Yes. It replaces our hayfields. It does all right but was much better for grass than wheat, in my opinion."

"What about corn instead? Is that a possibility?"

Riccardo grimaced. "No, not really. Il Duce insists on wheat."

Robert patted Stella's withers. "I read an article in the paper about his push to become self-sufficient, cut down on imports."

"Yes, this is his plan. But ..." Riccardo bit down on his lower lip. He was saying too much. He glanced at Robert, who gave him a quick nod.

"No need to say more, my friend."

Riccardo halted Lancelot. "We shouldn't discuss business. You're on holiday."

"You're right. As you've probably noticed, I'm not good at turning off the business part of my life. Perhaps you can help me with that."

When Lancelot gave an impatient dance, Riccardo loosened his hold on the reins. "How about a run?"

Robert grinned and called out, "You're on!"

Rebecca and Nancy talked far into the night, catching up on all the news, so everyone slept a bit later than usual. When Rebecca went downstairs, she found Carlotta directing traffic as the servants packed baskets of food for the trip to Sperlonga. Alberto and Lucia would travel ahead in the hired car, escorting the luggage and everything they'd need for the fortnight by the sea.

Before Rebecca could step in and offer her help, Ricci pulled her aside. Hands on his hips, he kept his voice low. "I'm concerned about our plans for the trip."

She searched his eyes for a clue. "What do you mean?"

"There are so many stops along the way. I know you want to show your friends everything our beautiful countryside has to offer, but I am anxious lest we tire Mamma too much. She would never say, and she wouldn't want to think we had changed our plans for her."

Rebecca worried her lower lip. Of course he was right. Why had she not considered this? She'd been too excited and caught up in her own plans. She gave a slight nod. "You choose the stops then. You will be our tour guide."

His handsome brow creased into a frown. "You are not going to argue with me? What fun is that? I was prepared for a battle." He grinned as he drew her into his arms.

"Ah, look at the lovebirds, Nancy," Robert said as he descended the stairs. On level ground, he pulled Nancy close to his side. "There is something about this place."

Ricci chuckled. "It is romance, my friend. It is in the air, and it is quite contagious. Just wait until you experience Sperlonga."

Breakfast was a light meal of dark Italian coffee, cheese, and freshly baked bread. The walls of the breakfast room reverberated with laughter and warm conversation. Rebecca didn't know when she'd felt so content.

"Remember the first time we met?" Nancy asked Rebecca.

"On board the *Mauretania*."

"You'd been seasick for three days."

Rebecca laughed. "Hey, better late than never. My poor maid stayed below the entire voyage."

"How long have you two known one other?" Carlotta asked Nancy.

"We met the summer of '24. It hasn't even been a decade." She glanced at Rebecca. "Is that hard for you to believe?"

Robert leaned forward. "So many things happened in those seven years. What will the next seven hold for us?"

Carlotta shook her head. "One ought not to ask. Taste each day as it comes then enjoy every moment of it." As if to illustrate, she sank her teeth into a slice of bread.

For a full minute, everyone was silent. Rebecca could appreciate her mother-in-law's words of wisdom as she scanned the beloved faces at the table. How dear they all were to her. She wanted nothing more than to slow time during this visit and savor each moment. She broke the silence. "You are so right. We are blessed to be here together."

Ricci held up his coffee cup. "To old friends and new ones."

They all touched cups and drank.

After breakfast, Ricci and Robert disappeared again. The two had bonded almost immediately. When she heard Ricci call him, "Roberto," Rebecca knew they'd be fast friends.

Just before noon, Alberto and Lucia departed. Carlotta kept Tito busy preparing for the next day's journey. It was decided they would leave immediately after a light breakfast. Today, Rebecca took Nancy riding. She couldn't wait to introduce her to Stella.

Nancy's face lit. "Oh, what a beauty—oh, Rebecca." She stroked Stella's neck. "And the saddle is like a piece of art."

Rebecca almost felt she should apologize when the stable boy brought out an ordinary brown mare Riccardo had borrowed from a neighbor. But Nancy seemed not to mind at all. She didn't even wait for assistance, but used the paddock gate to climb into the saddle.

Along the river, they dismounted and stood gazing at the mountains.

"The views take my breath away," Nancy whispered. "Do you ever get used to them?"

Rebecca looked at Nancy then scanned the horizon. "Not really. It's so changeable. Every season, or even every hour of the day can produce something entirely different. But it has always reminded me, just a little, of Perry's Landing."

"Yes, it does. Just a little. The river—the mountains—the yellow flowers. Only our yellow flowers are field daisies and goldenrod."

In the nearer distance, a small dust cloud followed a moving automobile. Rebecca watched it, wondering if it was the same one she had seen several times lately. It slowed and halted near the lower pasture. After several minutes, it inched forward then disappeared around a bend in the road.

"You seem far away," Nancy said.

Rebecca turned to her. "I'm sorry for ignoring you. My mind was wandering."

Nancy laughed as she returned to her horse. "That's usually my game. Though I haven't daydreamed as much lately."

Rebecca boosted her into the saddle. "I don't imagine you have much time for woolgathering these days."

"I beg your pardon," Nancy said, in a pleasant mocking tone. "I wouldn't call it woolgathering. No, it was far too cerebral for that. Who knows? I may write a book one day."

Rebecca laughed. "You certainly have a vivid enough imagination. And plenty of material for one." They set off at a gentle pace.

"Don't worry. I would never write an exposé. I'd change the names." She cast a grin in Rebecca's direction. "Actually, I like the idea of mysteries for girls. You know, the younger set. What think ye?"

"Oh, like Nancy Drew. How perfect. Let me know if you need any ideas. There's plenty of intrigue here."

Nancy gave Rebecca a lingering look. "Is there something you're not telling me?"

"No, just the excitement of living in a dictatorship. The possibilities are boundless." She tried to keep her answer lighthearted, but her heart fluttered with worry over the car she'd sighted earlier. It was probably nothing, just her propensity to worry too much.

Chapter Twenty-Five

Villa Carlotta, Sperlonga, Lazio, Province of Latina

From the street-side balcony at Villa Carlotta, Rebecca's gaze scanned the piazza for any sign of Ricci and Robert. How long did it take to examine the ruins of the old bathhouse?

When an early morning breeze brought the unmistakable aroma of freshly-baked pastries, Rebecca's stomach emitted a low growl. "Good idea," she whispered. Moments later, she stood in the queue in front of the small cafe, a basket on her arm, waiting for a portion of the newly baked treats.

Directly across from her, almost hidden in the deep shade, she noticed movement and heard the sound of an argument between a man and a woman. Not that unusual in Italy, but the woman's voice was familiar—Francesca. The queue inched forward, putting Rebecca at a better angle. She could just make out the dark entranceway where the two stood. Her head down as if preoccupied, she observed the scene from beneath lowered eyelids. Francesca let out a high-pitched noise of frustration then stomped away like a spoiled child. Behind her, a door slammed shut.

Rebecca's heart skipped as anxiety churned in her breast. What was that woman doing in Sperlonga?

A moment later, Francesca nearly collided with a middle-aged man standing on the corner. "What are you looking at?" she demanded when he glared at her. "*Idiota!*" Her gaze swept the crowd of onlookers.

Rebecca tried to make herself less noticeable. She dug in her purse for loose change to give the impression she hadn't just witnessed the scene between Francesca and whoever dwelt in that house. Finally, the woman turned away. Her spiked heels tapped out a staccato rhythm across the cobblestones of the piazza.

"Who is that?"

Rebecca jumped at the sound of Nancy's voice. When had she come down? She glanced over her shoulder at her friend. "Francesca."

After a swift intake of breath, Nancy leaned close. "*The* Francesca?"

Rebecca nodded.

"Next," the clerk called out from behind the counter.

Rebecca started forward then reached for Nancy's hand. "Come, we've more important things to think about. Which of these fine pastries shall we try?"

Later, they sat on the balcony, drinking freshly brewed coffee and munching the treats they'd purchased.

Nancy stirred her drink. "Are you quite certain there was never anything between those two?"

Rebecca dusted crumbs from her lips with a napkin. "Which two?"

Nancy set the spoon on her saucer and lifted the cup, holding it with both hands. "That woman and your husband."

"He said there wasn't."

"And you believe him?"

Rebecca fingered the handle of her cup. She should never have told Nancy about this. But she'd been so upset over it a few months back, she'd needed someone to talk to. After swallowing another sip of coffee, she set the cup down. "Ricci and I know enough about each other's past that there's no need for secrets between us. Neither of us was an innocent—you know that."

Nancy's nose crinkled as the corners of her lips lifted. "Georgio."

Rebecca lifted her hand. "No names, Nance."

"Touché. I haven't been called by that name in a long,

long time."

Rebecca squeezed her eyes shut. Why had she said that? She'd tried so hard not to bring up Nate in any of their conversations. She laid her hand over her friend's. "I'm sorry."

Nancy leveled her gaze at Rebecca. "It doesn't bother me anymore."

Rebecca wasn't sure she believed it. How could one not be bothered by such a tragedy? If someone kidnapped her and left her in a dark place to die, Rebecca was quite certain she'd be haunted by it forever.

At that moment, she caught sight of their husbands, strolling across the bridge. Thankful for the opportunity to change an uncomfortable subject, she touched Nancy's arm. "Will you look at that? Two of the handsomest men in Europe are headed our way."

Nancy stood and leaned against the railing. She blew out a low whistle. "Shall we go and greet them?"

Throughout the morning, Rebecca replayed the scene she'd witnessed between Francesca and the stranger. Was it creepy that Francesca showed up everywhere they went? Even in Sperlonga! And who was on the other end of that conversation? She drew in a deep breath and let it out.

"That sounds like a tired sigh," Nancy remarked.

Ricci took Rebecca's hand. "She ought to be tired. She has not slept properly for a month because she was so excited to see you."

Robert cleared his throat. "Well, she'll be tired of us in a few days, happily wishing us on our way."

"Never," Rebecca said, sending Robert a smile. "I'm so happy you're here. And Carlotta hasn't been so animated in a long time. You've been good for her, too."

Ricci let go of her hand and sat forward, his elbows on his knees. "Roberto has been a great help to me. His good advice may save us heartache down the road."

Rebecca looked at him. She'd seen the two men in several in-depth conversations and wondered what kept Ricci so spellbound. "What kind of heartache are we talking about?"

Ricci glanced at Robert. "Something we will need to discuss fully. Weigh and measure."

"About?"

Robert cackled. "I told you, Conte. She will not let it be. You may as well give her the nutshell theory."

Ricci turned his warm gaze on Rebecca and gestured as he spoke. "She has determination. This is certain."

Like most Italians, Ricci probably wouldn't be able to speak without the use of his hands. Rebecca smiled. He was such a dear.

He settled back onto the sofa beside her. "What are you smiling at, cara? You look like the Cheshire cat in that children's book you are reading to Chico." He twirled a lock of her hair around his fingertip as he continued. "Roberto made suggestions on ways to protect our holdings. He's heard rumors—just rumors, mind you—of the possibility of ... er ... not so good relations between the United States government and Italia." He wiggled his fingers and grimaced. "A little unhappiness between our leadership and ..."

"Most of the world," Robert interjected. "Your husband is being polite, Rebecca. These rumors are not so polite."

Something stirred in Rebecca's mind—Francesca's words—perhaps she had also heard the rumors. "So, what are you suggesting, Robert?"

Robert sat forward. "There are ways to protect your interests, but," he looked at Nancy, then back at Rebecca and spoke softer. "Quite frankly, the less you speak of them, the better. Your husband is right, Rebecca. You should take time and talk about it. Decide what is best for you."

Panic fluttered in her chest as Rebecca glanced from one

to the other of the men then shrugged. Sometimes she tired of being the subservient woman. Ricci may say, "We'll talk it over," but that didn't mean her opinion would count for anything. "All right, I'll be quiet. But it's going to cost you." She gazed into the bright blue sky outside the window then held out her hand to Nancy. "I've a mind to go shopping. How about you?"

The last night of the Emersons' visit, Nancy played the piano. Besides a few of their old favorites, she performed "The Star Spangled Banner," the new national anthem.

"I'm truly surprised they chose that one," Rebecca told her. "I preferred "America the Beautiful." But I suppose they wanted something more unique."

"You mean more masculine?" Robert stood behind Nancy, his hand on her shoulder. "More war-like, to show how tough we Americans are?"

"Precisely," Ricci said then whistled "Yankee Doodle Dandy," causing everyone to break into laughter.

After things settled down again, Robert addressed Nancy. "Did you tell Rebecca about our visit to New York?" He looked at Rebecca. "Next time you're stateside, we'll have to take you to see the Empire State Building. You can take an elevator almost all the way to the top. Can you imagine? There's an observation deck. Nancy wouldn't go. She's not too keen on heights."

Rebecca forced a smile. Who knew if she would ever return to New York? Tendrils of sadness crept over her heart. She gave a little laugh. "Can't say that I blame her. I saw the framework in the beginning and it was already massive. I can't imagine over a hundred floors."

"You've been higher in the Alps, I believe," Ricci said.

"But that was not straight up. I read an account of someone's visit to the observation deck. He said you could feel the building sway in the wind. I suppose it must be thrilling."

Carlotta entered, carrying a pot of coffee. "Dessert is served." She looked at Ricci. "Mio figlio, will you go and bring the other tray?"

Ricci winked at Rebecca before sweeping out of the room. They had planned a special dessert, a cake of several layers, expertly iced and decorated by a local baker. A lump rose in Rebecca's throat. When they'd made those plans, it had seemed such a long way off. Now her friends' departure was imminent. The thought sent a dagger through her heart. When would she see them again?

The sun's first rays woke Rebecca. She threw on her robe and stepped out onto the terrace, hoping for a few minutes alone. Farewells were not easy for her, especially when she didn't know if she'd ever see her friends again. If the rumors they'd talked about were true, a rift between the United States and Italy could close doors. Every time she thought of it, her heart constricted.

Moving further out onto the terrace, she noticed Carlotta perched on the stone wall, gazing out at the sapphire blue water. She'd draped a white shawl over a brown dress. Bright morning sunlight picked out silver highlights in her dark hair.

At Rebecca's approach, she glanced over her shoulder. "Good morning, my dear."

Rebecca scanned her mother-in-law's face. Carlotta seemed so much better, happier, even peaceful. As Ricci hoped, the fresh sea air proved good for her. Rebecca rested her hand on Carlotta's shoulder. "Good morning. I trust you slept well?"

"Oh yes, I always sleep very well here." She patted the flat rock wall. "Sit beside me."

For a few minutes, they were silent, gazing at the water far below them. Sea birds circled, waiting for their breakfast to surface. She drew in a deep breath, heavily scented with the sweet perfume of jasmine and roses. "I love it here."

Carlotta's eyes crinkled when she smiled. "I am glad. You know it is mine."

Rebecca wasn't sure how to respond. She searched Carlotta's face. "I heard you telling Robert yesterday."

"Yes, it was passed to me by my mother. You should know our history, but I won't burden you with it right now. We will be quiet and enjoy the daybreak, before the others are up." She patted Rebecca's hand. "But it pleases me that you love it here. You have become a daughter to me." She took a breath. "I never thought to have a daughter."

Rebecca blinked away moisture, determined not to spoil Carlotta's happiness. Once she had better control over her emotions, she leaned forward to kiss her mother-in-law's cheek. "And I never thought to have a Mamma."

Carlotta giggled behind her hand. "Oh, I am so sorry, dear. I shouldn't laugh at this. I hope someday you can forgive the wrongs done you by your parents." Her eyes roamed the water, as though she cast about for the perfect thing to say. Finally she turned back to Rebecca. "Your upbringing made you the person you are today. For this, I think you may be very grateful, because Rebecca is lovely, inside and out. And she is loved." Her voice broke as she uttered that last. She drew out a handkerchief and touched it to her eyes. "I say prayers for you, every day, and I believe God hears." She gestured toward heaven. "He understands."

They sat, shoulder-to-shoulder, for about a quarter of an hour. A contented silence fell between them, until they heard Ricci singing in his bath. Reminded of their honeymoon, Rebecca gave a little giggle.

Carlotta chuckled and squeezed Rebecca's hand. "He is very silly." She pushed away from the seat. "Well, our blessed quiet has ended. Let's see what we can find for breakfast."

Riccardo held back as Rebecca said her final farewells to the Emersons. He knew it would be difficult for her. Curiosity kept his eyes glued to her face. Did she regret her choice now? Was she homesick for America? Did she long to return there with her friends?

When she turned to him, he rested his arm at her waist. She leaned against him as the car pulled away.

He looked down at her. "Are you all right?"

She lifted watery eyes to his and smiled. "It was such a wonderful visit, but I have to say, I'm ready to return home."

Home. The way she said the word sent a little thrill through him. He led her to the street-side entrance of the villa, where Tito and Lucia were packing the car. Through the open breezeway, Riccardo caught sight of Mamma on the terrace overlooking the sea. Saying her private farewell. It was something she always did whenever she left Sperlonga.

His lips near Rebecca's ear, Riccardo whispered, "A few minutes into our journey home, she will say, 'I shall miss the sea, but it is good to go home.'"

A quarter of an hour later, as they rounded the last curve and turned away from the water, Mamma sighed. "I shall miss it, but I think even more, I will miss your friends, Rebecca. I liked them very much."

Rebecca smiled into Riccardo's eyes then turned to Mamma. "I'm so glad you liked them."

"I did. But it is good to go home."

Riccardo gave Rebecca's hand a light squeeze. "I agree, Mamma."

When they stopped for fuel, the ladies walked to the facilities. Tito spoke to Riccardo. "Signore, may I have a word?"

"Is there a problem with the engine, Tito?"

"No, Signore. I wondered if you noticed, we are being

followed."

Riccardo straightened. "That is not unusual, is it, Tito? Surely there are others taking the same route."

"This is an unusual automobile, Signore. One you might recognize."

A chill wind raised the hair on the back of Riccardo's neck. "You're sure it's ... that one?"

"I got a good look when I turned in here. It passed right by. I couldn't make out the face of the driver, and I didn't see a passenger. But it was a definitely a 520."

Boccali? Hers was not the only Fiat Tipo 520, of course, but the license number—Tito would definitely recognize it. He had always been good with numbers. "All the way from Sperlonga, or did we pick him up close by?"

Tito shook his head. "I first noticed him as we left the waterside, Signore."

Riccardo kicked at the gravel with the toe of his boot. Why would Signorina Boccali's driver be in Sperlonga? Did he have business or family there? Perhaps it was only chance that he ended up on the road behind them. He looked at Tito. "Keep a lookout for him as we start out again. I, too, will watch. Maybe it is coincidence."

Tito shrugged. "So many coincidences, Signore, don't you think?"

Riccardo met the man's gaze. So Tito had also noticed. Could Boccali's driver be some sort of spy? A year ago, he would have considered such a thought ridiculous. But in these days of political upheaval—a distinct possibility.

Chapter Twenty-Six

Mid-August, 1931

Unlike the breathless heat of summer in the states, August in Ginestra was quite mild. Rebecca left the grocer with only a few things in her basket. They didn't need much this time of year. Her weekly errands complete, she strolled across the piazza and down a narrow alley to the place where they'd left the car. Tito got out and walked around to meet her. She handed him the basket. He took it then stepped forward to open her door but drew up short. He looked away when she tried to make eye contact with him.

In a low voice, he spoke. "Say nothing, Signora. Only get in the car."

Odd. "Tito?"

He dipped his head and opened the door. "You must trust me, Signora. *Per favore.*"

Normally, she wouldn't think twice about trusting the man, but this uncharacteristic behavior stunned her. She quickly ducked her head and slid into her seat. There, her eyes rested on a lumpy form in the floor beside her. A slight movement caused her to draw back, sucking in a quick breath.

"Per favore, Signora," said a familiar voice. "Please do not be alarmed. Keep your eyes upon the scenery outside. I will explain everything, but we must wait until the walls of this city have receded into the distance."

Mayor Modesti. What on earth? Rebecca swallowed then wet her lips and tried to relax. But it was difficult with a small mayor huddled in the floorboard next to her.

She smiled and waved to two of the young girls with whom she'd attended catechism classes. Would they remember her? They waved then laughed behind their hands. Yes, they remembered her. She settled in to her seat, and folded her hands on top of her purse, breathing deeply. Going for calm. It worked, somewhat.

Once the road leveled out and the twists and turns of Ginestra's streets had ended, Rebecca waited for some reaction from the Mayor. Realizing she held her breath, she released it and that soft sound seemed to rouse him. Still, he did not uncover himself, but spoke from beneath the rough car blanket.

She bit back a smile.

"My apologies—Signora—for inconveniencing you. But you will see it is necessary. I must get out of the country, and your husband has promised to help me."

"He what?" Ricci had said nothing to her.

"I called him on the telephone this morning. We made arrangements then. I hope you will not be angry, Signora, with him—or with your driver—grazie, Tito."

"Prego," Tito answered.

Rebecca almost laughed out loud but quickly sobered. What awful thing had happened to send the man running like this? "I'm not angry, Mayor—"

He held up a palm to stop her. "I am no longer mayor, Contessa. I have resigned. But only because—"

She heard the break in his voice. He was struggling for control. She had heard of some trouble, but she had never expected him to resign. "Signore," she whispered, "I am not angry, just concerned."

What was Ricci planning? Would helping the mayor somehow injure him, threaten his reputation? Was this why there'd been the occasional car parked near their villa? Finally, the former mayor proceeded with his explanation.

"Pardon, Signora. I am still very much in shock over everything that has happened. Many accusations have been made, which are false. But I cannot fight them. My family has already gone. They left on the pretense of a visit with family in Switzerland, but they are going to America. I will eventually follow."

"But if …" she hesitated. Were they looking for him? What if they found him, and what if Ricci was also deported? Her heart began pounding in her chest. She drew in a deep breath.

"You mustn't worry, Signora. They don't know I am gone. Not yet. In the morning, they will know. By then—I hope to be well on my way."

"Where will you go?"

"The Conte, he has a plan. He said he would be ready."

Okay. She twisted her hands then realized she was doing it and stopped. She must remain calm. Defying a despot head of state was definitely a new thing for her, but if it was something Ricci believed in … O God. She bit down on her lower lip and mentally fashioned a prayer, mostly for herself to remain calm.

As they neared Tres Viti, Rebecca's gaze scanned the surrounding countryside for any sign of the black sedan she'd seen more than once. But there was nothing.

Tito pulled into the drive. Without turning his head, he addressed her. "Scusi, Signora, but you only, will exit. I will then take the car around to the garage."

"Behave as you normally would, per favore," Modesti whispered. "I am forever in your debt."

Ricci stood on the portico as they drew up. He stepped around to open her door. His eyes pierced hers, sending a silent apology. Or so it seemed.

Lucia hurried out, took the basket from Tito, then returned inside the house.

Then, as if nothing had happened, as if there was no man in the floor of her car, Rebecca got out, delivered a quick kiss to her husband's cheek, and began telling him about her day. She could do normal.

Inside, Riccardo directed Rebecca to the study and closed the door. At first, he couldn't read her expression, but now he was reminded of a wet hen. She was angry.

"Have you thought about this?"

He held up his hands. "Wait a minute. Before you say anything, please listen to what I have to say."

Her shoulders drooped. He stepped forward, took her purse from her hands and set it on the desk. Then he turned her aside to sit with him on the settee. She watched him like a hawk tracking its prey. He could be in trouble. Taking a deep breath, he released it and took her hand. "I will give the short version now. Later, when all this is behind us, I can tell you more. Modesti is being exiled. If we do not help him, he will be sent to Africa to serve there in the armed forces. We will never hear of him again."

"And what if they find out you helped him?"

Riccardo had never heard her speak in so sharp a tone. He had to reassure her, quickly. "They will not. I have a plan already in place. He will rest for a few hours in the garage. Later this afternoon, you and I will accompany him to Sperlonga."

"Sperlonga?"

He nodded then pushed away from his seat and crossed to the window. "Modesti will be in disguise." He tried but couldn't restrain the smile. "He will be dressed in something of Mamma's."

Rebecca blew out a quick breath before covering her mouth with both hands.

"It will work, I know it. Anyway, when we arrive in Sperlonga, we will have visitors at the villa. Someone you know—Eugene Lambert—and your mother."

She stood so quickly, she nearly overturned the small table beside the settee. Riccardo made a grab for it and her.

"Mother?"

"It is the perfect cover. They are making the journey by sea in his yacht. They will meet us sometime tomorrow. After a short visit, they will leave, taking on a passenger."

"The mayor?"

Riccardo nodded. "Modesti—he is no longer mayor. The adjutant is taking Modesti's place. Apparently, it was the plan all along."

"Are *you* in danger?"

He stepped forward and drew her into his arms. "This I cannot say, my love. I hope not. But I cannot tell you for certain. I, too, am guilty of dissension. Somewhat. And I have a very important enemy on the board."

She leaned back to gaze into his eyes. "The adjutant?"

He shook his head. "Francesca."

Rebecca sighed. There was that name again. The woman had a way of popping up at the most unexpected moments. Francesca.

Ricci released Rebecca and moved to the door. "Come, we must prepare for our journey. I expect we will only be away for two or three days, at most. But I have directed the servants to pack for a week, just in case."

"What of Mamma?"

"She will be fine. She is much better. The servants can care for her quite well while we are away."

Rebecca said nothing as they climbed the stairs, but when they were in their room, she turned to him. "Does she know—about Modesti?"

Ricci gave a quick nod. "Yes, she knows. The disguise was her idea." He grinned and reached up to rub the back of his neck. "Oh, cara, it seems we are not to be free of trouble. There is always to be something, I think."

She moved into his arms and laid her head on his chest.

His heart beat strong beneath her ear, warming her, giving her strength. "I'm glad we'll be together, at least. And I will be glad to see Mother."

"Let's hope she has good news of her life to tell you."

"I hope so." Mother's letters had been few since she left Tres Viti. Rebecca believed there was a degree of guilt involved. She suspected her mother was living in sin with Eugene. Such a thing was not uncommon among her contemporaries.

A tremor shook Rebecca. She stepped to the bed and checked the suitcase, already neatly packed by Eva. Everything she'd need and more.

But she'd miss a day or two, or several, with Alessio. He was growing so fast. "Do you need me to do anything before I go down? I want to spend a few minutes with Alessio."

"I thought as much," he said with an odd look on his face. "I hope you are not getting too attached, my love. We do not know what the future holds."

Her heart clamored to a halt then sputtered a few times. "You think you'll be deported."

He shook his head. "I am uncertain, as I have said. I will do all I can to avoid it. Believe me. But it may not be enough." A frown creased his handsome brow. "Trouble seems to follow me these days."

It was the first time she'd ever heard him say anything so pessimistic. He must really be concerned.

She relaxed her shoulders and returned to him. He needed her more than Alessio at the moment. She slipped her hand into his. "I've been called trouble before but never by anyone so handsome as you."

He chuckled and swung her into his arms. "You are by far the most charming trouble I have ever endured."

She leaned back to peer into his face. "Charming? Not beautiful, after I said you were handsome?"

He hushed her with a kiss.

A full moon shed its light on the white walls of Villa Carlotta as Riccardo followed Tito inside. After turning on lights and checking to make sure everything was all right, they returned to the car for Rebecca and Modesti.

The former mayor was not happy in his costume, but he had admitted it was effective. He wore a hat covered by a dark veil. Since Mamma had been ill, no one who saw them would question it.

Once inside, the man removed the hat and veil and insisted on being shown to his room so he could get out of those clothes. "I do not know how you women stand these confining garments," he told Rebecca, who sent a smirk Riccardo's way.

Riccardo was proud of her. She was a good sport to put up with Modesti's chatter for several hours. Tito unpacked the basket of food Mamma sent for their arrival. After everyone had settled in, they sat around the kitchen table and ate in silence. Riccardo watched their weary faces. They were all in need of a good night's rest, but it was more than that. Everyone's nerves were stretched taut with worry.

He'd feel much better on the next day when Modesti could move to the yacht. Until then, they'd need to keep him confined inside the house, dressed in servant's clothes. As long as he kept his head down and his mouth shut, they should be all right. Riccardo chuckled beneath his breath. That might be the tricky part.

Even after they'd gone to bed, Rebecca continued to giggle. "It was too funny. That deep voice droning on and on … from behind a black veil. That hat!" She buried her face in the pillow to muffle the sound of her laughter.

"I'm glad you can laugh at it," Riccardo whispered. "But we really must get some sleep."

He remembered nothing else until the piercing cry of a seagull woke him. Rebecca had already risen. He sat up and threw the covers aside then stood and stretched. Crossing the room, he gazed through the open window, hoping to make out a vessel on the water. There were several, but they'd be fishing boats at this hour.

No, it would most likely be noon or later before the Duca's yacht arrived.

Behind Riccardo, the bedroom door opened with a loud squawk of the hinges. Rebecca, bearing a tray. She wore a white dress with navy trim around a wide collar, reminding him of a sailor's uniform, only this sailor had more curves. She set the tray on a table. "I'm glad you're already awake. This door is ridiculous."

"It's the sea air. It causes rust. I'll have Tito oil the hinges later. I was just going to draw a bath."

She set a tray on the table beside the door. "I brought coffee. Thought you could probably use some." She gestured toward the terrace door. "I'll be outside."

He caught her hand and brought it to his lips. "Thank you, love of my life."

"For?"

"Putting up with all of this. I know it hasn't been easy."

She reached up and mussed his hair, which must look ridiculous. Her eyes flashed with mischief. "I've always wanted to do that."

"If we were alone, I'd make you pay for that."

Her chortling laughter echoed in the small room. "Go take your bath." She stepped lightly through the terrace door.

After his bath, he joined her, but she was not alone. Modesti sat at the wrought-iron table, sipping coffee. Tito perched on the edge of the wall, gazing out to sea. He was probably every bit as anxious as Riccardo to see this thing over.

"Did you have some coffee, Tito?"

Tito stood. "Si, Signore. Would you like me to bring your breakfast now?"

"Stay at your post, Tito," Rebecca said, with a wave of her hand. "I'll serve my husband." She turned to Riccardo on her way to the kitchen, which also opened onto the terrace. "Tito is watching for Eugene's boat. I gave him your binoculars."

Riccardo pulled out the chair across from Modesti. "Good. We need to leave as soon as we see the boat." He sank into the chair and reached for the coffeepot.

"I know you will be glad to be free of me," Modesti said. He used a linen napkin to wipe his mustache-less lips. "I'm sorry to have caused you so much trouble."

Riccardo filled his cup then offered Modesti a refill.

Modesti held up his hand. "I've had enough. I'm afraid I didn't sleep well." He blew out an exasperated breath as he mopped his forehead with a handkerchief.

Rebecca returned with a plate of bread and cheese. She set it in front of Riccardo then returned to her chair across from him. "I found him pacing the terrace at dawn. I made a large pot of coffee, and we've been here ever since."

"Your wife is a gift from God to you, Riccardo. I hope you know that," Modesti said.

Riccardo chuckled. "Oh, I know that, Signore. She won't let me forget."

Rebecca slapped at his arm.

Modesti laughed. "And you, my friend, are a prince among men. What would I have done without you?"

Riccardo swallowed the bite of cheese and bread he'd been chewing. "I appreciate your compliment, but this isn't over yet. You may thank me when you are safely away. Don't risk a letter or a telegram. Have someone send me word."

"I will do that, Conte." He pushed away from the table and rose. "And now if you will excuse me, I think I will go and prepare myself for what lies ahead."

After he had gone, Rebecca reached for Riccardo's hand.

He smiled into her vivid eyes. "What's going on in that mind of yours?"

"I'm trying not to worry, Ricci."

Was she actually going to tell him her thoughts? That was new and unexpected. "About this situation?"

"About the aftermath. What happens if—?"

In one swift movement, he set down his cup and touched her lips with his fingertips. He kept his voice low, mindful of Tito's presence. "Don't say it."

"I just wanted you to know how I feel."

He nodded. "We'll talk about it later."

"Signore, she has arrived," Tito said. He stood and laid the binoculars on the table. "I'll go and get him."

Riccardo stood and held his hand out to Rebecca. "Come my love. Let's get this over with."

Chapter Twenty-Seven

Bing Crosby crooned in the background as Eugene Lambert welcomed Rebecca, Ricci, and Modesti on board his forty-foot yacht anchored offshore.

Rebecca scanned the deck for her first glimpse of Mother, whom she hadn't seen in over a year. She hadn't long to wait. Dressed in a white linen day dress, her mother navigated the narrow stairs with practiced ease.

The picture of elegance, she breezed across the deck to plant a kiss on Rebecca's cheek then strode to Ricci and greeted him. "My dears, you look wonderful. I've missed you so." She caught sight of Modesti, now dressed as a deckhand. "Is that you, Modesti?"

His expression reminded Rebecca of a caged animal as he held up his hand. "Per favore, Signora. I am incognito."

Shooting a quick glance at Rebecca, Mother covered her lips with one well-manicured hand. "Oh, dear. I am so sorry. Of course you are. What may I call you?"

He accepted a drink from Eugene's butler. "Perhaps you may call me Bart. It is from my second name—Bartolomeo."

Rebecca bit down on her lower lip as she strode to the railing and stood looking out to sea, sipping the grapefruit juice she'd ordered. Grapefruit juice had always seemed to settle her stomach. A strong breeze ruffled the flag on the mast and almost drowned out her mother's next words. Rebecca turned her head in time to catch the very end.

"… So I am a duchess now." She faced Rebecca. "I had started a letter, but then we heard from Riccardo, so I decided to hold the news until I saw you in person."

In two long strides, Ricci moved beside Rebecca and

placed his arm around her waist. She nodded in response to his whispered, "Are you all right?"

"Yes. Of course." She faced her mother. "Congratulations, Mother—and Eugene. I … am … overjoyed with your news." She was more relieved than joyous, but there was no need to go into detail. Mother would most definitely take offense.

Eugene swept forward, took her hand, and bowed. "I do not attempt to take the place of your father. He was a man of unique qualities. But if ever you have a need, my lovely Rebecca, you have only to call on me." He nodded to Ricci. "And, of course, you are both most welcome to visit us at any time."

Ricci murmured a reciprocal invitation. Realizing she had forgotten to breathe, she sucked in a quick breath. To cover her confusion, she took another sip of the juice. Ricci tightened his hold on her. Glad of his support, she glanced up and smiled.

His gaze probed hers for a moment before he relaxed and sent a bright smile toward the others. "Perhaps you will come later in the year. We can celebrate."

"That would be wonderful," Mother said. "And remember Eugene has a chalet in the mountains as well as a villa in Bourdeaux. We'll go to Switzerland for the summer." She flashed a toothy smile at Rebecca. "You loved the Swiss Alps, remember?"

Rebecca forced her attention to remain on her mother's face though her mind was reeling. How could her mother move on so quickly as though Daddy had never existed? She swallowed hard and gave her mother a nod. "I loved Switzerland, yes."

"I think we must go," Ricci said, his voice low. "Our friend is most anxious to be on his way."

Eugene snapped to attention. "Why don't you all sail with us? We will have a celebratory dinner."

Waves of panic shot through Rebecca. She darted a quick

look at Ricci then relaxed. He was already declining the invitation.

"Perhaps another time. We left in such a hurry, we are not at all prepared for a long stay."

Mother touched Rebecca's face. Leaning in close, she whispered, "Darling, you are very quiet. I hope you are not having difficulties? You must be patient. It is not easy what you are doing. Living in the country, working with the peasants. If you need a break, you can come to Nice. We will always be happy to have you. You can stay anytime. Even if we are away. You know that."

Rebecca nodded then pressed a kiss to her mother's cheek. "Thank you, Mother. I'm fine, really. But I do appreciate your invitation, and I will keep it in mind."

As they were leaving, Mother tugged at Ricci's arm then whispered something into his ear. Rebecca watched him, but he kept his eyes averted until they were both on board the small motorboat that would take them back to shore.

"What did she say to you?" Rebecca asked when he sat next to her.

"She apologized for her former behavior. She says she is no longer having the problem with drinking."

The lofty position of his brows told her he was not convinced, but he would give Mother the benefit of the doubt. Rebecca had seen this expression many times, usually with herself as the subject.

After a short ride in the small motorboat, Riccardo helped Rebecca disembark. She'd been quiet since they'd pulled away from Eugene's yacht. Though she'd smiled and waved, she seemed on the verge of tears. How difficult would it be to see your mother moving on with another man? He'd never had to face that.

He tried to think of ways to cheer her up, but she refused

his suggestions. So he tried harder.

"Let's stay a couple of days in Rome. We'll have dinner in a fine restaurant. See a movie. What do you think?"

Her eyes lit as though someone switched on a light bulb. "I'd love to see a movie."

Tito was glad of a couple of days off. He was happy for the chance to visit friends in the city.

Riccardo secured their hotel room then asked about dinner reservations and tickets for a movie. Later, they sat on a terrace overlooking the city and dined on perfectly prepared pasta and seafood. After dinner, they walked to the theater.

Strolling down the street after leaving the theater, Rebecca seemed almost like her old self, the girl for whom he'd fallen so hard. He smiled as she chattered on and on about Marlene Dietrich.

But it was the newsreel that had captured his imagination. An airline had begun offering passenger service in the U.S. "Can you imagine, people flying from place to place just to visit? Would you do it?"

"Oh, yes. I have actually. Well, it was a small biplane. A friend of mine …" her voice drifted to a whisper.

"You were saying?" He pinned her with a sharp look. "One of your many boyfriends, perhaps?"

She rolled her eyes. "A male friend but not really a boyfriend. Of course, he wanted to be."

"Ah, you are bragging now, I think."

They strolled along in silence until she asked, "How about you? Would you fly in one of those passenger planes?"

He nodded. "I would. Perhaps one day they will fly back and forth across the ocean." He gestured toward the clouds. "Instead of a long sea voyage, we could be there in a matter of hours."

Her eyes widened. "It's so dangerous. So many of them have run out of fuel before reaching the mainland." She trembled against him. "I can't imagine a time when a larger plane could travel such a distance without refueling."

"They'll soon solve that problem. Perhaps in our lifetime, we will see planes as common as automobiles."

She shrugged. "Robert would buy one. He could fly back and forth to New York in a fraction of the time it takes to go by train."

Riccardo settled into bed, ready for sleep, Rebecca curled up next to him. Before he could drift off, she asked, "So what caused our friend's problem?"

He had promised to tell her later. So now it was later and she was asking. More than anything, he wanted to sleep and not talk.

"And don't just say dissension. I've heard that one. What does it mean, and why are you guilty of it also?"

He groaned then turned over and gazed at the ceiling. "Modesti's problems began several years ago, when he was a new mayor. On the advice of a friend, he hired a new secretary. Before long, he was getting a little too friendly with her. It is not uncommon in our country."

She pushed up to look at him. "He had an affair with—"

Riccardo covered her lips with his fingers. "You never know who may be on the other side of a wall in a pensione, cara."

"He had an affair."

He nodded. "Yes. As I said, it is not uncommon. Not everyone has great respect for the marriage vows."

"So, help me understand this. The same person who tried to seduce you, also had an affair with the former mayor?"

He gazed at her. Why was she still bringing this up? "*This person* began submitting unlawful procedures in the mayor's name for other men of her acquaintance. She wrote letters and documentation, which she easily persuaded him to sign. By the time he realized what was happening, it was too late. When he tried to extricate himself from her clutches, she handed proof of his wrongdoing to someone with proper authority. This person sent the adjutant to snoop around. And you know the rest."

"Does she also hold documentation against my beloved?"

He drew her into his arms and kissed her. "You know as much as I do. Maybe she has set spies on us to find proof of dissension or wrongdoing. I have honestly done my best to keep my reputation."

"Other than what you just did."

"Not only that, but I married an Americana. Two black marks on my record. But worth it."

Groaning inwardly, Riccardo faced Francesca's icy stare when he entered the mayor's office on Tuesday morning.

"Where have you been? Modesti disappears, and you are also away." She narrowed her eyes. "Is this coincidence?"

He passed by her to take his seat at the table. He'd known there would be questions, and he was ready. But he'd rather not give too much information unless it became necessary. "I went on holiday with my wife."

She brushed past him to reach her chair on the other side. In normal circumstances, Riccardo would have waited until Francesca was seated before he took his chair, but her thunderous mood this morning made him want to slink away. He hated that feeling.

Perhaps he should consider resigning the committee if this was any indication of his prospects. She could poison the interim mayor's opinion of him. Perhaps she already had. He'd hoped to form a friendship with Guerra by inviting him to dinner at Tres Viti, but the man invented so many excuses, Riccardo stopped asking.

As the table filled with his fellow committee members, Riccardo noticed two missing. Ernesto and Bastione, close friends of Modesti's. When Guerra entered and took his chair at the head of the table, Riccardo studied his face, watching for signs of trouble. There were none. Guerra kept a cool distance. He was all business, with no apparent interest in making friends. Even, Riccardo noticed with some satisfaction, with Francesca. Could it be Signorina Boccali held no sway in the new mayor's reign? He could only hope.

Guerra cleared his throat. "You will notice the absence of two of our comrades. In the wake of the former mayor's resignation, they have also stepped down. I will not tolerate gossip on this committee. So I will thank you not to discuss, either here or anywhere else, your opinions of what has transpired. They are gone because of dissension and outright rebellion against authority. Any activity of this sort will be dealt with quickly. Of this, you may be certain."

A chill danced up Riccardo's spine. His gaze trained on Guerra, he dare not meet the eyes of anyone else on the committee.

Thoughts of Rebecca entered his mind. He was uncertain why. With difficulty, he forced his attention on the meeting while Guerra laid out his expectations. There was no discussion. After dismissing the other members, he approached Riccardo.

"I hope you will forgive my former excuses, Signore, when you invited me into your home. But if you will renew your invitation, I will be happy to visit now that my wife and family have arrived."

Riccardo gave a little bow. "I am pleased to hear that, Mayor. I hope Thursday evening will be convenient for you? And of course your family as well."

"Thursday is good, yes. And I would like to bring the family. My wife, Violeta, is most eager to make new friends. And I have two sons of eight and ten."

After giving the mayor directions and agreeing on a time, Riccardo sauntered across the street to *la panetteria* for a few of Rebecca's favorite pastries. Driving home, he wondered what she would think of the new mayor.

"He has harsh eyes," Rebecca told Ricci after the mayor's family had gone. "And his driver. The man looks like a Blackshirt. But his wife seems pleasant enough. And the boys are certainly well-behaved. Chico could take lessons from them." She nodded her head toward the wall as a soft giggle emanated from behind the sofa.

Ricci grinned and slapped the sofa's back. "Chico, *andiamo.*"

Chico stood, his merry eyes alight.

"I believe it is past your bedtime," Rebecca told him.

Chico started to give a negative answer but paused when Ricci arched his brows at him.

"*Buona notte*, Signore e Signora," he said in a sing-song voice, backing through the doorway.

"Buona notte, Chico," Rebecca called after him. She snickered as he tiptoed down the hall, no doubt trying to hide from Nonna, who still worked in the kitchen clearing the dinner.

In their room, Ricci seemed reserved. He went straight to bed and was soon asleep.

Rebecca lay awake for hours, replaying the evening's scenes in her head. The mayor had wandered through the downstairs rooms, admiring the architecture and paying close attention to some of the older pieces of furniture. Violeta told Rebecca he was "obsessed" with antiques. Was that really the reason he'd cased the joint—an affection for ancient things?

Rebecca sighed. When had she developed such a mistrust of people?

She could almost trace it back to her first encounter with Francesca. The woman had ice crystals in her blood and an ulterior motive for everything she did. At least, that's how

Rebecca saw her.

Now, there was this new mayor, no doubt appointed by Il Duce, himself. But why? To exercise his explicit rights as supreme ruler? Perhaps it was a warning to all his constituents: do what I say, when I say, and don't complain about it, or you're out of here. That was putting it simply. That was fascist government, and she was right in the middle of it.

She'd never met Mussolini, but she'd heard him speaking on the radio. Others of their friends bragged about an acquaintance with him. The sound of his voice made Rebecca's skin crawl.

Snuggling into her pillow, she closed her eyes and tried to force herself to sleep. After only a few minutes, her eyes snapped open. Moving slowly so she wouldn't disturb Ricci, she rose from the bed, slipped on her house slippers, and into her robe.

In her study, she lit a lamp. She opened a drawer and removed a sheet of writing paper. Ricci had commissioned the paper with her initials at the top. She took out a pen and began a letter to Nancy. She couldn't tell her of all the doubts and fears that crowded her mind. She didn't want Nancy to worry. But also, she'd heard rumors that the private mail of certain individuals was being screened. It may not be true, but she felt compelled to keep her thoughts private.

Instead, she wrote of the weather and the crops. She wrote about Alessio and Eva, Ambra and her new baby, Constanza. Nancy would love that name.

It was three thirty when she crept back up the stairs. Finally. Sleep.

Chapter Twenty-Eight

September 1931

Rebecca bounced Alessio on her lap, made silly faces, and baby-talked. He laughed once then stuck out his lower lip again.

Eva reached for him. "He's teething, I think."

"Judging by the amount of drool he's producing, I'd say you're probably right." Rebecca used her hankie to dry a spot on her blouse.

Eva laughed. "Have you been reading the baby book again?" Alessio punctuated his mother's question with an impatient squeal. She settled him on her lap and nursed him. "There, that will calm you."

Rebecca tucked her foot beneath her as she settled into her favorite chair across from Eva and pulled out her knitting. It had been a quiet day. Ricci was in town at a meeting. Carlotta was sleeping off another headache. Rebecca tried hard not to worry about her. Carlotta's headaches came more frequently these days. Dr. Manfredi gave her powders to take, but Carlotta refused them. And the grape harvest was right around the corner. Rebecca's mouth watered with anticipation. Was there anything so delicious as newly ripe grapes?

"How many squares do you have now?" Eva asked, her voice so soft Rebecca barely heard.

"This makes four."

Eva chuckled.

Rebecca watched her friend's eyelids droop. Poor thing, she'd been up late at night with Alessio then insisted on continuing her work for Rebecca. It was too much. She leaned her own head back and relaxed. Let the knitting go a little longer. The ladies in the missionary society made faces at her squares anyway.

A knock at the door caused both of them to jump. Rebecca stood and laid the knitting aside. "You stay put. I'll see who it is."

Lucia was at the front door, talking to someone as Rebecca closed the study door. By the time she'd entered the foyer, Lucia was on her way back through.

"A letter for the Signore," she said, offering the envelope to Rebecca.

As soon as she saw the national emblem on the front, Rebecca's stomach pitched. But she smiled at Lucia as though nothing was wrong. "Thank you. I'll put it on his desk."

With a polite nod, Lucia returned to the kitchen.

Rebecca looked at the envelope, wondering what it contained. She glanced at the clock. Ricci wouldn't return for a couple of hours. Blowing out a breath, she trudged up the stairs to the tiny room he claimed as an office. It had actually been the nanny's quarters when he was a child, but no one needed it these days. She pushed open the door and crossed to his desk where a large brown envelope lay. The flap was open, but she couldn't see what was inside.

It was no problem reading the return address upside down. Woods-Sanderson, New York, USA. She stepped around the desk to double check. After setting down the special delivery letter, she pulled the papers out of the brown envelope and glanced over them. As she read the words on the form, her heart picked up speed until it nearly blocked her breathing. Her hands trembled as she returned the papers to the envelope and put it back on the desk.

How could he do this?

How could either of them do this?

Riccardo gazed at the official envelope in his hand, his heart sinking in his chest. He closed his eyes briefly then reached for the letter opener and ran it under the flap. Slowly, he unfolded the letter and read the contents. He bowed his head. The timing could not be worse.

A creaking floorboard brought him whirling around to find Rebecca, an odd expression on her face. The way she held her head told him she was angry about something. Did she know what the letter contained? He held it up to her and opened his mouth, but she spoke before he could utter a word.

"How could you?"

He opened his eyes wide. What had he done now? He thought back to the morning, tried to remember if he had forgotten anything. It wasn't her birthday or their anniversary. "Excuse me?"

She stalked past him to the desk and touched her fingertip to the envelope he'd received from Robert. She didn't say a word, just arched her brow. She was mad.

"I was going to talk to you about that tonight. It was late—"

"How could you even consider—" she glanced around then lowered her voice. "Consider selling Tres Viti?"

"We talked about this. I told you what Robert suggested."

She parked one hand on her hip and glared at him. "You didn't tell me it involved giving up ownership."

He closed his eyes and drew in a deep breath. Now was really not the time. When he opened his eyes, her face had flushed. He had to stop this before she worked it up into a major row. "I would like to talk to you about it but not now, please. This letter just arrived." He held it out to her.

She pressed her lips together then dipped her chin. "Yes, it was delivered today." She took it from him. Her expression as she read made him reconsider giving it to her. She tossed it on the desk as if it was a snake. "They can't do that."

He nodded. "Yes, they can."

Her eyes filled, her lips trembled, reminding him of a chastised child. "Why?"

He reached out to her. She moved into his arms. He felt her trembling and wanted to comfort her, even though his own mind reeled from the news.

She sniffed. "Why?"

He stroked her hair and held her, his mind racing. He had so much to do and only ten days to get it all done. His gaze found the brown envelope from Robert. It would have to wait.

Conscription. He'd never expected that. Still holding Rebecca, he turned the letter on the desktop so he could see the words, "Temporary Assignment." Perhaps it wouldn't be so bad. There was a shortage of officers to train fresh recruits in the Royal Army. Bari—the name glared at him. He swallowed. Not the best posting, but not the worst either. He'd served with the Alpine Division in their elite forces. They must really be in need of officers to send him so far south.

He cleared his throat. "It's a temporary assignment. Only six to eight weeks. I'll be home in time for olive harvest."

She shook her head. "I don't understand why they need you. You've already served."

He put his hands on her shoulders and took a step back, to see her face. "I am obligated. I am an officer."

"It's too much. This, on top of—that." She pointed to the brown envelope. "Too much." Her jaw trembled. She backed away from him.

Riccardo gripped the edge of the desk. How could he make her understand? He was desperate to hold on, keep Tres Viti secure. For her.

"Let me remind you of Modesti. You remember what happened to him? They took everything from him—his land—everything. I can't let that happen." He paused to draw a breath.

Rebecca looked as though she might collapse at any moment. He reached for her. She stiffened but allowed him to draw her closer. "These papers Robert sent, they are a means to an end. I realize we have never discussed this. I meant to. I wanted to, but it has been difficult for me. I'm fighting it, I guess, and looking for other solutions."

She slumped against him. "I can't believe this is happening again."

"What do you mean, happening again?"

"Losing everything. Again."

"No, no. No." He drew back, lowered his head to peer into her eyes. He pointed at her. "You. Me. That is everything. We are not losing that. If this house, this land, all we own goes tomorrow, we have what is truly important. As long as you love me."

She leaned her head against his chest. He knew what she was thinking. She was thinking it was all because of her, but it wasn't so. She was not bad luck, a bad omen, or a curse. She was the best thing that had ever happened to him. He wrapped his arms around her and held her.

"We are together. You remember that. We have each other, we have our faith, our God. What else is there? These things that burn up and dwindle away? *La famiglia—il mio amore*—this is the most important thing." La famiglia. The family. Not only the two of them, but Mamma and the Campis. Rebecca was slow at learning this. It was difficult for her, but he trusted God to show her.

She turned her face to his chest. Her voice came out muffled. "We haven't been apart, ever. You'll be gone."

"I won't be far. We can write. Every day. Like when you were in America. I waited so long for you." He lifted her chin with his fingertips. "You write such beautiful letters, cara." He chuckled. "Remember when you would devise secret messages within the text? Capitalize certain letters to make a word or a message?"

She gave him a tremulous smile and nodded. "Capital I. Capital L. Capital Y." She giggled. "It was so silly."

"I loved it. It was fun and zany and so … Rebecca."

A soft knock on the door pulled them from their memories. They moved apart. Rebecca turned to gaze out the window.

Riccardo opened the door.

Chico looked up at him. "Dinner, Signore."

"Thank you. We'll be right down." He turned to find Rebecca gazing at him and biting her lower lip. He held out his hand. "Shall we go, mia carissima?"

Heart racing, Rebecca urged Stella into a run, following closely behind Lancelot as he carried Ricci through the pasture amid patches of bright yellow broom. Within moments, Lancelot out strode Stella. He sailed over a rise and disappeared. Rebecca laughed as Stella picked up speed. Then with the suddenness of a bolt of lightning, Stella halted, nearly catapulting Rebecca from the saddle.

Breathless, she scanned the scene before her. A devastated landscape—burned grass—smoke still rising from piles of dirt. What had happened here? The sky darkened as the smoke blended into the clouds. And what of Ricci—Lancelot—where had they gone?

She strained her ears for the rhythm of the horse's hoof beats. Had he fallen into one of those gaping holes? There was no sound, no peeping of frogs, no scraping of crickets, no birdsong. Nothing.

"Ricci!" She screamed his name, but the sound dropped away as though it hit a wall. Something horrible had happened. He was gone, and she feared he wasn't coming back. Panic filled her breast. Something jostled her, sending her tumbling from the horse.

"Becca, wake up—you are dreaming—" Ricci pulled her into his arms and held her.

Confused, she lay against him, her heart beating wildly, gasping for breath. It was a dream? No, a nightmare.

Ricci smoothed her hair and kissed her forehead. "It was a bad dream, cara. This is all."

She pulled back to peer into his face. He really was there beside her in their bed. She had dreamed it, but it had seemed so real. She swallowed and relaxed against him. "We were riding, and you disappeared."

He drew in a deep breath and relaxed. "No, mia sposa, it will be all right. Only a dream ..." his voice drifted off.

She lay against him. His even breathing calmed her. She would like more sleep but feared a repeat of the dream. She'd no wish to go back there. When he slept, she rose from the bed, donned her robe and house slippers. The downstairs clock chimed three times as she crept onto the landing. A chill shook her though it was midsummer. The dream clung to her.

She boiled water and made tea then took the cup to the front parlor where she could watch the sun rise over the mountains. She didn't want to disturb anyone with a light, so she lit a single candle. Its flame glinted on the smooth, brown wood of the radio Riccardo had given her for Christmas. Carlotta didn't like it. She preferred the music of the Victrola. She hated all the bad news that came over the radio.

The clock ticked away the minutes, dragging, dragging. But the days had rushed forward. Ricci's departure drew nearer, like a ship on the horizon, ever nearer. What would they do without him?

Rebecca stomped her foot and squeezed her eyes shut. Stupid. Stupid. Stupid. Why had she picked a fight with Ricci today, of all days?

He didn't want her to go with him to the train depot. How had she responded? She'd thrown a tantrum and stomped away. Like a five-year-old.

She couldn't bear the thought of him leaving at all. She wanted to be with him every last second. Why did he not understand that? Because she'd been a … a crazy woman for the last several days. She couldn't even understand her own behavior.

Then she'd finally done it. She'd riled him to the point he lost his temper. He'd never blown up at her before. Of course he hadn't yelled like Mother and Daddy. He just left the room. Classic Ricci. Then he'd given her the silent treatment. Cool and curt, instead of the warm, vibrant man she loved so much.

Loved to distraction.

Rebecca had railed at him. She'd rivaled Carlotta in arguments. Her cheeks flamed at the memory. She swiped at tears with the heel of her hand.

The study door creaked open. Carlotta stepped into the room, her eyes red and swollen.

Rebecca studied her. It was like looking in the mirror. She bit her lip and stared out the window.

Carlotta approached, stopping beside Rebecca. "I know you love him." She drew a sharp breath as though it caused her pain. "Don't let him leave angry. Go to him."

Rebecca looked at her. "Is he angry? He doesn't shout like normal people."

Carlotta touched her arm. "It is his way. He is like his Papá. Not like me. You know when I am angry."

Rebecca darted a look at her. She whisked another tear away and caught her breath. "He doesn't want me to go with him."

Carlotta shook her head. She drew in a slow breath. "He's a man. What does he know? He doesn't want you to see him cry. He doesn't want you to think he is weak. You get up there and tell him you're going."

Rebecca gazed at her for several seconds then turned and dashed up the stairs. Carlotta was right. She rushed toward their room.

He wasn't there. She checked the bathroom. It was empty. Turning back, she saw him coming out of his office. She paused. He wore his uniform. She'd forgotten how elegant he could be, how—her eyes found his face—how angry he was.

He scowled at her then turned his back and started down the steps.

"No, Ricci, stop." She grabbed his hand.

He hesitated, then turned to look at her.

She took a breath. "I'm so sorry."

He stepped back toward the bedroom, bringing her with him, closing the door behind them. His eyes burned into hers.

The pain she saw in them pierced her heart. How had she been so callous? Of course, he was hurting, too. "I'm sorry. I've been so selfish." She covered her mouth with her hand as sobs rose in her throat. Why must she always cry? She couldn't seem to get through a single serious conversation these days without losing it.

His expression softened as he stepped close and folded her in his arms, leaning his cheek against the top of her head. For a moment, he didn't speak.

Relaxing against him, she listened to the steady beat of his heart. How could she live without this man?

After a moment, he raised his head. He lifted her chin and peered into her eyes. "My love, I am sorry if my words hurt you, but I am hurting, too. The thought of being so long away from you, it is difficult for me. I thought if I could hold on to the anger, it would be easier." He gave her a sad smile. "I planned to apologize in a letter."

She shook her head. "I wish you didn't have to go."

"I know, but I must. It is my duty. But at least I am an

officer. I will train younger men as officers. This will not be so bad. I won't be able to come home, but perhaps you'll be able to visit me."

Rebecca drew in a shaky breath, her heart throbbing painfully. She had this crazy fear that Mussolini would start a foolish war. All the talk she'd heard—could it be true? He wanted to build Italy into an empire. This was one of the things they had argued about most. "But what if—?"

He placed his fingertips over her lips. "Do not say it, my love. You must never speak it. Perhaps it will not happen." He caught her hand and drew it to his lips. "We must pray that it doesn't."

She gazed into his eyes and saw tears. It hurt to breathe. She gripped his shoulders. "I love you so much."

His fingers caressed her cheek as he lowered his mouth to hers.

For a moment, nothing else existed as she gave herself up to the sheer pleasure of his kiss.

Too soon, he released her but kept an arm around her waist as he drew her alongside him. "Come with me to the station. I find I cannot bear to let you go ... until I must."

The train whistle sounded. Riccardo tightened his arms around Rebecca as an unfamiliar ache spread through his chest. "You will take care of Mamma? I hate leaving her when she's ill."

Rebecca nodded. "I promise. I'll make sure she rests and follows the doctor's orders."

He pressed his lips against her forehead. "And you will write to me every day."

She caressed his cheek with her palm. "Every day. And I will do all I can to help Poppi. We'll be fine. You and I will be so busy, the time will fly."

He swallowed the lump in his throat. He wasn't sure about

that. And he couldn't seem to form the necessary reassurances.

Crowds milled about the platform, spending final moments with their loved ones.

After checking his luggage, he pulled Rebecca into his arms and held her as long as possible until the train whistle blew again and the final call sounded.

She looked very small and fragile as he stepped away, her face partially hidden by the train's shadow. He found a seat next to a window where he could watch until he couldn't see her anymore. Until the train rounded the bend and hid Foligno from his sight.

He leaned his forehead against the window as misery churned in his chest. Why did he feel so torn inside, as though he'd never see her again? Wetness trickled down his face. He smoothed the moisture away then gazed at his fingertips as though he couldn't believe it was real. Not sweat from his brow but tears from his eyes.

Chapter Twenty-Nine

Rebecca had never known pain like this before. How had she existed on her own? Could she go back to that? They were minutes away from Ginestra when she rested her hand on the back of the front seat. "Tito, would you stop at the church?"

"Si, Signora." His brown eyes held sadness. He would miss Ricci, too.

Father Antoni wasn't there, so she lit a candle and prayed then returned to the car. The beautiful vistas she usually enjoyed blurred before her eyes.

Tres Viti seemed barren without his presence. Like a shadow-world. Everyone spoke in hushed tones. Eva gazed at her with big, sad eyes. She understood Rebecca's pain. But even Alessio's baby smiles could not cheer Rebecca. She went to bed early and hoped for sleep to deaden her pain.

Her despair lessened over the next few days. She stayed busy, even made an effort to check on Poppi, but he was quite capable on his own.

"You needn't worry, Contessa. I will take care of everything," he told her.

She thanked him and headed back to the house, taking the path through the olive groves. Was it her imagination or did he prefer not to answer to a woman? He behaved with the utmost respect, but his message was clear. He needn't worry. She wouldn't bother him again. She'd watch the workers from a distance—on horseback or on foot. That way, she could tell Ricci what they were doing and behave as though she had some part in it.

It was a gradual process, a daily growth, but she slowly began to step out of Ricci's shadow. She had never expected to become so dependent on anyone, much less a man. She'd been so strong as a young, unmarried woman. How had this happened? Not such a bad thing—she'd love to welcome him home again, but she had to admit, this little bit of independence felt really good.

Three weeks passed without incident. She wrote to Ricci every day, though his letters were less frequent. She only heard from him once a week. He had to be very busy.

Carlotta spent her days sitting in the portico, beneath the ancient grapevine, or on one of the benches in her beloved rose garden. Her energy improved, but Rebecca knew she missed her son.

As grape harvest approached, the air filled with their fragrance. Poppi came to the house to talk to Rebecca and Carlotta. They sat on the portico enjoying a cool morning breeze. Poppi refused their offer of coffee. He removed his hat and lowered himself into a nearby chair.

"We will need all hands for the harvest—she is heavy—" he grinned, revealing a row of crooked teeth.

Rebecca returned his smile. "Will we have enough? Do you need to hire more?"

"I think not," he said, hunching his shoulders. "A few of the neighbors will come. Nonna will cook for everyone."

Rebecca knew the routine. The neighbors would help Tres Viti. Then Tres Viti would send workers to help the neighbors. "Thank you, Poppi. I will let Ricci know about the good harvest."

Carlotta touched Poppi's arm. "It means so much that we can depend on you. We will pray for good weather during the picking."

When Rebecca saw the tears standing in Carlotta's eyes, the slight quiver in her lips, she glanced away to the mountains. She'd cried gallons of tears already.

Poppi cleared his throat and stood, fingering the brim of

his hat. "Grazie, signoras, I bid you good day." He gave a slight nod then turned and strode toward the lane, pressing his worn work hat onto his head.

Carlotta sniffed. "He's probably anxious to be away from these weepy women."

Rebecca squeezed Carlotta's hand and smiled. "No doubt."

As Poppi had predicted, the grape harvest was good. They sent several loads to the juice factory, with ample left over for their private production of wine. This was Poppi's enterprise, and he enjoyed it very much. The Campis held a big celebration, stomped on grapes, danced, and feasted.

Rebecca and Carlotta put in an appearance, but Carlotta soon grew tired, which gave Rebecca an excuse to return to the house. After helping Carlotta to her room, she made tea and took a cup to her study. While the events of the harvest were still fresh in her mind, she wrote a descriptive letter to Ricci, knowing he'd be pleased.

In the fourth week of Ricci's deployment, Rebecca received a short note from him. Disappointment clouded her vision as she read it.

10 October, 1931

Cara,

I'm sorry to tell you they've extended my stay. I will be here at least eight weeks, possibly more. I had hoped you would be able to visit, but it is now not possible. We will soon be camping in the interior. I cannot give you details of course, but I am assured I will be home soon.

I so enjoyed your last letter. It is good to know the grapes are in and the harvest was a good one. Looks like I'll not be home for the olives. Tell Poppi for me to use his good judgment. I trust him completely.

I miss you, my darling...Your Ricci

Eight weeks or more? And he'd miss the olive harvest, too.

Would her fears be realized? Every day, she heard of skirmishes near the border of Italian Somaliland where Claudio was stationed. Would Ricci be sent there next? He'd said he was only called up to train volunteers. But Rebecca didn't trust the government. Only yesterday, she'd heard the Blackshirts had set up headquarters near Foligno.

She swiped at tears then folded the note and returned it to the envelope. How she longed for Ricci's strong presence, to feel his arms about her, his lips on hers, the sound of his voice. She tucked the letter beneath the blotter and pushed away from the desk. It was useless to feel sorry for herself.

The sun beat down on Riccardo's back as the sergente put his men through their morning routine. Riccardo ticked off the requirements and made notes on the men's performance. His evaluation was the final grade that would either promote the young sergente or secure him another round of recruits. After he and another primo capitano had inspected the weapons, they walked back to headquarters to turn in their paperwork.

The last hurdle came next—bivouac in the field—which consisted of three weeks of living in a tent. Roughing it to toughen up the raw recruits. Not an easy task in some cases. Once upon a time, Riccardo had enjoyed the exercises in the field, but these days, he only thought of Rebecca and returning home to Tres Viti.

After the field exercises, the men would be given a furlough before being sent to their various assignments. Riccardo hoped to return home at that time. This is what he prayed every night as he lay down to sleep. He prayed again as he rose up in the morning. Surely, God would hear and answer his prayers.

Letter writing had never come easy for Riccardo. He liked to have time to create perfection. But here, time was at a premium. He did good to jot down a few thoughts each day. He'd talked to Rebecca on the phone a few days ago, but the call had only made him more homesick. So he occupied himself with his work, though it was difficult to keep his mind from wandering home where she waited for him.

The officers' morning meeting lasted until the noon meal. After they were dismissed, Riccardo approached Colonello Provo, his commanding officer. "Do you have a moment, Signore?"

"Walk with me," Provo said. "What can I do for you?"

Riccardo fell into step beside him. "I was hoping you could tell me when I can expect to go home."

Provo returned the salute of an approaching sergente. "Are you tired of us already, Capitano?"

"I understood the assignment was temporary."

The colonello nodded toward an ancient stone structure that served as headquarters. "Step into my office for a moment, Capitano." He opened the door and stepped through.

Riccardo followed him inside. The place smelled old, musty—even though the recruits kept it spotless.

Provo waved him to a chair. "Have a seat."

Riccardo removed his hat and lowered himself into the straight-backed wooden chair. Acid churned in his stomach. He had no idea what to expect. He only wanted to hear that he'd be leaving soon.

Provo lit a cigarette then leaned back in his chair and blew out a cloud of smoke. He narrowed his eyes at Riccardo. "Capitano, you're a good man. I appreciate your hard work."

"Thank you, sir." Riccardo flattened his palms on his thighs, drew in a slow breath, and eased it out.

"Have you ever considered moving up in the ranks?"

Riccardo swallowed and met Provo's gaze. "At one time, I

did. Before my father died."

Provo nodded. "I see. Now you are expected to play the part of the Conte and look after the estate of your father?"

What was he getting at? "I am running the estate, yes, and taking care of my mother, who is not well."

"Right." He set his cigarette on the ashtray and leaned forward on his elbows. "As you know, we are living in difficult times. Should your ... situation change, you should consider advancing in rank. I will vouch for you."

His nerves stretched taut. *Should my situation change?* He studied Provo's face but saw nothing to clue him in to the man's meaning. "I appreciate that, Signore. And I will keep it in mind."

Provo stood. "You may go now, Capitano."

Riccardo hesitated. Should he press for an answer to his former question? He still didn't know if they'd dismiss him after the field exercises. He stood and saluted. "Yes, Colonello."

"Oh, and I'll make some inquiries to see when you'll be released from duty."

Riccardo nodded. "Grazie, Colonello."

The sun had yet to rise, but Carlotta couldn't sleep. She tiptoed toward the stairs, pausing near Rebecca's door. No sound came from within. Moving toward Riccardo's office, she crept inside and found the envelope Roberto had sent. Tucking it under her arm, she slowly descended the stairs. In the kitchen, she turned on the light and laid the envelope on the table. She filled the kettle with water and lit the burner then sat down and removed the contents of the envelope. While the water simmered, she read documents.

Rebecca's reaction hadn't surprised Carlotta. The girl saw it as giving up. But it was not surrender. It was a means to an end, as Riccardo had stressed to Carlotta. A way to possibly outsmart the government. Carlotta could tell Roberto had spent a good deal of time creating this document. He hadn't trusted it to the mail but had it hand delivered by an employee of his office located in Paris. He had taken every precaution. She was impressed by that. She liked Roberto. He was a good man even if he was an Americano.

When the kettle whistled, she got up and made the tea then set the teapot on the table. The moment she reached for a cup, the familiar pain stabbed behind her eyes. With one hand, she gripped the cabinet. With the other, she covered her eyes for a moment, until the pain lessened. Then she took a deep breath and exhaled. She returned to the table with her cup.

Riccardo first discussed the transfer of property with Carlotta while Rebecca was recovering from her latest miscarriage. A woman of Carlotta's generation respected the judgment of the man. It was Riccardo's decision, and she would go along with it because he believed it was best. Villa Carlotta was hers. So he had come to her and asked if she wanted to include it in the transfer. She spent three days in prayer and meditation. Then she sat down and wrote a letter to Roberto. The paper she now held in her hands reflected the intent of her letter. She was satisfied with it. And so, she had signed it. As soon as Riccardo returned and set his signature to the documents, they could return them to Roberto.

There would be money in the bank, and the property would be held in trust. Something Rebecca had missed when she'd first skimmed over the documents—there were two sets. One held the property in trust until the crisis had ended. Roberto would keep that copy in a safe place. The other copy showed only the sale of the property to a Swiss corporation. Carlotta flipped through the pages to find the name. She thought it was very clever. "EmerVera," she whispered.

Setting the papers down, she poured her tea. Balancing the cup between the fingers of both hands, she sipped it carefully.

Before Riccardo left, the three of them sat down together and went over every aspect of the deal. Now that Rebecca understood the plan, she felt better. And for a short time there was peace. But poor Rebecca's nerves had frayed to bare threads. The girl was upset over Riccardo's being called back into the army, as Carlotta also was. You couldn't trust the government anymore to do what was best for the people. They were apt to keep him, send him far away, and take his property.

Carlotta set the cup down and gathered the papers into a stack. She carefully slid them into the envelope and held it in her hands. She wished he had gone ahead and signed the papers before leaving. Perhaps then, she wouldn't worry so much.

Her head throbbed and her eyesight dimmed. Her eyes closed, she began to pray. Worry was fear and fear was not of faith. "I will not be afraid," she whispered. "I will trust in the Lord."

When the clock struck five, Carlotta rose from the table to go and put the envelope away. Any moment, the workers would arrive, and she didn't want anyone asking questions about its contents.

Rebecca pressed her fingers to her brow. Another dizzy spell had left her nauseous and unsteady. Thank goodness no one noticed. The women who gathered in their parlor had come to visit Carlotta, work on their granny squares, and gossip. Rebecca had no patience for it today.

Carlotta peered at her over the rims of her reading glasses. Rebecca tried to reassure her with a smile, but it didn't seem to work. Carlotta touched her forefinger to the teapot. Rebecca took the hint, rose from her chair and carried the empty pot to the kitchen.

Once there, she left it on the counter and sat on the nearest empty stool.

"Oh my," Nonna whispered. "You are not having a

wonderful time with the hens?"

Rebecca glowered at her.

Maria rinsed out the teapot and prepared more tea. She brought the refilled pot and set it in front of Rebecca. "Would you like me to take it in for you, Contessa—make some excuse for you?"

Rebecca sighed. "No. Grazie, but no. I'll do it." She slid off the stool and picked up the tea as Eva strolled in from the adjoining room, Alessio cradled in her arms.

"You are just bored because they won't let you do anymore knitting," Eva said, biting back a smile.

Several of the others giggled. Nonna shushed them, her own face reflecting amusement.

Rebecca resigned herself to another hour or so of total boredom. She refreshed several cups then sank into her chair.

After a few moments of blessed silence, one of the women leaned forward. "Contessa, how is your mother? Does she never mean to visit?"

Rebecca sat back in her chair as the air left her lungs. "We visited her recently. She's quite well."

"She's remarried," Carlotta added. This news met with a temporary silence as every eye in the room fastened on Rebecca's face.

Summoning every ounce of available strength, Rebecca pushed her lips into a smile. "Yes, isn't it wonderful? She's married the Duca de Archambault."

"She's married a Frenchie?" Rebecca wasn't certain who made that comment.

Carlotta shot her an apologetic look. "He's a very nice man, though he is French. And of course, he's Catholic. We can be glad of that, can't we, dear?" She smiled at Rebecca.

This added enough fresh fodder to keep the conversation going for a while. When the ladies realized the lateness of the hour, they got up and began to pack their knitting baskets.

Rebecca and Carlotta followed them out to their vehicles.

Carlotta leaned close. "Thank goodness they didn't decide to stay to supper. I don't think I could've lasted. I'm so sorry I brought up your mother's marriage. I was only trying to help. Instead, I made it worse."

Rebecca slipped her arm around her mother-in-law's waist. "You meant well. And at least, it's out. They'll feast on that for days."

As they turned to go inside, Rebecca's eyes caught on a distant glint in the sunlight. She stopped and stared at it, narrowing her eyes to make it out. A black car was parked behind the cypress trees near the wheat field. She watched it for a moment but saw no movement. Perhaps someone had parked there and had gone over to visit with Poppi? She made a mental note to ask him about it later. Right now, she was sorely in need of nap before supper.

Chapter Thirty

Tres Viti Verdi
November 1931

An odd noise woke Rebecca from a sound sleep. Something she shouldn't be hearing in the middle of the night. She sat up in bed. A car's engine? She reached for her housecoat, slipped into it, then stood for a moment, listening. Had she been dreaming? She moved to the window. It was too dark outside to see anything.

After a trip to the bathroom, she reentered the bedroom. The darkness seemed deeper. She held her breath as a chill danced up her spine—an eerie feeling—as if someone watched her. Creepy. Feeling silly, she released a sigh. She'd never get used to being without Riccardo. He'd be sound asleep right now, but she'd still feel safer.

Might as well get back to bed and try to get a little more sleep.

She turned but struck something that shouldn't be there. Someone, actually. She tried to cry out, but whoever it was pushed a wadded cloth into her mouth. She heard the bedroom door click shut then an odd snap.

A flame leapt up from a cigarette lighter, illuminating Francesca's face. And she was not alone.

Rebecca tried to turn around and look behind her, but strong hands gripped her elbows so she could only face forward.

Francesca lit a candle on the table then snapped the lighter shut. "Sit her down."

Forceful hands pushed Rebecca into the chair. She tried to swallow, the action made difficult by the dry wad of cloth in her mouth. Pushing against it with her tongue, she tried to get it out, gagging in the process. The person behind her looped a bandanna over her mouth and secured it, catching some of her hair in the knot.

She winced at the pain.

"Just until we finish our business," Francesca whispered as she drew a small pistol from her purse and pointed it at Rebecca.

Rebecca opened her eyes wide as her heartbeat sped up. What was going on? Did Francesca intend to shoot her?

Francesca slapped paper and a pen on the table then waved the gun toward them. "I need you to write something."

Rebecca's hands shook as she fumbled with the pen. She scooted closer to the table, smacking her knee against the leg.

"Quiet," Francesca cautioned. "If you do not do exactly as I say, you will pay the price."

Rebecca hooked a strand of hair behind her ear.

"Write what I tell you. Don't try anything or I *will* shoot you." Francesca pressed the cold metal of the pistol into Rebecca's temple.

Rebecca drew a shuddering breath, waiting for further instructions. Out of the corner of her eye, she saw the man behind her move to the door where he stood guard. She couldn't make out his face but assumed he was Francesca's chauffeur.

Francesca bent near, her voice a raspy whisper. Her breath stank of tobacco. "Address the letter to Riccardo's mamma— whatever it is you call her. Tell her you are going away. You are tired of living this lie. You are leaving with your beloved, Georgio."

Rebecca sucked in a quick breath as tears pressed against her eyes. She couldn't do that. The cold metal of the gun barrel now pressed against the back of her neck as Francesca bent near her ear. "You think I won't use this? I am not afraid to do it. But it will not only be you who dies. I will first let you watch as I put a bullet in the mamma's head. And it will be all your fault."

Rebecca squeezed her eyes shut as a tremor shook her. Tears ran down her cheeks. A deep breath helped her gain control. She straightened. What had Francesca told her to write? The facts were beginning to fall into place. She'd had a purpose in leaking the story of Rebecca's first marriage.

Rebecca closed her eyes briefly then began to write in a shaky hand. Only after she'd written the first sentence did she realize she'd just written it in English.

The letter to Carlotta written, Francesca ordered Rebecca to write another one addressed to Riccardo. Her mind screaming, Rebecca did her best to concentrate. At first, Francesca had become angry when she'd seen that Rebecca wrote in English, but Rebecca shook her head then wrote on a scrap of paper, "I always write in English. They would think it strange if I did otherwise." She hoped Francesca would accept that.

"You'd better not be lying to me." She smacked Rebecca's head with the butt of the pistol.

Stars danced before Rebecca's eyes as pain coursed through her head and neck. She swiped at tears and concentrated on a steady hand as she wrote. She must properly convey the message to Riccardo.

The letters written, Francesca left the one for Carlotta on top of the desk, a glass paperweight holding it in place. She folded Riccardo's letter and tucked it in her purse. "Now get up. Do exactly as you're told. Do not try anything. Make no noise. You know the consequences."

Rebecca did as she was bidden. Thank goodness her robe was quilted and somewhat warm, because Francesca was forcing her down the stairs and outside, the cold metal of the gunpoint firmly against Rebecca's ribs.

They'd left their car below the house at the edge of the lane, well hidden by live oak trees and scrub. Before opening the door, the man with Francesca grabbed Rebecca's wrists and twisted them behind her back. He wrapped a length of rough rope around her wrists several times then tied it, trimming off the loose ends with a knife. The dome light illuminated Francesca as she placed the gun back inside her purse and set the bag at her feet. When she sat back again, she held something in her hands. Rebecca lifted her gaze to Francesca's face, but the woman would not make eye contact.

The driver closed the door, plunging them into darkness. Within minutes, they were rolling quietly down the lane and out to the main road where he switched on the headlamps.

Rebecca sat on the right side of the rear seat, her hope fading with the last glimpse of Tres Viti. Weary, she leaned her head back and tried to relax, but that movement tightened the bandanna. She turned her head sideways, but it brought little relief. They drove for at least an hour on narrow, winding back roads. She had no idea where they were. With no sun to judge the direction, she was completely befuddled.

Where were they taking her? She fought for breath as panic overwhelmed her. Had Nancy felt thus at Nate's mercy? How had she survived it?

She forced herself to swallow then began measured breaths. Nothing could be gained through panic and confusion.

The driver spoke to Francesca. His words sent an icy chill through Rebecca. "*Fast geschafft.*"

Almost there—German!

Light flashed as Francesca lit a small battery torch. Resting it on her knees, she opened what appeared to be a flask. She leaned toward Rebecca and removed the bandanna then pulled the wadded cloth from her mouth. She raised the flask to Rebecca's lips. "Drink this. It will help you relax."

Rebecca twisted away.

Francesca grasped her chin with thumb and forefinger then poured the liquid into her mouth.

Revulsion shook Rebecca as her mouth filled with the bitter-tasting stuff. She tried to spew it out again, but Francesca applied pressure to keep her jaws clamped shut. Tears overflowed and ran down Rebecca's cheeks. She had no choice but to swallow then convulsed at the taste.

"Not a good year," she said, wishing she could rinse her mouth to erase the flavor.

Francesca held the flask to her mouth again. "Another drink. Don't be so stubborn. It will help you relax." After pouring another healthy dose into Rebecca's mouth, Francesca rolled down her window and tossed the flask and the rags they'd used to bind Rebecca's mouth. Then she snapped off the torch.

Rebecca forced herself to swallow the saliva collecting in her mouth. A tremor shook her. What had Francesca given her? And why had she tossed the flask out of the window?

The sky lightened. Rebecca blinked to clear her vision. Had she slept? She would need to keep her wits about her.

Carlotta's dream was interrupted by a rooster's crowing. She turned over in her bed. She should get up, but her head throbbed painfully. She closed her eyes, hoping for a bit more sleep. A soft knock sounded. She opened her eyes. "Yes?"

The door opened partway. "Signora?" Eva stood in the opening.

"What is it?"

"I went to wake Signora Rebecca, but she is not there."

Carlotta sat up slowly, cradling her head. "Perhaps she is in the bath."

Eva stepped into the room. "No, Signora. I checked and also the dressing room."

"I'm getting up. I'll be right out." She slipped on her house slippers, trying to push past the throbbing pain in order to think. "Has anyone checked the stables? Perhaps she has gone out for an early ride."

Eva picked up Carlotta's wrap and held it for her. "We sent Lucia to check the garden and the stables."

Carlotta followed Eva down the stairs to the kitchen. "She was sad last night, missing my son. Perhaps she has gone for a walk."

Seated around the table, the women sipped steaming hot coffee as Eva fed Alessio. "This is not like her," Eva said, her eyes on the baby's face. "Where could she have gone?"

When Lucia returned, she held out open palms. "No Contessa anywhere. No one has seen her, and her horse is still in the stable."

Carlotta massaged her temples. The headache impeded clear thinking. "She will turn up. We are overlooking something." She finished her coffee and pushed up from the bench. "I'll go and get dressed so I can help."

"I'll prepare you something for the headache, Signora," Nonna said, her hand on Carlotta's shoulder.

Carlotta forced a smile then shuffled out of the room. Of all days for this to happen. She'd been much better lately. She'd almost begun to hope the doctor had been wrong. Carlotta put on her blue work dress while Maria made her bed. Together, they descended the stairs and returned to the kitchen.

Still, Rebecca had not put in an appearance.

Were they missing something? Had she planned an early errand today and they'd all forgotten it? A quick search of the downstairs office revealed no clues. Rebecca's calendar was clear.

Carlotta stood in the office window, gazing out at her rose garden, bathed in early morning sunlight. She fingered the rosary in her pocket, whispering her morning prayers. Behind her, the door swung open. Carlotta turned to look, expecting to see Rebecca.

Maria stepped into the room, a sheet of paper in her hand. "I found this on the desk in the Signora's room."

Carlotta's hands shook as she read the note aloud. How was this possible? She squinted her eyes, struggling to make out the words written in English. "I don't believe this." The paper slipped from her fingers and drifted to the floor. She crossed herself. "Madre di Dio, help us."

Eva picked up the paper. "I do not believe it, either. Not for one moment. Rebecca would not do this. She would never leave Signore Riccardo, and she would never leave Alessio." She pointed to the words on the paper. "This does not make sense to me. There is something wrong." She gazed at Carlotta. "We must take this to Poppi."

Carlotta blew her nose. "Poppi?"

"Si. He will know what is what."

The tablecloth trembled then lifted as Chico crawled out from his hiding place beneath it. "I will go and get Poppi."

As the boy darted by, Carlotta crossed herself again. Stepping to the window, she watched until Chico disappeared through the trees.

Eva touched Carlotta's arm. "Will you sit down, Signora?"

Carlotta lifted her eyes to Eva's then gave her a reluctant nod. Once seated, she reached for the letter, still in Eva's hands. She reread it, translating as she read, hoping to make sense of it so she could tell it to Poppi. What he could do to help, she knew not. "It breaks my heart, Eva. I am loving her like a daughter, and she has done this? My poor, poor boy. What will he think? He is off serving his country, and she leaves him for this other man. Oh, dear. My heart—I feel as though it will break in two."

She cupped her hand over her forehead. The dull ache behind her eyes had returned. Voices sounded from the kitchen. Carlotta recognized Poppi's low drawl. A moment later, he stood in the doorway, drying his hands on a towel.

Poppi's thick brows drew together as a deep line furrowed his forehead. "What is this I am hearing?"

Carlotta held up the letter. "The contessa has gone away and she has written us a letter. She says she can no longer live this lie. She must follow her heart. She goes back to America with her Georgio." A tear rolled down Carlotta's cheek, but she ignored it. She shook the letter at Poppi. "How can she do this?"

Poppi handed the towel to Nonna, who had followed him into the room. He pursed his lips and stared at the floor.

Carlotta blew out a shaky breath. She laid the letter on the table and reached into her apron pocket for her rosary, raising it to her lips.

Poppi took a step forward. He pressed a gnarly finger to the letter. "What is this?"

Carlotta stared at him. Had he not heard a word she'd said? "It is the letter."

Poppi shook his head. "No. No—it is not our Contessa— she would not leave us a letter like this."

"This is what I said." Eva stepped forward. "I told la Signora it is not like her."

"It is not that," Poppi said, his eyes boring into Carlotta's. "She would not write you a letter in Inglese. She speaks as well as you do." He shook his head again. "No, Signora. This is a clue. La Contessa is in trouble."

Chapter Thirty-One

Carlotta gripped Poppi's arm. "You think Rebecca is in trouble?"

Poppi rubbed his chin. "Someone should go into town to look for her. It's been such a short time. Perhaps she is nearby."

"Wait a minute," Carlotta said. "First, I think we should pray."

Nonna moved farther into the room. "Yes, we should all pray." She reached a hand toward her youngest daughter. "Lucia, call your sisters."

There was no need. The women, listening at the door, hurried through the narrow passageway from the kitchen to join the others in the parlor. Several children followed along behind, eager to take part. The family gathered in an uneven circle around the room. As one, they crossed themselves and prayed the rosary.

Then Carlotta spoke, "Our Father in heaven, show us what to do. Bring our precious sister back to us. We need her. Riccardo needs her." She made the sign of the cross. After a moment's silence, she lifted her eyes to Poppi's face. "Send Tito to town. He will know where to look. If he cannot find her, he must go to the authorities."

The room emptied as everyone returned to their work. Only Eva stayed, watching Carlotta. "May I get you something, Signora?"

"Ask Nonna to make me a compress." Carlotta lowered herself into the chair as her head throbbed. She closed her eyes against the pain. How could such a thing as this happen to them? Oh, my poor boy. She stilled. Should she try to get in touch with him? In her mind, she considered what would happen if she called him. He'd be upset and for what if Rebecca turned up quickly?

No. She mustn't tell him yet. Hands folded together in prayer, she whispered, "Holy Father, helps us to find Rebecca. Bring her safely home before Riccardo need ever hear of it."

Nonna brought the lavender-scented cloth. "Signora, please. You should go lie down. You know these headaches drain you."

"I can't, Nonna. I must stay right here. What if she calls? What if—?"

Nonna settled the cold compress across Carlotta's brow then laid her cool palm on Carlotta's cheek. "You are warm, but this will help. I am going to make you some tea. You'll feel better then. Don't worry. We have prayed. Now we trust." Before leaving, she lifted Carlotta's feet and propped them on a padded stool.

She left so quietly, Carlotta never heard her go. She closed her eyes and breathed in the relaxing scent of lavender. Yes, now we trust. This had always been the hardest part for her. As much as she had resisted Rebecca's first coming to Tres Viti, one would think she'd be happy to see her go. But no. She had come to love the girl, to accept her as family. And she had no doubt Rebecca was God's answer to the prayers she'd prayed for her son. Father knew best when it came to love. While not precisely what Carlotta had expected or wanted, He had provided what Riccardo needed in a spouse.

"Why are you doing this?" Rebecca took advantage of her moments of lucidity.

At first, she thought Francesca might ignore her question. After a cursory glance at Rebecca, the woman began to hum as she pulled on her gloves. Long moments ticked by until her cool gaze lifted to Rebecca's. "You are a fungus—a cancer—

eating away at everything you touch. You've attached yourself to Riccardo, and he does not realize what you are doing. You will ruin him. He will be left with nothing."

Rebecca's heart beat faster, throbbing in her throat. Her vision blurred momentarily. Should she waste her time and effort arguing? What could she say that would make any difference to this vile creature? A drop of sweat ran down her cheek. Hands secured behind her back, she could not even wipe it away or calm the itch that ensued.

Francesca removed a cigarette case and lighter from her purse, opened the case, selected one. A small smile tugged at the corners of her lips as she snapped the thing shut again. Every move seemed studied, timed, as though she knew exactly what she was doing and how long she had to do it.

She lit the cigarette, closed the lighter, and then returned the items to her purse. Smoke filled the backseat as she exhaled, her cold eyes staring straight ahead. "You are to be pitied, I suppose. You thought you could march in here and take over. Make him love you." Her head turned slowly toward Rebecca as she spoke. "Fool his mother into believing you are like them. You would end up with his good name and all his property." She scoffed, took another long draw on her cigarette, and exhaled. "But you are very wrong. I will not let this happen.

"There are things you do not know. Things happening even now, that will wrest everything from Riccardo if you are still in the picture. He cannot take his place in our country's future if he has this … American wife." She spat those last words as though they sickened her before leaning forward to tap her cigarette on the ashtray. "I tried to end it before you came."

Sleep clawed at her, clouding her mind. She pushed her eyelids wide open, struggling to stay awake. What had Francesca said? Tried to end it before? "What?"

Thoroughly enjoying her game now, Francesca chuckled around her cigarette then removed it and blew a plume of smoke. "He did not tell you?" She held her hand palm up in front of Rebecca's face. "I had your sweet Riccardo in the palm of my hand." Withdrawing her hand, she tamped the ashes again. "I knew you could not be trusted as soon as I heard what happened to your coward of a father." She scoffed.

"What an idiot—your father. I offered to pay off all his debt. The only thing he had to do was discourage your engagement. Rather than go through with our agreement, he killed himself."

What? Rebecca's eyes clouded over. She blinked hard to clear her vision. The woman was psychotic. What was she talking about? Francesca had communicated with Daddy? The sickening smell of cigarette smoke added to Rebecca's confusion.

The driver slowed as he drove the car through a narrow, cobbled street.

Panic coiled in Rebecca's breast, squeezing her heart, stealing her breath. She had no idea where they were taking her.

Sounds penetrated her darkness. Rebecca struggled to open her eyes. The splash of water. The thump of oars. Her stomach lurched as the world careened up then down. A deep droning sound vibrated beneath her. Bright lights flashed.

Waves of nausea woke her sometime later. A breeze played with a tendril of her hair. She tried to lift her hand to scratch an itch, but her hands were stuck. Movement sent more waves of nausea. Rolling forward onto her belly, she lost the contents of her stomach.

A fat drop of water plopped on her back. Then another, and another, soaking through the fabric of the quilted robe. Tears stung her eyes as weak and defenseless, she lay in a pool of water and sickness and who knew what else.

When Rebecca woke again, the rain had stopped. She was soaked and chilled. A strong shiver wracked her body. Forcing one eye open, she closed it again. The light was too bright. After a minute, she slowly raised her eyelids. The world lurched again and her stomach roiled. She vomited once more, her body convulsed with the effort. There was little to come up. She collapsed, weak and panting for breath.

Hands still bound behind her back, she lay on her side in some sort of wooden thing. Her mind began to clear. Where was she? Overhead, a gull cried. A boat—had they set her adrift? Waves of panic joined the reeling nausea. The flask. What had that woman given her?

Relief coursed through her body as she stretched her legs. No pain. Using her bound hands, she pushed up slowly, but her arms were still too weak to support her. She managed to sit halfway up, barely enough to get a glimpse over the side of the boat. Water. Everywhere.

She eased back down, gasping for air. Deep breaths would help relieve the nausea and clear her head, but the foul smells in the boat agitated her stomach again. She had to get away from it. Rolling over, she pushed against the side of the small boat until she finally managed to lean her head on the frame, high enough for a breath. It was briny and fishy, but better than what she reclined in.

Overhead, clouds lay in thick folds, hiding the sun and its warmth. She shivered again, teeth chattering.

A strange fluttering noise came from behind her. She turned her head to see a white pelican perched on the bow, watching her. Creepy. Gathering her legs beneath her, she managed to sit upright and then to draw a deep draught of air.

Lightning struck the water in the distance as a rain-laden breeze swept over her. The pelican drew his head down, preparing for the onslaught. Rebecca curled into herself as well as she could, wishing someone had thought to leave a tarpaulin or a slicker. She eyed the pelican. "They didn't mean for me to survive."

By some miracle, she slept. When she woke again, the clouds had parted, just enough to allow a narrow beam of late afternoon sunlight that seemed to illuminate one spot. Hers. Words returned to her mind, from Nancy's long-ago letter, memorized from frequent reading.

As the sun steals through the smallest cracks and penetrates the darkest regions, so the Son will always find you. No matter where you go, or how far away you find yourself, He will be with you ... never forget.

How could she forget? Everywhere she turned, she met someone who wanted her to believe. And how could she not believe? Here she was, adrift on an unknown body of water, left for dead. Chilled, no doubt suffering from exposure, and God sent a ray of sunlight to warm her.

An odd gurgling snore drew her attention back to the bow. He'd sent her a companion as well. Her dry, cracked lips kept her from smiling at God's apparent sense of humor. Leaning back, she lifted her face to the sunlight.

"Okay, God, you have my attention. There's no one around to hear my confession or even to pray for me. If this is the end of my life, I ask you to forgive me for whatever sins may lie in my past."

Carlotta's face drifted before Rebecca. In her heart, she knew Carlotta prayed for her. She'd be kissing her rosary beads and muttering Hail Marys, but she'd be praying from the depths of her heart. Her own heart stilled. Did Riccardo know? Had they gotten hold of him—shared her letter with him?

Would he guess the letter was false? Surely his heart would reveal the truth. She peered heavenward. "Oh, please,

God, don't let Riccardo believe a lie. Please don't let—" Her eyes squeezed tight against the anguish of festering hate in her breast. "Don't let Francesca win."

Forgive, that you may be forgiven ...

The pelican chirped. Rebecca turned her gaze to the front as a chill danced up her spine. Had the bird also heard those words? She almost laughed aloud at the thought. But there was no denying the truth. It was a scripture she'd heard in class. If she truly wanted forgiveness, she would need to forgive—even this.

She felt like Jonah sitting in the belly of the whale. It was probably pretty smelly in there, too. If she could manage to forgive Francesca for trying to end her life and steal her husband, would this whale vomit her out onto a beach somewhere?

Now she was getting very silly. Must be the deprivation, or dehydration, or whatever this was. Her shoulders ached from her arms being drawn behind her back for so long. She leaned forward again and rested her head on the rim. Concentrate.

"If I should die before I wake ..." She rolled her eyes heavenward. "Jesus ... if you could forgive what man did to you, surely I can forgive ... her." She blinked into the blurry distance out beyond the bow of the boat. A movement nearby refocused her gaze.

A man, dressed in white, stood on the water near the front of the boat. "Do you love me?"

Rebecca blinked at him. "Have you come for me?" Her words came out slurred like the voice of a drunken sailor.

"Do you love me?"

"I'm trying to."

He took a step nearer. "Don't try. Do."

She nodded. "I love you."

"Love *her*, too."

"I forgave her. Isn't that enough?"

"Mother."

"I have to forgive Mother, too?" She leaned her forehead against the boat's rim for a moment then nodded. "I can do that. Can you take me with you, now? I'm so tired and sick."

Nothing. Just the quiet lap of water.

The shrill call of a gull pierced the air. Rebecca startled awake. Had she been dreaming? The man dressed in white … she gazed at the white pelican and smiled. "Was it only you I saw?"

But the man had spoken to her. Maybe He really had been there. She wanted to believe He had.

The gull cried again. Wait. If there were gulls and pelicans, she must not be too far away from land. She tried to sit up. Her gaze followed the line of the water now shrouded beneath a heavy mist. It must be early morning, and it looked like the sky might be clear.

She scanned the boat's interior. If only there was an oar. Even a loose board might do the trick. But her hands were bound. The scratchy rope burned her wrists. They'd been so wet, maybe the rope would stretch just a little bit so she could loosen them. She forced her hands apart, but in her condition, she didn't have the strength to stretch the rope.

She backed up to the side of the dinghy, rocking it. "Don't rock the boat, Rebecca."

The pelican stood and flapped its wings then flew away, cruising over the surface of the water, no doubt seeking food.

"Bring me some," she called after it. "I like mine broiled, with a splash of lemon."

Delirious. Evidently. Very, very silly. She leaned her head back and shrugged her shoulders to relieve the tight muscles. Now the rain had stopped, she'd be thirsty. Already, her throat felt parched.

Thrummm …

What was that sound?

Thrummm ...

She peered into the undulating mist and prayed it wasn't a ship headed her way, blinded by the fog.

Chapter Thirty-Two

The phone jangled, waking Carlotta. Before she could rise from the chair, Eva answered the thing.

"Si. One moment, please." She handed the receiver over. "It is the commissioner of police."

With trembling fingers, Carlotta gripped the handset. "Commissioner?"

The man began speaking so quickly, Carlotta found it difficult to keep up. Frowning at Eva, she whispered, "He says something about Francesca Boccali also disappearing. He wants to know have we seen her?"

Eva shrugged then shook her head.

"No, no one has seen her." Carlotta said.

"We will pursue this investigation, Signora," he said, "but I am thinking the two may have gone on a jaunt, this is all. Perhaps you will hear from them this evening."

"But the letter," she said. Too late—he had already hung up. The loud dial tone filled the parlor. She handed the receiver to Eva. "I don't think he's going to be much help." She sank back into the chair and massaged her brow. "If only Riccardo was here."

Eva hung up the telephone then turned toward the door. "Nonna has made you some soup. I'll bring it. You need to eat, Signora, to keep up your strength."

For the first time in a very long time, Carlotta wanted to weep—loudly. She had not been this troubled since … her dear husband passed. Tears coursed down her cheeks. She swiped at them, clearing the evidence just in time. Eva reentered the room, carrying a tray.

Carlotta sat forward, smoothing her skirt. "I should be

outside, helping serve the workers."

Eva set the tray on a table and moved it in front of her. "You must take care of yourself today, Signora. We have plenty of help for the dinner."

Carlotta draped the napkin over her lap. "I know, but this is not the time to have the headache. I must be busy. Who is caring for your child?"

"Lucia is in the kitchen with him. Shall I have her bring him in for a bit after you've eaten? Perhaps he will cheer you."

Carlotta doubted that. "I suppose it would at least keep my mind off things. Has Tito returned?"

"No, Signora. I will have him report to you as soon as he does."

"Thank you, Eva. Now, you go and help the others. I'll be fine on my own." She was hungry. The food tasted a bit bland but filled the emptiness well enough. She pushed the tray away as a knock sounded on the parlor door. "Enter."

Tito presented himself, cap in hand, and gave a slight nod. "Signora, I am afraid I have little to tell you. No one has seen la Contessa since late yesterday."

"I have spoken with the commissioner on the telephone," Carlotta told him.

Tito waved a hand in the air. "Yes, he said he would call. He seemed unconcerned."

"I thought so, too. But I cannot agree with him."

Tito lifted his chin. "I am at your service, Signora. Tell me what you wish me to do."

"The commissioner informed me the secretary is also missing?"

"Signorina Boccali. Yes, he mentioned her to me also."

"Are you familiar with her automobile?"

Tito nodded. "Si, Signora. I know her driver and her car— a Fiat Tipo."

Carlotta knew nothing of cars. She'd take his word for it.

"Good." She sat up straighter. "I think we must go farther afield."

"Signora?"

"Go to all of the surrounding towns and villages. See if you can find someone who has seen Signorina Boccali's automobile last night or early this morning. If you need help, find one of the older boys to go with you."

"Si, Signora." He bowed and started for the door.

"Tito." She smiled when he turned back. "Stop in the kitchen and have your dinner first. Then go."

He returned her smile. "Grazie, Signora."

Carlotta pushed up from the chair and padded to the window. She wasn't certain but sensed in the deepest part of her spirit—that Boccali woman had something to do with this. Had she not tried several times to drive a wedge between Riccardo and Rebecca? And all that business with Modesti. Shameless woman.

Carlotta's gaze traced the cloud bank forming in the south. Storms coming. They could use the rain. She turned away from the window, her lips moving in silent prayer.

15 November, 1931, Encampment, near Bari

Riccardo saluted his commanding officer then dismissed his men. As he strode to his tent, he caught sight of a dust cloud moving purposefully across the plain below them. An automobile, but who's? He approached the lookout who watched the progress of the vehicle through a pair of dusty binoculars. The man lowered the field glasses and saluted as Riccardo drew near. "Looks like an official vehicle, Capitano."

Riccardo squinted. Looked like a Crossley Coupe to him.

The car pulled into the compound, dust swirling as it came to a halt near the makeshift gate. After a brief conversation with the driver, the guards lifted the bar and allowed them passage. The driver got out and opened the rear door. Riccardo's mouth went dry. Francesca.

Before she could see him, he turned and strode off toward the tent he shared with another first captain. He'd almost made it through the door when one of the guards called out his name. "Capitano Alverá, you are wanted, sir."

Why had she come?

The guard waved him toward the colonello's headquarters, a larger tent with room for several tables serving as desks, and their radio communications. With a sinking heart, Riccardo entered the tent to find Francesca sitting in front of Colonello Provo's desk. He saluted as Provo rose. Provo returned his salute. "Capitano, I believe you know Signorina Boccali."

Riccardo ducked his head. "Si, Signore."

"She has asked to speak to you in private—a family matter—of great importance."

Riccardo frowned at Francesca. She kept a bland countenance, barely batting an eye. He nodded. "Yes, sir."

"You may sit here. I have business to attend elsewhere."

Riccardo waited until Provo left the tent before taking his place at the desk. A cursory glance around the interior assured him the communications officers were otherwise occupied. He folded his hands on the cool metal surface of the table and leveled his gaze at Francesca. She wore jodhpurs, leather boots, and a white blouse underneath a tweed jacket. A riding outfit?

She gave him a tilted smile. Her cold eyes bored into his, daring him to challenge her presence. "I have official business in the area on behalf of my superior. So the delivery of this letter fell to me." She presented an envelope.

Riccardo took it and turned it over. No address and unsealed. He lifted his eyes to hers.

"There was no envelope. I put it in one for the sake of privacy."

He steeled his limbs to keep his fingers from shaking as he removed the letter. He raised his eyes again. "You know the contents, then?"

She closed her eyes and gave a barely perceptible nod.

Riccardo dropped the envelope to the desk and unfolded the paper. His heart nearly stopped at the sight of Rebecca's stilted writing.

*Riccardo, **I** am so sorry to write to you in this way, but it is necessary. I cannot go on living this **L**ie. It is easiest for both of us if I go now, while you are away. When you return, I will be gone along with every memory of me. I am returning to America with my beloved Giorgio. **Y**ou know how I have struggled with my feelings for him. Please forgive me for this.—**RLA***

The contents of the letter puzzled Riccardo. Why had she written it in English? He studied it carefully, taking in the shaky formation of letters. If she was suffering emotionally, she would have a less than steady hand, and she may think in English, but she had always written to him in Italian. On closer evaluation, he noticed three larger letters. She wrote with flair, in artistic fashion, so the curling letters did not really draw attention, except to his discerning eye. The first "I" was larger. Then the "L" in lie, and later, the "Y" in you. He chewed at his lip. Just like the old days, in some of her earliest letters. And the date—14 November. Yesterday. How had Francesca gotten this to him so fast? He raised his eyes to hers. Still holding her gaze, he folded the paper and placed it back in the envelope.

Francesca removed a case from her purse, chose a cigarette, and tamped it before raising it to her lips. "Do you have a light, Capitano?"

He glanced at her. Why did she not use her lighter? He had never seen her without it. He found a box of matches on the Provo's desk and pushed them across to her.

After lighting up, she turned her head to the side and blew out a cloud of smoke. "I am so sorry to be the one to bring this to you. This, tragic news."

Riccardo folded his hands on top of the letter. "I'm sure you are."

She arched her brows. "You do not believe me?" After a puff of her cigarette, she flicked the ashes onto the dirt floor. "Or maybe it is the letter you doubt. You are free to contact your home, Riccardo. I believe they have received a similar letter. I'm sure by now they will be glad to hear from you. I can have them send you a telegram."

He picked up the envelope, folded it, and pushed it into his breast pocket. "That won't be necessary." He stood to go then paused and turned back to her. "How is it possible that you have arrived here so quickly, Signorina?"

"I told you. I am here on government business. They arranged a flight for me."

He drew back, studied her expression. Was she lying about the government business? Why would they send a woman to so remote a location? And who, in Ginestra's financially strapped government office, had the use of an airplane?

Riccardo gave her a slight bow and replaced his cap. "Ciao, Signorina Boccali." He strode away.

She jumped up from her chair and rushed after him. "I realize you are hurting, Riccardo, but the least you could do is thank me for making this effort."

He turned back. Two of the communications officers had swiveled in their seats at her sudden rise of voice. When Riccardo's gaze met theirs, they turned away again.

His attention settled on Francesca. Was she completely off her rocker? "I'm so sorry, Signorina. Thank you for taking the time to bring me this news from home. Now, if you don't mind,

I've a job to do. We are preparing men to go into battle. Perhaps I'll receive orders also. In that case, it is good to know you have done this for me."

She grabbed his sleeve and drew him back, speaking in a husky tone. "Riccardo, surely you must see this is for the best. Now, you'll be able to rise in the ranks. You can go home a hero and take your place in the government as we so often discussed. No one will think badly of you. With my help, you will be able to retain your title and your property. With the new realm that is coming, can you not see what a good thing this is?"

Riccardo tore his sleeve from her grasp. He could see it, all right. Everything working to Francesca's advantage. She had him right where she wanted him, headed in the direction she desired. He wanted to smash his palm against her smug expression, but he resisted the urge. Instead, he twisted away from her and stalked to his tent.

Inside, he tossed his cap aside before collapsing on the cot, his limbs shaking. Thank goodness, his tent mate was not there. Riccardo needed a moment of privacy in which to calm his roiling emotions.

A few minutes later, he sat up on the side of the cot and supported his head in his hands. He did not for one moment believe the lie written in the letter. He knew Rebecca.

He raised his head. She loved him with all her heart. And that sentence about Giorgio proved it. Riccardo was well aware of her struggle. And the three prominent letters—I, L, and Y. He smiled and whispered, "I love you, too, mia carrissima, more than you'll ever know."

But there was a mystery here. He drew the letter from his pocket, ripped it from the envelope, and unfolded it. He wet his lips, thoughtful. Why had she written such a letter? Lie—it was a lie. Perhaps she had also capitalized the L so he would know … it was a lie.

The image of Francesca's face drifted before him. His body went rigid. If that woman had in any way harmed his beloved Rebecca—he jumped up, stuffed the letter in his pocket, grabbed his cap, and dashed from the tent. He must find Francesca.

But he was too late. She had already left.

It took Riccardo only a few minutes to receive the necessary permission from his commanding officer to go after her. She could not be that far ahead. He had to find her to question her further. He'd been an idiot to lose his temper and let her get away.

He secured a car and his usual driver, and they were soon on the road, kicking up so much dust Riccardo had to cover his nose and mouth with his handkerchief. Blast these stupid ancient vehicles! There was no protection whatsoever from the elements.

He blew out a breath as they topped a hill. He needed to calm down.

The driver darted a cautious glance his way.

"I'm all right. I just need to catch that woman before she leaves." At that moment, he caught sight of a biplane taking off in a nearby field and his heart sank.

"Over there, Topi," he told the driver, pointing to the field. But by the time they reached the place, only the automobile she'd used remained.

A cursory search of the car turned up nothing. Riccardo couldn't shake the feeling something was terribly wrong.

The sun was high, the heat sweltering, as Topi steered the ancient automobile belonging to their battalion. It bumped along the road, battering every muscle and bone in Riccardo's taut frame.

"We should have confiscated that car," he said. "It was much nicer than this one."

Topi chuckled. "You are right, Capitano."

At the sound of a plane's engine overhead, Riccardo glanced up. Was she coming back? Perhaps she'd seen him and decided to return. The sun was so bright, he couldn't see the plane. He tugged at the bill of his cap to shade his eyes. In that moment, he heard a loud pop like a gunshot. Then another and their vehicle swerved. Riccardo glanced at Topi.

The look on the man's face reflected the fear in Riccardo's heart. His own expression must have looked similar. He grabbed hold of the door handle but quickly let go and raised his arms to protect his face as glass shattered. The car was picked up, as if by a giant hand, and tossed end over end.

Riccardo blinked. Odd, the thoughts that go through one's mind in the last moments … blessed Madre!

Chapter Thirty-Three

After a fitful night's sleep, Carlotta rose and stepped to the window. All was quiet, but the heaviness in her heart would not release her from the need for prayer. She dressed, donned her shoes, and threw a black shawl over her head and shoulders.

Moments later, she padded along the path to her garden where she felt closest to the Holy Mother. Here, she'd say her prayers and maybe ease the awful ache in her heart.

The sun's rays broke over the horizon, warming Carlotta's back. She stood, crossed herself, and drew in a deep breath. Her gaze drifted to the kitchen door just as Eva stepped out. Carlotta set off to meet her.

"Buongiorno, Signora," Eva said. "Tomas has come. He is waiting for you in the parlor."

Carlotta paused. The police. "Tomas? Have they found her?"

Eva shook her head. "He will only speak to you, Signora."

Carlotta steeled herself for whatever the young officer had to say. She had known him since he was a boy. If he knew something, he would tell her. She met Eva's gaze. "You will come with me."

Eva nodded and followed close behind her.

Tomas stood looking out the front window, his back to the door. He thumped his cap against his thigh.

Carlotta stepped through the doorway. "Tomas?"

He turned and dipped his head. "Signora Alverá, I have good news, we have located the young contessa. However, she is in the hospital in Perugia."

Carlotta drew in a quick breath. "Is she all right?"

"All I can tell you is, she is in guarded condition."

"What does that mean—guarded condition?"

He pulled out a notebook and opened it. "Dehydration, exposure, possible drug overdose."

Carlotta's jaw went slack as she stared at him. "But Rebecca does not take any drugs, Tomas."

He looked up from the notepad and shook his head. "No, Signora, most likely this person who allegedly abducted the contessa may have drugged her. This is what they think."

"They?"

He shrugged as if to apologize. "Since she was rescued near Perugia, their police force is handling the case. But they will know more once the contessa has regained consciousness."

"She's unconscious?" She repeated the words to Eva, who covered her mouth with both hands.

Carlotta faced the window, trying to bring her emotions under control. She grabbed at her pockets, seeking a handkerchief, then blew her nose before turning back around. Behind Eva, the entire kitchen staff waited. Carlotta had not heard their approach.

Nonna pressed through to join her.

Tomas took this opportunity to make his escape.

When Carlotta felt able to speak, she turned to Nonna. "Has Tito returned?"

Nonna gave an affirmative nod. "He has. Gigi, have him bring the car at once." She turned her attention back to Carlotta. "Signora, let me help you upstairs. You must get ready. Perugia is a long drive."

"I want to go too, please—" Eva touched Carlotta's arm.

"Of course," Carlotta whispered, happy to have someone accompany her. Like an obedient child, she took Nonna's arm and followed her up the stairs.

Thirty minutes later, Carlotta and Eva climbed into the car.

"It is like a dream," Carlotta said. "I don't know what to

think. If only Riccardo was home."

Eva patted her hand. "If the conte was home, this would never have happened."

Carlotta had to agree. "You are right."

The drive seemed so much longer than usual. Carlotta tried to ignore the dizziness as Tito navigated the narrow roads. She covered her lips with a folded hankie. Could she make it until they arrived? The more she tried to relax, the more nervous she became. Her head pounded, lights flashed before her eyes. She had to keep her wits about her. More than anything, she wished for Riccardo. She pulled out her rosary. Eva joined her. They prayed together until they reached the outskirts of Perugia.

The ancient, white building that housed the hospital loomed ahead. Tito dropped them off and left to find a place for the car.

A very kind sister led the two women to a waiting area. "Remain here. I will go and get Dr. Cozetti."

A young man, Dr. Cozetti, stood only a couple of inches taller than Eva. He smiled, but his eyes revealed weariness. "Your daughter is suffering from exposure and dehydration. We are still running some tests. It appears as though she was drugged. Her rescuers told us her hands were bound when they found her. She was in a small boat on Lake Trasimeno."

"She was taken from our home night before last," Carlotta told him. "We have been looking everywhere for her. The police were not at all helpful."

The doctor shook his head. "I'm so sorry. She has been asleep most of the time since she arrived here. But her rescuers said she was mumbling about Jesus and Francesca."

"Francesca," Carlotta said, glaring at Eva. "I knew that woman had something to do with this."

"Please, Signora, do not excite yourself," Eva said, rubbing Carlotta's arm. She looked at the doctor. "You said she was drugged?"

He nodded, glancing through the papers in his hand. "Most likely, it was some form of opiate. We are not entirely certain. She was found lying in … I beg pardon, signoras … filth, partly vomit. But vomiting may have saved her life." He shifted from one foot to the other. "When she is awake, we will send for you."

Carlotta drew in a quick breath and stepped forward. "She will be all right?"

The doctor nodded. "I believe she will make a full recovery, yes."

As Dr. Cozetti walked away, Carlotta noticed Tito, standing in the corridor, holding his hat. She waved for him to join them. "We must wait, but if it is too long, Tito, you must take Eva back to her baby. I can stay."

"You should go with us," Eva whispered. "They will most likely keep her a day or two. You can return after you've had a good night's sleep."

Carlotta shook her head. "No, my dear. I will stay." She looked from Eva to Tito then back to Eva. "If they say she must remain, I can go to my sister's. She is not far."

Eva nodded. "Should we try and contact your son?"

Carlotta considered Eva's question. Perhaps, if his superiors knew of this incident, they would allow him to come home. But by the time he received the message, there would be no need. Since the doctor said Rebecca would make a full recovery, perhaps it was best not to—he would only worry. "I think no, because I don't wish to upset him. He has much to think about where he is. When we are home again, then we can write to him."

Eva nodded. "Whatever you think. Does your sister have a telephone? Do you wish for me to call her?"

Carlotta sat and settled her purse on her lap. "She has no phone, but Tito knows where she lives. When you leave, you can go by there and give her the message."

After waiting nearly an hour, Tito left to find them something to eat. When he returned, one of the sisters led them to a quiet spot in the garden where they could enjoy the food.

She assured them Rebecca was sleeping peacefully. "Someone will come for you as soon as she wakes."

"… Deliver us from evil. For thine is the kingdom and the power and the glory forever … Amen."

Rebecca heard a man's voice praying. A priest? She tried to wake up but couldn't. Panic flooded through her. She was suffocating. *Am I dying? Are they saying last rites over me? Oh, God—I'm not ready—I thought I was. But to never see Ricci again.* Her breath came out as a sob.

A hand gripped hers. Warmth. *I'm not dead. I'm not dead.*

Peace spread from her head to her toes. She opened her eyes to a large room filled with light.

A nun in a white habit stood looking down at her. She had very kind eyes. "How do you feel, Signora Alverá?"

The woman knew her name. Rebecca swallowed. Her throat was parched and sore. "Thirsty."

The sister turned away for a moment. Rebecca heard the sound of water being poured into a glass. Then the nun returned to help Rebecca drink it. It tasted wonderful. Cool, refreshing water. So much nicer than that awful wine Francesca had forced down her throat.

"Now, if you are comfortable enough, I will go and get your family. They are waiting to see you."

Rebecca tried to make sense of the woman's words. Her family? Was Ricci here? Mother? Surely not. But before she could organize her thoughts, the woman had gone.

She tried to push herself up, but the effort left her dizzy and tired and confused. She lay back down, but not before she'd seen the other beds. She was on a ward. And just across the way, a man talked quietly with another patient. He was the one who'd prayed. She recognized his voice. Was he a priest? Would he also visit her?

Hurried footsteps sounded nearby. Carlotta appeared beside her bed. Then another kind face hovered over Rebecca. She smiled into Eva's eyes. "Eva—" then turned to Carlotta. "Carlotta."

Carlotta bent to kiss her cheek. "My dear, we have been so worried for you."

"You mustn't worry, remember?" Rebecca reminded her. "Always pray about all things."

Eva chuckled. "We have taught you well, I think. How are you feeling, my friend?"

"I've been better."

"Do you remember what happened to you?" Carlotta whispered.

Rebecca frowned. "Francesca had a gun. And that awful man. He's German, I think."

It was Carlotta's turn to frown. "What awful man?"

"Francesca's driver. They communicated in German. They didn't know I understood." She grinned at Eva. "I'm ambidextrous."

Eva giggled. "I think you mean you are a polyglot— multilingual."

Rebecca tried to concentrate, but her mind wasn't cooperating. "Possibly."

Carlotta patted her shoulder. "You mustn't tire yourself. A policeman is coming to speak to you, so I think we must go. But we'll be close by, cara."

The loving faces of her family were soon replaced by that of a stranger. A thickset man in a brown suit brought a chair and sat down beside her bed. Dark eyes, rugged face, salt-and-pepper hair. The smell of cigarette smoke and body odor assaulted Rebecca's nostrils.

"I am Inspector Rossi, Contessa. I am here to ask you some questions regarding your recent experience. I am told by your family you were abducted from your home by force. You will please tell me about it?"

Rebecca told him her story as well as she could.

He made notes in a small, black book. After Rebecca told him all she remembered, he asked questions. "Why Trasimeno? Is there some significance to that?"

"I had no idea where I was, but no. I have never visited Lake Trasimeno." Weariness crept over her, a result of his constant prodding, but she fought it. She hoped for answers. Why had Francesca done this?

But when the inspector had finished, he rose to go, shoving the pad and pencil into his jacket pocket. *"Arrivederci,* Contessa."

"Inspector, please—what will happen now?"

As he donned his hat, he worked his lips as if he mulled over his answer. "We will investigate this. If I need anything further from you, I know where to find you."

Would they ever know the answer? Perhaps the woman had gone crazy. She couldn't lure Ricci away from Rebecca, so she'd tried to murder Rebecca and make it look like she'd run off with Giorgio. Perhaps Francesca never expected the boat to be found before it contained a skeleton. But Rebecca had outsmarted her. Or maybe that really was the Savior out there on the water. Or possibly an angel—her guardian angel. She smiled at the memory of the pelican.

Her eyelids drooped as sleep overtook her. Maybe she'd wake up and find it all a dream.

A chill coursed through Rebecca as she listened to Dr. Cozetti's summary of findings. "It is apparent to me, and to those who have examined these reports, you were never meant to survive this attack, Contessa." He glanced from one to the other before flipping to the next page of his chart.

"Most amazing of all, your child is also fine. I think we are seeing a miracle."

Rebecca's gaze flitted to Carlotta's face, where a slow smile lit her countenance. No hiding it this time. *Sweet Jesus, please don't break her heart again.*

Rebecca hadn't known she was expecting. She hadn't even been sick, just tired and confused sometimes. And so emotional. Now she understood why.

The doctor's words reverberated in Rebecca's mind as she dressed in the clothes Eva sent. Her favorite blue dress, her everyday undergarments, seemed foreign to her. Part of another life. A life that had nearly ended just a few days earlier.

And she could not forget the encounter on the water. The visitor in white. It had seemed so real. Her heart warmed at the memory and threatened to overflow with love. She suspected her family may attribute it to the drug she'd been given. Perhaps it was, but she chose to believe it was real, so she kept it to herself.

The sun warmed her face as she walked out the front doors of the hospital onto the street.

Tito ran forward to assist her. "I am so thankful you are well, Contessa."

"Thank you, Tito."

Carlotta patted her hand and smiled. "I know you must be as happy as I am to be going home." Carlotta had spent her evenings with her sister. Each day, she returned to the hospital. Sometimes her sister came also, but most of the time, Carlotta came alone.

Though Rebecca suffered guilt over it, Carlotta seemed happy.

"It is good to have time away," she'd told Rebecca. "Good

to be needed. And when we return, it will not be many days before our Riccardo will come back, and we will be a family again."

Rebecca rubbed her wrists, still sore from the rope burns. She couldn't understand why they hadn't heard from Ricci. Had he received that awful letter and believed it? But no—she remembered Carlotta telling her—they'd sent him a telegram after they knew she'd recover. He knew, so why had he not come to her? Surely in such a case as this, the army would release him or at least give him a few days off.

Tito threaded the car through noonday traffic outside the city. Traffic that included hand-pulled carts, donkey carts, and ox-drawn wagons, as the farmers headed back to their homes.

"I spoke with the fisherman who rescued you," Carlotta said.

Rebecca looked at her. "The fisherman?"

"Yes, he stopped by the hospital this morning to see how you were doing. He said a large pelican drew his attention to the dinghy, and he was able to swerve just in time. Then they circled back and found you, unconscious."

Rebecca gave a little chuckle. Had the pelican saved her life? "I remember a boat. I thought it was going to hit me."

"The man was very happy to learn you were going to be all right. He was worried since you kept talking about Jesus. He thought you may be close to death." She reached for Rebecca's hand and gave it a squeeze. "I know God was looking out for you. I'm so glad you were spared. I've had such a bad feeling in my heart of hearts."

Rebecca turned to look out the window. So had she. As though their world had changed and would never right itself. If only Ricci were here to hold her. She closed her eyes as longing consumed her.

She had hoped to remain awake, to let her eyes feast on the beautiful countryside nearer home, but Rebecca's eyelids soon grew heavy. She woke when Tito opened the door.

"We have arrived, Contessa."

Eva was there, ready to help her out of the car. She gathered Rebecca into a loose hug, as if she feared hurting her. "You don't know how happy we are to welcome you home. Everyone was so worried."

Rebecca kissed her cheek. "Grazie, Eva." She looked at all the other smiling faces flanking the front of the house. "Grazie—it's so wonderful to be home."

Carlotta had also fallen asleep so Tito helped her inside the house. Eva made them both comfortable in the parlor then left to bring refreshments. Rebecca hoped it included Nonna's raisin cakes. She'd not been allowed sweets for the last several days.

Carlotta wiggled her toes as she sipped hot coffee. "It is so good to be home. I only wish for Riccardo." She set the cup down. "I can't stop thinking of him."

Rebecca swallowed the lump that rose in her throat at the mention of his name. "I know. I wish we could hear from him. I thought perhaps there'd be a letter, but Eva said no."

"It has been overlong, which leads me to believe they may be someplace inaccessible." She touched her pocket where she kept her rosary.

Rebecca knew she was saying a silent prayer.

Something was definitely wrong. The uneasiness returned as soon as Rebecca woke. She gazed at the ceiling and whispered a prayer for Ricci. Where was he? Why had she not heard from him?

She had never desired or expected to be a soldier's wife.

"Don't get up," Eva said as she entered, carrying a tray. "Well, unless you have to. I've brought you breakfast in bed."

Rebecca allowed Eva to fluff her pillows and adjust the bedclothes. Then she positioned the tray and sat on the chair beside the bed. Rebecca gazed at her friend, noting the shadowy circles beneath her eyes. "You don't have to do this. I am quite well."

"I know," Eva said.

"Besides, you are more tired than I."

Eva sighed. "Alessio was awake too much last night."

"I hope he's all right?"

"Oh, yes, just fretful. He's sleeping soundly now."

"Why don't you take a nap while he's resting? You'll be no help to anyone if you're tired."

She shrugged her shoulders. "Maybe later."

After a leisurely breakfast, Eva helped Rebecca dress and prepare for the day. Rebecca descended the stairs with a smile on her face, ready for whatever mess awaited her in the study. She had carefully avoided it since her return.

Everything was as she left it. A few more letters lay in a neat stack. She organized the envelopes according to importance. Most were bills that needed her attention. There was a letter from Mother. She placed that aside to read later, since she was fairly certain it would rankle her.

She was just thinking of paying a visit to the kitchen when she heard noises outside. Eva, her face pale, and eyes bright with emotion, hurried in. "Andiamo, Rebecca—it is an official vehicle."

An official vehicle. Rebecca stared at her. What did she mean by that?

"Andiamo!" Eva insisted, waving her forward.

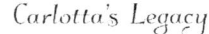

Chapter Thirty-Four

Rebecca forced her feet to move. When she crossed the threshold onto the portico, she understood Eva's alarm. A black sedan with the national symbol on the side advanced along the drive toward the house. Something had happened to Riccardo—or Claudio. She glanced at Eva.

Was it silly of them to presume the worst? She pressed her hand to the base of her throat, willing herself to breathe.

Eva gripped her arm.

Behind her, Rebecca heard a swift intake of breath. She turned to find Carlotta, her face contorted with emotion. Rebecca pulled her close. "Have faith, Carlotta."

The car pulled up and stopped near the steps. The driver got out and moved to the rear door, opened it, and reached inside to assist someone.

Tito ran forward to help.

Rebecca kept her eyes pinned to Tito's face, noting the slight hesitancy when he reached the car. He gave no other indication. A moment later, the two men had the occupant on unsteady feet. A white bandage covered most of his forehead. His shoulders slumped forward, his arm bound to his body by a sling and straps.

Rebecca's throat constricted. She could barely breathe as she pulled away from Carlotta and out of Eva's grasp. "Ricci!"

She stumbled—Eva caught her—but not before she made eye contact with Ricci. A sob broke loose at the pain in his eyes. Questions filled her mind. What had happened to him? Why were they bringing him home like this?

Alberto came running from the stables, Sandro at his heels. Alberto helped Tito support Ricci. Rebecca had only a moment to touch his face. Noting his evident pain, she withdrew. She stood still until they'd made it through the doorway then followed with the others.

Carlotta looked too stunned to react at all.

Nonna began barking orders. Her voice rang out inside the house. "Get him to the parlor. Gigi, run and get a blanket and pillows. Maria, start water for the tea. Lucia, help the signora."

Ricci gasped when they lowered him into the chair.

Sandro brought a footstool and propped up Ricci's legs.

By now, Gigi had returned with the pillows and a blanket. Within moments, they had him situated.

Nonna herded everyone out, but Tito stood just outside the parlor door.

Ricci extended his palm to Rebecca. She knelt beside him and laid her hand in his, swiping at her eyes with the other hand.

His eyes brimmed with moisture. His voice trembled when he spoke. "I heard you had gone away."

She stared back at him. "How? Who told you that?"

He blew out a breath. "We'll speak of it later."

She brought his hand to her lips and kissed it then held it to her cheek. "What happened to you? Why have we heard nothing of this?"

Nonna returned with a cup of her olive leaf and lavender tea, which she handed to Rebecca. "Give him this. It will calm him."

Rebecca released Ricci's hand then lifted the cup to his lips.

After swallowing, he rested his head on the pillows. "Thank you, Nonna. I have longed for your healing teas." He looked at Rebecca, his eyes lingering on her face. "It is not so bad. I wouldn't let them send word. I was worried for Mamma." He moved his gaze to Carlotta's face.

She leaned forward to pat his knee then left her hand there

as if she needed the physical contact with her son.

After another sip of tea, Ricci continued. "They were going to make me wait another week. I bribed an officer to send me in the car. I've a letter ... somewhere ... from Provo, informing you of my injury."

Rebecca made eye contact with Carlotta. "We knew something was wrong. You'd never stay away on purpose."

His gaze burned into hers as though he drew strength from her. "Just as I knew you would never leave me."

Between sips, he closed his eyes and rested. When he had taken the last few drops, Rebecca tucked the blanket around him.

After a few moments, she rose and sank into the nearest chair. She and Carlotta sat on either side of him, watching over him as he rested.

A few minutes ticked by on the clock before Carlotta whispered. "His legs seem fine. It is only his arm or shoulder. And the left one."

Rebecca smiled into her eyes. "And the head injury."

"Of course," Carlotta said, lifting her hand toward his forehead. She drew up short of touching his face.

"You know I can hear you," Ricci whispered. His lips curved in a slow smile. He drew in a deep breath and exhaled. "I am much better now that I am home." He opened his eyes and scanned the room, halting at Tito. "Will you help me upstairs? I would like to go to bed now."

Tito darted forward and helped Ricci rise. "Are you all right to climb the stairs, Signore? If not, I will call Berto. We can carry you."

Ricci laid his hand on Tito's shoulder. "I can make it with your help. It's good to see you, by the way."

Tito grinned. "And you also, Signore."

Alberto showed up as the two drew near the bottom of the stairs. He stayed directly behind them, ready to help if needed.

Eva had gone ahead of them to turn down the bed, so Rebecca followed behind Alberto. He still hadn't told them what had happened to him.

Alone with Ricci, Rebecca sat on the edge of the bed and stroked his cheek.

He yawned behind his uninjured hand. "I am so tired. I hope you don't mind if I sleep."

"Of course not, dearest." She leaned forward to press a kiss against his temple.

He caught her hand and pulled her close. "Kiss me like a wife who has been longing for her husband."

She drew back a couple of inches to look at him.

He had the audacity to grin. His hand slid behind her neck as he pressed his lips against hers.

Like the first sustenance after a prolonged fast, Rebecca reveled in the taste of him. The smell of soap and antiseptic tingled her nose, but she didn't care. Oh, to be able to embrace him fully, but she dare not, for fear of causing him pain.

When he released her, he seemed to sink back into the pillows. "I want more than kisses," he whispered.

She smoothed his dark hair away from his eyes. "I know you do, but first you have to heal." Should she tell him now— of the gift God had given them?

His eyes drooped, his brow creased.

No, not yet. He was too weary and obviously in pain.

When he snored softly, she walked around the end of the bed, picked up his pants and hung them over a chair then did the same with the jacket. Two envelopes slipped to the floor from the inside pocket. She stooped to retrieve them. One was badly stained and battered. The other was crisp and clean.

The newest letter was from the Department of the Army. The letter from Provo he'd mentioned. It was addressed to her. She laid it aside. Her stomach lurched when she realized the stains on the other envelope were dried blood. Was it Ricci's? She removed the letter and unfolded it. Her handwriting—her letter—written at gunpoint, a lifetime ago. A shudder ran through her.

Had Francesca mailed the letter? Rebecca picked up the envelope, turned it over. No address. How had he gotten it? Special messenger? But even then, it would have his name on the envelope. Puzzling.

That's why he'd said, "I heard you had gone away," because he'd read her letter. Had he understood her meaning? She glanced at his face, so peaceful in repose. Perhaps this was why he'd put off the conversation. Was he upset with her? She closed her eyes and remembered his kiss. He hadn't seemed upset.

She returned her letter to his pocket then took the other one downstairs.

"What a confusing day," Carlotta said, as Rebecca entered the kitchen. "It's nearly time for dinner. I think we skipped a meal. I don't remember."

Rebecca held up the envelope. "I have the letter."

Nonna handed her a small knife which Rebecca used as a letter opener then handed it back. The room grew very quiet. Rebecca scanned the contents before raising her eyes to Carlotta's face. "It's from his commanding officer, Colonello Provo. It is for both of us."

Carlotta touched her arm. "You read it."

Dear Signoras Alverá,

It is my solemn duty to inform you that your husband (son) has been injured in the line of duty. Be assured that he is being given the best care available. You will no doubt hear from his surgeon soon, with a summary of his injuries. I am told he is expected to make a good recovery. Please call on me if you have any questions or concerns.

Primo Capitano Alverá is a fine officer, and it is my honor to serve alongside him. He has my best wishes and most fervent prayers for his recovery.

Sincerely,

Col. A. Provo

Carlotta gave a little chuckle. "So he says nothing. But it is nice of him to write."

The women in the kitchen giggled and a hum of conversation replaced the former quiet.

Rebecca folded the letter. "And he spoke very well of Ricci."

"Well of course, he did," Carlotta said. "We know what a fine man our Riccardo is." She patted Rebecca's cheek. "Are you all right, my dear? You are not too tired? How is—?" She sent a quick glance around the room.

Rebecca gave her a smile and whispered, "We are fine."

Carlotta nodded. "Why don't you rest until dinner?"

"Both of you go and rest until dinner," Nonna called out from the sink where she scrubbed a kettle. "We will call you when it is ready."

More than anything, Rebecca wanted to curl up beside Ricci for the night, but she didn't want to disturb him. She didn't want to leave him, either, so the overstuffed chair would have to do. Weary from all the day's excitement, she soon fell asleep.

Near dawn, Ricci cried out. She rushed to his side. He sighed and, though it was dark, she sensed his eyes were open.

She brushed his cheek with the back of her hand and whispered, "Are you awake?"

He stirred then reached for her hand. "Lie next to me."

She pulled back the covers and climbed in beside him.

"Every part of me is hurting right now."

She drew back. "I'm so sorry."

"No. It is all right. I have a prescription in my bag. But I don't want it right now. I want a clear head."

"I understand." She cradled his hand in both of hers.

His voice was low when he spoke again. "Being close to you is enough. I only wish I could hold you in my arms."

"You will again."

"I know." The words came out as a sigh. "Now, tell me what happened. Why did you write that ridiculous letter?"

She hesitated, but decided it would be best to tell him everything. "I was awakened in the middle of the night …"

Early morning sunlight filtered through the curtains as she finished her narrative. She looked at his face. "How was the letter delivered to you?"

He lay still for so long she thought he'd fallen asleep. Then he opened his eyes, cleared his throat, and tightened his grip on her hand. "She came to our camp."

"But … how did she find you?"

"She has ways. Believe me. She said she had business there and decided to personally deliver the letter to me since it was of great importance."

Rebecca scoffed. "She must have gone straight there."

"I suppose so. I have no memory of anything that happened after the accident until I woke up in the hospital in Bari." He caught his breath as he repositioned his bandaged arm.

"I'm so sorry you're in pain. May I get you something? Do you need your medication?"

"Maybe after I have something to eat."

She started to get up, but he held on to her.

"Not yet," he whispered. "I'm sure Eva will come soon."

She relaxed against the pillow. "About your accident, how

did it happen?"

"I didn't tell you? Funny. I clearly remember telling you. Must have dreamed it." He drew a shaky breath then exhaled. In brief terms, he told her about Francesca's visit. "After I stalked out of Provo's office, I reread your letter. I was afraid she had harmed you. She'd already left the camp. I chased after her. With a car and driver, of course, as befits an officer."

Though she found this part of the story humorous, his intonation led Rebecca to believe he was angry. Why was that? And he'd avoided saying Francesca's name. Interesting.

"We came upon her plane, but it had already taken off by the time we reached it. We turned around and started back. Within minutes, I heard what sounded like gunshot. Then another. I think the tire was hit, or maybe more than one. We were going so fast when the tire blew it sent the car flying in the air. I held on as long as I could, while the car flipped end over end. I thought I was most certainly … dead."

"Oh, Ricci. You could've been killed."

He was silent for a moment. "Topi—my driver—was killed. The car landed on him. I was thrown free."

No wonder he was angry. She leaned her head against his shoulder as thankfulness coursed through her. "I'm so sorry, Ricci." A new thought struck her. "Who shot at you?"

"I don't know. I'm uncertain—but a moment before I heard the first shot—a plane flew over."

Chapter Thirty-Five

Riccardo watched as Berto ignited kindling beneath a small woodpile in the outdoor fireplace behind the house. Soon the flames took hold, making the outdoor room cozy and warm. Riccardo wanted to be in the open air, to hear the birds sing. He felt the need to look over his property and enjoy the day and perhaps take his mind off the ever-present pain.

Mamma dozed across from him, a smile on her lips. So good to be home. He frowned into the flames. Home—this peaceful place—had been violated. His family's life threatened. Not only theirs, but his also. Had those shots been fired from the plane? Suspicion wormed its way into his mind again. No matter how hard he tried, he couldn't forget. The worst part was not knowing. Not knowing why. Not knowing if she … or they would try again.

He couldn't voice his suspicions. He worried about repercussions. Signorina Boccali had gone, but she had ties to some very important people. He didn't dare make accusations. Not yet, anyway. Not without proof.

Not many minutes passed before he heard the sound of a car on the drive. He groaned inwardly. Had the neighbors heard he was home and had come calling? He didn't feel ready to entertain.

Rebecca's voice sounded in the hall, answered by a masculine one.

Mamma stirred and sat up as Rebecca and two men stepped outside. She introduced the first man. "This is Inspector Rossi from Perugia and, of course, you know Commissioner Franco. Please sit down, gentlemen. I will order the coffee."

"Buongiorno, Conte." Inspector Rossi offered his hand to Riccardo then took the chair nearest him. He wasted no time, but began at once. "I spoke with your wife in the hospital. That is where I started my investigation. I followed up with Commissioner Franco." He nodded at Franco. "We have worked together to bring this case to a satisfactory conclusion."

Riccardo liked the sound of that, but doubt stirred in his mind. How had they done so without his input?

Maria entered with the coffee tray, followed by Rebecca, who sat next to Mamma. Rebecca's eyes found his. Was she nervous?

He drew a deep breath and eased it out.

After the coffee was served and pastries offered, Rossi cleared his throat. "There was initial doubt about Signorina Boccali's involvement. I will explain that later. We pieced together the facts from what the Contessa was able to tell us. And then what Colonello Provo was able to discover."

Riccardo lifted his head. "Provo?"

Rossi nodded then sipped his coffee. "Very good coffee, Contessa. Thank you." He set the cup down, picked up a file folder, then flipped it open and thumbed through the pages until he found what he wanted. "The colonello became suspicious when he found the two bullet holes in your vehicle. They located a witness who reported seeing a biplane fly over. According to the witness—a local farmer—a person in the back seat of the plane seemed to be holding a rifle. When the farmer heard the shots he hid behind a boulder. After the plane disappeared, he found the wreckage of your vehicle. It was he who hauled the two of you back to the camp. I believe you know the rest."

Riccardo nodded but kept his eyes on his coffee cup. He knew part of what the inspector had shared. Since there was a death involved, he'd been subjected to an inquisition as soon as he was lucid. At that time, Provo assumed the accident had been the result of a blown tire.

"The farmer remembered the number and color on the side of the plane," the inspector continued. "We traced the origin of the plane to an airfield outside Rome. I cannot, at this time reveal any names, regarding ownership, etc., but we were able to follow the trail as far as Bari. We found the abandoned plane in a nearby field. As far as we can tell, the pilot and passenger then left by sea. It is there, we lost the trail."

Riccardo looked the man in the eye. "You are certain it was Signorina Boccali?"

"We are certain," Franco said.

Riccardo turned to him.

He sat with his arms crossed over his chest, brow deeply furrowed. He turned to look at Mamma. "Signora Alverá, let me apologize for my … seeming disinterest in your initial request for my help." He unfolded his arms and shifted in his chair, settling with a hand on each knee. "You see, we had a report from … er … the signorina that the contessa—" he darted an apologetic look at Rebecca then back to Riccardo. "That the contessa had run off with a former lover."

"What?" Rebecca's face flushed again as she gazed at Franco.

Riccardo wanted to box someone's ears, but Franco was not really to blame. He held up his good hand. "It's all right, mia cara. They now know it is false."

Both men nodded.

Franco resumed with as much humility as ever, which in Riccardo's opinion, was not enough. "So there was some delay in our investigation until I had a phone call from Rossi. At that time, I pledged my full cooperation."

Rebecca's brow arched.

Mamma sat forward, ready to blast Franco. Riccardo knew that look.

Before either woman could say anything, he spoke,

keeping his voice calm. "So now you are certain of Boccali's involvement?"

Rossi nodded. "We have solid proof of her involvement, Signore. We found items belonging to Signorina Boccali in both the plane and the automobile abandoned in Bari."

"In the plane, we found her lighter trapped beneath the seat. You know the one, surely?" Franco asked.

Riccardo nodded, remembering her request for a light. He'd wondered about it at the time.

"Once there was reasonable suspicion, we searched Signorina Boccali's residence and found enough to tie her not only to the abduction, but also to the attempt on your life, Contessa. And also I don't know if you were aware," Franco leveled his gaze at Riccardo. "The signorina had you and your wife under surveillance for some time. She kept very accurate records of this."

"And she left all this accurate information where it could be easily found?" Riccardo looked from Franco to Rossi.

Franco shook his head. "No, it was not easily located. At first, we found nothing. But one of my men chanced to step on a loose board in the floor. He pulled it up, and we found these things in a metal box beneath the planks."

Rossi closed the file folder. "Have you any other questions, Conte?"

"I'd like to know who owns that plane," Riccardo said, with a glance toward Rebecca. "It's difficult to feel safe, knowing someone may still be out there."

Rossi nodded. "I do understand that, Signore, and I assure you, we will follow through with every detail."

"In the meantime," Franco added, "we will be vigilant, as I know you will also be, Conte."

Riccardo exhaled then lifted his eyes to Rebecca. "Do you have further questions?"

Her gaze shifted from his to Rossi's. "I only wonder why

she did it."

Rossi stood and Franco followed suit. "That is the question we are all asking, Contessa." He looked to Riccardo. "Have you any idea, Signore?"

Riccardo shifted in his chair. All eyes were on him. Everyone waited for his answer. What could he say? He had no idea why. Why had she targeted him—from the very beginning of their acquaintance? He drew in a deep breath and released it with a huff. "She wanted something she couldn't have," he said, gripping Rebecca's hand. "Something that belonged to another."

Rossi nodded, as though he understood, as though in agreement with Riccardo. "Arrivederci, Conte. It was good meeting you. We may meet again one day if we manage to locate the signorina."

Franco bowed to Riccardo and Rebecca. "Ciao, Conte, Contessa. We will be in touch."

Mamma stood and fussed with her shawl. "I will see you out, Signores."

Rebecca hated being so emotional. She wanted to jump into Ricci's arms, but of course she couldn't do that. Instead, she leaned to kiss him. "Are you all right? Do you need to go up and lie down?"

He held on to her hand. "No. I need to digest this. I don't know what to think."

"Neither do I." She pulled a chair close and sat in it, facing him. "I've thought about it for days now. I can't figure out why she did it. Other than what you said, of course. She doesn't like rejection. But still, to risk everything—her career, her life—on retaliation."

"She is bitter. I saw it when she was at the camp. I think she really expected me to be happy you had gone away." He smiled into her eyes. "But she didn't count on you, mia cara.

She never even guessed, though I know she read the letter."

"Oh, she read it before we left here that night. She didn't like that I had written both letters in English. I told her I always wrote in English, and everyone would question it if I did not."

He smiled and squeezed her hand. "You are a genius."

She shook her head. No way could she accept praise for this. "It was God, Ricci. I was only half awake. And I was scared, so when I started writing, it was in English. When I thought about it, it seemed a good tactic if I could make her believe the lie."

Ricci chuckled. "Which of course you did."

Carlotta padded into the room. "Are you telling him your news?"

Rebecca looked at her then back at Ricci. "I was just about to."

Ricci's attention had been on Carlotta. His eyes snapped to Rebecca's face. "What news?"

"Dr. Manfredi is coming in the morning," she told him, doing her utmost to keep a straight face. "I suppose he can assess both our conditions during the same visit."

Ricci continued to gaze at her, one brow tilted up. "You are still under a doctor's care? I thought you said there was no permanent damage."

She grinned at Carlotta. "No damage. He's going to check on my ... condition."

"She's in the family way." Carlotta clasped her hands together.

Ricci's eyes flashed as something akin to fear flitted across his face. "Before all this happened?"

Rebecca nodded. "Apparently. I was as surprised as you."

"You are all right? I mean—the baby—will it be all right?"

"Only God can answer that. But the doctor in Perugia said the baby appeared unharmed."

Carlotta sank into her chair and folded her hands on her lap. "I think we should send her to bed for the rest of the time, however long that is."

Ricci caressed Rebecca's cheek, his dark eyes boring into hers. "I agree with Mamma. I think I must have a talk with Dr. Manfredi."

Rebecca blew out a sigh. "If that's what I have to do to bring a little Ricci into this world, then I'll do it." But she certainly hoped it wouldn't be necessary.

Rebecca rejoiced that Dr. Manfredi didn't send her straight to bed. But, after checking her vital signs, he did caution her to take life easy.

"You've made it farther than you have in the past. And with all that has happened, I would tend to agree with Dr. Cozetti. We may have witnessed a miracle. I say that with some trepidation." He folded the stethoscope and returned it to his bag. "We will see. In the meantime, I will have the midwife begin her visits right away."

Ricci and Carlotta were not so lenient. No physical labor, no riding the horse, no lifting Alessio. It was going to be a long nineteen weeks.

When she'd made it past the halfway point, she wrote Nancy the news. Should she tell Mother? She may feel obligated to come. Rebecca's first reaction to that thought was not a good one. But the presence on the water … she couldn't dismiss the memory. She'd more or less made a vow to love her mother. Perhaps this child would help heal the rift between them.

She kept herself busy on the accounts until she got so worked up over the finances, Ricci took that away, also. But taking them away from her didn't keep her from worrying.

"I know what you are doing," Carlotta told Rebecca, offering her a cup of tea. "You are trying to make things work as you did when you were at home, having to clean up the problems left you by your parents."

Rebecca shot a glance at her mother-in-law. What was she talking about? She accepted the tea and set it down with trembling hands.

"It is no longer your responsibility, *mia figlia*. It is the responsibility of your husband." She sat down across from her and wrapped Rebecca's fingers in her own. "You need to let him do it."

Rebecca closed her eyes. Carlotta had an uncanny way of seeing into a person's soul. "I know you're right."

How many times had Rebecca stepped in and corrected wrongs done by her parents? She'd even sold her own jewelry. She was barely nineteen when she had to close up a house and prepare it for sale. Her parents had dismissed the servants with no prior notice, and no final pay. She'd gone to each of them, supplied them with a letter of recommendation she'd written herself, and a small cash settlement.

Now she was trying to stand in the gap again, only this time, it wasn't her place. It was Ricci's, and he was doing the best he could.

After the holidays had ended, he sat down with her and drew out a familiar brown envelope. "It's time for us to talk about this."

"I read it through after you left for Bari," she told him. "I think I understand it better."

He considered her for a moment. "As we stand right now, barring a miracle, at the present outrageous tax rate, we will be out of money in two years."

Rebecca bit back all the responses that tumbled through her mind. Ricci watched her as though he understood her conflict. She drew a deep breath and released it slowly. "This sale will supply us with cash to hold on longer. Is that your intent?"

"It is one reason. Roberto will set up what he called a 'dummy corporation,' which will dissolve when it is no longer needed. We will have first rights to repurchase."

"The contract seems airtight."

"It is. He covered all contingencies. He has no need of the properties. He's not looking to take anything from us."

"I know. I've always known. I was taken by surprise, that's all. My only question is, can he protect the land. Can this 'dummy corporation' keep the title safe from the powers that be?" Mussolini's reach had already extended into Umbria, as he dispossessed families who opposed his tactics.

Ricci nodded his understanding. "No one can be certain. But this will tie it up legally. It will be owned by a Swiss company. It has a good chance."

She watched him frown over the paperwork. The last few weeks had held many changes for him. He'd resigned the committee after two of his friends were dismissed. Guerra was already ousted and replaced by a man known to be a fascist. Rebecca couldn't help the anxiety that threaded its way through her heart at the thought. She tried to hide it with a smile she hoped held reassurance. He would notice even a slight hesitancy. "So you feel good about it? I'm sure you've prayed over it."

"I have. Often and fervently."

"Your mother and I talked it over. She seems in agreement with you."

"She has given me her blessing." He sat forward and picked up the envelope. "The arrangements for Villa Carlotta, she made on her own. I notice those papers are not here. I think she has them in her room."

"Oh, Ricci. Does she need to give up her property as well?"

His lips quirked. "Mamma has made a change to her will. She wants you to have Villa Carlotta."

Rebecca drew in a quick breath. "Shouldn't it be yours? Or one of the Dominicis?"

He shook his head slowly. "It is her property, her decision. And she did this some time ago. Not long after we returned from there, when the Emersons visited."

The memory surfaced of Carlotta telling Rebecca about her ownership of the Villa. And then she had called Rebecca her daughter. Dampness trickled down Rebecca's cheek.

Riccardo dried it with his thumb. "I know she told you how it is always passed from mother to daughter. And so she is passing it to you. We have come to love you very much, my sweet."

She gave him a small smile. "I've always had a way of growing on people."

"Like a pearl in an oyster, you grow on us. A very precious pearl." He leaned in for a kiss, which she gave gladly.

Chapter Thirty-Six

4 January, 1932

Rebecca broke down and cried when they got the news. Francesca and her German chauffeur had been apprehended while trying to cross the Austrian border. She didn't understand why it affected her so. Possibly it was something to do with the pregnancy.

Inspector Rossi sat in the parlor, sipping excellent coffee and nibbling one of Nonna's cakes. "I have a cousin who is a border official in Austria. We had just been there to celebrate the wedding of his youngest daughter, so we talked about this case." He barely suppressed a smile. "Now I ask you—what are the odds they should choose that particular crossing?" He grinned, obviously proud of himself.

Ricci shook his head. "Providence."

The inspector nodded. "You are right."

Rebecca blew her nose. "What happens now?"

Inspector Rossi finished his coffee and set down the cup. He licked his lips. "There will be a trial, Contessa. But you mustn't worry about it. We have plenty of evidence."

Ricci shifted forward, a faraway look in his eye.

Rebecca watched him. What was he thinking? She glanced at the inspector. No doubt, they both held back because of her presence. Attempted murder was a crime punishable by death. Tears welled up again. She excused herself.

"I'm so sorry, Contessa, for upsetting you," Inspector Rossi said as she left the room.

Instead of climbing the stairs, she stepped into her office and closed the door. She stood in front of the window, gazing out, but seeing nothing.

After the inspector left, Ricci opened the study door. "Are you all right?"

She nodded. "Yes. I didn't want to embarrass myself further. I suppose it's my condition. I'm so emotional."

He crossed the room in two long strides and pulled her into his arms. He kissed her neck and caressed her swollen belly. "I love that you are emotional because you carry my child."

She released a pent-up breath and did her best to hold back another rush of tears. Several moments passed until she could speak without choking on the words. "Did he say anything else of importance?"

"No, only what you would expect in the circumstances." He kissed the top of her head. "I am so relieved."

"So am I. Maybe that's the reason for the tears. I've been half afraid she'd show up again."

"I, too."

She drew back to look at him. "Really?"

"All those months, she watched us. Everywhere we went, she was there. Did you not notice?"

She nodded. "I did. I thought at first it may be coincidence."

"And she was able to come into this house, unnoticed by anyone."

She raised her eyes to his face. "You know, she told me she wrote to Daddy and offered to pay off all his debt if he would forbid me to marry you."

Ricci stiffened. The furrow of his brow deepened. Perhaps she shouldn't have mentioned it.

He drew in a breath and held it for a moment. "Did he— forbid you?"

She shook her head. "Do you have to ask?"

His expression cleared. His eyes probed hers.

She leaned against him, listening to the steady thrum of

his heart.

Rebecca shivered but not from cold. "I wonder why she was going to Austria. Just passing through, maybe?"

Ricci took a step back. He lifted her chin with his fingertips. "She wasn't going to Austria, cara. She was leaving Austria. She was coming back to Italy."

She drew a quick breath as understanding dawned. "Oh." What energy she had drained away. Her knees gave out.

Ricci caught her. "Do you need to go upstairs?"

"No. I'm fine, just … surprised." She gripped his arms. "So is it really over?"

He drew her into his arms and held her tight against him. "Yes, mia carissima. I believe it is over."

The trial took place in Rome. Riccardo went alone. Out of respect for Rebecca's condition, she had not been summoned.

For the first time, he heard the tale of Francesca's early years. What wasn't brought out in the trial was written of in depth in the newspaper. Though he hated the public display of it, Riccardo felt drawn to the story. He read it over breakfast on what should be the final day of the trial.

Francesca started life as Frantiska Nemecek, of Slovak origin. Her father was killed in World War I when Frantiska was only twelve. Her mother managed to flee to Italy with her daughter where the mother later succumbed to an unnamed disease, leaving Frantiska an orphan. The girl survived on her own for a couple of years. She was later taken in by a man of some importance in Rome. His name was not mentioned in the newspaper article.

Riccardo humphed. Someone was paying for this to be kept quiet. Probably the same one who owned the plane. He folded the newspaper and laid it on the table beside him. After finishing his coffee, he paid for his meal and strolled down the street. One more day, until he returned home to Tres Viti, to

Rebecca, and Mamma. How he hated this separation. The reason for the separation left a bad taste in his mouth. He longed to distance himself from it.

The news story had only hinted at what followed. The girl's name had been changed. She grew up as mistress to this unnamed man. He later described her in a letter as cunning, shrewd, and possibly, quite dangerous.

This was how the article had ended, leaving no doubt of her character. Leading the reader to believe she was unredeemable. Riccardo prayed it was not so. He prayed for her soul and hoped she would renounce her past, show remorse, at the very least.

But she did not. Two days later, she was hanged. Riccardo was on his way home when it was announced on the radio. She was dead. Now, it really was over.

26 February, 1932

Riccardo strode out of the bathroom and plopped down on the edge of the bed. The midwife had insisted Rebecca stay put the last few weeks of her pregnancy. Though Rebecca was at her wit's end, Riccardo felt only relief. He needn't worry about her now.

She frowned at him. "Where are you going today?"

"I'll be in the vineyard. Poppi has a couple of ideas he wants to run by me. I won't be long."

She shrugged. "Nothing for you to do here. I would only have to beat you at cards again."

He kissed the end of her nose. "We can't have that, can we?"

Truth is, he hated leaving her. She was brilliant and vibrant in the best of times, but these days, she seemed dull. It was starting to get her down, and she had far too much time to worry.

A bright blue sky greeted him, making the chill in the air

more bearable. Ricci loved the outdoors. What would he do if he were trapped inside like Rebecca? Not something he wanted to contemplate. He wound a wool scarf around his neck and ambled down the lane. This was lining up to be a grand year. There'd be money coming in with the sale of Tres Viti to the EmerVera Corporation. Most of the money would go into trust, but they'd have enough to pay the taxes and keep up the property. The Alverá family had always been able to feed themselves with their produce.

He hoped Papá wasn't turning over in his grave. Riccardo had no wish to go down in history as the one who lost *Tres Viti Verdi*. He figured there would be talk, at least initially, but he could weather it, if it was for the greater good.

Worldwide, things were happening as well. The market made slow gains. Tourism bloomed again. Even here, in their remote little corner of the world, visitors flocked to visit Assisi, the cathedrals, and castles. They were mostly English and a few Americans, but they had money to spend.

Riccardo felt hopeful about the future. Though he didn't like the new mayor, the man kept the citizens of Ginestra somewhat content. Riccardo didn't trust him. He couldn't really say why, but there seemed always something just behind the man's eyes. As if he knew things no one else did.

28 February, 1932

"I have never been so bored in all my life," Rebecca told Eva, as the day dragged on.

Eva's laughter trilled. "This room is always filled with visitors. Chico comes to chatter about the numerous fish he's caught. Nonna comes to check on your bad knitting. You are only bored because you can't run about and poke your nose into everyone's business."

"That's right. I've no freedom at all." She grinned as Eva set Alessio on the bed beside her. Rebecca held out her hands.

Alessio moved onto her legs and settled back against her swollen belly. She tousled the boy's hair. "What shall we read today?"

Eva handed her a book. "What else? He loves this one."

Rebecca cleared her throat then began to read. "Chug, chug, chug..." How many times had she read it? *The Little Train That Could*. And every time, she had to laugh. It reminded her of herself.

After Eva and Alessio left, Carlotta came to sit with her. She'd spent hours these last few weeks talking of the old days, flipping through old photos. Rebecca had enjoyed every minute of it. She couldn't help thinking of those first days—Carlotta's cold greeting—her begrudging offer to move to the guest house after Mother left. She almost laughed out loud at the memory.

Dear Carlotta. Now look at her. Surely Rebecca had memorized every line of the woman's face, every timbre of her voice. Carlotta was the kind of mother Rebecca had dreamed of as a child. Someone who really cared, prayed for her children, desired the best for them. The kind of mother Rebecca hoped to become. She reached for Carlotta's hand and smiled into her eyes.

"Would you mind very much if I call you Mamma?"

Carlotta sat back, blinking away tears. "My dear, I would be honored." She gave Rebecca's hand a gentle squeeze, drew in a long breath and released it with a contented sigh. "I only wonder that you've waited so long."

After Carlotta left her, Rebecca settled back, hoping for sleep. Today had been her worst day yet. She'd been nauseous all morning, but in the afternoon, she wanted to get up and do something. Rearrange the furniture, scrub the floor, anything to be busy and moving about. To make the hours pass.

Her gaze drifted to the view outside their bedroom window. The distant mountains loomed blue, still capped with white patches. Winter was passing, but she couldn't really enjoy the approach of spring. She fought worry constantly. If the baby didn't kick as often as yesterday, if a pain caught her when she moved a certain way—panic. She hated being weak. Why couldn't she have a normal pregnancy like everyone else, strong as she had always been?

Mother had written an unusually long letter. She, too, had problems in her pregnancies. "Yes, dear," she'd written, "I also suffered a miscarriage. Then after your birth, the doctor had to perform a partial hysterectomy. Which is why you never had a sibling." Quite a shocking confession but how illuminating for Rebecca. Mother went on to say that she and Eugene were abroad until summer. They'd stop in then and visit. "How odd that I will be a grandmother. I think I will need a unique name to define myself. What do you think?"

Rebecca drew in a few deep breaths and prayed a few Hail Marys to calm down. These memories weren't really helping. But she did manage a quick prayer for her mother. That was saying something.

At least she needn't worry so much about Ricci. His injury would keep him out of the service, at least for a while. He still had not gained back full use of his shoulder, but he was much better. He worried about his facial scar, of course. The man had such an ego. Didn't he know it made him more handsome than ever? She'd told him so on more than one occasion.

She opened her eyes. Had she slept? The western sky glowed with pastel shades of peach and lavender. Wonderful aromas drifted up from the kitchen, along with the usual chatter of the women. She lay back, contemplating a delicious meal, when a sudden pain caught her around the middle. She'd had some pains in the last few days, but this was definitely stronger. She tried not to cry out, but it tightened like a vise.

Footsteps thundered up both sets of stairs. The doorway filled with faces. Rebecca lay back, breathing in little gasps.

"That was a hard one."

"Run and get Nonna," Eva called out. "Here, Gigi, take Alessio. I'll stay with Contessa."

Ricci was beside Rebecca in two long strides, kneeling beside the bed. He gathered her hands in his. "Are you all right?"

By now, the pain had gone away. Surely it was isolated. She was probably fine. Goodness, would she have to give birth in front of an audience?

She shrugged her shoulders. "I'm okay. Really, everyone, go back to what you were doing. Have your dinner. Live your lives."

"Now you are being sarcastic," Ricci said, a smile on his handsome face. "That is more like the old Rebecca."

Another pain began. Rebecca opened her eyes wide as Nonna stalked into the room. "Everyone out. Dinner is on the table. We have sent for the midwife—now go!" The little woman shooed everyone out like hens from a hen house.

Ricci hesitated, but he was no match for Nonna. He kissed Rebecca's forehead. "I love you more than life."

She lay back, closed her eyes, and prayed she'd be worthy of such a great love.

1 March, 1932

Rebecca's ordeal ended a few minutes past midnight. Dominic Riccardo David Alverá was officially two weeks early, but Rebecca was not complaining. She gazed at her newborn son, completely and utterly in love.

"What a lot of trouble you were," she whispered. "But worth every single moment."

The midwife giggled. "Oh my, yes, you are right. He is quite the handsome boy."

Ricci gave her one of those long, mind-melting kisses then stole his son to show him off to all those waiting below.

Carlotta wept. "Happy tears," she assured them. "I am too blessed. Overwhelmed with God's goodness. I won't sleep a wink this night." Half an hour later, she snored softly in Rebecca's favorite overstuffed chair.

At long last, everyone retired for the night. Ricci and Rebecca were both too excited to sleep. She lay in Ricci's arms and watched their tiny son breathe. Was there any greater blessing in the world?

She closed her eyes and gave thanks to God. "You answered my prayers and gave even more than I could ever have believed."

About the Author

Betty Thomason Owens writes romantic comedy, historical fiction, and fantasy-adventure. She has contributed hundreds of articles and interviews to various blogs around the Internet and is an active member of American Christian Fiction Writers (ACFW), where she leads a critique group. She's a mentor, assisting other writers, and a co-founder of a blog dedicated to inspiring writers and serves on the board of the Kentucky Christian Writers Conference.

Her writing credits include *Annabelle's Ruth*, Book 1, Kinsman Redeemer Series (2015), a 20's era romance, *Amelia's Legacy*, Book 1, Legacy Series (2014), both through Write Integrity Press. She writes contemporary stories as a co-author of *A Dozen Apologies* and its sequels, *The Love Boat Bachelor and Unlikely Merger,* (2015). She has two fantasy-adventure novels, *The Lady of the Haven* and *A Gathering of Eagles*, in a second edition published by Sign of the Whale Books™, an imprint of Olivia Kimbrell Press™.

Connect with Betty online

Amazon Author Page

http://bettythomasonowens.com
https://twitter.com/batowens
https://facebook.com/betty.owens.author
https://pinterest.com/btowens
https://writingpromptsthoughtsideas.wordpress.com

Other Books by the Author

Amelia's Legacy
Available on Amazon:
Paperback and Kindle

It's the Roaring Twenties and anything goes ...

Orphaned and living with her grandmother since the age of six, Nancy Sanderson desires only her freedom from her strict grandmother, Amelia Woods Sanderson, who divides her time between Nancy and a successful career. Her grandmother's plans include a wealthy, smart, and well-connected young lawyer named Robert Emerson, who bores Nancy.

Instead, Nancy seeks the company of the wild-hearted Nate Conners. When her rebellion turns deadly and her dalliance with Nate leaves her in trouble, Nancy turns to Robert, who promises to protect her. But Robert has underestimated Nate's thirst for revenge.

As hidden truths become known, can Nancy find the strength to forgive herself and gain true and lasting freedom?

Book One in the Legacy Series.

The Heart Seekers Series

Three books in one, plus added bonuses!

Available in Paperback and on Kindle

A Dozen Apologies:
Mara Adkins, a promising fashion designer, has fallen off the ladder of success, and she can't seem to get up. In college, Mara and her sorority sisters played an ugly game, and Mara was usually the winner. She'd date men she considered geeks, win their confidence, and then she'd dump them publicly. Now, Mara stumbles, bumbles, and humbles her way toward employment and toward possible reconciliation with the twelve men she humiliated.

The Love Boat Bachelor:
What's a sworn bachelor to do on a Caribbean cruise full of romance and love? Brent will either have to jump ship or embrace the unforgettable romantic comedy headed his way.

Unlikely Merger:
If her best friend has her way, Mercy will simply marry one of the single, available men she meets, but they overwhelm her. So handsome and kind. And so many. Even if she felt obliged, how could she ever choose?

BONUS MATERIAL!

Updates on many of your favorite characters!
Videos from two of our authors!

AND:

The Christmas Tree Treasure Hunt:

Grace takes delivery of a package and her life is turned upside down by nine sealed mystery envelopes from her late grandmother. Grammie's instructions require Grace to take the journey of her lifetime, not only to far off places, but also into the deepest parts of her heart. As she follows the trail laid out for her and uncovers her family's darkest secrets, Grace is forced to confront the loss and betrayal that has scarred her past and seek the greatest Christmas Treasure of all.

For the first time, all four stories are offered in this "boxed" set. And for the first time, they're all offered in a single print volume.

Unlikely Merger

No longer needed as her father's nurse, Mercy Lacewell attempts to step into his shoes at his acquisitions firm. That means travel, engaging strangers, and making final decisions—nothing she feels equipped to do. If her best friend has her way, Mercy will simply marry one of the single, available men she meets, but they overwhelm her. So handsome and kind. And so many. Even if she felt obliged, how could she ever choose?

Available on Kindle

Jerusha Agen   Marji Laine
Theresa Anderson   Fay Lamb
Julie Arduini   Elizabeth Noyes
Joan Deneve   Betty Owens

The Love Boat Bachelor
Available on Kindle

Romance is a joke.

After the love of Brent Teague's life came back into his world only to marry someone else, Brent is through with women. He might be through with being a pastor, too.

Brent was so sure that God brought Mara Adkins home to him so they could marry and live happily ever after. Six months after her wedding to another man, that theory is obviously a dud. If Brent could be so wrong about that, who's to say he's not mistaken about God calling him to pastoral ministry?

Tired of watching Brent flounder for direction, Brent's feisty older sister boots him out of Spartanburg and onto a cruise ship. Brent's old college buddy manages the ship's staff, and he's thrilled to finagle Brent into the role of chaplain for the two-week cruise.

As the ship sets sail, Brent starts to relax. Maybe a cruise wasn't such a bad idea after all. But there's just one little thing no one told him. He's not on any ordinary cruise. He's on The Love Boat.

What's a sworn bachelor to do on a Caribbean cruise full of romance and love? He'll either have to jump ship or embrace the unforgettable romantic comedy headed his way.

A Dozen Apologies
Available on Kindle

Mara Adkins, a promising fashion designer, has fallen off the ladder of success, and she can't seem to get up. In college, Mara and her sorority sisters played an ugly game, and Mara was usually the winner. She'd date men she considered geeks, win their confidence, and then she'd dump them publicly.

When Mara begins work for a prestigious clothing designer in New York, she gets her comeuppance. Her boyfriend steals her designs and wins a coveted position. He fires her, and she returns in shame to her home in Spartanburg, South Carolina, where life for others has changed for the better.

Mara's parents, always seemingly one step from a divorce, have rediscovered their love for each other, but more importantly they have placed Christ in the center of that love. The changes Mara sees in their lives cause her to seek Christ. Mara's heart is pierced by her actions toward the twelve men she'd wronged in college, and she sets out to apologize to each of them. A girl with that many amends to make, though, needs money for travel, and Mara finds more ways to lose a job that she ever thought possible.

Mara stumbles, bumbles, and humbles her way toward employment and toward possible reconciliation with the twelve men she humiliated to find that God truly does look upon the heart, and that He has chosen the heart of one of the men for her to have and to hold.

Look for other books

published by

www.WriteIntegrity.com

and

www.PixNPens.com

Thank you for reading our books. If you enjoyed this one, we would greatly appreciate a brief review.